YOU
ARE
NOT
YOU

YOU ARE NOT YOU

Simon Rosenberg

Published by Simon Isaac Rosenberg

LEGAL DISCLAIMER

As a product of the author's imagination, all the characters in this book are fictitious, and any resemblance to actual persons or events is entirely coincidental.

A catalogue record for this book is available from the British Library.

paperback ISBN: 978-1-9996754-0-0
e-pub ISBN: 978-1-9996754-1-7

Cover design by Vince Haig
Design by Wordsense, Edinburgh

The anaemic blue light in the narrow windows either side of the front door could indicate twilight or dawn. Lorraine March assumes it's dawn, which at the very least establishes some kind of order. The last thing she remembers is going to bed in a hotel room in the city; now she's standing in the hallway of her family home in Totteridge, and she doesn't have a clue how she got here. When she tries to think about what happened between then and now, it's like peering through a mental fog, and her mind becomes sluggish and her head feels heavy.

She sways slightly, rocking on her heels, blinks and rubs her eyes. She turns, to go and splash some water on her face, but her foot is obstructed by something heavy.

Her husband is staring up at her from the floor. No, not at her, at the ceiling directly above him. Scott's eyes are blank and glassy, and his mouth is hanging open the way it does when he's lost interest in what she's saying. It's an expression that ordinarily infuriates her, but right now it doesn't even cross her mind to be irritated. Because beneath his chin there is another mouth, yawning wide, its lips ragged and its gullet deep and red.

Air sucks into Lorraine's throat with a high-pitched whistle. She staggers backwards and her high heels slip in the blood that is spread across the parquet like a rug. She reaches out to stabilise herself and, when she opens her hands, something clatters to the floor. Her eyes flick towards it momentarily, and then back to the body of her husband. The shock of seeing him there is still greater than the small anomaly of what it was she was holding. But as her limbs tremble at the terrible sight, her mind processes what she has glimpsed only briefly, and the warmth drains from her body. Her head slowly rotates towards the object that has come to rest against the blood-spattered skirting board.

It's a knife. A kitchen knife. A knife from her kitchen.

Beside the knife there is an oversized stuffed-toy elephant. Scott won it at a fairground a couple of years ago, and it has sat there ever since. Now its friendly face is flecked with dark spots. And seeing it makes her think of her children. And the horror, the paralysis, is replaced by an immediate need.

She rushes up the stairs, screaming their names. But the silence of the house mocks her. She checks their rooms. They are empty. The kids are not in the house. A helpless suspense overcomes Lorraine and she sinks to the floor of the landing and buries her head in her knees and sobs until the sobbing subsides.

Unable to bear the sight in the hallway, she covers her eyes as she comes down the stairs, goes into the kitchen and shuts the door behind her. The gleaming tiles and granite surfaces look exactly the way they always do. And shut in this room she can almost forget what has happened, write it off as some horrific nightmare. It would be so easy to just sit and try to forget about it. But instead, she goes over to the phone. She dials 9, then another 9. And then the toy elephant flashes through her head, and the knife beside it. She grabs the address book from its hook on the wall and flicks through it until she finds the name she's looking for. It has several lines scored through it. Scott must have done that. But she can still just about make out the phone number. She dials.

"You have reached Roberta Klein." The recorded voice is instantly soothing. "If you are a prospective client, please leave your name, number and an indication of when I can call you . If you are an existing client, just leave a brief message and I'll get back to you at the earliest opportunity."

The answerphone bleeps.

"Please..." Lorraine hears herself say, her voice sounding alien, as if someone else is speaking, "... call me..."

The phone drops from her hand and bounces on its springy coil. Lorraine retreats to one of the stools at the breakfast bar. She sits down and holds herself, curling her head into her arms and closing her eyes. And she breathes deeply through her nose and out through her mouth and she tries to find a way to a safe space, somewhere far away from here. And in the black behind her eyes, she hears a voice, very clearly, the way she sometimes hears her mother calling her name when she's on the edge of sleep.

You are not your thoughts. You are not your past or your future. You are only your body and this moment right now.

And the blackness behind her eyes begins to deepen. Until it is not just a blackness but a space. There is a musty smell; the smell of earth, and the sensation of pressure, of being in the earth. There is warmth, a close warmth, warmth that comes from bodies. Enclosed by bare brick, flaky with the remains of paint that may once have been white, only a few of the large gathering are visible, caught by residual streetlight from a tiny barred window at the top of one wall. They stand with their heads downturned at a forty-five degree angle, their eyes closed. Like they are asleep on their feet. She doesn't know who any of them are, but she feels as if she knows them. She can almost hear what they are thinking.

There's one guy. Skinny, unruly hair, a strong nose like a beak, his glasses throwing shadows up across his forehead. She definitely recognises him. Though she struggles to think from where. He's a friend of Scott's maybe? Scott. Dear Scott. But she's not sure. And then she hears a name whispered somewhere in the back of her mind. Maybe by him, maybe by someone else, and the voice says,

Sam

but her attention is pulled away from him. Pulled away from the other sleepers who are not asleep to the centre of the room. The centre where there is an opening in the crowd. And in that opening a shape begins to materialise. It rises, huge and black, and its blinkless black eyes are as large as her head. And it spreads out its wings, reaching to the very edge of the room, casting its protective shadow over all of them. The sleepers who are not asleep.

Part One:

Roberta

Chapter One

HOPES AND FEARS

A black bird. It stares at Sam from where the sloping wall of the attic room meets the ceiling. Four years he's been coming here and he could swear he's never seen it before. It must have always been there, but the shock of discovering it, crouched up behind his head like that, leaning over the chair where he's sitting, makes him strangely ill at ease. He stands and walks over to the stuffed bird, reaching up towards its sharp black beak.

"I wouldn't touch that," says Roberta, entering with a steaming mug of tea. "It's a bit fragile."

"How have I never noticed it before?" says Sam.

"Sometimes we only notice what we notice."

Her small black eyes maintain contact for a length of time that would be unusual for anyone but a lover. Sam shuffles his feet, puts his hands in his pockets and looks away. Roberta sits down in the armchair opposite his and they begin.

"So how are you?"

"I'm not sure. I just read some disturbing news."

Roberta inclines her head, inviting him to continue.

"They found Scott March dead yesterday morning. Murdered in his own home. It was in the papers."

Roberta blinks, but shows no sign of emotion. "It's terrible. I didn't realise you knew Scott."

"We chat sometimes in the café round the corner, before his session and after mine, while he's waiting for his wife to turn up. I haven't seen him for a while, but I never thought... They came to see you together didn't they?" A little light bulb goes on in his head. "You're not... Are you still seeing her?"

"I really can't talk to you about my other clients, Sam."

Of course, he should know this; and the look he gets from Roberta makes him feel like a naughty child.

Then her face softens. "But of course, it's a shock for all of us. Why don't we talk about something else?"

"How do you do that? Just switch from something so big to, you know, business as usual."

"Because it's my job." Her fingers curl around the arms of her chair like she's piloting it. Like it's her instrument. "Let's talk about you. That's what we're here for. How was your date?"

"Which date?"

"You had more than one?"

"No, obviously, I just, I don't know why I said that. It went well, really well."

"Do you think you'll see her again?" She leans forward and her bottle-copper curls jangle around her moonlike face.

"I really hope so."

"That's wonderful. I am so happy for you." Her smile is like skin on a tanning rack.

"I feel like I should be thanking you."

"Not at all. It's you that's done the work."

"No, I mean specifically... there was something you said that really helped me."

She raises one of her pencilled eyebrows.

"Well, we were in this bar and I knew I was going to kiss her, I just didn't know when. And she looked so beautiful and all I could think was when, when, when? How can I make it happen? And as long as I thought that, I felt kind of paralysed. And then, out of nowhere, this thing floated into my head. Something you said once. Something like

You are not your thoughts. You are not your past or your future. You are only your body and this moment right now.

And the next thing I knew I was kissing her."

"And what was that like?" Roberta's puffy face is flushed, like she's caught up in a Mills and Boon.

"Nice. Kind of weird, but nice."

"Weird how?"

"I didn't really feel anything."

"Emotionally, you mean."

"No, physically. I couldn't feel her lips or her hair brushing against me. I couldn't taste her. Nothing. And when I think about it, I don't even know how I got there. I don't remember leaning in. One minute I was sipping my pint and the next I was kissing her. It was like there was... a blank in time. Like I was absent from myself."

The attic room heaves with a dry silence. Her staring eyes are like holes.

"But of course it's going to be weird," she says; then gives him one of the warmer smiles in her repertoire, her teeth showing just a little. "This is the first time you've kissed a woman since Caroline."

Streetlights, cat's eyes, white lines. Lines and lines moving past. The

road is dark. And the sound of the wind is furious. Billboards flicker by. Images pass through images of recent memories. Her pure grey eyes, the brightness of her smile. Her light floral perfume. Her hand brushes against him. She's in the seat beside him. The warmth of her body, so close that it's almost touching. But he needs to focus so he closes his eyes and then he opens his eyes. And he's in a...

It must be one of those sharing groups. It's years since Sam's been in one of these and he wonders what he's doing in one now. From the looks of it they're in the middle of someone's living room, but the furniture's been cleared away and the peeling orange and brown wallpaper looks like it's from the seventies. The windows are night dark, reflecting the bunch of them sitting around in a circle on plastic chairs. They've all got their heads down, like they're meditating or something. He's the only one with his eyes open, watching them all. It feels a bit naughty and he worries that if someone else was to see him he'd be in trouble.

He looks around at the others. He doesn't recognise any of them. There's a balding man with longish hair at the back of his head and a leather jacket; a slight, pixieish blonde woman; a tall, thin man in a suit with one of those city-boy shirts that's a rainbow of coloured lines, open at its white collar.

"It's going to get difficult soon. You know that, don't you?" The blonde woman is speaking. Her head is up, her eyes open. She is looking at him. "You know that this isn't going to last. It can't last."

"You're going to have to tell her who you really are at some point. What you're really about." Now the balding man is looking at him. "And when you do, she'll run."

Sam opens his mouth to respond, but before he can their eyes close and their heads drop and somehow he understands that speaking to them is pointless.

"What would she want with you anyway?" Sam's head jerks towards the city-boy, right next to him. His face is hard-edged and lean and acne-scarred, his narrowed eyes are cold. "What have you got to offer a woman like that? You were pissed when you hooked up. Neither of you knew what you were doing. In the cold light of day she'll see you for what you are. A loser. A mopey bastard who just hangs around by himself doing fuck all 'cos he can't get over shit. And anyway, what do you care? You'd rather have your dead wife, even though she's been in the ground long enough that what little was left of her has probably crumbled to dust. Not that a dirty little necrophile like you would know what to do with a real live woman if she bit you on the dick."

Sam wants to strike the man, to knock his stupid, arrogant chin around the other side of his head. But his hands are glued to the underneath of the plastic chair he's sitting on. And like the others, the suited man's head turns down and his eyes close and his face becomes as peaceful as a sleeping babe. Sam scans around the circle, his nerves and muscles twitching as he anticipates the next speaker. But while he looks at them, he finds his eyelids becoming heavy and his head tilting towards the floor and he –

Slams into wakefulness. He's sitting up in bed and his room is dark and everything is dreadfully quiet. Hushed. Only the occasional sound of a car passing on the road below. Streetlights cast a forest of imaginary shapes on the ceiling. They soothe him. And already he's forgotten the whirling disorientation that clung briefly to him as he woke from his dream. But still, those voices echo in his head. Those people, whoever they were, their faces already fading from his mind as he lays his head back on the pillow. And now when he closes his eyes, they fade with his consciousness.

Teeth. Bared and gritted in the bathroom mirror. Smiling, flapping his lips, he picks at his teeth and flosses them, going through string after string until his gums bleed. What if she runs? He keeps asking himself. What if she runs? If she runs she runs. That's what Roberta would say. And he tries to remind himself not to place such an emphasis on the outcome. To just enjoy Nina's company while he has it. That dreams are just dreams and reality is reality. And never the twain shall meet. But that's not the fear, is it? That she might run. The fear is that she might not be right. Nina might not be right. Because right now she feels so right. And that makes him happy. Not just not depressed. He's got a real shot at it. Happy.

Nina's summer dress clings to her on this sultry evening. She walks at a measured pace along the South Bank, where the billion lights of London twinkle and play across the swelling darkness of the river. Heels always make her feel like some sort of gawky creature on stilts. Like she might topple at the slightest sigh of an adverse breeze, or the shoulder of a brusque passer-by. But it isn't just balance that's keeping her from rushing. Her pace is also dictated by a mixture of anticipation and apprehension. And as she approaches the bar where they've agreed to meet, her lips whisper a little prayer:

Dear Lord, please don't let him be an arsehole. An arsehole or a psycho. And don't let me get too pissed and make a silly mistake. 'Cos if you do, I will be filing a negligence claim. Kind regards, Nina.

And by the time she's finished, she looks up to see the doorway of the bar looming over her.

He watches her float in on a wave of cool air. Lights along the river sparkle behind her head. She's tall and elegant. Her black hair trails around her shoulder in a coil, her summer dress is caught by the wind and a gauzy pashmina drifts around her shoulders. She looks left and right. A smile on her lips twitches at the edges. She should have seen him already – it's too early in the evening for the place to be busy – but she's so full of anticipation that she's looked right past him.

She walks into the middle of the floor and does a sweep. There's a guy playing the piano, there's three businessmen laughing. And there he is. Sitting in a dark corner watching her with a little smirk on his face. And she puts her finger on her nose and points at him like it's a game of charades. And he lifts up his hands: here he is.

She floats over to him. And they're just looking at each other and smiling. He puts a hand on her arm and leans in to kiss her, but feels her twitch away, and his kiss lands on her cheek.

She sees him back off, the way his lips fold. She didn't pull away on purpose. And he's about to say something, but instead she places a hand on the side of his face and plants a kiss on his lips.

And while their faces hang, touching, he can't suppress a grin and he chuckles and they both do. And then she pulls back and looks at him with her lively grey eyes, and he can see little lights dancing in them and all she says is–

"Hi."

But somehow it's the warmest greeting and it reassures him to know that they are both nervous.

Before long the stuttering awkwardness has passed and they are into the delight of conversation without meaning or effort. He finds everything she talks about fascinating. It's not so much the content as the way she expresses herself. Her colleagues, the little events of a day at chambers; to hear her talk about it you'd think she worked in a sitcom.

But she tires of talking about herself and takes a swig of her drink to indicate a new paragraph in the conversation.

"So what are you going to do now that you've sold Blue Mountain?" she asks.

"I don't know." His gaze trails away. "I wasn't really doing much anyway. It basically ran itself."

"It can't have been easy, though. Selling the company."

"All I did was sign some papers."

"Well, Caroline was such a big part of it. So..."

He looks straight at her and blinks once. Twice.

"I thought we were talking about *your* work," he says.

"I'm sorry, I just, I don't mean to pry, but... I just want to know more about you." A small smile, a softening around the eyes, "Tell me about her."

The colour drains from his face. Real, raw, fresh sorrow crowds in. Valiantly trying to smile through it, he says,

"What, how... how she died?"

"No, Sam," she takes hold of his hand across the table, "you already told me about that. Don't you remember?"

"I'm not sure. I was a bit tipsy."

"Understatement of the year. But yeah, we both were." And she squeezes his hand and it brings out a smile in him. "Look, I'm sorry if I was out of line. I don't want to spoil the mood or anything, even though I probably have, but I just... Tell me about the good times. Tell me how you met."

He folds his arms and looks away. Then back to her.

"Okay." The muscles in his face relax and a calm settles on him. "Okay then. It was at university. I was queuing up to register on the first day. I was nervous and I didn't know anyone and I was looking up and down the corridor at the other students. Everyone seemed so confident, you know. I was, like, dazed, caught in the glare of all of this too-much-going-on, too much new stuff.

"So I was rooting in my bag for some papers or something and I looked up and saw this girl standing in front of me." His eyes grow far away and a smile lights his face. "She was short. Blonde hair cut in a bob above a white polo neck. There was something about her. I couldn't stop looking." He looks at Nina now, his eyes alive with the memory. "But that whole time standing in line I didn't see her face. I was just looking at that polo neck. The way her hair curled down over the edge of it. The way its lines stretched and expanded and grew around her..." he flushes, "um, shape."

"You mean her tits."

"Yeah, I mean her tits," he chuckles. "Anyway, we reached the end of the line and she hooked her hair behind her ear while she dealt with the registrar and I caught a glimpse of this rosy cheek. And I was just staring at her and it took a while for me to notice that a guy behind another desk was saying 'Next. Hey. Excuse me. Next please.' but when I did, I just motioned to the guy behind me to step forward. He didn't understand why I was being so polite but I insisted. And my display of chivalry must have charmed her because she turned round and our eyes met. And – her smile. Her smile was so bright. I don't think I even smiled back. I couldn't move."

Nina's eyes are wide, and emotion plays visibly on her face.

"That's beautiful," she says. And she finds herself wishing to be loved like that. When he gets up and walks around the table and gently touches her elbow, lifting her to stand, she floats upwards. And she's lost in his eyes as he says,

"I don't think I've ever been able to talk to anyone like this before." And he places his lips on hers, and she melts. In between kisses, she breathes against his cheek,

"Why don't we get out of here?"

It had taken Nina a while to fall asleep. But now as the half-memories of the evening come back to her, she is filled with a warm glow and she reaches out for Sam, to burrow into his embrace. But she finds the other side of the bed cold, the quilt thrown off. She puts her glasses on. There is no light behind the curtains. It must still be the middle of the night. She flips over to look at the clock. It's 3:36 am. She wonders why she's even awake at this time. Maybe Sam woke her when he got up, or perhaps he went to the toilet or couldn't sleep and went to the lounge to read. It's not always easy getting used to sleeping with somebody else. But even with these completely reasonable explanations, she has a sinking feeling.

It's troubled her enough to wake her up fully, and she sits up in bed, breathes on her glasses and polishes them and calls out for Sam. The only reply is the whistling of the wind outside the tall windows of her top floor apartment. She hugs herself, trying to deny what she feels already, and gets up.

The bathroom door is open and the lights are off. And even though she knows she'll find nothing there, she switches on the light. The glass and tiles and white porcelain that she spent so long polishing earlier gleam at her. They look like they have never been used, like no-one even lives here.

The lounge is similarly spotless. The large format floral photographs, the creams and pastels, the night and the city lights stretching on forever outside the windows. They abstract the flat from its surroundings, it's like a showroom apartment. The only signs of life are the half-full wine glasses on the coffee table, flanking the vase full of cut roses that he brought with him, and the rumpled and squashed cushions of the pale pink couch where they fumbled together before making their way to the bedroom.

Even though she knows there will be no answer, she calls out for him again, and the sound of her voice is less like a call anticipating a response, and more like the plaintive cry of a wounded animal. Her teeth grind against the flush of anger that rises within her. She still can't make sense of it. It's not like it's the first time it's happened to her, but she didn't expect it of Sam. He seemed like a really sweet guy. Not the type to fuck and run.

She drains the remaining wine from each abandoned glass and goes back to bed. Sleeping is the last thing she feels like doing now – not with all these boiling emotions – but she can't afford to further compromise her energy levels for work tomorrow. Especially not for the sake of a man who has left her in the middle of the night. She huddles under the covers and holds herself, trying not to fight the tears that come, hoping they'll pass in time for her to get some sleep.

The truck comes every morning, reversing slowly towards her prone body. It'll run her over if she doesn't wake up in time to move out of the way.

Nina jolts into a sitting position and lets the alarm bleep on in an attempt to drown out the cold feelings of disappointment and force herself to get up and out to work.

A groan beside her gives her a bigger jolt than the alarm. And she looks round to see Sam right there in her bed, pulling a pillow over his head to block out the sound.

Relief balloons in her chest and emerges as an irrepressible smile.

It's like waking from a dream of a childhood Christmas morning to realise that it is in fact the 25th of December. She reaches out towards him, only half convinced that she will touch anything real.

He takes hold of her arm and drags her towards him, mumbling, "Mmm, turn it off and come here..."

But she pulls back from him and frowns.

"Where did you go?"

"Uh... very lovely... floaty... sleepyland?"

"Sam." She turns his face to look at her. "Really. No joke. I woke up in the middle of the night and I looked round the whole flat and you weren't here."

"Hmm... You're funny..."

"I told you, I'm not joking."

Sam's face freezes. He's heard her now.

"I don't know how I feel. It's difficult to know how to feel about something you don't remember."

"Well, start with the not remembering."

"I felt confused. And kind of like I've lost something. Like I've missed out or something's been taken from me. And scared."

"Why scared?"

"Why scared? Well, because of Nina. I mean she's been really good about it, but you should have seen the look on her face. It really freaked her out." His fingernails pick at their quicks. "Roberta, I don't want to fuck this up."

"You're not going to fuck anything up, Sam. Nina's a grown woman. She'll make her own decisions. You're you. She's her. Let's for get about her for now. Let's focus on you." Roberta leans towards him, her hands in her lap swallowed by her enormous bust. "How are you feeling generally?"

"Fine. I feel fine."

Roberta smiles, "I think you can do better than that."

"It's just... kind of out of control. I mean just when things are starting to get better, I feel like I'm losing my grip."

"Tell me something, do you think this... nocturnal wandering, somnambulism, whatever you want to call it, that it might be related to anything else? Do you see any kind of pattern?"

"Not that I can think of..." he screws up his face and looks down at his lap.

"Didn't you have a dream after you first met Nina?"

Sam shivers,

"You mean the one about the people standing round my bed?"

"Yes, that one. Tell me about it."

He folds his hands into the sleeves of his pullover, "Do I have to?"

She gives a slow, deliberate nod.

"I dreamt that I woke up in my room. It seemed totally normal and then I noticed these five long shapes around my bed. Like standing stones. But they were people. I lay there absolutely still. I didn't know what they were going to do. But they didn't do anything. They just stood there, straight, with their arms by their sides, and I realised that they weren't actually looking at me. Their heads were all turned down to the floor and they had their eyes closed. Like they were asleep on their feet."

"And what did you do?"

"I couldn't do anything. But as I lay there I began to notice words. It was like they were speaking to me but their lips weren't moving. I was hearing their thoughts."

"What were they thinking about?"

"Well at first it was a jumble of words. Meaningless things, football scores, song lyrics, shopping lists, whatever. But then it resolved into one word. All of them thinking it at the same time and nothing else."

"And what was that word?"

"Sleep."

"That's right. And then when you kissed Nina for the first time?"

"Yeah. Yeah, that's right." His head snaps up and he points his finger at the empty space between them. And somehow, he doesn't know exactly how, what she says makes sense. "It feels connected, but I'm not sure..."

"You said you felt – how did you put it? Absent from yourself?"

"Yeah, but it was just like a... How is that significant?"

Roberta smiles and leans back in her chair,

"What we're talking about here is the emergence and development of romantic feeling. And we're tracking a corresponding pattern of subconscious response to that." She holds her head at an elevated angle. "You see Nina, you fancy her, then you have a dream about sleepwalkers where you are paralysed and they are telling you to sleep. You kiss her and you have a kind of out of body experience –"

"I wouldn't call it that."

"However minor, you felt alienated from your own body. Like you weren't controlling it. And then, after you sleep with her for the first time, you sleepwalk out of her flat with no memory of where you went or what you did."

Sam's arms tense, his fists clench. It's like being read a list of his crimes. He doesn't know how to respond to them. All he does know is that he feels a strong desire to resist this narrative, to fight it somehow. If only he knew how.

"Sam, I think it's time we addressed the elephant in the room, don't you?"

He avoids her gaze, looking around as if actually expecting to find one.

"Do you think you might, in some way, in some deepest, darkest recess of your subconscious, feel like you're betraying Caroline?"

Air hisses back through his teeth,

"What's this got to do with Caroline?"

"You don't want to talk about her? Why do you think that is?"

It's not really a question. Sam knows this. It's Roberta's way of insisting that this is exactly what they need to talk about. He turns away, his jaw ticking, unable to meet her gaze. Little wooden animals line the windowsill, painted in bold colours. One of them is, in fact, an elephant.

"What do you feel when you think about her?"

He'd happily talk about anything other than the memory of his dead wife. But to try to change the subject now would be pointless. The more resistance he shows, the more it will convince Roberta that she's on the right track. And so, he tries to give her what she wants, to go with it. The oranges, yellows and blues of the parade of little animals distract him. And while he studies them, words begin to come.

"I feel like I'm in, like, a really stuffy room. Somewhere where you can't breathe. Where the air is tight and close. And it's dark and the curtains are closed even though it's the middle of the day and only a little light gets in and you can see all those tiny bits of dust floating in the air, the ones that you're breathing in. The ones that are suffocating you."

"Where is this room?"

And in his mind's eye, he turns and looks over his shoulder. The shapes are vague. Everything cast in shadow. But as he looks closer they resolve and he can make out a figure under a sheet. It's barely a figure. Barely there at all. It's like a bird skeleton. How can this be good for her? he thinks. This place where my lungs instantly constrict, she's in here all the time. Day after day. Hour after hour. Breathing in those motes of dust. He can hear the liquid rattling of her lungs. A straw sucking at a nearly empty glass. And he thinks does it even need cancer? Surely this room is enough to kill her on its own. But there's nothing he can do about it. All he can think is get out, get out. Get away from her.

"There's something we need to find," says Roberta.

Sam's watery eyes blur her shape into a black inkblot.

"The thing that's holding you there. We need to dig it out and look it straight in the eye."

And he tries to focus on her but he can't. Her face multiplies and divides in front of him.

"How do you feel about hypnosis?"

The bedroom is dark. She shivers. It takes a moment for her to realise that this is not her bed. She can still smell him. But she is alone. The quilt is half thrown off her and it is cold. She pulls it around her. Scoots herself back to sit, wondering why she is awake. There's a sound coming from somewhere, a regular, rhythmic scuffing. She squints across the dim room, but without her contacts all she can see are the dark, blurry shapes of furniture. Something moves. Floats up. A draft hits her and for some reason she's thinking about how clearly she can hear a car passing on the road below. She reaches for the bedside light– click–winces from the brightness.

The movement was the billowing-up of a lace curtain. A window is open. The scuffing sounds are coming from outside it. She calls for Sam with a wavering, uncertain voice. But he is not here.

Adrenaline begins to pump around her body. And she has to dare herself to stand, to shed the quilt and expose herself to that naked cold. Shivering. Holding the stiffening skin of her arms.

Things fade into being as she pads across the rug. There's something there. Something in the far window. Perched on the sill. At the chair where her clothes are draped, she reaches inside her jacket for her glasses and puts them on. She is about to put the jacket on too. But drops it to the floor.

It's Sam. Sam is there. That's him. Sitting in the window. She asks if he's all right. And then if he can hear her. Because he's not responding. He's just sitting there with his back to her and there's that scuffing noise. It must be his feet kicking at the wall below the window, idly swinging back and forth, like a child sitting on a bridge.

"Sam?"

And still he doesn't respond. His back is a closed book. She stares at the back of his head, willing herself to see through it and read the expression on the other side. She reaches out to touch his shoulder. And stops. Her fingers hover inches away from his skin. If her touch startles him, if he is sleepwalking and she wakes him... It would take so little for him to slip. And drop. And smash below, where the lonely cars pass in the lonely night. She thinks about it happening. About losing him that way. And in that moment the question poses itself with absolute clarity. Does she love this man? She has no answer. But the thought of losing him feels like the worst thing in the world.

The rattle of a shutter from below. A pair of arms reaches out from the newsagent's across the street and drops a stack of papers to the pavement with a solid thump.

Nina's heart is a wire, vibrating her whole body. She needs to do something. She leans one way and then the next, trying to get a glimpse of Sam's expression through the adjacent windows. But all she can see is the edge of his jaw.

She reaches out on either side of him, joining her hands in front of his chest. His shoulder is damp and cold against her cheek. The man from the newsagent's is now outside, staring up at them with his face slack and his eyes dull like he's watching telly.

She tightens her grip and leans back, attempting to ease him inside. Where it's safe. Where there are no sudden drops. He rocks back slightly. She feels his head turn against hers and looks up to meet his eyes. They are empty.

"Caroline?"

The dead name sends a shiver down her spine. She grits her teeth and her grip constricts.

They fall backwards together. The impact knocks the breath out of her. And in a moment of disorientation she has the sensation of the street outside rushing up to meet her, whirling behind her closed eyes. She slips out from under him and scrambles to her feet, groping for the edge of the desk and holding fast to it.

He is lying on the floor, curled up into a ball and shivering. His skin looks almost blue and the breath susurrates between his lips like he's hyperventilating. His eyes bulge, wide and brown, their veiny edges straining. Tiny pupils are fixed on her. His skin seems thin. She can see his skull through it.

The lounge is like another planet, an island of warmth in the dark cold night. They sit together on the couch, blankets wrapped around them, steaming mugs clasped between their palms. At the edges of the light, all of Sam's clutter – piles of books, boxes, computer parts and old magazines – crowds in around them like a nest.

"The first thing I remember after we went to sleep is looking up from the floor to see you standing above me."

"You called me Caroline."

He sees the distress in her eyes, the deep concern folding her brow. He hangs there, his mouth open, desperate to say something to make it better. But he can't think of anything.

"I thought you were going to jump," she says. And it hurts him to see the expression on her face that saying this elicits.

"I don't *think* I was going to."

The expression stays. He has done nothing to alleviate her concerns. He reaches out and slides his hand along her forearm. But something about the gesture brings tears to her eyes and her face curls down towards her lap. She stands and steps away, the blanket sliding off her. He stares at her back, which is hugged by her strappy pyjama top. Shoulders, spine, waist, hips, her shape is so strong, so graceful, so beautiful. Like nothing that could harbour the vulnerability that played on her face a moment ago.

"Sam, I really love being with you," she says, her face obscured by the curtain of her hair, "but maybe you're not ready for this."

Nina turns to him, her expression etched with sympathy, "I want you to know that I'm here for you, you know, whatever happens between us, I'll be here to support you. But... if you have issues that you need to sort out, things that are going to cloud our relationship and maybe make it impossible, then I'd rather just step out of the way and be a friend until..."

He leaps to his feet and closes the distance between them to take hold of her shoulders. And he looks into her eyes and they are darker and shinier than usual and there's a frailty fluttering about their edges.

"No," he whispers. "No, no, don't say that."

"Sam, what's going on with you? If your therapist says that..."

"Roberta." The breath evaporates from his lungs.

Nina peers at him, at the far away look in his eyes, the haunted expression.

"Sam, what is it?"

And his thoughts return to his last therapy session. To hypnosis. And a great and terrible notion crystallises in his consciousness. A large black bird, peering down at him from the wall with beady, beady eyes.

He's early. Tired and out of sorts, he sits on the wall outside her suburban semi and watches the birds in the trees. The little things flitter and jump from branch to branch. There's a sense of peace about the place and a fresh smell in the air.

At 4.14 he's standing on the doorstep. He watches his watch. Watches the second hand travel around the scratched face. It irritates him that he's still observing this propriety. And so, with thirty seconds still to go, he hits the bell. A tiny act of rebellion. And waits, staring down at the rough, brown weave of the doormat. The faded "Welcome" emblazoned there.

She appears with a waft of incense. Greets him in her customary manner, her head tilted to the side as if in sympathy before he's even said that he requires any. Today she's wearing dangly necklaces that pile up on the shelf of her bust. She tells him to go on up while she goes to the kitchen to make a cup of tea. He stands there for a moment, his fists balled at his sides. And it's just long enough that she stops in the kitchen doorway and turns to him with a questioning raise of the eyebrows.

"Smells like a hippy shop in here," he says.

She explains that she's had a bit of a damp problem. He folds his lips in imitation of a smile and makes his way upstairs.

He looks at her chair. Its worn brown leather moulded to the shape of her body. And he wonders what the room looks like from her point of view. He can't resist. With half an eye on the door, he gets up, edges towards her chair and sits down.

The seat is still warm. Opposite him, the chair that he thinks of as his looks tired and empty. The black bird is crouched over where his head would normally be, beak stabbing down. Ready to peck at his brains.

He leans forward, transfixed by the bird, unaware of his hand travelling towards the trestle table beside her chair. A clump and a rustle of paper startles him, and he looks round to see Roberta's notebook on the floor. "Shit." He picks it up. There's a pen lodged between the pages. He opens it to the place that she has saved and scans down the scrawled notes that detail their last conversation. There are some codes and abbreviations that he doesn't understand but little that betrays her thoughts about what he's said. Until he comes to one note, very clear, in the middle of the page in block capitals.

NINA = PROBLEM

His eyes defocus and he sees his fingers trembling above the words, stalled where they were tracing the lines of her scrawl. It could mean any number of things. But seeing those words written so starkly... He looks at his fingers and realises he can't feel the ends of them.

Footsteps on the stairs. Have they just started, or was he so distracted that he's only just noticed them? He lurches to his feet. Takes a step. Stops. Returns to the trestle table to adjust the notebook. The door handle turns and he all but falls into his seat.

He stares dead ahead, eyes glued to Roberta's empty chair. He hears her come into the room. Her necklaces jangle and clink as she pads softly around him. It's like she's walking deliberately slowly. But he doesn't dare look up at her.

She settles herself into her seat. Her brow creases. And she places a hand on the book and tweaks it a degree or two. As if she knows exactly what he's done and what he's seen. But the frown disappears so quickly that he's not even sure it was there. And she looks up at him, and smiles a familiar kind of smile. The kind that doesn't touch her eyes.

He lets her get through the initial questions. Sits, detached from the conversation, as she asks how he is. She seems blissfully unaware of the tension in him, of the tight-lipped one-sentence answers that he gives her. Her red curls bounce as her head tips from one side to the other, metronomically gauging the rhythm and cadence of her questions.

Until she asks him what news he has and he tells her, trying to keep his tone as matter-of-fact as possible in clipped. Brief. Words. About how Nina found him on the windowsill that night. And Roberta takes it like the bombshell it is. She drops back in her chair and unpacks a face of serious concern.

"It's a little bit important, don't you think," says Sam, "that you tell me what happened when you put me under."

"I know what you might be thinking but hypnosis is perfectly safe. There's absolutely no reason to... "

"Just. Tell me."

"Okay, okay." Roberta raises her hands. Then her podgy fingers find each other, interlacing in front of her mouth, elbows resting on the arms of her chair. "I took you back to that room. To Caroline's deathbed. I described it to you, much as you have in our previous sessions: you standing by the window, your back to her bed. And you were there, right in there. I tried to bring you close to her.

Evoke the feelings that you felt when you were there. And you felt them. It was hard to watch. Really, really desperately sad. My heart went out to you.

You started getting restless. I didn't realise at first, but you were fitting. I thought that maybe I was taking you in too far, somewhere you weren't ready to go yet. And I tried to pull you out but you weren't responsive. You had no control of your body. And you jerked yourself out of the chair and onto the floor and I began to get really worried that you would do yourself an injury – never mind what might be going on, you know, in there." She taps her temple. "I put a cushion under your head and I held you and I tried to bring you out of it again. But you still weren't responding – instead you started muttering and you were telling me the dream, you know, your reoccurring dream that you have."

"What dream?"

"The same one you always have. The one where you're driving."

And he feels the rhythm of the road. The undulation of the tyres as if he was sitting in the car right now. It's calling to him, taking him somewhere. But then he thinks of Nina. Of Nina = Problem. And his need for answers. He flashes Roberta a defiant glare and she flinches oddly, her head twitching back like she's surprised.

"I don't see what this has got to do with Nina finding me on the windowsill at three in the morning."

Whatever that reaction was, it has now been replaced by her default illegible smile.

"It's all connected, Sam."

"Oh really? How is it connected?"

"Caroline, Nina. You really don't see it?"

He just stares.

"Your wife dies, your world collapses, everything breaks

down." Her fingers place each point in the air, like imaginary bricks. "You build yourself slowly back up until you reach the point where you're almost ready to become a functional human being, you sell the company, you're letting go, and then you jump the gun and meet a woman and suddenly everything in your life is about her. And then, oh, surprise, surprise," she sweeps away her invisible construction, "you experience a run of disturbing life events surrounding Caroline, and orbiting around time that you spend with Nina. And, hang on, you actually during this latest episode, confuse Nina for Caroline. I suggest to you that maybe, just maybe," she holds her thumb and forefinger together, "there might be a tiny chance that you feel like you're betraying Caroline. You don't want to accept it, though. And then at the very moment that you're trying to distance yourself from her spectre, that guilt kicks in and it just," clicks her fingers, "pops back up again."

Sam sits absolutely still.

"Look, I recognise that the appearance of this woman in your life has given you hope; given you something to live for. She's like an anchor, drawing you into the future. But what happens when this woman... goes out of your life. What will you do then?"

He picks up the musty smell of damp beneath the cloying incense.

"You'd like that wouldn't you?" he growls.

Roberta's lip twitches. She passes her tongue across it, as if to lick away the betraying gesture.

"What is it about her that you don't like?"

"I don't like or dislike Nina. I've never met her."

"Are you trying to split us up?"

Roberta's eyes narrow.

"Did you tell me something while I was under hypnosis? Give me some kind of instruction?"

"I don't do that."

"Well I wouldn't be any the wiser if you did."

There's a tremor under Roberta's cheek, a tiny jerk of her head, "Oh, that's childish."

"Childish? I'm moving on with my life. You should be happy for me. But no, you've got some other agenda. As far as I can see, Nina's doing more for me right now than you are."

"This is exactly why she's no good for you!"

"Aha." Sam smiles and opens his hands.

"Sorry, I didn't mean to snap. I'm just being straight with you, Sam. It's what I'm here for. If you don't like it, there's not much I can do to help you with that."

He looks down at the floor, breath coming hard through his nostrils. His fists clench and then he stands up,

"What are you helping me with anyway?"

"Wait, Sam–"

He turns his back on her and starts for the door.

"Sam!"

He looks over his shoulder to see that she has got up out of her chair.

"It would be a very bad idea for you to leave like this." Her voice is quivering.

"Really?"

She steps towards him and places a hand on his chest. The intimacy makes him uncomfortable but he stands his ground.

"If you leave now, your problems are only going to get worse. The blackouts, the dreams, the aberrant behaviour – until you've faced up to your feelings around Caroline, they're only going to increase."

"Well, *if* that happens I can always see someone else."

He turns to go but her hand tightens into a fist and grips his shirt.

"Seeing another therapist would be a huge step backwards. Four years, Sam. Four years we've been working together. I am the expert on you. You'll never be able to replace that relationship." He can feel the heat of her body. Her small black eyes boring into his. "You walk out of that door." He tries to turn away but she grips him tighter; her breath smells of coffee, "You walk out of that door and you'll never be happy."

And he looks at her. Really looks. And he sees makeup cracked by crows' feet. He sees cheeks rouged by emotion that just shouldn't be there. He sees a lonely woman in her fifties who'll say anything to stop him from leaving. She has been so solid for him. He has relied on her for her strength and stability. But it's a façade. And it's crumbling. Underneath it all there's just an insecure mess of emotions. The thought of how much power he has given this person over his life is terrifying, and all he wants is to be as far away from her as possible.

He twists away and runs down the stairs.

It's only when he gets outside, into the fresh air, the slam of her front door still ringing in his ears, that he notices that one of the buttons on his shirt is gone. It must have come away in her hand.

Nina waits outside Piccadilly station, watching the flitting crowds as the daylight tilts towards sunset. A shaft of light breaks through the clouds, shining from amongst the flickering shades of grey and the deepening purple of the sky. A rare moment of stillness and beauty, seemingly unnoticed by anyone but her.

Her peripheral vision picks a movement out of the throng and she turns to see Sam striding towards her. He sweeps her up in his arms and his embrace is warm and strong and his face lit by an elated grin. It thrills her that he's so pleased to see her. And he pulls her close and kisses her deeply and firmly and when they part, their breaths steaming in the evening chill, she grins back at him and says,

"What's got into you?"

"I did it," he says, cheeks bright and pink, "I did it. I quit."

It takes her a moment to connect the dots and realise that he's talking about Roberta.

"I feel so light," he says, "I feel free. It's, Nina, it's the best thing I've ever done."

She feels a plunging inside her when she realises that this joy is not for her, but she pushes it aside. She congratulates him. For inasmuch as she can't really know about the interplays and importance of this aspect of his life, she can see that it means a lot to him and she's glad, for her part, that he's managed to distance himself from that awful woman.

He takes her by the hand and they step lively down the street, their arms swinging together.

"Where are we going?" she says.

"I don't know. A bar somewhere? I fancy a bar. What do you think?"

"Sure," she shrugs, "might as well celebrate, I guess. If that's the right term."

"I think... Yes, I think it probably is."

And then they are ensconced in a cosy corner seat in a lively bar, their heads and shoulders leaning together as they work on a bottle of wine. She's enjoying his company, but she's distracted somehow and while they talk, she catches a pair of eyes on the other side of the room. Sam nuzzles her ear and she's brought back to him.

"Are you thinking about getting another therapist?" she asks.

"Hmm," he says, finishing his glass and pouring another, "I hadn't really thought about it yet. In fact, I'm kind of really enjoying not thinking about it. I mean, don't you think that life might be just, I don't know, better, easier, without this constant navel-gazing and over-thinking and questioning everything? All this heavy shit weighing on you all the time?"

As he weighs up the pros and cons of getting another therapist, the crowd parts and she sees the man sitting on the other side of the room. He's tall and thin and dressed in the uniform suit and tie of any city worker. He could be anyone. But he's looking at her intently. Brazen. He knows that she's there with another man, but he doesn't give a shit. Nina decides to ignore him and turns back to Sam, interrupting his flow to kiss him on the lips. He grins and apologises for being dull.

"Can we talk about something else now?" he says.

"Of course," she shrugs. "But, look, I know it feels good to be away from Roberta, but maybe we should look into other therapists. I mean, she might be a shit therapist, but that doesn't mean they all are. I could help you find one if you like."

He agrees in principle, but demurs that he'd like a week or two to enjoy himself, to spend a little unburdened time with her. And the sentiment pleases Nina. But even as he begins to discuss ideas of what they might do together during that time, her eye is drawn back to the man in the corner. He's still there. He's still staring at her. And the intensity of his stare makes Nina feel a little tickle at the base of her spine that sends a chill up her back. She turns back to Sam and tries to focus on the conversation, but the whole time she can feel the stranger's eyes.

The next time she checks, he's gone. She wonders when he

left: whether it was the moment before she turned to look, or if the intervening sensation of being watched was the work of her imagination.

Above their sleeping bodies, streetlights cast a forest of imaginary shapes on the ceiling. Shadow fronds sway in an implied breeze. Sam and Nina sleep peacefully beneath the canopy.

It's the same dream he always has.

He's moving down a dark road. It's so dark that all he can see are the points of light. Streetlights, cat's eyes, white lines. Lines and lines moving past. Billboards flicker by. Images of recent memories. Nina astride him, her face alight with ecstasy. Roberta's hand gripping his shirt. His signature spidering across the contract that sells the company he and his wife built together. He puts his foot down, eager to move forward. The images flash past ever quicker, until he can no longer see what's on them. There's something in the road, hurtling towards him at speed. It's a chair. A brown leather armchair. Worn to the shape of someone's body. He swerves around it. But there are more obstacles. A china ballerina, smashed in pieces all over the road, his wheels crush it to dust. A baby's cot. An oversized stuffed-toy elephant, spattered with dark spots. He swerves around them, but loses control. The car lurches dangerously left and right. He tries to fight it but the steering wheel is whirling, spinning out of his grasp. He slams his foot on the brake, but it doesn't work. He grasps the key and yanks it out of the ignition. But when he looks back there is another key in there. He pulls that one out and another takes its place. He turns back to the steering wheel. But there is no wheel. The car hits something in the road and turns over. And he's upside down, tumbling in the dark, not sure which way is up. Everything starts to fade and wobble. It becomes unbearably hot. Flames lick at the windows, melting the glass. The whole interior of the car is bathed in red and orange. There's red and orange and black, the deep endless black beyond the windows. He's upside down in his seat, held in place by his seatbelt. And he looks to his left, and sitting in the passenger seat, there is another person. A woman. Her hair is cut in a blonde bob, and she's wearing a white polo neck and the lines stretch and grow around her shape. And then she turns to him, unperturbed by the flames that lick around her, charring everything black. And her eyes are perfect wide ovals that shine with unsullied brilliant whites, and inside them pearlescent blue laps around pupils so large it's as if she's on some kind of drug. And at their heart, two pricks of light shine out at him. Twin stars that burn a thousand times hotter than the flames that now engulf them.

Chapter Two

FORMLESS THINGS

It's one of those shitty, shitty days when the rain keeps on coming and the sky is nothing more than a smear. Nina is uncomfortable in her heels when she comes out of the tube station. She's still in work mode with a handbag hanging from her shoulder in a straight line to her hip. But her professional façade is doing little to protect her from the elements. Raindrops spatter and mark her clothes despite the newspaper she holds over her head. And by the time she makes it to the underpass, it's little more than a sponge. She discards it and stands, shaking herself off, in that low-ceilinged space where she wouldn't ordinarily wait for more than a moment. Even as she entered it she noticed a couple scampering out the other end upon hearing her footsteps. But the dodgy feel of the place and the smell of stale urine isn't enough to make her sacrifice shelter.

Dawdling the length of the tunnel, she unties her hair, pulls it to one side and wrings it over her shoulder. At the far end, she peers out to see the rain coming down in sheets. So she waits for a bit. She checks her phone. There are several missed calls from Sam and she mutters a 'fuck's sake' half-directed at him for pestering her and half at herself for not having found the time to take his calls. She dials and gets his answer phone. Smiling at the sound of his cracked voice on the recording, she leaves a message. I'm sorry. I do this. I know. I didn't mean to. She hangs up. Looks out at the rain, holds a hand out and brings it back in wet. Cursing under her breath, she rearranges her clothes, preparing to brave the elements.

A scuff. A shuffle as if someone walking has stopped abruptly. She turns. Nothing. No-one's there. She becomes aware of the silence and the cut-offness of this place. It is an almost dead space. It's the middle of rush hour outside but here it feels like there is no-one else in the world. But there is. And she tenses up as her eye is drawn to something down by the bottom of the wall at the tunnel entrance. Just poking out. A black shoe. Taking a grip of herself, steadying her voice, she calls out, "Hello?"

The shoe doesn't move. She stands there, everything bristled, alert. She calls out a second time and the shoe slides out of view. For a brief, insane moment she considers going to see who's there. But then she turns and dashes out into the rain. It was probably just another nervous commuter; the two of them jumping at each other's shadows the way everyone does in the city. That's how people eat each other alive. The fear is good for you, she thinks as she jogs through the rain, it helps you turn a profit.

His sleep has been getting worse and worse of late. On nights when Nina's not there, he'll lie awake half the night waiting for rest. It always goes the same way. The feeling of warmth and comfort as he pulls the quilt up around himself. The closing of the eyes. Darkness. Peace. And then a growing restlessness as his awareness fails to dim. And sleep feels like an unknown, distant thing. The quilt becomes hot and uncomfortable. Cotton chafes against him as he turns over. He turns again and again. Until he is barely lying still for more than a second at a time.

This kind of sleeplessness is not something that he remembers experiencing since the darkest days in the wake of Caroline's death. This is something that he had almost forgotten about. Something that Roberta had cured him of. And he experiences a feeling of gratitude towards the spurned therapist. And a return of the desire to be back in her room, sitting in his chair, facing that illegible smile.

It feels like a couple of hours have passed by the time he opens his eyes. But it's barely twenty minutes. He blinks at the blurred landscape of the room. His shoes; one standing, the other on its side. The lines of the floorboards are just visible, coming out from underneath the large faux-Turkish rug. In the murk its fringes curl up into strange characters; they undulate like waves or tangle and grow spider legs. Occasionally he thinks that some of them are moving. The tricks of an overactive brain that refuses to do his bidding. That won't be turned off. The notion that ordinarily he persists in believing – that he is his mind, that his mind is him – does not appear to be true. It seems more likely that it is nothing more than an organ. And in the same way that a stomach ache might refuse to settle no matter how much he wants it to, his mind is equally uncontrollable. It makes him wonder who and what he is. If he is not a brain carried in a vehicle which it controls, is he some kind of spiritual consciousness to whom the mind is just another of the many tools at its disposal? Is he a soul? Does he believe in a soul? Does this mean that there is more in this world than he perceives? Does this necessitate the existence of a god? How does he feel about God?

He decides that it is this frenzied thinking itself that is preventing him from sleeping. And he tries to empty his mind. He turns onto his back, folds his arms over his chest like a corpse and slows his breathing right down. Big long breaths in through his nose and out through his mouth. The hope that his body is responding to this wilful imitation of sleep. That it is being fooled. That it is sinking back into the mattress. That the softness enveloping him is not just the comfort of his bed but is in fact the embrace of sleep itself...

Something brushing against his lips. He thinks maybe it's Nina. Her hair as she turns in her sleep. Then more like fur. And at the same time fingers. Brushing. Brushing. Soft, gentle. It is a pleasurable sensation. And they begin to push into his lips, prise them apart. Something foreign. Fibrous. Like he's ordered a drink at a restaurant and on the first sip found something left in his mouth; looking down at the glass to see some residue floating there, a lipstick stain. The liquid swimming with an oily rainbow on the surface. Tainted meniscus. He tastes bitterness. He sees lips and mouths and faces. The faces of strangers. The lacquered lips of women. Crumb-encrusted lips belonging to old men. Tramps. Dirty fingers. Heroin addicts' fingers stained with something indescribable and dark and brown. Reaching out as he hands them his spare change and tries not to touch them. Not to touch. Those fingers. Those lips. Entering his mouth. Another tongue like a living creature inside his mouth. A mouse. Fur. Foreign bodies. Flakes. Pastry. Crumbs. Fibrous small flecks. He begins to retch and spit and there's that bitter tang. Something acrid and horrid and dank like the smell of a broken-down freezer or his block's communal rubbish bins in the summer. His nostrils twitch. His throat begins to convulse. Feels like it is collapsing in on itself. Is there someone standing over him as he sleeps? A shadow overlooking his prone and vulnerable body. Who is it? Who's there? Has Nina come home? And a surge begins in him, a subtle convulsion of his whole body, a mind-vomit. And he feels as if he is spasming and spasming again as he is forced by some part of his consciousness into wakefulness. Wake. Wake and wake again. Seeing himself wake, he jerks. And finally his eyes really do open and panic thumps away inside him but as he begins to clear he sees that the room is empty.

In the cool darkness his head whips round, jarring his neck. Who's there? Is anyone there? He feels inside his mouth. His tongue searches and he finds nothing and still he can't shake the distinct sensation that there was something in there but a moment ago. When he was unconscious. Like a dream of falling that leaves him sitting up with a sensation of vertigo.

He's awake. When is he ever going to sleep? Is it even worth trying? He throws the quilt aside and swings his legs over the edge of the bed, ignoring the blast of cold that hits him. His feet hit the floor and now he's up and standing. He's still wrapped in the arms of a host of grasping dreams that don't want to leave him. He takes a step. And they start to lose their grip on him. He leaves them behind, impotent and fading and with each step his awareness grows, his conscious mind coming back to its full power. He walks out of sleep and into wakefulness. Like he is stepping from one part of his mind to another.

He gravitates towards the open door of the lounge, seeking to step once again to another place. His shin cracks against the leg of a chair. Letting out a cry, he realises that he has just transcended another level of awareness, that he was perhaps more asleep than he realised. That he may never quite reach the end of these folds within folds. Is his whole existence, he wonders, a dream within a dream? Another unknown state of awareness could be available to him. Is this what he's trying to reach through therapy, perhaps?

A vantage point from which he can look at the whole of his mind from the outside?

At the doorway to the lounge, he turns and looks back at the bed. The quilt cast aside. The impression of his body. Considers holding an entire conversation with the part of him that was there a moment ago. To sit and speak and drink coffee and discuss matters known better to either of them than they are to anyone else. But is that not what they are already doing? They? He. Him. Me. I.

A scuff. A heavy, solid, sound. Sam spins back to the lounge and sees, he could swear, a foot sliding out of view in the doorway. As if someone was hiding, has just ducked around the corner. He grows heavy with fear as something in the back of his mind somewhere is confirmed. He is not alone. Icy-veined, he moves towards the doorway. Pauses. Takes a deep breath. Holds it. Listens for any sound; for the rustle of cloth or the faint hiss in and out of breath. But he can detect nothing.

"Hello?"

It rings out like a gunshot. And after it's gone the stillness of the place is so marked that it feels like there couldn't possibly be another person in here with him. He's alone, firing guns at shades, chasing the images behind his eyelids. He steps through the doorway:

TV, couches, coffee table, pictures on walls, the kitchen hatch. Stainless steel pots and pans catching the moonlight on the draining board. The back of his neck bristles. He spins the other way. Dining table. Vase. Nina's flowers starting to droop. Windows. Curtains. Could the intruder have worked their way around to the other side of the room without him noticing? No. Of course they couldn't. He chastises himself for his ridiculous illogic. And then his eyes return to that hatch through to the kitchen. If there's one place a person could be...

He steels himself and crosses the floor, bare feet leaving shadows of themselves on the wooden boards. As he approaches, the hatch offers a changing perspective and he leans this way and that to try and get a more comprehensive view of the room beyond. But it still leaves out vital areas. Hiding places. What is there but stillness and, and, a man hiding with a kitchen knife in hand. Ready to stab him, cut his throat, gut him, wear his genitals as a hat. Oh God.

But the room is as empty as any of the others.

Returning to sleep is clearly a fruitless exercise. So he turns all the lights on. Takes a book and he sits down on the couch in the lounge and reads.

Two pages in, his stomach begins to churn and gurgle. Not with any serious discomfort. Just a gastro unease as if he has eaten something that was a little undercooked. Something that his gut can deal with that will pass soon. But as long as it's happening to him, there's always that gnawing discomfort that it could develop into full-blown food poisoning. Vomit. Diarrhoea. The works. It doesn't though. It doesn't escalate. And he ceases to think about it. Not because it has gone away but because something else steals his attention. Since the moment he started feeling odd, he has been reading and rereading the same paragraph. And even though the words are now as familiar to him as his own name, he can't get any meaning out of them. As if it's a foreign language. And the more he goes over the paragraph, the more oblique they become. He thinks about skipping it but when he moves his eyes to another part of the page, the words swim in front of him. They are fuzzy, shifting. Uncertain. Their order becomes mixed. Soon they migrate and drift, even crossing the boundaries between pages. The effect on Sam is something not unlike car-sickness and now he's not sure if the nausea that's creeping over him is coming from his gut or from his head. From these churning pages. He lets the book drop to the floor. Blinks. Blinks again. Pinches his eyes. Looks up. Around. Shakes his head. Feels a little better. Stands. Inhales. Exhales. Lets his lungs expand to capacity and the fresh night air from the open windows purge him of these unwelcome sensations.

A surge. Downwards. A swing. A swoon. The whole flat moves around him. He can hear the concrete of the building straining as everything becomes uneven and the floor slides down away from him and the ceiling tilts up. This, this is... Sam doesn't know what it is. He steps, spins, wobbles. Tries to walk towards a doorframe, to find something solid to hold on to but he can't put one foot in front of the other without twisting off in another direction. This is not what he wanted. Why is he going that way? Can it be anything other than a falling falling falling through the floor? He twists his head at the doorway, tries to step towards it but his foot just slides across the floor. He lands in a crouch, his hand planted on the boards. And the doorway tilts down at him, towering up over him. And the shadows in the room beyond coalesce. They are becoming something else: a figure that steps out towards him. The shadows still cling to it and it remains dark even as it steps into the light. And then, behind it, another steps out. And another and another, until there are five of them, surrounding him. Their faces are confused and jumbled by patterns. Each one is a shifting mass of geometric patterns. Living, writhing masks. He asks who they are but they do not respond. And as he tries to focus on them, he sees faces emerge through the chaos of shifting geometric patterns. He doesn't recognise any of them, but their heads are downturned towards the floor, their expressions dead. And they close in on him and they grow in size until they are tall as mountains. Two of them reach down, from either side and grab him by the arms and he finds himself rising until his feet flap jelly-like and find the floor. And one in the centre comes forward and his human face becomes a grinning devil and just breathes and breathes and doesn't speak and Sam can't find words to say anything but all he can think is why are you not speaking, why the hell are you not speaking? And that devil breathes lowly and full in his face with a sound like the shifting of mosses through the earth and it smells of rot and speaks not speaks not speaks not and Sam tries to stutter something but all he can manage is to – the devil's arm comes up and –

Slam.

Slam.

Slam.

Sam's head rips back and the ceiling curves into an arch above him as his vision is severed into blackness with each successive blow and a pain so bitter spreads through his face from the fragile bone of his nose to the base of his skull. And the next thing he sees is the floor. Tiles. Wet tiles and blood. He's in the bathroom. Shards of silver glass around his head. He scrambles over to a corner, eyes darting left and right and he realises that he is alone. Then a flutter. A flutter before his eyes. Like an insect or a fly or a butterfly. He feels his heart pumping. And every beat is an earthquake from inside him. He rubs his hand over his face and pain ignites once more. And he looks at his palms and they are covered with a dark smear. Like the stains on a junkie's fingers.

Out – out are the lights – out all.

First there is the sound of knocking. Then there is pain. Then there is awareness. He drags himself along the floor, lips kissing tile and dragging dry.

He opens the door and Nina's face blanches. Sam spins as if he can't carry himself and stumbles back into the lounge and leans against the back of the couch. Nina is still standing at the front door. Tears sparkle on her white cheeks. In shock, she stares at Sam's swollen face. The darkening mass of bruised flesh under three broad stripes of black: one over his brow; one across his nose; the other wrapping from his chin around to his cheek.

"Sam..." Is all she can say. But she doesn't dare move. Doesn't take another step. For what seems like ever she is locked into where she stands on the floor.

He doesn't know what to tell her. They sit in Accident and Emergency and he waits for stitches. He feels convinced in one moment that there was someone else there, and in another that he was alone and that whatever happened was a product of his own mind.

"But this," she says, indicating his injuries, "this isn't in your head. You can't have done this to yourself. How can you possibly have done this to yourself?"

Back at home, he points out that the medicine cabinet mirror in the bathroom is shattered. There's a chip out of the porcelain of the sink. The way the blood and damage is spread out. He says, "I was sure that they, he, those things, did these things to me, but now, now I just –"

And all Nina can say is "A person can't do that. Can't smash their..."

And the thought of what he must have, might have done makes her feel ill. She realises that despite her words, despite everything she says, she feels that the opposite might very well be the case.

They lie in his bed in their underwear. He is curled into himself in a little ball and he stares away at the curtains brushing the floor. She has her arms around him and sobs into his shoulder. She lifts her head and looks at the wet stain left on his t-shirt.

"Think about it. Sam. Logically. If there was someone here, who could it have been and what would they have wanted with you and why is it that it's so confused?"

"And if there wasn't." His voice is empty of inflection. Without the "if" you'd never know it was a question.

"Then you need to work out..." she tries "why..." but she can't complete the sentence.

"Why I would do this to myself."

She buries her face in his shoulder and tears come anew.

"I need to speak to her."

"No. Why? Why her?" And she looks up to see his gaze resolute, if far away.

"Because she understands me," he says.

She lurks in her chair, a soft black shape. Her lined face is severe, despite its roundness. The eyes are little glass pebbles like you find on a stuffed toy.

"You shouldn't have stopped coming," she says. "Do you need any more proof of that than this?"

"You think it happened because I stopped coming?"

"Yes. You had a full-blown psychotic episode." She lets the words settle. "Sam, there is something inside you that you're hiding from, but the harder you push it down, the harder it's going to keep coming back up. Don't you understand that yet? I would have thought after all our time together you'd..."

"But what if it wasn't?"

There's something furious in her expression when he says this and it makes him feel weak and stupid. He wishes he could take it back. But she cocks her head and waits for him to continue. So he proceeds haltingly to explain that there is, could be, maybe a possibility that there were people in the flat with him that night. She asks him, if this is the case, how he can explain all those other sensations. He says he doesn't know.

"It was clearly an hallucination."

A pronounced judgement. A final, definitive view. That's how it is. There's no going back from it. Sam looks at her. Looks at her really hard. Concentrates on those eyes, trying to read her soul. And while she's asking him questions about the practicalities of what it would mean if there had been people in the room, who they could have been, why they might want to do that and why, why might he think that he's going to such lengths to explain away what happened as something external to him, he's just staring and staring at her. And he doesn't answer her questions even though she stops, waits for him to answer, then asks another and another. He just looks. And this is what he reads from her: nothing. Absolutely nothing. No kindness, no anger, no hate, no love, no sympathy, no self-doubt.

"What if it was you?"

He puts the question to her like a bullet. But it doesn't kill her. She doesn't die. It doesn't hurt her. It doesn't even seem to surprise her.

"You did the right thing coming back here," she says. "Well done."

Sam blinks at her in disbelief. The response has him regressing back to a small child being patted on the head and he feels the cushions of the chair rising up around him as he shrinks, shrinks and shrinks.

"I don't think you realise how significant that is. But it's huge, Sam. It shows that you want to conquer this. You really do."

By now he's not even sure what she's talking about. Her lips move but the things she says cease to have meaning. And then she smiles. Not a real smile, of course. Just the kind of smile she gives to her clients.

"Why do you think it could have been me?"

He doesn't say anything. He just glares and the longer he looks the stronger his hate becomes.

"Did any of them look like me?" she asks.

"No."

"Why do you think you would want to think it was me? Come on, let's unpack this."

"No."

"You say they didn't look like me, but you still think it could be me?"

"No."

"Keep it up. We've still got half an hour. If you want to spend that time behaving like a toddler, that's completely up to you."

He stands. Takes out his chequebook. Fills out a cheque. Tears it off. Lets it drop to the floor and then walks out without another word.

In the innocuous quiet of the suburban street, he walks in circles, breathes deeply. Ideas swirl in his mind. He can't get away from the feeling that whatever the reality of his situation is, this woman does not mean to help him. That nothing she does or says is designed to get him anywhere but in that chair for more and more hours. What does she want him for? Does she really care about him or is it just about the money? Is she some kind of weirdly obsessed psycho? What the hell is she playing at?

The front door opens. He doesn't even turn to look. And when she starts to say things to him, he covers his ears and starts walking. And he walks and walks. Even though his car is right outside her house, he just wants to be moving in the fresh air and anywhere away from her. He passes things that he hasn't seen on foot before. Things that were previously just a uniform blur of masonry. Featureless rows of houses become real places. Solid, motionless features of the landscape. They are channels. Funnels down which he is directed, that offer no option for a sideways move. Only two directions: to move forward and end up where they want you to end up; or the other, retreat.

After an hour of walking around the almost identical residential roads, he finds himself back at Roberta's. But he doesn't go in. Instead, he sits in his car and he waits. The world is so unbearably quiet sitting where he sits. Every incidental sound muted by the closed windows. He becomes acutely aware of himself in his seat, in his car, in his situation in time. Of minutes ticking by and the idea that whatever the truths are, he will eventually die one day and none of this will matter. Why is he sitting here watching his therapist's house like some kind of stalker. Is there anything illegal in what he's doing? No. But it feels wrong, doesn't it? He's stepping over some boundary. A rule of the relationship he has with this inscrutable woman – he's waiting to see other parts of her, parts of her that he's never allowed to see.

Footfall on the road is not massive. Every so often someone passes from one direction or the other. And as they approach, he evaluates the possibility that they might be her next patient. Too young. Too old. Too together. Then a scruffy woman in her forties. Possible. Possible. But no, she keeps on walking. Watching her, he has failed to notice the man on the other side of the road, crossing now in front of the car and making a beeline for Roberta's door. But now that he does, Sam's heart starts thumping in his chest. His skin feels electric. His awareness zeroes into a hyper-alert funnel, focussed on the man.

His brown mac covers a city-boy's outfit, stripes and a white collar, which is open, his tie removed. He carries a briefcase. He's around forty and the kind of wiry person that looks like they are made up mainly of ropes under their skin. His Adam's apple is like the dorsal fin of a shark. His face is pocked with acne scars.

He's one of them. Sam is sure of it. The people in his flat were unclear, fuzzed and fizzed by hallucinatory static, but now that he sees him in the plain light of day, Sam remembers his face. From that night. But more than that, he's so familiar that even though he has never spoken to him, doesn't even know his name, he feels like he knows him. Flicking back through his memories of the 'psychotic episode', he sees that the picture has sharpened now. Resolved into something clear and definite. He can see this man standing in his flat, with his eyes closed and his face downturned with his arms reaching out towards him. And now he's right there, right there in front of Sam, and he's outside Roberta's house, and he's knocking on her door.

It opens. Sam doesn't see Roberta, but he just about hears the chime of her voice welcoming him. He goes inside and the door closes behind them.

Sam sits there, his hands twitching on the steering wheel. He's desperate to get inside, to overhear their conversation. To know why he's here in this street and what his connection to Roberta is. Is he just another client? Is it something else? Will he now occupy Sam's chair, a chair that he probably feels as much ownership over as Sam does? Maybe one day they'll fight over it. And whoever wins will get to take it home with him. He wants to burst in there and ask them both. The impulse is so strong that he has to remove himself before he does something stupid.

He finds himself on a main road. There's a smattering of local shops, a bank, an estate agent. Stuff. More stuff. He goes into the coffee shop. Orders something frothy and sits down, letting his thoughts and emotions settle as he sits and sips at the too-hot drink. It scalds his lips but he barely feels it. A group of four children bounce by the window as their mother tries to corral them in some useful direction. The waitress sits at a table in the otherwise empty shop. She is young and beautiful. Her jeans are black and tight. Her top is almost sleeveless. She is on the phone, chatting about something so hip that Sam doesn't understand it. She notices him looking at her and her black lashes flicker, she gives him a little smile. He looks away. A bus thunders by and he imagines that the whole world is shaking.

W. Ross v Blue Mountain Ltd., page fourteen of 146. A tiny pain niggles at Nina's temples. She puts down the papers and rubs at the sides of her head. Leaning back in her chair, she stretches, sighs, sits up again. She thinks maybe it's something to do with that particular case. Taking up another file, she pulls off the pink ribbon and tries with that one. But it's no different. She has a nagging feeling, a heaviness, like her body is hanging off her bones. And she wishes she could just go home.

The phone rings. It's one of the clerks. He's quite a junior fellow and he ums and ahs and stumbles over his words as he asks her something trivial and then begins to repeat the same information that he told her in his last phone call. By the end of the conversation her patience is worn thin. She hangs up while he's still speaking.

And then she's angry with herself for being so short with him. It wasn't his fault. Not really. Although he should learn not to bumble so. That will come with time, she guesses. She wonders if he's quite so nervous around the male barristers.

She goes back to the file, and doubles her resolve. Headache, fatigue or no, she pushes through it and the machinery of her brain begins to grind into life. When the phone rings again, she tunes it out and lets it ring and ring. Until it goes to answerphone.

"Hi Nina, it's Sam."

This throws her right out of her zone.

"Um, listen, something's... I went back to see Roberta. And while I was there, I just got this feeling like, I don't know –"

She reaches out to pick up the phone.

"Like she was in on it, you know?"

And stops.

"And, well, I put it to her. I said it to her. I accused her. And, she wouldn't really answer and then... and, anyway, then I went outside and I waited outside her flat."

Her hand recoils all the way back into her lap.

"And there was this guy. I mean, I don't know who he is and I'd never seen him before, but the thing is: I *had* seen him before. Like, as soon as I saw him I knew he was one of those people in my flat. The ones that attacked me, it's... it's *real* Nina." He pauses, breathing hard. "Just give me a call, okay?"

Then the line goes dead and the office is quiet except for the muffled burr of conversation in other rooms, the dampened trill of other phones ringing. Nina feels cold. Reality sits heavily in her stomach. She thinks to herself, what do I really know about this guy?

The thought shocks her. It's never occurred to her before and she doesn't know why. But isn't it obvious? For all his loveliness and his niceness he's a fucking wreck. Exactly how much of a wreck, she doesn't even know. Yeah, he might have been something useful once but it's all lost in this mire of obsessive navel-gazing – and who knows what else? She reaches for her coffee cup and her hand is shaking. Shouldn't she have learned from her mistakes by now? She's been burned before.

Obsession. Compulsion. Psychosis. Again?

And then she stops herself. Chastises herself for having this thought. Feels a flare of anger directed inwards. How would she have felt if someone had made this judgement against her way back when... She's just had a shock, that's all. She probably shouldn't even be at work today. She should probably be talking to a therapist... And that tingling comes at the corner of her eyes. Her tear ducts prick and moisture comes there. And she feels an exquisite sense of loss because she knows that something has begun to crack. Something very valuable to her. She looks back at a little piece of herself that was living just a moment ago and is now shrivelled up and grey.

An hour later the door opens and Roberta's voice can be heard again. City-boy walks back into view. Crosses the road, oblivious to being watched, and continues on his way. Sam follows him at a distance until it becomes clear that the guy is not going to get into a vehicle of his own. He pulls over for fear of alerting the guy to his presence with the slow crawling, gets out and trots after him.

They turn through suburban street after suburban street. It's a fair fifteen-minute walk until they reach a new-built block of flats. Sam watches the guy go in and curses inwardly. Following him any further could be tricky. He crosses the road and watches the windows of the block for lights coming on. A wind stirs the trees around a patch of grass out front, catches Sam and chills him through his insubstantial jacket.

There's a dull throbbing in the base of his skull, a caked thickness in his temples, a fug of mental catarrh that he finds it difficult to see through. It's something like a hangover. The aftermath of his episode, perhaps.

The lights come on in a third-floor flat and from where Sam is standing he can just about make out the heads of taps and some hanging pots and pans. City-boy appears and he potters with something out of view. He stands and sips from a can of beer whilst staring blankly out at the night. Sam ducks behind a parked car, but then remembers that the brightly-lit interior will prevent city-boy from seeing out into the dark. So what's he looking at? Some lights in another house? His reflection? But he doesn't display any preening behaviour. No leaning forward and flashing his teeth or playing with his hair. He'd just be staring at himself in the room, staring with all the interest of a man on the tube who has forgotten his book. Could he be looking at nothing? He stands there like that, sipping his beer for some minutes before he walks out of view.

Sam ponders ploys and plots for a while. He could say he's a Jehovah's Witness. That wouldn't get him in. Pretend to be a neighbour, perhaps. It's London. In all likelihood the guy has never spoken to his neighbours. Would he know if Sam had just moved in or not? But then why wouldn't he have a key? That blows that one out of the water.

Sam hits the buzzer. It's a guess. Looks like there are two flats per floor, which would make city-boy's either five or six. He goes for five. There's a pause, during which Sam holds his breath. Then a hissy sound from the machine. A woman's voice says, "Come on up."

A woman's voice? The door clicks and Sam pushes it and he goes in.

Reaching the third floor, Sam finds the door to number five ajar. Except that it's on the wrong side. He knocks on six. A moment later city-boy opens the door and stares at him with a look of weary enquiry.

"Yeah?"

Sam glares at him. His hands ball into fists by his sides. City-boy squints at him like he's just seen a strange new kind of insect.

"What do you want?

"Don't you recognise me?"

City-boy shakes his head.

"You work with Roberta."

City-boy's eyes bulge. But before he responds, the door opposite is pulled open and a woman in a kimono dressing gown emerges saying, "Dan are you... Oh."

City-boy glares at her from under a sunken brow. He looks hostile now. The woman meets his gaze with equal malice, her arms folded, jaw clenched. He turns abruptly and walks back into the flat, motioning for Sam to follow.

"You're not Dan, are you?" says the woman.

Sam shakes his head.

"Did you see a man down there? Oh never mind."

She disappears into her flat and slams the door.

Sam follows city-boy into his spartan lounge. Everything is made out of identical flat-pack MDF. There isn't a picture or an item that gives a hint of personality in the entire place. He's leaning against the back of a white leather couch, his arms folded, staring at Sam.

"Fucking bitch," he says.

"You don't get on with your neighbour?"

"Worst neighbour. She's a whore."

"You and she..."

"God no," he laughs, bending forward as he does so, "I mean she's a whore. Literally." He shakes his head, puffs out his cheeks and looks away towards his reflection in the black window. "Some people have to go to work in the morning, you know?" He takes a money clip out of his pocket and squints at Sam. "Look, how much do you want?" he says, and starts peeling off notes.

"What?"

"Who do you work for? Phillips? I bet you work for Phillips, the little cunt."

"You really don't recognise me?"

"No, why should I?" His stare is vacant and his mouth hangs open moronically.

"You work with Roberta, right?"

"Not that I'm publicly acknowledging anything, but off the record, as I suppose you have evidence anyway, yes. Followed me back here from hers, did you?"

"How can you be working for her and not recognise me. You were in my flat just the other night, you... She put you up to it, right?"

"Wait, wait, wait." Waving his hands in front of him. "I said I work *with* Roberta, not *for* her. It's just how therapists say it, isn't it? Great working with you. Like you're doing something together and not paying them for a service. If anything she works for me, but this... I really have no idea what... Why don't you just tell me who you are, alright?"

"My name's Sam. I'm also a client."

City-boy's eyebrows rise, and then he breaks out in a shark-like grin.

"Neil," he says, and leans towards Sam, holding his hand out. The shake is strong. And there's something in his eye that speaks of camaraderie.

"You don't mind that I..."

"Oh, mate, I'm just relieved. I thought you were snooping on me for someone at work. Little shits'll do anything to get one up on the competition and, heh, I know it's not a big thing, but I work with guys all day and they have no idea I see a shrink and if they found it'd make me look weak. Never mind that I'd be fucking mortified."

"What do you do?"

"Trader." Twitch of his cheek. "You want a beer?"

"Thank you, I... sure."

"Hey, how crazy can you be? No crazier than me, right?"

"And how crazy is that?"

"Fucking loopy. Have a seat."

Sam sits. He looks at himself in the reflection in the large window. Looks at himself in the space. It doesn't seem to him to be a space that a person could live in. It doesn't bear the scars of a life. It's just a space. Blank and empty. In the centre of the longest wall, there's a huge television. Below it a tower of DVDs, some twenty or thirty in all. About half of them seem to be something to do with football. How many times can you watch a football match, Sam wonders. There are no books. On the dining table behind him there's a briefcase and an open laptop. Papers spread out.

Neil returns with a "heads up!" and throws him a perspiring can of Tyskie. He slumps down in the armchair opposite, a leg hanging over the edge. He undoes the second button of his shirt. His chest is hairy. There's a thin gold chain.

"You married?" he says.

"No. Seeing someone. I was. Before."

"Me too." He takes the chain out from under his shirt. There's a wedding ring on it.

"I'm sorry. Did she... pass away?"

"I wish," he chuckles, turning his face up to the ceiling. "Worst mistake I ever made. I keep this to remind me of what a fucking burden it was. You know, like what's his face in Lord of the Rings."

"Frodo."

"No, you know, the guy, fresh-faced kind of... Elijah Wood, that's it."

"Right. Yes."

Neil is clearly enjoying their exchange. If he had anything better to be doing, he'd be doing it. If he had anywhere to go, he'd be there. If he was busy, he wouldn't be here shooting the shit or entertaining such an intrusive visit.

"So why is it you think I should recognise you?"

If he was in Sam's flat that night, then he's either pretending he wasn't or he doesn't remember.

"Can you... Do you mind if I ask you about why you're seeing Roberta?"

Neil twitches again, a minute tightness comes and goes over the acne-scarred skin of his cheeks.

"Fraid not, mate. You can tell me about you, ask what you want to ask about her, but I'm not talking about my shit with you. Heh. That's what I pay her for."

"Will you tell me how long you've been seeing her?"

"Let me think." He leans forward, beer clasped between his knees. "Probably about, yeah, must be seven years."

"Wow. Me about four."

"Uh-huh. So I'm the veteran here."

"I don't know how to put this exactly but, um, have you ever noticed anything strange about her?"

"Apart from she's uptight and doesn't ever get fucked? No, not really. She does her job, I do mine. That's it."

"Has she ever hypnotised you?"

"She does that kind of spooky shit?"

Sam nods.

"Jesus. I wouldn't let anyone get anywhere near me with a swinging watch chain. What's it like?"

"I don't know, really. Can't quite remember." He chuckles to hide his discomfort. "You ever have any... blackouts, memory loss, strange dreams, that sort of thing."

"Sleep like a baby, mate."

"Have you ever considered ending therapy?"

"No. Tell you the truth I enjoy it. I can afford it. You know, it's nice to have someone to talk to so why stop it, you know what I'm saying? Even if it is all a bit touchy-feely."

"Hmm."

"Actually, you know, hang on. There was one point. Way back, it would have been a good few years back. But I do remember I got a bit fed up of it at one point. I don't know why and you know it's so many years of talking I can't remember every detail. But, God, when was it? I... funny, you know, I just can't put it in a place or time."

"I know what you mean. Don't you wish you had a record of everything you'd ever talked about with her..."

"What, like read her notes or something?"

"Yeah, yeah. Exactly. You could ask her. Let her show you her notes on you. See when exactly that was. 'Neil thinks about quitting' – I bet she's got it in big red marker pen." There is a spark behind Sam's eyes, a breathy excitement in his voice.

Neil looks at him with a wry smile. And then shakes his head, "What does it matter to me? Why do you even care?"

"It might help you to put the pieces together. I... it's hard to explain, but I'm interested in whether your urge to quit coincided with anything, you know, psychologically major?"

"Like what?"

"You know, hallucinations, voices, strange urges or desires, weird sort of acting-out and stuff."

"What, like a proper nutter? No, I'd remember if any of that Vincent van Gogh shit had gone down. Why? Has it with you?"

Sam tightens his lips, shuffles his feet.

"Wow, it has, hasn't it? You're proper loopy, aren't you?"

Sam winks.

At the door Neil says, "Listen, let's keep this between you and me, eh? I quite like the idea of having an eye on the inside, you know what I mean?"

Sam smiles at him. Nods. "It was a pleasure to meet you Neil."

They shake.

There are new voicemails on Nina's phone. It grates on her that he's left so many messages, surely one is enough. She's in her pyjamas, all fluffy and wash-aged, the kind of thing she would never let herself be seen in by a lover. She's curled up on the couch, battering her way through a bottle of wine with a dull, aimless look on her face. The television she's watching is so mindless that when she switches it off and goes to find another bottle, she wonders in disbelief at how she could have been occupied for the past two hours by so much reality shit.

She is in the kitchen opening the bottle when she hears the letterbox clunk. Her brow creases. Who would be posting stuff through her door at this time of night? It could only be another resident. A junkmail-flyerist wouldn't have been able to get past the entry phone. Even if they could, bothering to come all the way up here would be somewhat over-zealous. She sighs. It must be another one of those tedious residents' association round-robins. Uncorking her bottle, she pours another glass. Takes a healthy slurp.

But there is nothing on the doormat. So, what, someone just flipped her letterbox for the fun of it? It's possible that the kid from the neighbouring apartment could have run past and given all the doors a rattle. He is a wild one. Half-curious, half not really thinking about it, she saunters towards the door. And then stops. It registers that there *is* something there, and even before she can really recognise it for what it is, she feels a churning deep within her. Revulsion. The hairs on her arms stand up.

On the lip of the brass letterbox there's something gleaming. Something messy. Gelatinous. Something that gives her the same sensation as seeing a dead animal or encountering rotting waste. She reaches towards the door handle. But then her hand retreats. The whole door has taken on the aspect of something infected, something contaminated. That little drip of jelly seems part of it now, as if it has seeped through the wood and impregnated the door handle. She shakes herself. A fragile bravado is easy to come by with a whole bottle of wine to fuel it. Telling herself not to be so goddamned stupid, she opens the front door.

The outside is worse. The semen clings to the front of the letterbox in two milky ropes. She gags and staggers back into her flat. Turned away from the front door, she shivers and holds herself as a greater, more terrible notion comes to her: beyond revulsion at the thing itself there is the thought that there was somebody, some man, who did this. This is not the act of a stupid kid that runs up and down hallways making a racket, this is a personal, directed attack. This can only have been meant for her. Someone has sneaked into the block, come up to her floor, found her door and ejaculated on it – and not only that, they have made sure to get it through the letterbox. To open it and penetrate her private space. They want her to know that this is a message.

When she wills herself to turn and look at the still-open door, she gags again. And again. And the reflex keeps coming. Her throat aches with the force of the convulsions. A violent cough shakes her and a dark red splash is ejected from her lips, staining the floor. With the sour wine taste in her mouth, she looks down at her pyjama top with its little teddy bears and the rancid dark splash across it. Tainted. Filthy. She can't even contemplate closing the front door, let alone cleaning it. She runs back into the flat and tears off her pyjama top and throws it into the laundry basket. But her skin still feels creepy and soiled and disgusting, and all she can think is who? Who could have done this?

The police are running tests on the semen. She didn't give them Sam's name because she's pretty sure it's not him and she doesn't want to send any more trouble his way. After they leave, she heads out. And the whole way there, she's debating the matter in her head. She's sure it's not him. But if it's someone else, who could it be? The police assured her that her ex is still locked up. But that's less reassuring in a way. That's the most disturbing part. It could be anyone. Anyone male. But she's sure it isn't Sam. It's just the timing. Really bad timing. And his incessant phone calls don't help. But isn't that normal when you're in a relationship with someone? It's her that's been giving him the cold shoulder of late after all. Of course he'd want to know what's going on with her. And right now she needs to be needed. She needs comfort and reassurance.

Sam's block towers over her. Grey concrete reaching up in an endless pillar towards the overcast skies. A sharp wind whips at her jacket. She lingers on the threshold, finger poised over the buzzer. Rests her index pad on the button. Then removes it and steps away. She walks off a few steps. Stops. Returns. Oscillates between the two positions. She can't help it, even in spite of everything she tells herself. It's fear, and it's inexplicable. It's not something she can control.

There's a scraping sound above her.

Sam opens the window and looks down at his girlfriend, who stops mid-pace. He calls out to her and the pale disc of her face appears as she turns her head up to look at him. At the top of his voice, he asks her if she's all right. But she doesn't answer. She stands there for a moment, two dark spheres blinking, too far away to read. And then she turns and walks off down the street.

Sam bolts away from the window and races through his flat, overturning a chair on the way. He fumbles with the front door, pulls it open. It jars. The chain is still on. He closes it, trembling fingers struggling to unhook it. Then it's open and he's out into the corridor and shuttling down the stairs with feet that barely touch them. He slams out into the street. But she's already gone. There's nothing there but cars and cold and noise. And he looks round and shouts "Nina! Nina!". He runs down the street a way. But she's gone. Probably in her car by now; halfway home. There's confusion and anger rattling around inside him, bumping together and knocking chips off each other. He tries calling her but she doesn't pick up. And so he stops, stands exhausted there. And it's only after a little while, after he's run out of steam, that he notices that the shirt he's wearing offers no protection against the cold and he's shivering. Even so, he can't muster enough energy for anything more than a slump-headed shuffle back to his block.

He rings her four or five times again. And on the last attempt he leaves a message saying just "Nina. What the hell is going on?" And when he flops backwards onto the couch all he can think is: NINA = PROBLEM. Roberta. It's got to be Roberta. But what could she be doing to make Nina run away from him like that? The idea seems ridiculous. And yet, there's so much he can't explain.

He wishes he could tell Nina about all of this. Just discuss it with her. And in thinking about this, his thoughts dissipate into abstract longing. And then he lifts his head and peers through a fog to find himself sitting in his flat where the bright light of day penetrates through the tall windows and is cold and piercing and raw. And he doesn't think about much else. He's just here, awfully present. And the silent flat looks altogether sparse. It used to be so much cosier in here before Nina helped him declutter it. Some few sounds filter in from the street outside, others from other flats. A baby is crying. A television set blares. A chair is dragged across the floor. And Sam has the sensation of being terribly, awfully alone.

He calls Nina a few more times. And by the time he's finished, by the time she's not answered, night has begun to fall. He pulls the curtains closed with resignation as the words of Nina's voicemail circulate in his head. I can't get to the phone right now. Leave your name and number. I'm sorry I. Phone right. Nina. Call you back. Nina. Name and number. Name and – And something clicks in his head.

If Neil is somehow in thrall to Roberta without knowing it himself, then might there be other such clients? Couldn't she also be using them? Wouldn't it be great if he *could* see her notes, as Neil suggested. Not just to track his own therapy sessions, but to see who her other clients are. Maybe he knows some of them, too.

He gets out of the car and walks through the benighted neighbourhood. There is not a light on anywhere. No signs of life. It is as if all the people living here had just got up and moved out. He strolls along like any old pedestrian, with nothing to do, going to no particular place. He's just walking. Almost does that sort of tuneless whistle designed to designate non-suspicious activity. He ambles past Roberta's, looking casually towards it as he goes. The windows are dark. But it's too cursory a glance, so when he reaches the end of the street, he turns and swings by for another pass. Satisfied that there is no-one awake, he steps towards the front door.

The place bursts into colour. Security lights. Sam bolts. He runs down the road with his heart thumping and stops around the corner and thinks that now he understands why people have those things. He leans against the hedge and thinks. He needs to get inside, but he hasn't broken into a house before. It would be far simpler just to make an appointment and swipe her notebook while her back is turned. But she'd know it was him. She always knows. Those searchlight eyes are always watching, scrutinising his every inner motivation. How could they fail to see something as big and glaring as that.

Rounding the corner of the next street to return to his car, Sam notices something he has never seen before: an alleyway that runs in between the backs of the houses of the adjacent streets. A scrubby, overgrown no-man's land. Like any public space in this suburban London, it is unloved. The places that do not belong specifically to any one person do not receive attention. Care is not lavished. Ugly places surround the domestic fortresses of this city; an ugliness that is accepted and indeed confirms for its residents the hostility of the world around them.

He begins to make his way through.

There is almost no light here. Brick walls rise on either side. Rubbish underfoot, everything from crisp packets to car tyres to children's toys. Sam picks up a plastic football and tosses it over the wall thinking there's a fair chance that a child might be grateful for its return. Mistake. Security lights flare up beyond the bricks. A dog barks. Sam crouches in the rank grass. The disturbance sets something scurrying down there. But all he can do is stay put and try not to bolt when the alarmingly heavy something scurries across his foot. He hopes it's a squirrel – although he's fairly sure that the night is the traditional domain of another, less sympathetic variety of rodent.

Soon there is silence again. Stillness. Sam continues his advance, counting properties until he arrives at the back of the therapist's den. He reaches up – jumps for the top of the wall. He remembers climbing fences as a child and finds it alarming that those memories no longer incorporate the scratching and strain on his hands, the hardness of a brick surface when his knees press down on it, the infernal pittedness of brick that is rough and jagged and scouring. Heaving himself to the top, he finds himself eye to eye with a black cat. It's a cat he recognises. Roberta's cat. He hisses and it flies down into the scraggy alleyway. Sam drops down into the back of Roberta's garden.

He finds himself in a clump of bushes and is grateful for the cover, although the foliage ends about halfway down the garden where a paved patio leads up to the back wall of the house. A thud beside him. He gasps, almost letting out a shout as the cat makes a reappearance. It dashes through the bushes towards the house. The bright lights burst into life and Sam watches it zip through a cat flap in the back door. The sudden illumination is alarming, but he is reassured by the idea that Roberta may well be used to the security lights being triggered by things other than intruders. He wonders if any clients have ever attempted to break into her house before. And silently thanks the cat.

Taking careful note of where it was triggered, he waits for the light to deactivate. And then, sticking to the side of the garden in an attempt to skim the edges of the sensor range, he creeps forwards. The light comes on just as he reaches the end of the bushes. He makes a dash for the house, flattens himself against the back door and stands there, not daring to move. In the bright light he feels as if the whole world can see him. He is seized by a paralysing fear – thoughts of discovery, the police, other consequences. All he can do is wait there until the light eventually fades, and he can breathe again.

He casts around for a plant pot, a brick, something under which a key might be stored. There are several possibilities. He crabs to his left, edging towards a stack of pots, ever fearful that the light might come back on again. It doesn't, and he feels safe in the darkness. He reaches for the pots and tries to lift them, but they're heavy and precarious. He crouches. Heaves. The top one totters. Nothing but woodlice. Lets them down. He leans forward, taking a crouched step and reaches out for a loose brick. The light comes on and he almost screams, but stays put. Picks up the brick. The nothingness beneath it glares in the brightness. Across the other side of the garden there's a barbecue. Another furtive sortie. And still nothing. There are a few other possibilities: a garden gnome, a bench, a table. But none seem especially promising and the journey to each of them is guaranteed to bring the light flashing back on. Not worth the risk.

Sam seethes with frustration. He hasn't planned this at all. It is only now that the complete madness of the endeavour becomes apparent to him. The whole theory that he is trying to prove is built on nothing but air and suspicion – "Fuck" – and, it pains him to admit, no small amount of self-denial. He wouldn't even be here if Nina was talking to him. It's probably his agitation over that that's driven him to focus on this ridiculous narrative that he's constructing. But then he *did* recognise Neil. Not that his recollection of that night is incredibly clear, or trustworthy for that matter. It could easily be that they just bumped into each other outside Roberta's at some point in the last four years and he's forgotten the incident but remembers the face. And even having met Neil, that doesn't explain the special effects, the sensations, the visuals, the sounds...

Sam shakes himself as if to physically fling off these doubts. He takes in his situation. Looks up. Looks around. Breathes deeply in and out in an attempt to calm his nerves, to channel the adrenaline. He shuffles along the wall until he reaches a drainpipe. Flicks it. Ping. It's metal. Sturdy. He leans back. The pipe passes within a foot or two of the attic window – the window to Roberta's office. He takes a deep breath. Will he even be able to open it when he gets up there? Most likely it will be locked. And if it's not locked, it's definitely shut. So what's the worst that can happen? He has to come back down? No. The worst is that he could fall and break his neck. Wouldn't it be more sensible just to have come to see her for a session... but it's her gaze, her scrutiny that he fears. And in fact, it is so fearful that when he looks up the length of the drainpipe, it seems like nothing in comparison.

Sam grabs the pipe with both hands and jumps up, bracing his feet below him. It already feels precarious and the strain on his hands and feet is considerable. He is not sure if he will be able to support his own weight. He looks up at the pipe again. And thinks, isn't this the problem with this whole therapy thing in the first place? You spend your whole time thinking, running round in your head, never doing anything. And the only cure is action – the only cure that therapy doesn't seem to offer.

He reaches up. Pulls. Advances. Reaches. Pulls. Advances. He is surging, powerful, driven, possessed of a strange elation that makes him relish this challenge. And before he knows it, he is passing the second floor. The attic window draws near. To his relief, he finds a small pediment running across the wall below it. And gaining it makes him feel some small amount more secure at this height. But as he holds himself there, calming his breathing, he realises that the distance between the pipe and the window is far greater than he had estimated while on the ground. It's a distance he's not even sure he could make. And there are no handholds around the window itself. Maybe the frame would be thick enough to hold onto. But maybe not. The pediment couldn't support him alone – it is little more than a thin cement strip. He can just about get his toes on it.

He tests. Reaching out with his leg. Reaching as far as he can. And his foot comes within inches of the window. He thinks about making a lunge for it. Looks down – and the garden yawns beneath him. So far down. His head whirls with vertigo and his leg clamps back towards the pipe. There is no chance. And it's crushing. That he's come this far and still has such a risky descent to get back down. And to have no chance. No chance. He looks over at the window again. Thinks about saying 'fuck it' and making the leap. And the window frame itself begins to fizz and stutter. It seems at once less solid, like it's not really there and somehow more there than any other part of the edifice. The edges blur and tremble and then with a sucking sound, they separate into two separate windows. Sam's stomach dips and his skin tingles. And oh my God, he thinks, what is this? Another episode? A flashback? He has to get down. Now. Just looking down is terrifying. He needs to concentrate on his feet. Try to shuffle them off the pediment to grip the pipe. He stares at his feet, willing them to move, but they just won't obey. And now the pediment itself is beginning to shake and vibrate. Turning to jelly in front of his eyes. His feet detach. He drops, clinging on with his arms for a second until his feet find their grip. His cheek presses into the cold pipe and he breathes in and out, eyes squeezed shut. Then opens them. Continues. And realises that the descent is somewhat easier. It doesn't require the same strength. Just a sure, steady pace and a cautious eye. Not to let himself move too fast. He feels in control. Until the pipe itself starts to bend and fold in his hands. He's not sure where his feet are going or what to do. The pipe seems wet, almost fluid. He lets his feet down to the next position on the pipe. They cross over with nothing between them. The pipe turns to liquid between his hands. And he plunges into darkness.

A white ceiling. A fringed lampshade hanging above him. The softness of cushions below him. The arm of a couch under his head. A damp cloth is smoothed across his brow. An arm sweeps across his vision. He looks in the direction of its owner. And Roberta smiles down at him.

He starts to speak.

"Shhh, shh, it's alright," she says. And her smile is so beatific that she could be an angel straight out of heaven. "I found you in the back garden. I don't know what woke me but I sat right up in bed and I saw the security light was on. And then I looked out and there you were, spread out flat on your back."

"I..."

"I know it's confusing. You don't need to speak. I'm guessing that you must have had another of your episodes – and that for whatever confused reason you were desperate to come and see me and you felt that you needed to get in the back door. I don't know, maybe you'd already tried the bell. I'm quite a heavy sleeper."

"Yeah," he manages. His mouth is sticky and dry. It's difficult to get words out. "Yeah, that's right."

"Oh poor dear. Poor dear. My heart goes out to you. It really does. You must be so confused. It must be terrible."

"You're not... angry?"

"Don't be silly. Look, you can stay here on the couch tonight and we'll talk about it in the morning, okay? How does that sound?"

"Uh... Uh-huh."

"Now you stay right there while I go and get you a blanket."

Sam watches her waddle out of the room. That plump form seems so innocuous. Her whole being speaks of motherliness and caring.

Strangely, Sam doesn't feel much in the way of pain. He notices a scrape on one of his arms and a slight discomfort around one side, but he doesn't seem to have sustained any major injuries. He does feel sleepy though. And he knows enough to know that if, as is most likely, he has sustained a head injury of some kind he should avoid going to sleep. But it's hard here in this stuffy room with the heating up high, lying on this ever so comfortable couch. He wonders if it would be a good idea to advise Roberta of this. It doesn't seem like a good idea. How would he explain that he fell from her drainpipe. What on earth was he doing up there?

Or maybe she already knows. Maybe she's just playing like she doesn't, to further perpetuate her caring façade.

He looks around and realises that although he has been to this house many times he has not been in this room before. It is a sitting room. Not a lounge, or a living room, but a sitting room. The carpet is so thick that the air feels as if it is full of fluff. The couches – the one he lies on and another matching one – are a beige-coloured fabric with lacy cloths laid over the edges of them. The coffee table is empty but for a bowl of shiny, round pebbles and a stack of coasters. It looks like a room that should belong to a woman in her sixties or seventies. And he would put Roberta in her fifties at the most. There is a television tucked out of the way in the corner, slightly overlapped by the other couch. Bookshelves full of books. Everything so pedestrian, so pleasant, so plain, so inoffensive. Unremarkable. Pastoral prints in gilt frames.

But then Sam notices that there is something slightly odd about one of the pictures. A wide, rolling field, a farmhouse, a cart loaded with hay, the figure of a farmer in front of it. Only he is sitting on the grass, cross-legged, his head in his hands. And on the other side of the cart, the horse's legs are poking out into view – indicating that it is lying down, possibly dead. In another image, an olden-days family sits at a picnic table in front of a twee little cottage. Off to one edge of the picture, the woods fade into darkness – and just before the lines indicating the trunks of trees disappear into muddy brown-black, Sam discerns a figure glaring at the family from the shadows.

Roberta returns carrying a blanket over her arm and a big smile on her face. It occurs to Sam that a possible concussion might be the least of his worries. And that falling asleep is something he definitely should not do. But Roberta refreshes the cloth on his head and lays the blankets over him and tells him to relax, soothing him with calming words and gentle whispers.

"How old are you?" asks Sam.

And he's not sure why he's asking the question. But for some reason it feels good to talk. Roberta smiles and her head tucks back, giving her an extra chin. "You know you shouldn't ask a lady her age," she says, not quite looking at him.

"Should. Ought."

Roberta rolls her eyes at Sam's invocation of therapy no-no words.

"Okay, you got me. I'm forty-eight. Why do you ask?"

"Don't know."

"Aw, look at you, you're completely tuckered out. You should really get some rest."

"Maybe. No. Maybe." He's finding it difficult to stay awake, to focus, to string words together. But he fights it. "What," he fumbles. Mouths words for a moment. Redoubles his concentration. His brow creases and he tries to sit up. But Roberta places her hand on his shoulder and gently pushes him down again with shushes and instructions to rest.

"Roberta?" He says.

"Yes, dear."

"Do..." Blinks a few times. Fixes her. "Do you really care about your patients?"

"Well, of course I do. I care about them, well..." she looks away towards the darkened window. A reflection of her there, sitting on the edge of the couch beside Sam. People in a space. And her gaze lingers there. "I care about them more than anything else in the world." Turns back to Sam with a tilt of the head and a kindly smile. "That's my job."

"That's what I mean. How can caring about people be your job?"

She raises her eyebrows and her mouth tucks, "Perhaps calling is a better word. Here, take this." And she places a pill between his lips. "It'll help you relax." He spits the pill out and it bounces down his chest and tumbles into the recesses of the couch. With a barely perceptible frown, she produces another and presses it in firmer, her fingertip penetrating the inside of his mouth. It tastes of lemon. He is too drowsy to resist. When she raises a glass of water to his lips he can't help but swallow. And his eyes close. And internally he feels a spike of alarm, a clamour of ringing bells desperately screaming No! No! No! But they become faint. And then they are silent. And then there is black.

A stirring. In a space of non-awareness, disconnected from all reality and time, there is only shifting black and folds and folds of black. Above him a dark cloud hangs in negative, swaying with a rhythmic motion. He feels a softness all over him that soothes him with a heavy but not overbearing weight. A sensation of being enveloped in it. And in the darkness, Nina's face appears from out of the cloud, smiling down at him with such tenderness that it almost makes him sob. He aches in his chest. Her hair brushes his face and he becomes aware of a rubbing. That pendulous motion. A smooth wet warmth. And he realises that he is hard. Aroused. Terribly, terribly aroused. A fierce hunger to consume. And the weight bears down on him. And he feels it pressing against his eyelids – which now struggle and flutter against it, willing themselves to open – like a gloved hand over his eyes that he barely has the awareness to shift. But as his arousal mounts, he forces them open.

Roberta hangs over him, her red curls swinging about her chin. The expression on her face is unlike anything he has ever seen there before. She could be a different person. It is one of lightness and joy, her eyes sparkling with excitement and her mouth open, transformed by ecstasy into the upturned curve of a comedic mask. Her tongue lolls from her pink lips and it is slick with saliva. Her cheeks are flushed and she looks so alive, aglow, almost beautiful. Her breasts hang, enormous now that they are uncovered, great swinging sacks. And when she rocks forward they cover his chest and compress against him in a way that produces an irrepressible physical excitement in him. And even though it feels as though he is fully hard, he gets harder and harder.

He gasps and she notices that his eyes are opened. She does not speak. Nor does her expression falter as she rides him. But her hand comes down and covers his eyes, leaving him in darkness with only the feeling of her, the smell of her heavy perfume and, beneath it, a tang of body odour. And the sound. The hard breathing that quickens as she rides him harder. Softness of her hair over his face. Her wet lips against his ear, the warmth of her breath, which quickens and rises in tone until it becomes moaning, inarticulate expressions of delight. He ejaculates. And though he remains hard and Roberta's motions only increase in ferocity, he feels a shrivelling inside and his energy begins to wane. And for a moment, before his eyes close under her hand, he feels a sense of shame. And disgust.

Sam wakes with the daylight. The curtains are open and outside the garden is alive with the industry of birds feeding at pendulous nut-cages and darting in and out of a dozen bird boxes that line the fences on either side. He stretches, feeling comfortable, warm and safe. At ease. But as his arms retract, the image of Roberta, sweating and half-naked comes back to him and his insides curdle.

He throws the blanket off him. His clothes are intact. His belt buckled, his zip zipped. But when he inspects it he finds that the belt is fastened two holes wider than normal. He pulls a hair – a long, twisting red hair – from his shirt. He doesn't know what to feel. It's as if he feels nothing. Was it rape? Is that it? He sits, back straight, and looks around the anodyne room. His head is clear and the world seems normal. Although there is something about this space. He feels like an intruder here. He did after all come with the intention of committing burglary. It reminds him of being a teenager and waking up on the floor of some friend's parents' house to see pictures of their family surrounded by spilled beer bottles and cigarette butts in the carpet. His clasped hands press in between the cushions, as if for warmth. And he feels a small object down there, rolling against his fingers. He picks it up and looks at it. It's a blue pill, diamond in shape. He shoots to his feet, suddenly desperate to get out of there. He doesn't want to be around when Roberta appears. Can't think of anything worse than having to look her in the eye and talk to her. He takes a step to leave. And then stops. The carriage clock on the mantelpiece catches his eye. It is just after five o clock in the morning. And then he remembers what he came here to do.

On the second floor gentle snoring emanates from one of the bedrooms. The door is ajar and through it he can make out the end of a bed. He moves across the landing as lightly and as carefully as he can. Mounting the next set of steps his foot produces a creak. He freezes. Listens for the snoring. And continues when he is sure that the regular in-and-out has not been disturbed.

As he mounts the last few steps up to the attic he begins to tremble. The door looms above him, cast into shadow in this lightless staircase. And the surge of adrenaline fuses with a bitter determination, a fired hatred. It's a struggle not to charge into that door with his shoulder. But he restrains himself. Keeps up the steady pace. Lays his hand on the door handle. Grips it tightly. It occurs to him that it might be locked and he feels a spike of panic. Twists. And the door bows aside to usher him in.

Sam struggles to recognise the attic room as the place that he came to for his first session; that he has visited week on week in the intervening years. Once, it was warm and welcoming. "A safe space." Now it has the clinical air of a laboratory, where harsh experiments are carried out on test subjects that have no capacity for understanding just how they are being toyed with. The only thing that he hasn't changed his feelings about is that big black raven crouching at the top of the wall – behind his chair.

And once again, he takes the time to walk over to her chair and settle himself into it. He sees his own chair facing him, the raven squatting above it, beak stabbing down towards the space in which he now pictures himself and then countless other patients sitting with a whole spectrum of emotions flickering across their faces. Tears. The number of tears shed. Insights shared. All gobbled up by that fat black bird. He looks down at the trestle table beside him. And there it is: Roberta's notebook. He picks it up and flicks through it. There are names, details, scrawled longhand notes, even doodles. But he doesn't have time to read it now. He takes it and gets up, eager to be away from this oppressive room. But something stops him leaving. In a corner, tucked away out of view from the client's chair, there is a shelf completely devoted to Roberta's notebooks. Pay dirt. Drunk with adrenaline, he pulls them from the shelf, but there are too many to hold at once and they tumble to the floor with a loud slap, slap, slap. He freezes. Listening for the snoring, or for sounds of stirring, but hears neither. Hears nothing. Only the silence of the house. A room of secrets telling him nothing now.

Chapter Three

THEY WHO COME AND GO

For a long while he does nothing. Sits on the floor with the notebooks spread around him like a messy fan of cards. The flat is cold and empty and silent. Nothing but a space for wind to blow and rain to fleck in through the wide-open windows, spattering the blown lace curtains. But it is a cleansing wind. And to some small extent it removes from him the stink and staleness of that big old house that feels like a grandma's and belongs to a woman with no children but many dependents. It eases him. But it doesn't cure him. Like tap water running over a burning finger. The injury still smoulders and will return full force should it be exposed to the air again. He thinks about her body with a mixture of arousal and revulsion and underneath it all a deep, deep sense of shame. He shivers and notices that his shirt is soaked with sweat. Occasionally the wind will cause something to flutter or scrape somewhere in the flat and he will jerk his head round as if in fright. As if observed. He looks at the books but does not pick them up. They reek of her. And he would push them away, send them scattering to the corners of the room, if he but had the strength to move.

The clock ticks. Strength does not come. Only the knowledge that it is futile waiting on strength. And with trembling hand and a bitter taste in his mouth he reaches for a book. And begins to read.

The notes are extensive and complicated. Taken session by session they skip between so many disparate ideas page by page that understanding any one client is as hard as trying to compose a coherent picture from the messy web of anyone's thoughts. This is Roberta's job: and she is good at it. She has training and tools that Sam does not. There are occasional underlinings and jotted correlations, but Sam has no way of telling what they refer to and for the moment they are less than helpful, perhaps the most obscure things on these pages. His limbs become leaden. A drowsiness takes hold which only departs when he breaks away from the page and sits up. He fears that he lacks the intellectual aptitude to draw anything from these notes. And he flops onto his back and lies in the middle of the floor with his arms stretched out for some minutes. He is consumed by thoughts of what he went through to get them. And though he is trying to bury it deep, to keep away from the aggressive emotions of betrayal and emasculation, he can't help picking at the edges of it. The threat of full-blown images returning to the forefront of his mind looms large, causing his muscles to jump uncontrollably in anticipation of their arrival.

And then something snaps. He sits up. Wipes it from his mind with a discipline that felt impossible a moment ago. He doesn't know where it has come from. It is not anger. It is not a hate-fuelled drive. It is just clarity of purpose. Taking the books into the bedroom, he stacks them in a neat chronological pile. Then he opens his laptop and, starting at the beginning, begins to collate information into his own file on each patient.

Nina sits at her desk. She stands in court, tall and gaunt-looking in her wig and gown. She sits in meetings. And while she does these things, her personal life stays far from her mind. It's only when she retires to her flat at night that she begins to fret. And so she has taken to carrying a fat folder of homework back with her every night, often falling asleep over it with a glass of red wine in her hand and waking up to a new stain on the carpet. The mornings are hell but she can battle through them and once she's back at work again everything's fine. Only occasionally, very occasionally, in a moment alone, will she stop and think about Sam. About how his calls have stopped coming. And she'll have a little cry, quickly dry her eyes, and face the next business of the day.

On the way home she does her best to get involved in her surroundings: to look at the people on the tube; read every advert; see the dirt and the grime, her eyes scanning the tracks looking for mice. She's desperate to notice every one of these details and not let them smudge into the background blur.

She steps out of the station and the fresh air brings a welcome hit of wakefulness. The wind is high, but it's crisp and not too cold. She surges out with the usual flood of commuters, some of whom she recognises and sees every day, although it's not like she's ever spoken to any of them. Instead of waiting for the crowd to pass the way she often does, she keeps right in the middle of the herd. It's a bustle and a jostle and the sense of hostility between these bodies that crave space but sacrifice it in the name of efficiency is palpable.

As they funnel into the underpass, she thinks about the day when she saw someone lurking at the other end. At the time, she had rationalised it as someone waiting to have the underpass to themselves, perhaps just as scared as she was. But now she could say with something approaching certainty that that someone was following her. A predator.

And she stops. Right in the middle of the underpass. Stops and turns and looks back. She half-expects all of the other people walking through to stop too, or at least to look at her with a frown and wonder what the hell she is doing. But they don't. None of them do. And she stands there and watches them file past. Countless people. Each one unique, and each one made featureless by the sheer volume of uniqueness. She tries to make eye contact with someone, anyone, but no-one reciprocates. She is just another face in the crowd, invisible. She finds her eye drawn to the end of the underpass. Watching as each new person enters. Thinking that any one of them, any one of the men there could have been responsible, could be shadowing her everywhere she goes. Could have defiled her door, her home. But if he's among them he doesn't show it; he doesn't meet her eye with a flicker of nervousness or a sly smile. Part of her – a part she is reluctant to acknowledge – wonders what would happen if Sam was to come through…

But before long the flood has passed and she is alone in the pissy light of the underpass, surrounded by dirty tiles and graffiti tags and clods of unnameable filth, breathing in the stale air that hangs and coagulates in this place. She can feel it oozing into her, impregnating her clothes. But still she waits, staring at the end of the underpass.

A clicking of footsteps. Beginning to echo stronger in the low place. Broken and repeated sounds. She bristles. She can't help it.

The woman comes round the corner. And she stops. She is a slight blonde in a mauve raincoat with a shiny leather handbag held tightly on her shoulder. She narrows her eyes at Nina's obstruction of the underpass. Nina stands her ground, staring her down until she averts her gaze and stands cowed, looking off at a point on the floor just to the right of her feet. Nina feels a little bad. She steps to one side and the woman hurries on past with her head down. A man follows shortly after her, but he doesn't pay Nina any attention. She traces the line of his eyes, and sees that he is ogling the small blonde.

Nina sighs. She chastises herself for her silliness and then remembers that it's not silly at all. All these feelings, these strange behaviours, are to be expected given what she thinks could be happening to her. Given what has happened to her before. She starts walking and is just at the end of the underpass when she hears another pair of footsteps echoing down towards her. And despite having levelled herself out, despite her reality check, she stops.

And the footsteps stop too.

What she feels now is real fear. It's that knee-shaking fear when you're not sure if you could control your bladder properly if you needed to. She stands there, eyes on the filthy, tiled floor. And her skin turns cold, as if there was a wind blowing right through her clothes, right across her naked body – and at the same time she can feel sweat evaporating off her in almost visible waves, condensing and collecting on the sides of the tunnel. Dribbling down the walls, pooling on the floor. On the floor where she notes, a little way ahead of her there is a discarded condom. A used condom. And all she can think is who would have sex down here? And even though she wants to turn round and see who is behind her, she can't. She just keeps staring at that condom and thinking that same thought over and over again. Who would have sex down here? Who?

She bolts. Runs towards the end of the underpass and steps quickly up the steps. And just as she passes under the end of the underpass, she hears again. The footsteps starting up again.

Starting up. She gets to the top and breaks into a run. Not far now. Not far now until she gets to her car. But then, but then, but then. An avenue of trees up ahead of her, outlining the cut-through away from the main road. Another difficult space, another sheltered and vulnerable place with no-one to see, no-one to help. She wants to get in and through it as quickly as she can, keep well ahead of whoever's behind her. But then, but then. She clip clops towards the cut-through. But then! She shudders to a halt and spins round her arms and coat flung wide, breathing deep an audible sucking-in of air. There, now further away than she thought, are the steps leading down to the underpass – a hole in the ground, half-hidden by its surrounding wall, about to disgorge...

Nothing. There's nobody there. And as she stares at it a tension grows and she can almost see someone appearing, head first, a step at a time, then shoulders, emerging from the depths. An irritation builds inside her, a fidgeting frenetic itch, until she has to turn and race away, away through the cut-through.

Fences on either side of her. Bushes and trees poke up over their tops. Glimpses of private back gardens; intimate, safe spaces that are also forbidden, fortified. Barbed wire skims the top of the fence in more than one place. The cut-through turns at right angles and she hurtles around a corner. At the end she narrowly avoids the concrete bollard in the middle and spills out onto the suburban street where her car is parked. It's there, right opposite her. All she has to do now is cross the road, unlock the door, put her foot down. But she doesn't. Instead, she stays rooted to the spot. Caught between conflicting desires to run and to get to the bottom of this. She finds, somewhere in her, a rising, indignant determination. And sidesteps.

Waiting off to the side of the cut-through. Her fingers twitching like a gunslinger. Minutes pass. Nothing. She stays rooted to the spot, eyes glued to that opening, waiting for something to happen.

And then, faint at first, footsteps. Heavy ones. A man's footsteps coming down the cut-through. Her pulse quickens. Her hands ball into fists. As the steps grow louder, she sees again and again a man step through that gap. Always the same man. A man she feels she knows but whose face she cannot quite see. And then the footsteps are right there on the other side of the fence. If it wasn't for the wooden planks between them, they'd be able to see every detail of each other's faces. And the blood thunders inside her as she is brought into a more real, more visceral contact with life than she ordinarily knows. There. Right in the moment. The abrasion of the air against her skin. Adrenaline channelling into her arms and legs and her fists and then in that very very raw moment, he steps through. A large figure in a dark coat. And before he has time to do anything, Nina throws her leg in front of him.

The man, obviously in a hurry, catches her leg with his feet and tumbles face first into the pavement. There is a horrible dull slap as he hits it. And she moves in, fists rising, and she shouts "Who are you?"

Her teeth are clenched so tight they might crack and spittle clings to her lip as she spits the question again and the air whistles in through her nostrils and her eyes stare, great and bulging, from her head. And she doesn't know what it is but something somewhere makes the drums in her ears begin to subside and she finds herself receding from that moment like she's being sucked through an aeroplane window and she can hear him whimpering

"please, please, please..."

A horrible sinking sensation. She could almost puke. She doesn't know this man. This man with his face glued into the pavement.

This man who does not dare move except to raise his palms slightly in a gesture of surrender. He's tall. Dressed smartly in a business suit under his coat. His shoes are polished to a sheen. There's a fleck of blood on his city shirt collar. And as powerful as he might look ordinarily, he is broken. She has broken him. And even though she can't see his face, she knows that nothing about him, nothing about any of the other thousand things that she is now seeing in immediate close up detail tells her that she knows him. He is a perfect stranger. She has never seen him before in her life. All she can do is run straight across the road, throw open the door of her car and put her foot down.

And as she squeals away, narrowly avoiding another parked car, she looks into her mirror and sees him lying there on the floor. Face down. Not daring to move. Or in too much pain.

Nina's keys jangle to the floor. She fumbles to pick them up like her fingers are tied together. Every bit of her is shaking. She staggers into the lounge and throws her heavy bag of files on to the table. It skids off and lands with a thud on the other side. She falls onto the couch. Stares up at the ceiling breathing too quickly her heart still pounding and all she can think is fuck. And she knows right now she's right in the middle of it. Whatever this thing is that's happening to her, it's properly got a grip on her now and there's no avoiding it. Whoever is after her – whatever is going on – even through these small actions – they have upped stakes and moved right in and planted their pitch in her head. And they're going to squat there until – until what?

All she wants right now is to be held. She wants Sam. She wants him right here right now. But even if she disregards the police DNA report that said there were no matches in their criminal database, even if she ignores the cloud of suspicion that still hangs over him and that she quietly wishes she had asked him to be tested, she doesn't quite know how to explain the way she's been acting the past week; and with every hour that passes, the thought of calling him becomes increasingly daunting. She wants to. Oh, she wants to. But... She checks her messages. Four voicemails. All work. None from Sam. That's hardly the actions of a... She doesn't dare use the word – even in her own head it's a doorway she's not willing to reopen. It can't be him. It can't. And she knows that if she called him he'd coming running straight over and into her arms and as soon as she explained everything would be forgiven. But how can she explain that she thought he might... And she just doesn't. She doesn't have the strength in her now. All she can do is curl up on the couch and hold herself. And then the tears come.

Gillian Downey strolls down the street in time for her 9.15 appointment. She is a willowy woman in her late thirties. Her hair sweeps around her face in long blonde strands, sunglasses reflecting everything and giving her the air of a movie star. Although in fact she is a mature student, returning to studying after seven years as a doctor. There is nothing about her that gives away the deep-rooted instability and self-loathing that she has come to nurture. This is her second spell in therapy. The first was during her career, when she suffered something of a breakdown. Stress-related. At the time she was married, although this seems to have had little bearing: when the marriage ended, she just kept on working and it didn't seem to make a difference to her life. She says that she didn't have time to attend to the divorce and was happy to let her husband take her to the cleaners while she wasn't looking. She cared about it all that much. But then a year ago she found herself overtaken by an unbearable sense of sorrow. She couldn't face work and decided she had to quit. As much as she believed in her calling, she had sacrificed her life to it and could not forgive herself for doing so. And she missed her husband, Phil, who had by this time remarried. A period of acting-out followed her quitting work during which she threw herself into a life of hedonism and careless nightclub encounters, for which she feels no small amount of shame.

Sam looks at her: her floral skirt fluttering around her knees as she stops to stub out her cigarette before ringing the doorbell. He can imagine her dancing in bars, stumbling in and out of hotel rooms, walking down pavements in the morning, heels hanging from her fingers as she lifts her arm to hail a cab.

During Gillian's hour with Roberta, Sam pulls away and drives to the café around the corner. Sitting at a table by the window, he reads through Roberta's notes. He is beginning to tease out some threads and patterns. He stirs his coffee and turns a page, refracted sunlight forming a stripe across it that is pleasantly warm and as he reads he moves his hand in and out of it. There seem to be two types of client: long term and short term. The short-term clients will only see Roberta for a handful of weeks. But it is not clear exactly why they don't last. There is no note of them wanting to end therapy. There is no note at all, really. They just stop. Their entries limited to a page or so. It points towards there being a period of evaluation during the first weeks. Sam doesn't really understand a lot of the terminology, but there is a sense of a move towards a decision of some kind.

He returns to the street in time to see Gillian leaving. She is walking away from him and he cannot see her face but there is a heaviness in her carriage that was not there before. Why do we do this if it just makes us feel worse, thinks Sam. And he remembers that it does not always make him feel worse. But even when it does, isn't the idea that confronting things makes it better in the long run? Isn't it about the feelings that are always there and which cannot be escaped? Learning to deal with them. But Sam feels that all of the emotions that have weighed him down in the past are still right here on his shoulders, and though he might have learned to bear them a little better, he still resents it. He wishes he could cut them out of himself. But it is not possible. Even the arrival of new feelings that attack the heart with more violence does not shift these deep wounds. It just packs them in tighter.

Ten minutes later, a man arrives. Sam checks a flip pad in which he has recorded the timings of all Roberta's current appointments. William Ross. William is an entrepreneur in his mid-fifties and has been a patient of Roberta's for a long time. He wears a leather jacket and jeans and has a spring in his step. His open-collared white shirt bulges a little from his belt but he is not really overweight. It's a healthy spread for a man his age who is conditioned to fine living. Sam considers that it must be a source of frustration to William that his youthful energy, persona and dress are countermanded by his almost completely bald head, across which a few lines of brown hair streak back, and wonders why he doesn't keep it shaved short. But there is something in the longish curly hair on the back of his head that speaks of his spirit.

Sam has learned from the notebooks that it is undoubtedly the case that William feels he has benefited from his time with Roberta. His life has blossomed. When he started seeing her, he was running a very successful estate agent's firm, but all of his time was spent in managing it and he felt swamped beneath the weight of administration. He had not worked this hard for his life to be spent in this way. And so with Roberta's help, he came to see that he should sell the firm. And not just sell the firm. He also left his wife and children. And this seems to have made him immeasurably happier. Now he spends his time buying and selling businesses and having a grand time of it all. He has some regret and anxiety about this decision and he misses his children. He does not miss his wife.

Next. Mandy and Jeremy Vickers. It seems from the notes that they cannot stand each other even though, as they approach the house, they are holding hands and smiling at each other. He makes an inaudible joke and she laughs. He is a short man, and though she is of average height for a woman, she dwarfs him. He has a funny sort of face; she is bland-looking. Her short haircut emphasises the oblongness of her head, the flatness of her face, which, even when she laughs barely moves at all. Remarkably, the notes show that Roberta is determined to keep them together. Even though she has identified fatal flaws in their relationship, her reflections on the pair amount to a rabid formulation of strategies to prevent its inevitable demise. In one of their most recent sessions, Roberta writes that they said therapy was the only thing that has kept them together. She has circled this many times, turning it into an elaborate sun-like doodle that sends rays out across the page.

This is the last appointment before lunch. Sam considers that now might be a good time to head home. Nevertheless, he returns to the coffee shop for the third time that day. The pleasant-looking young girl behind the counter says with a smile, "Back again. We must be doing something right."

He decides he probably shouldn't come here anymore. But for now he orders a sandwich and a coffee. Sits and sips and flips idly through the pages of a notebook he has read before. And he is quite content and laments the fact that it might be the last time he gets to sit here because it probably looks weird him coming and going like this.

His phone rings. "Hello?"

A long silence. Long enough for him to ask hello again and then who is it.

"It's Nina."

For a long time, he doesn't say anything.

"I..."

It occurs to him that this might be the most stilted conversation ever.

"This might be the most stilted conversation ever," he says.

And she laughs and they both laugh and it's an unnatural forced laughter that goes on for so much longer than the observation warrants. And they both know it but they keep laughing anyway. He rocks backwards and forwards in his seat and then he looks up and catches the eye of the waitress, who is the only other person in the place, and she shrugs. Sam's laughter peters out and he nods and shrugs back. In the meantime Nina's saying something. He turns away to the window.

"I'm sorry, what?"

And then she says,

"I said I'm sorry and, and I miss you. And I want to see you."

"I want to see you too. Where have you been? Did something happen?"

"It's a long story. A long, stupid story. Well, not stupid. But I'll tell you later."

"That time when I saw you outside my flat, what was –"

"Look, I've got to go, I'm at work."

"Okay. Bye then. I –"

But the phone is already dead.

Sam sits there in his plastic chair. His mouth is dry. He takes a hasty drink of his coffee, which is now lukewarm. Swallows it down thirstily. The waitress asks him if he would like anything else.

"Heh," she adds, "it's not like I've got much else to do round here. I might as well give you a silver service."

He turns and looks at her and she says, "My. It looks like you've seen a ghost."

He stands.

"Are you okay?" she asks.

He pulls out his wallet and places a twenty-pound note on the table.

"Thank you," he says. And leaves without further comment.

It's open. The front door. Roberta is ushering Mandy and Jeremy out of the house with a warm smile on her lips. A smile that sends a stab straight to Sam's heart. He puts his foot down. Surges past. Swerves. Pulls into the side of the road. Hopes his rash driving hasn't given him away. That Roberta was too busy with her patients to have noticed him. In any case, if he stays in his car and waits on her road and she has seen him, he'll find out soon enough. After all, she surely already knows that he's stolen her notebooks so what further damage could be done by her seeing him there? And on the other hand she fucking raped him. He realises that what he's actually anxious about is that he might see her face to face and have to talk to her. That none of this skulking around is down to not wanting to be caught. It's down to not wanting to be looked at. Not wanting to be eye-raped by this woman with her unreadable, superior expression while she pretends everything's normal and treats him like someone who still needs her help.

In the mirror he sees Mandy and Jeremy walking off down the road. They walk separately now. She's a little way ahead of him. There are storm clouds over their heads. Sam can almost see Jeremy glaring daggers between Mandy's shoulder blades. And sourly, without words, he wishes them a good week.

Nina is shaking all over. The urge to run is as powerful as it was the last time she was here. Standing back from the entrance, she looks up at the concrete of the building's façade. From this angle it seems to go on forever, right up to the sky. The clouds above it look like they might burst at any moment. And for all the time spent getting ready, she feels completely unprepared. Like she could fall apart with the slightest breath of wind. And as she stares up at that sky, the first drop of rain falls straight down towards her and hits her in the eye. She winces, wiping at it. The buzzer goes.

In the lift mirror she notices that she has managed to smear mascara across her cheek. Curses and dabs at it with a handkerchief, which drops out of her fingers. She bends to pick it up and when she stands the lift doors are open. And there's still a faint smudge.

She is standing in the corridor, dabbing at herself in her compact mirror when Sam opens the door. His hair is cut, he's shaved, his shirt ironed. He looks good. And at the same time she can see the small boy in him reaching out for her. He takes a deep breath in. His chest expands. He stands straighter. And now he's a man, his shoulders erect, his gaze strong. She feels something shift in her. A shift in her brain chemistry and now she's not even the same person. Not scared and anxious, something else.

"Oh, there you are," he says.

Neither knows whether to move. To step forward or step back. She begins to apologise, trying to control the tremble in her voice,

"I was scared. I thought it was because of something else, but now I know it was because I'd just, I'd made it so big in my mind.

The thing I was scared of. Now that I see you I don't think it was even real."

"Wouldn't you rather talk about it inside? A glass of wine, maybe?"

She smiles and tucks her hair behind her ear.

"The neighbours are really nosey."

And even manages a laugh.

He steps back, holding the door for her. She pauses on the threshold and places a hand on his chest. She can feel his heart beating. And she looks into his eyes and a sad smile creeps onto her lips. She closes the distance between them and their kiss is tentative. Lips opening slightly against each other. She loops her arm around his waist and presses herself against him, the breath coming hungrily through her nose. And he responds, but he doesn't lose himself. His hands stay where they are. She rests her head against his chest and then steps back. He's right. They need to talk first.

She sits with her legs curled under her on the couch. He passes her a large glass of red. She swirls it in front of a candle and picks up the orange highlights and purple lows. She takes a long, slow sip and sighs.

"It was bloody expensive," he says.

Her mouth curls with a little thank you. And uncurls. Her hair falls across her face and casts her into shade as she stares into her glass.

"Not so long ago, I was in therapy too. But, well, much as it's the trendy thing to do with some of my friends, the idea of dissecting my life never really appealed to me. I was a difficult teenager and I'd been there before. I was over the romance of it. No. It was a much more, a practical thing." She looks up at him. "About five years ago I had a stalker. It was pretty bad."

"Nobody deserves that. Least of all you."

"Of course nobody deserves it." She catches herself. "Sorry. I mean, it's not about deserves. It's just a thing that happens to a person. It happens a lot. Can happen to anybody. Anyway, you're probably wondering why I'm telling you this."

Sam doesn't know how to answer. He does his best to look sympathetic.

"When you are stalked," she continues, "when there is a person following you everywhere you go, who could pop up at any time, you develop a kind of extra sense. Like a sixth sense. You're more alert to the presence of somebody in your peripheral vision or standing right behind you. Except that it's not a sixth sense. It's not a sense at all. It's just fear. It's a persistent state of fear that he creates in you by appearing at just the right times so that you're always on guard. If a car slows down in front of you, or if someone loiters near you on the street or walks back up and down more than once while you're waiting at the bus stop. You're aware. You're always aware. And your ears prick up and the hair stands on the back of your neck and it feels like you could catch the vibrations in the wind. Except you can't. Because like I say it's not a sense, it's fear."

"I understand."

"Thank you. But you don't. If it hasn't happened to you, you can't. That's one of the things that it takes a while to get your head around – only those who have experienced it directly know what it's like. It doesn't matter how close a person is to you, if they're not a target they'll never know what you're going through."

"Sure. Okay. It's just..."

She looks up suddenly. Sam's eyes are downcast, his fingers at his mouth.

"Just what?"

"There are some things I need to tell you. But you, you carry on first."

"Okay..." She eyes him warily, not quite sure what he's intimating. "So, anyway, that sense. That fear. It's been switched back on recently. There have been times – I don't know how many times – but I swear I'm just about at that point where I'm about to start counting, you know, recording things. I could have sworn, Sam, I was being followed. There's footsteps or there's you know, the feeling that there's someone there, hiding just out of view. I've even seen glimpses of a person. I've been so sure that someone's really there that I've even done stupid, really stupid, irrational things."

Sam looks scared. Really, fundamentally scared. And Nina feels a tingling around her eyes like you get in your nose when a sneeze is building up. Sam sees her face transform. She is about to cry and he reaches out to her, but she withdraws.

"The thing is, Sam. When my, when it happened to me before, it... was my ex-boyfriend and. And so when whatever it is, whatever the fuck this thing, this nothing, this fucking nothing started happening, I just couldn't get away from the thought that..."

"Of course."

It takes her a little off-guard.

He gets up.

"I mean I'm hardly a beacon of stability in your life. Shit, Nina, I," and he's speaking into his chest, almost to himself as he paces up and down the floor's wooden boards, "you've got everything going for you. And I know, I know I'm a total mess and you know what, I wouldn't hold it against you in the slightest, not for a moment if you decided you never wanted to see me again."

"Oh, Sam, don't."

"No. Really. Because, you see, this is kind of... it is my fault." And he's on his knees before her, hands holding hers in her lap.

"What do you mean?"

She's trying not to freak out. But it's hard. It happened before once. A man on his knees in front of her, begging forgiveness for his crimes. And she gave it. She gave it again and again in the mistaken belief that he would stop, that maybe this time everything would be fine.

There's redness in Sam's cheeks, pushing at the surface now and he's grinding his teeth like he can't bear to hold it in and his voice comes out in chattering, percussive notes.

"Roberta is – there's – something – truly fucked – about her."

And she doesn't know why, even though she's relieved he hasn't turned round and told her yes, yes it was me all along, but there's something in the conviction with which he says this that she finds disturbing.

"Sam, what's this got to do with her?"

And he's up on his feet again, striding away to the other side of the flat, then bounding towards her with his arms swinging, fingers crooked and a fire in his carriage.

"The woman's broken into my flat at night, she's drugged me, beaten me, lied to me, tricked me, hypnotised me, played me for a fool. And what for? What for? To keep me in therapy? She raped me, Nina."

"What?"

"Yes. And now she's following you."

She paws at the arm of the sofa as if wanting to get away, but to stand would only bring her into closer physical proximity to him and right now she still doesn't know whether she wants to hold him or run, run far away, as far away as anybody can run. This can't be true.

"It was a man."

"What?"

"I don't know who it is that was following me, but I am definitely, I am one hundred per cent sure. It was a man, Sam. How could it have been Roberta?"

"Maybe it wasn't. Not directly. You remember that time when you found me out on the window ledge? That was after the hypnosis, right?"

"Right..."

"So how many patients do you think she's got? Don't you think that she might use some of them to get at the others?"

"What, by hypnotising them?"

"Yeah."

"Oh, come on."

"Hypnosis, maybe. I don't know what else. NLP? Telling them that it might help them if they did X Y or Z? Suggestion. Whatever."

"Sam, this is..."

He rounds on her, wild with conviction, nostrils flared. His lips are peeled back from his gums like some kind of mad preacher. There is a certainty in him which, if it were anyone else, she would have to dismiss. But she can't. She's got to listen to him. Even if only with a part of her. Because she's invested here. And ultimately, she's got to kill or cure and either reaction involves bearing all sorts of emotional fallout.

"I've got the proof."

"What proof?"

He strides out of the room, returning a moment later.

"There!" he shouts, and throws the slew of notebooks on the

ground. "That's all her patient notes going back years. It's a big old mess of stuff, but in there there's a catalogue of divorces, break-ups, domestic abuse, personal redemption and self-actualisation. And there's always a thread running through all of them. It'd take you a while to see, but whenever it gets better, it gets worse. She does something, or suggests hypnosis or some other treatment and just when they think they're out they're back in. Not one patient in there that's been with her for more than a few weeks has ever, ever stopped coming. Not one."

"Maybe she's just good at what she does."

"Shut up. No. Sorry." Breathes. "The things... the things that happen to them. She makes them stronger and just when they're ready to pull away from her, they'll find some new thing. Whether she recommends some other therapy or brings up an issue, or it's something external. They never get away."

He's staring at her so hard his eyes are beginning to ache.

Then, like a wisp of smoke, the spirit leaves him and his frame slumps. He's expelled it all. He's got it out. He's finally told her and now he's exhausted.

All he can see in her face is disbelief. And a deep, deep sadness. He turns from her and drags himself over to a chair. Sits down backwards on it, leaning over, staring at the floor.

"Where did you get these from?"

"From her house."

"How?"

He is silent. His eyes close. He swallows. She stands and steps tentatively towards him.

"Sam, there's a part of the story that you've kind of glossed over here. You mentioned it like a glaring red hot thing and then you just sort of dropped it."

"Yeah."

"Tell me what you meant when you said she raped you."

"I meant what I said."

A breeze flutters the net curtain behind him, the light isolating him from the background, bringing him sharply into focus before her. She closes the distance between them and lays her hand on his shoulder. He clasps it.

"Are you okay?" is all she can think of to say.

He stands and holds her tight. And they stay there like this for minutes.

"Have you got any beer?" she says, "I feel like a beer."

He nods.

"You want one?"

Nods again.

"I'll go get us a beer and then we'll talk this thing through, okay?" Then, "I'm here for you, Sam. I am here for you. You know that, don't you?"

"I'm..." but he doesn't complete the sentence.

Placing a heavy kiss on his lips she leaves him to go to the kitchen.

She opens the fridge, takes out two bottles and is about to close the door when something gives her pause. It's a strange object to find in a fridge: a kind of clay pot. Glazed in swirling yellow and brown. Wrinkling her nose, she pulls it towards her. It's surprisingly light, cool and dripping with condensation. She screws off the top. There's a tight seal. Inside there's a plastic bag. She stops before reaching in, thinking what if it's his mother's ashes or something? But then why would it be in the fridge? Inside the bag are three sheets of paper, separated into tiny little squares by perforations. On each of the squares, there's a little green man.

A shiver.

Nina returns to the lounge without the beers. She places the pot on the table beside him.

"Sam, what's this?"

"Huh?" A dopey look and a sniffle. "Oh. Oh that."

"It's acid, isn't it?"

"Yeah."

And he looks at her unapologetically, like there's nothing at all strange about having enough acid to send a roomful of people to Mars in your fridge. And then he twigs.

"Oh. Oh, it's not mine."

He stands, hands on her arms, almost laughing.

"It's not mine, it really isn't."

She wriggles away from him.

"It's hers. I found it at her house. It must be how she manufactured my episode."

"And when you said you had proof you thought it would be better to show me a stack of undecipherable notebooks, rather than a large quantity of a controlled substance that you found in her... Fuck! Sam, what were you even doing there anyway?"

"We were about to get to that part."

Her hands fly to her hips. Her face stinks of indignation and she bears down on him with a stare that must scare the hell out of ordinary mortals in court.

"Listen to me, Sam. You better be telling me the truth. Because if you are fucking with me I am going to put my hands round your neck and strangle the life out of you. I know this is scary. But it's scary for me too and if this turns out to be a bag of bullshit, then I don't know what –"

"If you don't believe me, all you have to do is walk out of that door and never speak to me again."

Nina falters.

"And I wouldn't bear you the slightest malice."

"You just..." something about it makes her furious, but it's too much to express. So instead she says, "You got this from Roberta's house. Yes or no?"

He opens his mouth to speak. There is a knock. He shuts it again. Turns towards the door, alarmed.

"Who?"

"Sam."

He turns back to her. Her teeth are clenched.

"Yes, yes, I already told you I got it from her house," he witters, "but..."

The knock again. Heavy. Officious.

"Mr. Peoples? This is the police. Open the door please."

Sam's eyes are glued to the door. "I never thought she'd..."

"Shit." Nina can see he's not going to do anything. She grabs the acid. "You know what it means for me if I'm caught with this stuff?"

She runs into the bedroom. Opens the window. Looks out at the street. No police in evidence. Lets go of the pot and watches as it sails to the pavement and bursts into smithereens.

She turns round. Through a crack in the bedroom door she sees Sam talking to two policemen. One of the officers crosses to the spread of notebooks in the middle of the room and bends down to examine them. He nods to his colleague, who turns Sam around and puts him in cuffs. Sam offers no resistance. He just calls, "Nina. Nina."

But she can't move. She sits down on the bed and stares through the gap in the door as Sam is removed from the premises. The door is shut behind him.

And she is alone.

Sam lies back on the hard mattress. He had imagined that a police cell would be a dank place, smelling of piss or worse, but it's not like that. It smells of nothing in particular. It's a no-place, like a waiting room. Perversely, it's here that all the concerns of the real world seem to be furthest away. He can almost forget about them. He imagines all the people that have occupied this space before him. Though there is no trace of them. It's as if he is the first person ever to have used the cell. As if it was built for him. Were they all hardened criminals, reprobates, drunks, the dregs of society, he wonders, or just people like him: mixed up in the head, or mixed up in something? And it's that thought that gets him. He's not mixed up in the head. His thoughts are clearer than ever. When he started this, everything was looking up and the future was bright. How could he have believed it? Even for a moment. That he might actually have a shot at being happy one of these days. It really seemed like it was in sight. A dream. Sharp, focussed, clear, drawing within reach. Sure there was a lot of stuff that was still up in the air, but that one element. It seemed so right. Nina. They could really have been happy together. And it's Roberta, the bitch, who's put it all in jeopardy. Right now, it occurs to Sam, there's nowhere he'd rather be. Sitting here rotting in this cell is just perfect. He closes his eyes.

Nina hasn't left Sam's flat. After the police took him she sat there holding herself, shivering, and then eventually lay down. Now she is staring up at the ceiling, watching the shifting patterns of light reflecting up from the street outside. She finds herself drifting between two thoughts: help him or get as far away as possible. She's a barrister for fuck's sake. They've got him in a cell. She should be down there doing everything she can to get him out of there as quickly as possible. And if she's not pursuing that option, well, the other writes itself doesn't it? If she doesn't help him, what's he going to think while he sits there with nothing but his thoughts for company. He's going to get angry. He'll look to blame. He'll know that her doubts have overcome her feelings and that'll be that. And she understands that she doesn't have a choice. Unless she acts, the decision will be made for her.

She tidies her mascara in the rear-view mirror and looks across at the police station. Its lights burn brightly in the night. One of those places, like an airport or a service station, that never closes. An oasis of activity in the loneliness of a dark, sleeping world. The shapes of police officers drifting past windows. It reminds her of her early training, of time spent paralegalling while she was applying for pupillage.

All business, she strides across the car park, her heels cracking like whips. Through the glass door she can see the waiting room, reception desk. Posters advising citizens to be vigilant and discouraging them from committing crime at the same time. The desk sergeant seems alert for the time of night. He writes something and puts his pen behind his ear as he looks up at the short, plump lady standing across the desk from him. Nina takes a deep breath and pushes the door open.

"We can't just drop the charges," says the officer. "They're criminal charges."

"Oh, come on Ross, you know me. I'm telling you there's no need to hold this guy. He's not a criminal." Nina watches the woman gesticulate as she speaks, red curls shaking on the back of her head. "There's no point keeping him in here, you'll never make a conviction stick. Especially if I say that nothing was stolen."

"That would be wasting police time. You wouldn't waste our

time now would you, Roberta?" Nina moves round to the side and watches Roberta as she sighs and leans on the desk.

"Look, is Brian in? Maybe if I could talk to him."

"You'll have to wait 'til tomorrow."

Nina steps into the space and interjects: "The way I see it, PC 114 Munroe, you're holding a man on a charge that doesn't really exist. I think you'd better let him go."

"And who are you?"

"Nina Trevanion, Barrister, 3 Inner Temple."

"Right. Er, let me see. Just bear with me a moment."

The sergeant disappears off into the back. Roberta turns to Nina. Her smile is genial, as if there is nothing wrong in the world. As if they are the best of friends.

"Nina. Oh thank God."

Nina doesn't return it.

"You were trying to pull some strings?"

"Oh, yes. I do some PTSD work around here. They all know me."

"PTSD?"

"Post Traumatic Stress Disorder."

A nod. "You have to know how to talk to them. You were just pissing them off."

"Well, you're the expert, I suppose."

Nina thinks to herself 'a little rusty maybe' but chooses not to engage in polite conversation any further. If Sam is to be believed this woman is a monster. But right now she looks completely innocuous. Her whole presence speaks of calmness and support and general love of humanity. From her round, gently smiling face, to the dowdy clothes, the home-knitted cardigan. Even the girlish copper curls that are surely coloured. And yet as Roberta looks back at her, waiting for her to speak, Nina has a creeping sensation up her spine and even with all the police in the building, she feels distinctly unsafe. Belying Roberta's casual body language and relaxed expression, her eyes are active, as if they are reading all of Nina's thoughts from underneath her skin. Nina breaks eye contact and looks away towards the front door. The world outside seems dark and hostile, pushing at the edges of the bright space reflected in the glass, where she and Roberta stand in the bland waiting room. It is as if the worst of humanity might burst in here at any moment and tear them both to shreds. Nina kicks at the floor.

"Nina?"

She turns back to Roberta.

"I just wanted to say that I think it's so good that you're standing up for Sam like this, you know, that you're there for him. When someone's going through what he is, it can really make all the difference to have someone you can count on."

And you know what, it'd be impossible for anyone to think she didn't mean it. This is madness, thinks Nina. More specifically, it's Sam's madness. And it feels like it's infecting her. She is unable to do anything other than nod and offer a tight smile.

"Of course," Roberta adds, "I understand that it must be very stressful. If you ever find you need to talk to someone..."

"What? You going to offer me your business card?"

Roberta laughs. A good-natured, rolling laugh.

"I don't think that would be appropriate. But I can recommend someone if you like."

And Nina feels bad for her snide ambulance-chaser quip.

"Can I ask you something?" she says. "Why did you report the theft and direct the police to Sam if you don't want him locked up for it?"

"I needed my notes back."

"You could have just asked him for them."

"I don't think that would have worked."

There's something grating in her buoyancy. Something patronising. Like I know something that you don't. I know him better than you.

"How did he get them in the first place?"

"Sam turned up at my house in the middle of the night. He wanted to talk to me. I let him stay on the couch and in the morning he took the books and left."

Nina furrows her brow, "And there wasn't anything else that happened that maybe..."

"I'm sorry, Nina. I really can't talk about it. I've probably said too much already. I'm afraid it's between me and Sam. You can ask him if you like."

"Ah," Nina almost-smirks. "Hippocrates, eh?"

"Hippocrates."

"Did he take anything else from your house? Apart from the books, I mean?"

"Like what?"

"Anything."

Roberta raises her eyebrows and is about to speak when a voice interjects, "Evening Roberta. Ms Trevanion."

They turn to see a balding man in his forties approaching. He has bags around his eyes and a coffee stain on his shirt. The duty sergeant walks behind him like a servant.

"Hi Roger," says Roberta. Roger leans on the desk propping his head up and yawns, "Okay, here's what we're going to do. We'll release Mr. Peoples into your care, Roberta, like you asked. Perhaps you'd like to speak to him first? Assess his state of mind."

"What?" Nina interrupts. "He's a free man. He's not being charged. You should be letting him go. That's it."

"I'm afraid I can only defer to Roberta's judgement here. He's her patient. It was her complaint."

"Patient? Hardly. She's a counsellor and he's her client. Actually, strike that, was her client, but has chosen not to retain her services."

Roger sighs, "I am releasing him into Roberta's care as a psychotherapist at the Ross and Waverly Clinic where Mr. Peoples is registered as an outpatient."

Nina looks like she has been slapped.

"Oh," Roberta takes Nina's hand in both of hers, "he hasn't told you." Her eyes are wells of sympathy. "You'll have to ask Sam about it, my dear. I'm afraid it's not something I can discuss." Her smile drops and she turns to Roger, unwavering, completely cool, professional. "First and foremost, I'd like to get him out of here. Then I'd like to have a chat with him. The rest is up to him."

"Very well." Roger walks off, leaving the sergeant holding the desk.

Roberta turns to Nina, "You'll have him back in no time, sweetheart. But," she purses her lips, "might I suggest that in the meantime you get some rest and give yourself a little time to think. This is a very tense, very extreme situation and I think a little time alone will give you some much needed clarity."

"And what is it you hope I'll find when I have this 'clarity'?"

"I'm not a fortune teller, Nina."

And something in Roberta's smile is ever so slightly repugnant. A smugness given away by the tiniest upcurl of one side of her mouth: victory.

A while ago a drunken-sounding woman in the next cell was singing

Fairy Tale of New York at the top of her lungs. She's stopped now, but it was actually quite pleasant. In a way, Sam is more relaxed than he has been in months. Which is why it surprises him when the sound of the key in the door causes him to jump out of his skin.

"Alright, you're out of here," says Roger.

"How come?"

"You've got friends in the right places."

"That doesn't sound entirely legal, officer. Don't you have procedures to follow or something?"

"Just a turn of phrase," Roger winks and beckons, "Come on."

"And I was just getting used to the place."

He gets up with a groan and follows Roger out into the corridor. Halfway down, he stops.

"Hang on. Friends, you say? Is Nina here?"

"Would that be Nina the barrister?"

Sam follows him down the corridor, glowing inside. And when Roger asks, "You're not nailing that, are you?"

Sam can't help but crack a big cheesy grin.

"Bastard."

Roger opens the door to usher him through, offering an oblong section of the reception desk and the waiting room beyond it. Between the two, Roberta looks up at him. Sam's elation turns to ice.

"What is this?"

"We're releasing you into her care."

"What do you mean 'her care'? No. No you're fucking not."

He spins and charges back up the corridor. He doesn't even see Nina step into view alongside Roberta. Roger grabs hold of him and he struggles and bucks and kicks with all his might. But the officer is experienced with this sort of thing and when the sergeant joins him they have him locked down, clamped on the floor. They exhort him to calm down, calm down, calm down, but he keeps shouting, "Get her away from here! Get her away from me! I'm not going out there until she's gone!" Until his shouts become inarticulate ragged screams and then, exhausted, they break down into short percussive barks of 'No Nah No Nah' that bounce off the hard walls of the corridor.

"Sam, it's okay. Sam I'm here."

At the sound of her voice all the tension leaves his body and he falls slack in the arms of the officers. They help him to his feet and he sees Nina standing there at the entrance to the corridor. And the look on her face speaks of something like shock and horror and her arms are folded tight across her chest. Not that it matters to him. She's here.

"I'm all right, okay," he says and walks unaided towards her. She throws her arms around him and kisses the side of his head and for some reason that Sam can't quite understand, she keeps saying, "I'm sorry. I'm sorry. I'm sorry," as she walks him out into the waiting room.

In front of Roberta, Sam becomes defiant. He finds some strength and stands straight-backed, Nina beside him with a hand on his shoulder.

"I'd like you to come with me. We're just going to talk, okay? We can go to a cafe. It won't take long."

Sam's eyes jump between his girlfriend and his therapist. "Why would I want to do that?"

"I think it's a good idea," says Nina. Sam almost puts his neck out as it whips round. "And then you bring him straight back to me. I'll wait up."

"I don't... what are you..."

He doesn't know whether to feel betrayed or safe. Is Nina looking out for him or has Roberta talked her round? What the hell is going on? Roberta inhales and slowly lets the breath out through her nose. And when she has their attention she continues, "Nina, I'd like it if you considered what we discussed earlier. I will take Sam for our little chat and when I'm done and he's back at his flat, he can give you a call."

Nina narrows her eyes and then nods.

"What did you discuss?" But they ignore him. It's like he's not in this conversation. He could be an item of furniture or a pet.

"You may wait up until then. It shouldn't be long. But then get some proper sleep. Doctor's orders."

"You're not a doctor." Again, he is ignored.

Roberta turns to go and then stops and motions with her head for Sam to follow.

"Nina?" It's the smallest of voices.

She throws her arms around him. And when she releases him it's time to go.

Nina turns on the television. She has no idea what to watch. Once upon a time she would have had favourite soaps or programmes but she can't even remember what those are now. The news is too depressing, too real. It's like letting the rest of the world in. There's a couple of movies but one's a horror and the other's a thriller and neither of those have appealed to her for a long time. Love stories are too romantic. Comedies are too goofy, insubstantial and irritating. Suddenly the world seems so dumb. Like everything is made for idiots. She settles on an archaeological programme. And it's only when she settles on it that she realises that it was the act of channel surfing that was what she really wanted. Because even though it provoked some base-line irritation it had kept her mind occupied.

And now, as she tries to focus on the gentle tones of the narrator talking about Ancient Egyptians, she finds images of the pyramids displaced by the violent surging of a screaming mouth. Sam, in paroxysms of fear, his eyes splitting and reasonless as his arms flail and spittle flies from his mouth. His teeth clench. And the officers's arms tighten around him and they bring him down. And they bring him down. And they bring him down again. And again.

Her eyes squeeze shut and she rubs her temples. But the images flash even stronger in the darkness. She downs the rest of her glass and pours another. And then returns to channel surfing. And at the back of her mind she's hoping that Sam's conversation with Roberta goes on forever or that because of some other reason, some change of heart, he never calls her.

It's an all-night coffee joint, Insomnia, the name. And it's surprisingly busy. Cabbies. A group of students hugging the corner, laughing and talking loudly. Which should make him feel safe. But it doesn't. Because safety isn't a thing that occurs to him. Because right now he's just angry. And that doesn't leave room for much else. If, however, he were to look round at the faces, each one animated differently by the varying nature of their pursuits, he might have cause to ask himself 'do any of them know her?'

"I'm not upset with you," says Roberta. "I want you to know that."

She is clutching a coffee in both her hands, leaning over it with unflinching sincerity. It's one of her therapy faces – one that's reserved only for times of specific need. "How do you feel?"

He stares back at her through slitted eyes, his jaw twitching. The expectation to speak is like something she secretly piles onto him. As if she's standing behind him adding a teaspoon at a time. And as much as it causes a tightening inside him, a desire to blurt something out, he doesn't rise to it. He won't give her the satisfaction.

"You don't feel like talking? That's okay. I didn't really bring you here to talk. This isn't a therapy session."

No because you're buying the coffee, he thinks.

"I just want to check in with you. To see how you are and to tell you that I don't hold a grudge. That everything is okay with us and I want you to come back to therapy and we can talk all of this through. All of it."

And as if to demonstrate this she sweeps her hands in front of her and brings them together like she's tying up a sack. She stops short of throwing it over her shoulder. It's all he can do not to punch her in her smug middle-aged face. And he holds on. He holds it back with all his might. But he can't hold back the words. Not anymore. And they strain out, stretching as they catch on his clenched teeth.

"I'm not coming back. Not ever."

She doesn't flinch. Nothing. No trace of a reaction. Just the words, "I think that would be a bad idea."

He folds his arms and sits back in his chair, kicking his legs out like a child.

"Come back. Just the once, if you like. And tell me what you think. Tell me what you think about me. Everything you think. I'm not here to judge. I won't contradict you. I'll just listen. That's what I'm here for."

He mumbles something incoherent that gets lost in the tightness of his mouth.

"Sorry, Sam, what was that?"

"Everything? Really?"

"Everything. Anything."

"How about we talk about it right now."

"It's not really the time or the place. We should make an appointment. It's important to respect the boundaries of..."

"How about when you raped me?" he says. The words are so flattened by tension that they sound robotic.

"What? Is this a..."

She turns to the window for inspiration. And back.

"Is this some kind of metaphor?"

Sam smashes his cup off the table. Leaps to his feet. Slams his hands down on the table. Screams at the top of his voice, "How about when you fucking raped me, bitch! How about we talk about that!"

And he's leaning over her, his breath coming in snorts through his nose and he feels a rush of adrenaline. And then a clarity. Like something inside of him has been pinched out. Expunged. It's a feeling of liberation that's almost intoxicating. And as the calm washes over him, he notices Roberta. She's flinched back into her seat. An arm half up covering her face, anticipating violence.

A reaction.

And it feels good. So good. To see her afraid.

And then not so good.

Roberta sits up straight again and in no time she has collected herself. A snigger. The students in the corner cluster together like a bunch of monkeys, hiding their faces behind their hands. A titter escapes one girl. And Sam becomes distinctly aware of how preposterous this must look. Him saying that to a woman like her in a tone like that. Perhaps they are laughing out of discomfort, but perhaps it really is inherently ridiculous.

"Not the time or the place," Roberta says.

Sam can't look at her. He storms out of the cafe, slamming the door.

"I want to see you."

"I can't."

"I want to see you."

"I can't."

Tick.

"I can't do it. Not right now."

She can hear defeat in his silence.

"I'm exhausted. We're both exhausted. What's the point?"

Now when Nina comes to the underpass, she automatically feels terrified. Before she's even at the steps she's contemplating whether she can avoid it entirely and get across the busy road another way. She thinks through her mental map for some long way round but there isn't one. The A-road cuts a clean swathe through the area, dividing everything, not just space but people, class, occupations, ethnicities and property prices. She shivers. It's been a long day and it is getting dark already. She wishes she had left her car in the tube station and paid for it and damn the expense, but frugality is in her genes, she can't help it. The unbroken stream of traffic whizzes past, its roar reminding her of an angry and weather-tossed sea. Lights are already coming on. Side-lights, headlights. And she contemplates trying to clamber over the barrier, wondering whether there might be a long enough interval for her to get across. And despairing when she realises that it would require two such intervals. Thinking about standing in the middle of the central reservation as the light fades and the weather undoubtedly worsens.

And then she tells herself to stop being so stupid and just use the damn underpass.

And she does. And all through it she's in a heightened state of awareness and she's jumping at every noise. Hurrying, on the brink of running. And when she gets back to her car, she can't think of anything to do but phone him.

"Sam," she says, her voice tight with tension and shaking with nerves, "Where are you? Can you just hold me? I can't take this anymore."

And they hold each other. He meets her at her flat and they stand there for minutes with their arms just wrapped around each other like that. And after a while he asks, "Do you want to go out? Get some dinner?"

And she looks up at him fearfully and says, "I'm not sure I want to be... out there. I'd rather be here where it feels safe."

And he replies that that's exactly why they should go out. "You are safe," he says, "You're with me."

They go to Silvio's, a modest Italian restaurant, local to him. The food is good and the service is friendly. They sit across from each other. She is thumbing the tablecloth. He tells her to have a glass of wine; relax. Even though his own hands play with the cutlery, looping knives over forks, forks over spoons and back again.

"Roberta told me that you are an outpatient at some clinic."

The cutlery stops looping.

"Shit," he says. And he looks up at her with moist, sunken eyes. "I'm sorry. I should have told you."

"Should you?" Her face is a mask.

"No. Look, it's, it's not that big a deal. I mean it is. It is and it isn't. I was there for a while after, you know, after... That's, actually that's where I first started working with Roberta. But it was a long time ago and, hey, look I didn't even know I was still on their books. I'm sorry Nina."

"Don't be." Her eyes are big and round, her smile calm. "I haven't told you everything about me, why should you need to have told me everything about you?"

"Well, this is a bit different."

"Look, it freaked me out, okay. At the police station. I got turned around in my head. That little nugget she dropped, you freaking out. I think... I think maybe she was trying to create a certain label for you in my head. But it all makes sense. The way you reacted there. I... I mean God forbid I was in the same situation I'm sure my reaction would have been pretty extreme." And her face breaks into a smile. She reaches across the table and grabs his hand, squeezing it tightly. Simultaneously, they let out a gasp. Relief. Weight lifted. The gasp becomes almost a laugh. But then Nina steadies herself, cutting the air with her other hand. "Let me look into it," she says. "I'm not sure that we'll be able to make much of what has happened to you stick, but let me see if I can find something on her. If she's as bad as you say she is, there's bound to be something."

"Thank you," and for the first time in ages he feels some security. "This is not going to last," he says. "We'll get her."

"Now," she gulps down her wine, "no more about her. Not tonight. Can we talk about something else?"

"Of course," and he smiles in that charming, understanding way he does, "talk about anything you want."

But she doesn't. And neither does he. They try a variety of topics but they can't seem to hit on something that enthuses them both. And Sam experiences a sinking feeling in his stomach and Nina recedes into the distance, as if the table was elongating and pushing her out of the room. And he worries that maybe they don't really have anything in common. Nothing besides this. And the horrible possibility occurs to him that far from driving them apart, as he had thought she sought to, Roberta is now the only thing holding them together. If none of this had happened, would they have gone their separate ways by now? And even though Sam thinks back on how they were and knows that this couldn't possibly be the case, he hears the hollow echo of what it feels like to be alone in the world.

Nina doesn't read any of this in his face and when her voice returns to his sphere of attention she is talking about something work-related. He feigns interest. And he knows that she knows that it is feigned but also that it doesn't matter – all that matters is that he makes the effort to listen and she makes the effort to speak.

They have had a little to drink. The same, but it's hit her a bit more and she stumbles and laughs while he struggles to fit his key in the front door of his block. He steadies her with a hand on the small of her back and she feels good, warm and pulsing beneath the fabric. She grabs the lapel of his jacket and tells him with a sly half-smile that when they get upstairs he's in trouble. It has been too long and they're both feeling a quickening of the blood that is drawing them together.

"Come on, let's get inside," she breathes in his ear.

"It doesn't... seem to fit."

"Are you sure it's the right one?"

He giggles drunkenly. She grabs the keys off him and fumbles with them.

"What have you got so many keys for?"

He shrugs.

"How about this one?"

And he blinks but it looks like she's holding up nothing, like an imaginary key.

"What are you..." He shakes his head in mock disapproval. "Gimme those. How drunk are you?" And he grabs the keys off her, locates the right one and opens the door.

They are just about at the lift when he says, "Hold on, wait a second."

"I don't think I can."

"Just a sec, okay."

"What? You're serious?"

She's got a broad smile on her face, she thinks he's playing with her. And he half plays along, chuckling as he holds up a finger and turns away. He walks over to the letter boxes near the front door and she's calling after him, "Sam, come on, the post can wait 'til tomorrow. What you doing?" The lift is open beside her, waiting for them to step in.

His shoulders stop shaking. He's looking at the boxes and she can't see his face and she is confused. She lets go of the lift button and walks up behind him. Even from his back she can tell that the joy of a moment ago seems to have left.

"Sam?"

When he turns his face has dropped.

"I knew it."

"What?"

"Harding. Rosanna Harding." And he presses his thumb against the letterbox. "I knew I knew it from somewhere. Jesus."

"What?"

"She's one of Roberta's."

"One," Nina swallows and steadies herself with a hand against him as she tries to make herself feel a little more sober. "One of

Roberta's what? Patients?"

"Yeah."

"So?"

They should be having sex now. But instead Nina is sitting at the kitchen table nursing a mug of coffee while Sam expounds his theory. Roberta's spy. Someone to keep an eye on him. Someone to keep watch. Someone to sneak in at night and administer drugs, support delusions, ratchet up the psychological tension with sneaky little twists of the knife. And it sounds plausible enough. But it's the way he's talking about it. The rage. The fervour again. And of course it makes sense. Of course he's right to feel angry if it's true – which, of course, is still an unknown as far as Nina's concerned. But she wants to believe it. She really does. It's just the extremity of his feeling. It's unsettling. She can't help but think, what if that animosity was ever turned against me? What would I do? Even though she knows it never would be. He's just too good. He couldn't. Could he?

"I should go round there right now," he says, "Just knock on the door and see what the fuck she has to say."

"That's a bad idea. If you absolutely have to, then at least wait until the morning."

"Wait until... Nina, with a viper right in our nest? Who knows what she could do while we're fast asleep. While we think we're safe. I mean she's done it before and she's obviously got keys to the place."

"So put the chain on. Leave a chair in front of the door, whatever."

"No, I have to... You're here, Nina. Don't you see, I've got a responsibility to you. I can't put you in danger."

"I can look after myself."

He sits and fumes, arms folded, staring down into their junction.

"Hey, tell you what, Sam, if it makes you feel better you can prop a bowl of water on top of the door. That way when she comes in it'll tip all over her and wake her up out of whatever semi-trance hypno-robot state she's in."

"It's not something to joke about."

"I know, I know," she takes his hand. "I was just trying to lighten the mood."

He's still not looking at her. When she calls his name, his head lifts, barely makes eye contact with her and then turns away to the window. Darkness. City lights.

"Sam," she says again, "Sam, look at me."

And now he does.

"It's important that we keep a level head about all of this and part of that is that you keep calm. What she's doing, it's emotional attrition. If you let it unbalance you then she's winning. Don't you see that?"

He nods.

"Take the night. Think about it. Sleep on it. Then work out the best way to approach the issue when you've got a bit of clarity."

A smile creeps onto his face. "I don't know what I'd do without you."

A little blush. That sweet, sensitive side of him. That's the good-heart. The soft centre. It's what she loves about him. The thing that supersedes all the bullshit and confusion that surrounds it. And with his hand still in hers, she stands and, swinging it playfully drags him towards the bedroom. He watches her hips as she walks with crossed feet and begins to unbutton herself with her free hand. And he says, "You know, as long as I've got you, I think I'll be alright."

And she looks back over her shoulder and smiles at him and says, "I know you will."

The bedroom is dark. He stands by the window staring at the faint orange glow of streetlights through the curtains. She's asleep now and he doesn't want to wake her. He wonders why he's standing there if she's asleep. He thinks maybe out of a desire to be close to her. But whatever the reason was, he can't quite remember it now and all he can think is that out of some stupid, forgotten impulse he has put himself in this place. This room where it's too hot and the air is so thick it's like breathing in soup. And he feels a tickle in his throat and he wishes he could just reach down inside himself and scratch it. He needs to get out of here. But when he turns away from the window, he finds himself night-blind. He cannot see her bed or the door that lies beyond it, but knowing the layout of the room so well, he tries to feel his way out, expecting at any time to come into contact with the bed or the desk or a chair or something to help him get his bearings.

He doesn't know how long but it feels like forever that he is groping through the blackness. And as every second passes, he can feel his throat getting tighter. The breath being squeezed from his body. And the heat is so close and the sweat is making his clothes heavy. And he keeps taking small steps, feeling around, always prepared for some impact, some connection with something but nothing comes. He gropes through empty space, eternal hot breathless blackness. He begins to take larger strides, a panic growing as he thinks that he must be walking round and round the room in circles and that he will never be able to leave. And he turns over his shoulder left, turns over his shoulder right, looking back to try and find that dimly lit window but finds nothing. The suffocating darkness around him is total. And all he can do is stumble ever forward his arms sweeping in low circles.

He hits it hard. There is a rattle and a clatter of equipment and the bed jogs on its wheels and he thinks shit shit shit and has no idea whether he has disturbed his wife or worse, maybe damaged some of the vital equipment that sustains her. And he tries to feel his way down to the bottom of the bed and round towards the door. But stops.

Her breath begins like an old motor car kicking off into life. And the sound of it, the massed mucus in the infected chest cavity. Its wet rattle and suck. As loud and articulate as speech. The body speaking alone without the assistance of the brain, speaking and saying nothing but I am in pain. Hideous, horrendous pain. Pain above and beyond anything you have experienced in your short and lucky life; short but still longer than mine. And he prays to a God he's not sure he believes in anymore. Prays that this is just the reaction of a sleeping body stirred, that he has not woken or damaged her in any way.

But then there is the stirring of sheets, rubbing together like folds of dry skin. Scratching each other. And he has a draining sensation as he hears her moan. A sob of grief as she wakes to realise that she is still here. That she is in terrible pain and she is still dying and her dreams were nothing but a temporary respite from this living hell, no matter how frightening or sad they may have been. Which they must have been because dreams are only made of the stuff of daily life, the fringes, the edges of it melded and reimagined. And the stuff of which her life is made is only terror and tragedy and self-pity. From the moment she wakes to the moment she goes to sleep. And necessarily beyond, with her, taking it all with her as she submerges in her subconscious, vulnerable and exposed to everything, every worst idea.

He searches the blackness, craning his head towards her sound, eyes searching blindly. But he cannot see her. There is only the black. Not even a faded outline. And he is too afraid to reach out for her because he does not want to touch her or stir her or possibly injure her fragile body and add yet another note of misery to her life if he were to dislodge a drip-feed or rupture a sore, or rip her delicate skin. And so he continues, feeling his way around the bottom of the bed, trying to find the way out and praying that she has not woken.

Her voice is so faint it is barely there at all. Like the reflection of a voice. The final reverberation of an echo. And he freezes. Swallows. Hopes that if he stays absolutely still she might think that she had only imagined him present and he will be able to slip away. But she keeps calling his name. Nagging and insistent like a child. He stands there in the black not responding. A note of sadness creeps into her voice and in between his name he hears what sound like sobs. Sniffling sobs, so small and incomplete. But they shake her. They shake her. He knows. He has seen. When she cries, as she often does, the sobbing shakes her whole, entire being. Her body vibrates as if it might fall apart. A hot tearing of the lungs. A fibrous wracking immolation of her throat. Her tear ducts seem like they are about to burst and shed pus-filled tears.

But he cannot bring himself to announce his presence and he stands stock-still, staring into the black.

And in the black. Something rises. Faint at first. Fading into view. Something he does not want to see, cannot bear to look at, but cannot turn away from. Cannot even avert his eyes. Cannot even close them. Because he knows that if he does it will be there again and again under his lids and a hundred times worse than the thing that confronts him now. If that is even possible. Because now that it is rising into his vision he feels everything that he is beginning to desert him and that he, like it, is becoming nothing more than a paper-thin chrysalis, discarded and left for the worms to consume. Fragile, vulnerable and beyond salvation.

Something starts like a nag. A tiny thing in the distance that forces itself to the forefront and dominates her perception. It is a sound of alarm, an immediate, wrenching sound. Nina bolts into wakefulness and slams upright. The room spins around her. Sam is screaming in his sleep. His arms flail in front of him and she grapples with him to pin them down and guard herself from injury. And he's lying on his back and flipping, bucking, struggling against her, or not her exactly but some unseen thing and she pins his arms with all her weight and bends over him and shouts his name into his face again and again and shakes him until he bursts awake and his head whips up and they almost collide and he looks her right in the eyes, his own dancing with terror.

"Caroline."

It provokes as much anger in Nina as it does concern.

"No. Not Caroline. It's me Sam, Nina."

"Nina. Thank God."

"You were screaming in your sleep."

"I was?"

She nods solemnly. "Are you okay?"

"Yes, yes, I think so."

She bids him go back to sleep and strokes his hair and lies close to him until he drifts off. And she stays like that watching him until the minutes roll into an hour and she realises that she is not feeling tired at all. And with a grunt of frustration she rolls over onto her other side with her back to him and rearranges her pillow until it is comfortable, gathered between her arms and her head and she can sink into it and she feels a relief, a weight lift. But still she doesn't fall asleep. Not for the whole night. Not until daylight begins to intrude upon the sanctity of the chamber.

Chapter Four

MUCH OF MADNESS AND MORE OF SIN

"Shit."

Nina's back, upright on the edge of the bed. A lean expanse of bare skin, the shape of shoulder muscles, the ridge of her spine, shoulder blades. Sam blinks his gummy eyes and smiles to himself as he watches it. Watches it move. She stands, pulling on her underwear, and he says to her, "Morning."

She speaks without turning round, "I have to be in court in two hours."

She pulls on her skirt. Zips it.

"Can't you just stay?"

"No."

She busies herself with the rest of her dressing and then stops and thinks and says, "Sorry. I'd love to. How about you come round for dinner later?"

Puppy dog frown turns into a smile.

"Any special requests for the chef?"

He places a finger on his lips, eyes turned heavenwards.

"Let me guess. Steak and chips?"

He nods enthusiastically.

"What are you going to do today?"

He lies back, stretches and grins.

"Bastard."

He chuckles.

"Hmm. Maybe I'll go speak to the Harding woman."

Nina stops what she's doing and looks at him pointedly. She's not comfortable with the idea, but she hasn't got the time or the energy to get into a discussion that might very well lead to an argument.

"Don't worry," he says, "I'm not going to do anything stupid."

Nina continues to dress.

"What do the notes say about her?"

"She's in her thirties. Single. Think she's an ad exec or she works in TV or something. Sounds like a bit of a whiner. Mainly moaning about relationship issues. Bouncing from guy to guy and complaining that she can never find Mr. Right, all that bollocks."

"Hey, watch it."

Nina's got this look on her face and her arms are folded and she's squinting across at Sam and he says, "What?"

"I just don't like the way you're talking about her. Like she's got nothing to be complaining about. Like her feelings don't deserve attention or they're not worthy of, you know..."

"Come on, Nina, it's not like there's a big issue here."

"There could be. How do you know?"

"There's nothing in the notes."

"Yes but," she frowns, "anyway, that's not the point. I'm saying I know how she feels. And it might be common or ordinary or boring but it's real and it can, you know, make you really sad. Being alone. Being lonely. It's not like you need someone to die." Nina immediately regrets what she said. "Sorry."

Sam breathes. Then smiles.

"It's okay," he says. But she still looks mortified so he reinforces, "It's really okay. It really is."

She sighs and turns away. Sam watches her collecting her effects, conspicuously busying herself.

"What did you mean?" he asks her.

And she responds with a noncommittal "Huh?" as if nothing in their recently truncated conversation could really be of any significance.

"You said you knew how she felt?"

Fiddling around in the contents of her handbag, she half mumbles, "I used to feel like that."

Sam swells with a great golden glow and he can't help himself from beaming all over the place. He walks over to her and puts his hands on her shoulders and she half-turns over her shoulder and says "What?" and he says nothing so that she is forced to turn to see him and she says "What?" again but this time there's a half-smile on her lips because she's seen his bright eyes sparkling at her and full of life and love and so very, very excited about something.

"You used to feel like that?"

And she nods coyly and tucks her hair behind her ear.

"When?" he says.

"You know," she still can't quite look at him, "till a little while ago."

And when he places his finger under her chin and lifts her face to look at him she can't hide a big fat smile that bursts on her face and then quivers as her cheeks turn grapefruit pink and she tries to hide it, keep it down, keep it from bubbling up but she can't quite and Sam just says "Oh yeah?" and lowers his face towards her and his lips touch hers and they press firmly together and part as she leans back in his arms.

She's gone. Sam's in such a great mood that he's almost forgotten about his plan. He's still walking on air like he's in a tacky song. He smiles as he laces up his shoes and thinks about how amazing it is that something so insubstantial, something as small as a comment, as a word, can effect such complete and total change. A smile. A look. And all of a sudden he's flying. But it's more than that. It's something major. Something that she's felt for some time but only feels able to share with him now. It is significant. Big or small, it is truly significant.

Sam checks himself in the bathroom mirror. Slaps his cheeks. Shines himself a cheeky grin and reminds himself of how great he is. How cool he feels. How attractive. He knows that he's great and as long as he has her belief, there's nothing that can get to him. Nothing at all.

It occurs to him that he's never been to any other floor of his building before. He emerges onto the second and is struck by the way that it's almost identical to his own, the sixth. It has the same flooring, the same wallpaper, the same light fittings. The only tangible difference is a bicycle in the hallway. It has a note pinned to it: "Please move your bike". Sam chuckles. But there is something else. It feels different. Like a foreign country. And even if you removed the bicycle and put the plant pots from number twenty-one in front of number six, it would still feel different. Somehow colder. Unwelcoming. Not home.

And as he draws towards number six, Sam begins to feel increasingly like he shouldn't be here. As if every wall and cornice and door is watching him. Beady-eyed peepholes, ready to report, comment, extrude, call the police, have him thrown out for encroaching on a space that is not his. Trespassers will be eaten. The neutral wallpaper and neutral lino suddenly seem anything but – they are aligned with the enemy and they close in like a prison of beige. There are smells here. Foreign ones. Cooking. The stink of rubbish. A stain on the floor.

Sam arrives outside number six. In a hurry to get this over and done with, he goes to knock. But stops. And gazes at the door with a growing sense of unease. All of those things pressing on him, the environment rising to meet him. He could walk away from this corridor and let it disappear forever, but as soon as he knocks it will become a permanence in his life. He will be connected to this place.

He paces up and down. What is he going to say to this neighbour? How will he ingratiate himself with her? What can he do to put her at her ease? What story to concoct? Hi, I live upstairs I was wondering if you had a cup of sugar. I'm from the residents' committee. Downstairs has a leak and I was wondering if I could have a quick look at the bathroom. Hi, you don't know me, but... but you do know me, don't you? You do.

He stops. Tempus fugit. He's here, now. He must do it. Things, time, space will change. He doesn't know why but this feels like it might be his only chance and it is slipping through his fingers with every moment he deliberates. He wills himself to act but his feet won't move. He can only stand and stare helplessly at these unmoving walls. And then before he has even thought it, he is at Rosanna Harding's door and he is knocking. He has knocked.

A deep sickness settles in his stomach.

There's a rattle and a clunk as the door jars open against the chain. A green eye peers out at him, blinking under a yellow fringe.

"Hi I'm..."

"What do you want?"

He can see teeth and curled lips through the gap. Like an angry dog. And his palms begin to sweat and he brings a hand to the back of his neck and it is wet there too and a trickle slides all the way down his spine and he says, "My name's Sam, I'm..."

"I know who you are. What do you want?"

Sam misses a breath. The corridor stretches and swims in his peripheral vision and that stench of rubbish is becoming stronger. Rich and shitty. And at the centre of it all there's that eye, those teeth, the snarling lips. And he stutters through a dry mouth,

"You know who I am?"

He can see her hands are shaking on the door; stretched across her brow, the chain trembles.

"Bastard," she says. And she leans in towards the door. But Sam catches the movement before she throws her weight against it and shoves his foot into the gap.

"If you don't go, I'm gonna call the police and have you fucked out of here."

"Why would you want to do a thing like that?"

"Like you don't know," she spits. And then a bare heel comes down on his foot. A dull smash against his toes but nothing unbearable. He's lucky she's not wearing shoes. And so he keeps his foot there and he pries his hands into the gap, pulling at either side and he leans into it so his face is pressing in to look at her and he says through gritted teeth "Look. I need to talk to you. I promise as far as I know I have never seen you before."

"You're lying, you're lying, you fuck."

"Listen. Shut up! Listen to me will you?"

"You fuck. You bastard. Have you had e-fucking-nough? Don't you think you've tortured me enough already? Just go back to the hole you came from and –"

"Roberta"

"die"

"Roberta"

"hope you fucking"

"therapist"

"arsehole"

"ROBERTA!" and he pushes his face into the gap, shouting through it, desperate to penetrate this inexplicable wall of abuse and something makes her stop. Claps her mouth shut. Is it that she's recognised what he's saying? "Do you..."

A scream wrung from within her. Abject terror. And she runs away into the flat. And he can't think of anything but that she must be completely deranged. And his blood's up so high that he doesn't even recognise that she's a terrified woman alone in her flat wearing nothing but a dressing gown and that he's got his face pushed through her door like Jack Nicholson and he's flushed and red with righteous indignation and his hands look big and strong enough to tear the door open and snap the chain. Which is exactly what he does.

And he thunders in after her and towards the lounge just in time for the door to slam on him and he bats it back with his forearm and storms in and there she is behind an armchair, curled up on the floor and she's holding a cushion up in front of her like it might actually protect her from something and now she's not swearing or spitting or cursing.

Rosanna's face is streaming with tears. It has moved beyond fear or terror to a state of complete abandon, her mouth is wide and her cheeks hang loose below her eyes and she begs "please, please, please" without even being able to specify what it is that she is begging for. She looks so small and pitiful and vulnerable and bereft. And her dressing gown is open, a small breast exposed. The nipple is erect. And somehow this absurd detail gives Sam pause. He steps back, averts his eyes and flushes with shame and says, "Shit, I'm sorry."

From behind his hands he peeps out at the room around him. The cushions are all torn and patched with gaffer tape. Wallpaper is stained and curtains are ripped. There are candlesticks on the mantelpiece and there's a dusting of broken china around their bases and, in the fireplace below, there are more remnants of smashed ornaments. It was a nice flat once. But something terrible has clearly happened here. And Sam realises that the stench of rubbish is coming from the next room. And without looking at her, hoping that she will correct her modesty, he says

"I don't know what's happened to you. But I'd like you to tell me. And I think I can help you."

"Yeah, right," comes her trembling answer. "Just do what you've got to do. Or do you leave that to your mates these days?"

And Sam wants to turn to her snarling and say what the fuck are you on about but he has the presence of mind to realise that that's not going to help him here. That he's not the only victim. And instead he says, "Look. I think we're both missing information here..."

"Oh, are we?"

"Just hear me out. I'm here because we share the same therapist, we live in the same block and I think that there's more to that than coincidence. But apart from that as far as I'm concerned I've never heard of you or seen you before in my life. And yet you not only think you know me, but have some kind of grievance. Can we just talk?"

But all she can do is huff and puff with indignation and disbelief.

"At least tell me what you think I've done. Imagine you've never seen me before and that you're telling me about the things that happened, like I was a completely different person."

She seems to mellow a bit. Well, maybe not mellow, but she descends into a kind of steely, suspicious calm, her arms folded and her eyes little slits staring at him and she almost says something a couple of times and then stops breathes and says, "I can't talk about this stuff to just anyone. That's what Roberta's for."

Sam looks her in the eye and he smiles. And it's a genuine, sympathetic gesture and she recognises it and he says, "Try."

"You are the thing that I fear. You are the face that I see when I wake up in the middle of the night. You are the destroyer."

She glares at Sam from under a lowered brow. And as if she is pushing him away with her mind, he staggers back a few steps. He turns pale, his frame losing the solidity and certainty that it had a moment ago. And Rosanna asks if he's okay and he nods and tells her to please go on. And for some reason seeing him weaken in this way allows her to let her guard down a little more and she says, "Sit."

And he does.

She takes the armchair across from him and sits turned away with her knees tucked together. She twists her head to look at him and then her gaze falls to her lap and from this position, as if talking to no-one, as if praying, as if confessing to a silent God, she tells her story:

"It happened one night. I woke up in the early hours. I had no idea why, but I just felt agitated. Alarmed. I rolled around in bed a while coming to and trying to figure out which way was up and where I was in my room. You know, you ever have that thing, where you think you're looking at the door to your room and it takes a few moments before you fully wake up and you realise you're really looking at a cupboard or the window?"

"Yes."

"Disorientation in the most literal sense. Anyway, after I figured out where I was I started to calm down but I was awake now and not really sleepy so I walked through to the kitchen to get a glass of water and then I went into the lounge and I was about to switch the light on when I saw someone sitting there in the darkness. Right there. Where you are."

"Shit."

"Yes, I was terrified. And I said who are you and it was a man and he was sitting there with his shoulders hunched and his hands clasped together and staring down at the floor in front of him and I started to freak out a bit so I said who the fuck are you and he turned to look at me and his face was serious and drawn together, lips pursed but he didn't answer me and he just kept staring at me and I began to shake, I realised how completely vulnerable I was and I couldn't speak for a moment. And I could just see his eyes shining in the dark, staring right at me, blinking occasionally. And he did nothing and eventually I summoned up my courage and I said what are you doing in my flat and still he didn't answer and I didn't know what to do. And then I said if you don't leave now I'll call the police. And he got up, just like that, and walked out."

"Jesus."

"No. That was only the beginning. But the man," her green eyes flick towards him, as if he should know, "it was you."

Sam's fingers curl and his nails scrape along his forearms. He looks down and sees long red wheals and recoils as he realises what he is doing. Until her voice snatches his attention back to her, "I tried to forget about it. I went straight back to sleep after and I wasn't even sure if it was real or if it was a dream. I spoke to Roberta about it..."

"What did she say?"

"Well, she assumed that it was some kind of a dream and maybe that fits because I think that was the way I was thinking about it at the time and probably the way I was portraying it to her."

"Tell me, before this happened, what was going on in general? In your life, I mean."

"Nothing much. I was feeling good. Things were fine. I think... yeah, I think I'd just started seeing a guy that I quite liked. His name was Francis. Turned out to be a bit of a flake in the end though, so I dumped him. Actually, it wasn't long after that that the next thing happened.

"It was the same. Jerking out of sleep unnaturally and then walking through into the lounge. And it was weird because I had this kind of fear that it would happen. I knew something was wrong. It was that feeling of apprehension and I recognised it."

"And I was there again?"

"Yes."

"And what did I do?"

"No, but you see, it wasn't just you this time. There were four of you there. You and three other guys. All sitting around in here with your faces turned down to the floor. You weren't talking to each other or looking at each other. There was a real sense of solemnity amongst you. Like a commonness of purpose."

"So what did you do this time?"

"I didn't say anything. I couldn't. I could barely breathe. And then after a while, when you didn't do anything, when none of you said anything or moved or acknowledged me, I sat down right there," she points, "on the couch next to you. And still you paid no attention to me but I didn't dare speak or interrupt whatever was going on, this strange unbreakable communion between the four of you. I didn't know what would happen if I did. And once I was sitting down I didn't dare move. I don't know how long it was we sat there. It felt like an hour, maybe more. And every moment of it was interminable. And then, after a while, you just got up and left again."

"And Roberta?"

"She said that it seemed like I was having some kind of episode. Perhaps something, some dream-state or waking-fantasy brought on by intense depression at my break-up. Except I wasn't depressed. I didn't feel it, you know, in my day-to-day life, when I was walking around everything felt fine. Except for this nagging feeling that maybe something was truly, deeply wrong with me."

"How did you feel about the break-up?"

"Fine. Good even. Really good. I felt like I was moving on from a sort of habitual thing of forming relationships with the type of guys I knew would always disappoint me in some way and I thought I could tell, you know, when I met the next one, I thought I'm closer to finding someone. And everything else was just ticking along just fine. So... And then..."

"It kept happening?"

"Every now and then, yes. But Roberta had me on some stuff and I was feeling great most of the time. And that was when I met David. David is perhaps the best man I've ever met. Even now I feel like I could just marry him and have kids and be happy forever with just a click of my fingers."

"So what happened?"

"David..." and she breaks off and holds her temples. Her body trembles. She breathes in deeply to settle herself. "David got into a horrible situation. A mugging gone wrong. He was, he was badly beaten and ended up in hospital for a few weeks. And I tried, I really did, to go and see him all the time, to be supportive, bring him stuff. But seeing him weak like that, not just physically but also cowed, you know, jumping at shadows. There was this, this creaking sound every time somebody walked into his hospital room and after a while I realised that it was his bed, that his body was shaking. And the whole effect of this thing was that I couldn't quite... Everything I felt for him, it just started falling off, you know. But I tried. I really did.

"And then one day I got home and my flat had been destroyed. Completely turned upside down. And I was shocked and I didn't know what was going on and I began to get very confused. And you started showing up again. Every night. Sometimes alone, sometimes with the others and I was convinced that you were going to do something terrible to me and there was nothing I could do about it and no-one could protect me. And every time I would fix my flat up I would turn round the next moment and find it overturned again. Worse than before. I replaced the broken flowerpots and my cushions would be slashed. I replaced them, they'd be slashed again. I taped them up and then my curtains would be torn."

Sam leans forward, "We need to help each other. Tell me. What did Roberta say?"

"She said that it was guilt, that I was expressing anger that I had repressed because I was making myself look after David out of loyalty, out of a sense of 'should' even though my own feelings had left me. And this was the only way I could express it. By destroying my own home."

"Had your feelings left you? I mean, I know it sounds like it was hard for you but from what you said a moment ago it sounds like you still have great feelings for David."

"For a fantasy David maybe; the old David."

"That's what she would have you believe."

"No. She may have suggested it... or maybe I did... but it's ultimately up to me isn't it? What I believe. How I interpret my life." She smoothes back a loose strand of hair and holds herself. "I don't know what I feel. I just don't."

"What if she's doing all this to you?"

Rosanna's eyes switch on him and her brow creases and several things seem to pass under the skin of her face like waves and then she turns her whole body to face him. And holds him with a look.

And then she bursts out laughing. But there is no levity in it. And the louder she laughs – her mouth opening wide, her body shaking, clutching her sides – the more worried Sam becomes. Because this isn't real laughter. Rosanna howls and bawls. She collapses sideways in her chair and drapes her arms over the edge as the laughter pours out through her like vomit until, exhausted and breathless, she looks up at Sam with a smile still on her face and she says,

"Now that would just be so ridiculous." And she sits up, correcting herself, adjusting her gown. "And yet it would make so much sense. It really would explain everything, wouldn't it? You see, Sam, I actually, you know, thinking about that, I find I really want to, I almost do believe it. But at the same time I know that it's because it's just the most convenient answer, the easy fix. It's right on so many points..."

"That it must be true." He finishes her sentence for her and she falls silent for a moment. Her lips press together, mouth bunching with little lines.

"No," she says. "No. There's still holes in it. You don't even know that you were here."

"I have some ideas about that."

"But still. 'Cos, see the thing is that even now, even right now in this moment, I don't even know if this conversation is really happening. It feels like it is and, and I know that it is. But, and I realise how stupid this sounds, but I don't know what I'll think in the next moment. When you're gone I might realise that this was actually some kind of an episode and I'll have that terrible thing fighting myself over whether I can even believe my own version of the recent past. But the longer I sit here talking calmly with you the more I begin to think that, yes, it is real and that maybe I'll be able to hold onto that." She breathes out a sigh and turns to look out the window. "But, I suppose that the now will soon become the past and things will become unclear and muddy again and," she covers her eyes with her hands, "Sam, I don't trust myself to hold on to what is real and what is not. I can't."

And he says, "Try."

The phone drags Nina out of her drudgery and she is relieved for the interruption. Relief transforms to gladness when she hears Sam's voice. She sits forward in her seat and curls her head inwards, as if trying to hide her girlish smile from her colleagues, even though she is alone in her office. And then he tells her he went to see Rosanna.

"Riiight..." her smile drops and now her elbow rests on her desk. Her fingers twine around a pen and flick it from side to side as she listens to everything Sam has to tell her. "You did what?" When he tells her he broke the door in. "Oh, okay," when he gets to the end of the story, "so she's not pressing any charges?"

"On the contrary," Sam says, "I think she'll help us. Nina, I think it's pretty clear that something pretty fucked is up here. And now there's two of us, it's not just my word against Roberta's, is it?"

Nina closes her eyes and pinches her temples. She's not sure what to make of all this yet, needs to give it some serious thought without Sam in her ear.

"Nina?"

"It –" she breathes out a long sigh, "look, it depends on what you're thinking about. Yes, you've got someone else who can add to your account, but we could do with finding something, something where you've got common ground and both of your testimonies can be weighed against hers."

"What if we had more people?"

Nina sits up straight, "That's an excellent idea."

"I think I know where to start."

"Okay, why don't you see what you can do. I'll make some inquiries and I'll see you for dinner later on, okay?"

"Can't wait."

"You can bring – what's her name again?"

"Rosanna."

"Yeah, bring her too if you want."

Dressed, Rosanna could be a different person. She shimmers with sheen and gloss. Her hair is pulled back into a neat ponytail. All of her clothes are immaculate, even her jeans. Taller in her boots, she shrugs on a leather jacket and fastens her earrings.

"I doubt you'll need those."

"Always be your best," she says. And flicks a strand of hair away from her face, smoothing it back over into where it forms part of the perfect lick of fringe and will descend, fluttering over her forehead adorably at the right moment. She gives Sam a sharp lipgloss smile and says in a bright, forthright tone,

"Let's go."

He's not back from work yet. They wait and Rosanna smokes and they fall into a series of uncomfortable non-conversations. Every time a subject is raised it is too heavy, too deep to go into. Sam explains his theory: that in the same way Roberta has used him to interfere with Rosanna's life, she has used Rosanna to get into his flat, to spike him and induce episodes. And Rosanna takes it all in a matter of fact way that shows nothing but disguises a deep internal conflict. And now they are just standing there outside a block of flats in a suburban street, waiting for Neil to get home. There's a light breeze that stirs the tops of the trees in the leafy forecourt. And she smokes. Stubs one out. Lights another. Sam watches the birds in the trees, chattering and going about their business unimpeded. Unharassed by challenging thoughts or double-thinking. Able to act without considering first one thing then another, then returning to the first. Action is clear and definite. Fly. Pick up stick. Build nest. Dig soil. Eat worm.

Neil's BMW hand-brake-turns into the car park and squeals to a halt. He rocks forward in his seat and grins with satisfaction at his manoeuvre. He loosens his tie, gets out, slams the door. He turns towards them and pauses for a moment, his eyes lingering on Rosanna. A different kind of smile falls over his face. A hungry one. She looks on without reaction, sucking on her cigarette as he saunters towards them.

"Sorry Sam, got caught up at work." He looks her up and down. "Not bad. Is this her?"

"Who? Oh. No. This is Rosanna. She's also a client of Roberta's."

Neil's head tilts to one side and his smile splits into a wolfish grin. He turns to her and extends a hand,

"Hello Ro..."

She's staring at him. Her cigarette trembles in her fingers, hovering in front of her lips.

"You alright?"

She snaps out of it with a sharp intake of breath,

"Sorry." Looks at Sam. "He was there. One of your... pals, I mean."

"In your flat?"

"Yes."

Neil narrows his eyes,

"What the hell are you talking about?"

"It's a long story."

Neil's tie hangs in two strips on either side of his collar. He stretches out on the couch opposite them, yawns and shakes his head.

"You know, Sam, I thought it might be good to have some dirt on Roberta, just 'cos, you know. But I can't buy into this." He holds his can of Tyskie aloft. An aluminium crack as he squeezes the last few drops out into his mouth. "What do you think?"

"I don't know," says Rosanna, "I don't know. But I want to find out."

Her jaw is set with a determination that is incongruous with her uncertainty before. This is the driven career woman that she has still managed to be despite everything that's happened in her personal life and in her mind. She looks at Sam and nods her support.

Neil chuckles, "You are as mad as he is, aren't you?"

She folds her arms.

"I'd still fuck you though."

"Jesus, who do you think you are?"

"Reckon I've got a better idea about that than you do about you."

He gives her a wink and her thorny façade cracks as a giggle forces its way up. She looks away and when she turns back she's serious again.

"Can you think, Neil," says Sam, "where and how has she directed you in your life, pushed you in the direction of certain decisions? There are gaps in our memories. We have to work with what's there."

"Look, there's no gaps in my memory. I think you two are both fucking cuckoo. You should speak to someone about it. Honestly. Probably her."

"You told me before. There's things you can't quite remember. You remember thinking of quitting therapy but you can't remember when it was. Do you think it might have been around the time you got divorced? Do you think it could have anything to do with that?"

"Now you're just being silly," he raises an eyebrow and a finger, "and I might add a little insensitive."

"Neil. Just bear with me. You're appointment's tomorrow right?"

"Nope. Had to move that one. It was yesterday."

Sam holds his breath and looks from Neil to Rosanna. She shrugs.

"What?"

"Yeah, what?"

And they're both looking at him with questioning glances.

"I don't know. I just felt a shiver. Do you think she knows that we've been in contact?"

"Course not. Why would she even think to ask me that?"

"'Cos she fucking knows everything!"

Unstable adrenaline vibrates behind Sam's eyes as they dart from Neil to Rosanna. A worried glance passes between the two of them.

"Mate, you gotta get a hold of yourself. I mean have a bit of common sense. Who's the therapist and who's the patient here? If I was you I'd take a deep breath and go and have a good long look at myself in the mirror." Neil's arms are folded, head tilted up, looking down at Sam with all the arrogance in the world. "Go on, you can use the one in my bathroom if you like."

Sam sneers and looks to Rosanna for support but her creased brow is far from reassuring.

A trill breaks their impasse. The phone. It's the landline. Neil gets up from his seat without even an excuse me. Picks up the handset and gives them both a look and a shake of the head before disappearing into another room. The echo of the door slamming behind him quickly deadens into an unhealthy silence. In the blandness of this barely-lived-in, characterless, life-vacuum of a flat, Sam and Rosanna are left with only each other to look at. Their eyes meet and then part as it becomes awkward to maintain contact in the wake of each one's failure to speak, to know what to say.

Sam's ears prick up, straining to hear the murmur of Neil's voice through the wall, for some nugget of conversation to lift him out of this stagnancy if nothing else. But he can hear nothing. Apart from the repeated groan of a floorboard as Neil paces back and forth in the next room. Surely his voice should be louder, Sam thinks, surely at least its tone should filter through; he is not, after all, a quiet man. He is loud and brash and offensive.

"It's odd, isn't it?" says Rosanna. Sam's head twitches round to look at her. She takes the kind of halting breath that you take in a job interview, where your every movement and physical process is being observed. "I mean he makes some good points and I know you thought he'd be on your side and that's a bit of a surprise but I guess it's fair enough – but you'd have thought he'd at least be, you know, interested."

Sam rubs his forehead, making a noise like paper in the sound-dead room.

"I know. It's, shit, it beats me."

"Especially as it's, like, he was up for helping you before, right?" She hisses inward. "Ach, maybe he's just a prick."

But Sam's feeling a creeping sensation all over him now. The return of the shiver he felt a moment ago. His hands clutch and reclutch themselves.

"No." His lip curls up. "I mean, he is. But such an abrupt change." And he looks at her with eyes startled wide and a haunted shadow beneath his cheeks. "What if she got to him?"

Rosanna's eyebrows twitch up for a moment. And then her neck tucks in and she squints.

"Oh, come on Sam don't you think that's a bit..."

The clunk of the door opening goes off like a bomb-blast in the quiet. Neil strides out of the room and chucks the handset onto the table without bothering to return it to its cradle. He grabs his coat off the back of a chair and shrugs it on, not noticing his loose tie falling to the floor as he does so.

"You going somewhere?" says Sam. But Neil ignores him and moves through to the hallway. "Hey, Neil, wait a sec."

"I haven't got time for this." The voice echoes from beyond the door. A flash of his acne-scarred stubble-cheek as his head darts back in. "Come on, get up. Out, you fuckers, out. I got somewhere to be."

"Where you going?"

"Look, I've had enough of this bullshit. You're boring me and I'm going out. And I don't need hangers-on. Specially not mental ones. Got it?"

He stands in the hallway, holding the door open for them as they shuffle out, not quite sure where to put themselves.

"Take my advice," Neil says, "get some bloody therapy." And he laughs. But underneath it, somewhere back there, back behind his temples, there's thunder.

"What a cock," says Rosanna, a little too loud, as Neil walks away towards his car.

"Weird." Sam folds his arms and peers after him through narrowed eyes. The BMW's security system bleeps and the door handle thunks.

"What if there's nothing in this, Sam?"

Sam scowls at her. And then a light bulb goes off. He takes a sharp breath in, spins on his heel and all but runs towards his car.

"What – where are you going?" she calls after him, catching up with a half-hearted jog.

He squints back at her and opens the door, "I'm going after him. I want to see where he goes."

"What? Oh come on, Sam, leave it."

He gets in, ignoring her. She walks round to the other side of the vehicle. Opens the door. Sits in.

"Are you not going to drop me home first?"

"How am I supposed to follow him if I have to drop you home first?"

"Well how long are you going to follow him for? Unlike *someone* I've actually got work to do."

"I don't know!" Sam's hands twist on the wheel. His teeth clench with a buzz of irritation. "Either come with or get out. Do what you want. I don't care."

There is a flash of ire in Rosanna's eyes and she gets out of the car, "Twat," and slams the door.

The BMW pulls to an abrupt halt at the side of the road. So abrupt that Sam shoots past it. He swoops into the first available space, having to pull across the traffic to park on the other side of the road. He watches his mirror, panting, hand on the door handle, ready to follow Neil on foot. But Neil doesn't get out. His car just sits there. Sam leans forward and peers closer at his mirror. He can just make out Neil, sitting in his car, not moving. And then he sees the lips move. Realises he must be on the phone. But there's no phone. If he's hands-free why has he pulled over? It's probably just a work thing, or a girl maybe. Something he wants to concentrate on. Sam waits. The air in the car is getting stale. He winds the window down and the traffic noise comes in. A loud, chaotic blast. The cacophony makes him flinch. He thinks about closing the window, sealing himself back up in his little bubble where he's safe from the vagaries of the world, insulated from people and their passions and their dirty day-to-day earthly dealings.

Neil's car whips past him. Sam tries to pull out but two lanes of traffic going the other way stream past relentlessly. He forces his way through. Horns blare. A red-faced man-in-a-van swears at him, the angry shape of his mouth more offensive than the fingers he raises. But none of that matters to Sam and he pushes on into the traffic going the other way. A grey saloon has to slam on its breaks. And as he drives on he sees the woman in his mirror, glaring at him with evil eyes.

But it's fruitless. The time it has taken him to get back into the traffic has allowed Neil to slip away. He's no longer in sight. But he can't be far ahead. Sam accelerates into a gap on the wrong side of the road to overtake. Pushing back into the correct lane, he almost forces a blue Golf up onto the pavement. Still no Neil. At the next opportunity he swings out wildly into the oncoming traffic again, puts his foot down and races past three or four cars towards a gap. And there he is. Up ahead, Neil's BMW turns left. Sam breathes a sigh of relief and goes to return to the correct side of the road but a car behind him pulls obstinately into the gap, refusing to let him back in. Sam puts his foot down and turns into it anyway, clipping the vehicle with his rear bumper. The incensed driver spins off onto the pavement and shudders to a halt and Sam glimpses him getting out of his car and shouting inaudibly as he swings left in pursuit of Neil.

Just as he has it in his sights, Neil's BMW rockets away down the single carriageway road. Sam doubts that he's trying to give him the slip. From the way he's driving it doesn't seem like he's aware of him. It's just a stretch of quiet road. The opportunity perhaps for Neil to let the boy-racer out to play. Unfortunately Sam's old Ford can't quite keep up, complaining with a pleuritic cough as the needle hauls itself over each notch while the BMW gets smaller and smaller. Then larger. Rapidly larger and larger. Neil has slammed to a halt. Sam grits his teeth, his breaks grind and wail as his car shudders and bucks to a standstill. He stops. Stalls. Neil is still stationary ahead of him. And Sam stares at the back of his head, at his mirror, looking for any flicker of eyes in his direction. Any sign that he has noticed him. But there is none. Despite their bumpers being only inches apart.

Neil moves on, driving at a normal speed now, as the old lady that pulled out in front of him happily chugs down the road.

Sam follows Neil into a supermarket car park. His quarry meanders around rows and rows of parked cars, breaking occasionally to allow shoppers through. And then at a seemingly arbitrary moment, he comes to a halt. He sits there. Right in the middle of the road. Not parked. Just stopped. A car behind Sam honks its horn and Neil winds his window down and waves them on. Sam echoes the gesture and the annoyed mother in the car behind him pulls past them both. If Neil was going to notice him at any point it would surely be now. But there is nothing about his behaviour or his movements that betrays recognition.

Neil stays absolutely still. Minutes pass and nothing unfolds. Just Neil sitting in his car in this weird limbo of actionlessness. Around them, shoppers bustle to and from their vehicles. Teenagers. Mothers and children. Trolleys, baskets. Boots opening and closing, muffled clunks just audible through the window of the car. Bags are loaded in. Uniform plastic sacks, the logo of the supermarket repeated over and over again, being sent in little parcels of branding to all of these peoples' homes. Like body snatchers' pods.

The roar snaps Sam to attention. His head whips forward, a jarring in his neck as the BMW rockets off. Sam puts his foot down and tries to catch up to it as it hand-brake-turns around a row of parked cars and disappears behind them in a cloud of dust and food wrappers. Hitting the turn, Sam breaks and twists the wheel but it whips back the other way, spinning out of his hands. He hits the break hard. His car skids and comes to a halt just feet away from a woman clutching her child in her arms and staring at him as if he was death itself.

Nina shifts the shopping bags around in her hands. Four of them.

She moves them back and forth, trying to balance their weight. In the end she has one with bottles and juices in her left hand and the other three in her right. She lifts them and lets them down, feeling the weight settle on either side of her. Then looks up, back straight, and sets off through the car park. In front of her three young boys run screaming ahead of their mother's trolley as she shouts after them. It brings a smile to her lips and she feels a little chuckle inside. She doesn't see the car when it hits her.

She doesn't feel it either. There is the sensation of being lifted by a strong and steady hand. The ground and the cars and the people and the car park all sink slowly as she rises up, the buildings becoming smaller. Like she's taking off. And there's a drop in her stomach, the feeling you have when a rollercoaster crests the top of its tallest peak and turns downwards. The buildings and the tops of people's heads fall away and then all she can see is sky. Blue cracks run in little rivers between puffy white clouds that are so deep and textured, all their vastness compacted into miniatures of intricate and exquisite detail. A plane moves slowly across the middle of the picture, carving a channel through the white puffs and parting them into fibrous strands. It moves slowly. The way aeroplanes always do. And she watches its leisurely transit and it feels like she is hanging there forever while the plane crosses from one corner of the sky to the other. She wonders what kind of plane it could be. Her mind seems to focus on anything but what is actually happening and every little detail seems possessed of the most fascinating intricacies, throwing up questions that have never occurred to her in her life before. Not when she has lain on a grassy hill in the sun, or on a beach at night looking up at the stars.

And there's a thump. Something slamming into her back. And it's only really now that it occurs to her that she has been hit by a car, except that it is confusing because it feels like it has slammed into the back of her. And she wonders if she could have been hit by two cars. One before and one now. And then all of this whimsy is whipped from her mind as the breath rushes from her body, pressed out of her in one swift, sudden compression. And her lungs seem to suck together, collapsing on the vacuum opened within them. She gasps for breath and all the veins and rods in her body, in her neck are standing out as she tries to inhale. The edges of her lips feel like they will split with the stretching-wide of her mouth and her throat aches and she sees her hands, fingers curled like bony claws paddling the air above her as if trying to scoop it back into her body. And then there is a slow, building sensation that begins as a dull ache in her core and spreads outwards, radiating across the whole of her. And as it spreads, the ache rises in pitch until it becomes brutal throbbing pain. And she begs it with every increment not to get worse but it does, it just gets worse and worse and all she can think is this isn't fair, this isn't fucking fair, this is some kind of sick evil joke how can it possibly get worse and she almost feels like laughing but there is no air left in her lungs to laugh with and anyway even the thought, the notion of doing such a thing, any consideration at all like that disappears from her mind as it is replaced by nothing but the fierceness of a pain that she does not know how to deal with and eclipses and wipes out all rational thought from her mind as it occupies every part of her being. Even her vision cannot cope and it begins to split and blur and the sky and the clouds above her seem to get smaller and further away and to shift out of focus and become dim. And as this happens, the sounds around her come to her attention, growing loud and raw. Voices. Screaming. Children crying. Men shouting. Car wheels churning and squealing. Doors slamming open and closed. All of this beyond her sight, leaving her only to guess and fumble at what might be producing them, whose voices they are.

And before she sees anything she feels a shadow slip across her. And it is a cold shadow. Like an unwelcome breeze on a warm day. And a figure appears above her in silhouette, its features cast completely in shadow and she feels an intense foreboding and as she stares into its eyes and behind it the sky splits and blooms into an indefinite white glare and the features of the man become visible she thinks that she recognises him and at the same time does not recognise him. It is a face she feels like she has seen, but only out of the corner of her eye, only in a snatched glimpse. Someone that she does not know but who is always there. And then before the image of his face can crystallise, he splits and blurs again and his features reshape and reassemble themselves into a new and far more familiar visage. Sam leans over her and he is screaming something, his mouth wide and his face twisted with tears and flushed. And he's saying something, he's trying to tell her something but his words are lost in the muddle of sounds that rise and circulate and coalesce all around her. And she thinks she can just make out his voice in the chaos but then it slips away and becomes inaudible. And everything washes out, fading to nothing, to silence. And with it Sam's face is lost in darkness and even that bright sky disappears, subsumed in a swirling blackness.

"Nina! Nina! Nina!"

Sam screams at her, but her eyes close and her head drops to the side. Her face is almost totally white, without any colour – apart from a cloud of bright red speckles around her mouth that seem to have been expelled with her breath. He looks around at the gawping onlookers and screams "Somebody call an ambulance!"

And doesn't even listen to the responses. People saying that they already have. Instead his head swivels and his body follows it and he sees his own recently abandoned car standing right there behind him and across the next row of parked cars, he sees Neil's BMW squealing away out of the car park and he has this sudden urge to go after him, to catch him. And he looks back at Nina on the ground and for a moment he is torn, each half of his body trying to go in a different direction until he sees Neil disappear from view and turns back to Nina, who is now completely still, and knows that his place is here. Right here beside her.

Sam is sitting cross-legged on the tarmac beside her when he hears the screaming of sirens drawing closer. Until they are right here, blocking out everything else. Nina has not moved. But he can see that she is breathing, her chest rising and falling so minutely that it would be possible not to notice it had he not been scrutinising her prone form for what feels like an hour but has in fact been only slightly more than ten minutes. And then the sirens cut out and all the surrounding noise returns. Sam looks up and an ambulance fills his vision. The back doors open like a gateway to another world and two men are bustling around him like worker bees bringing equipment over to Nina and listening to her body, taking her pulse. And then Sam is pulled up and back by two pairs of hands under his arms. He doesn't see who they belong to. He can only watch Nina as she is lifted onto a stretcher, wheeled the short distance to the back of the ambulance and there's a clunk that he thinks can't be good for her and then she is swallowed into the dark back of the vehicle with all its shelves and draping pipes and the worker bees buzz around her, settling her, strapping her in, plugging her in. Sam moves on legs that he can't really feel towards the back of the ambulance and he is telling the bees that he is her boyfriend and he wants to come with but they are too busy and paying no attention to him. And then he feels a hand on his arm and he turns and there's a policeman right there who says that he needs a word. And now the paramedics are out of the vehicle and the back doors are slammed shut and Nina is no longer visible and Sam shouts "Hey! Hey!"

A paramedic looks at him and then at the policeman who shakes his head and he says that he should come on to the hospital when he's ready. He becomes aware of the policeman's low burr buzzing in his ear and he turns to him, "What do you want?"

"Just a little talk, Sir. Do you think you could tell us about what happened?"

And Sam starts to speak but the policeman walks him over to a low wall and sits him down and says, "First things first. Can you give me your name and address?"

"What for?" asks Sam.

"We need it for your statement."

But it doesn't feel like a statement. It feels like an interrogation. As the interview progresses, Sam gets the sense that this policeman is far from the brightest bobby on the beat. He's got everything all topsy-turvy and he seems less interested in what Sam is trying to tell him than what pieces of information he can take to incorporate into his own strange and fragmented version of events. A version that bears little resemblance to what Sam witnessed. And he can't quite understand where this policeman has assembled his story from, how in the tiny space between his arriving at the scene and this moment has he managed to construct his narrative.

"No, no, listen to me. Listen to me!" Sam shouts at the dunderhead bobby, but all he gets in return to his insistence is "Now calm down, sir. I know this is a very stressful situation but you need to calm down and tell me plain and simple what happened."

There's a nagging pain at the sides of Sam's head. A tremulous, quivering tone. He breathes out a sigh and bends forward, his head dropping between his knees. He squeezes his temples.

"I really need to get to the hospital. I should be with Nina."

"I don't think you should be driving anywhere right now."

"Well, I'll take a cab then."

"Just tell me what you think happened."

"What I think happened? I've already told you. I followed Neil Allen here from his flat. Then he drove into my girlfriend."

"So you think it was this Neil Allen that knocked her down?"

"Yes!"

"And where is Mr. Allen now?"

"He drove away. Fled the scene."

"Why were you following Mr. Allen?"

Sam looks around for inspiration, "It's really difficult to explain. I thought he might be up to something."

"Why?"

"I..."

"Is he a friend of yours?"

"Sort of. We have the same..." Sam trails off. It dawns on him that it might not be best to get into the whole Roberta thing right now.

"Same what?"

"No, it's um..."

"If it was this Mr. Allen that hit your girlfriend, how do you explain the dent in the front of your car?"

Sam's head snaps up. It is like someone has snapped him out of a dream. The policeman's eyes are narrowed, his dense eyebrows peaking. Sam looks at his car sitting in the middle of the tarmac behind the bobby. It does indeed have a nasty dent in the bonnet.

"I..." He doesn't know what to say. He has no idea what could have happened to his car.

"You think I did it? You think I hit my own girlfriend?"

The bobby just cocks his head and says, "The bump?"

"I... I don't know. I must have gone into the back of Neil's car when, when it happened."

The policeman's mouth creases in a way that could say 'plausible' – if it was a word short enough to be present in his vocabulary.

"Have you even spoken to any of the witnesses yet?"

The policeman gives him an unimpressed look, "You do your job, sir, I'll do mine."

"My job?"

"You know what I mean."

Sam turns away and mutters "Fuck's sake" to himself. It seems to prick the policeman's ire but he lets it go this time.

"Can I go now?"

"We'll be in touch."

Sam gets up to go.

"Oh, and leave your vehicle here please. We'll return it to you when we're done with it."

"Fine. I'll call a cab. Thanks for all your help."

They hit traffic. Sam's fingers fidget with each other and he asks for shortcuts but the cabbie has none. After a while his adrenaline subsides and a calm settles over him. He gazes out of the window at the traffic with his mouth hanging slack like a gawping child. Lost in non-thought. Then a moment of anxiety. He sits up in his seat and shifts to the left and right, looking to either side of the cabbie's head as if doing so might enable him to spot a gap in the traffic, as if it was him driving, as if it was in his power to do something. But he doesn't say anything to the driver. He's sure he's already doing the best he can. Sam rubs his hand across his face. And is surprised when he feels himself smear two thin lines of tears. And now he knows it is there. Sees it coming and building clearly, like a shark approaching in the deep ocean. And there's nothing he can do but let it come. And come it does. It's a dark, throbbing sensation, a deep bitterness, a moment where he realises that the world has lost all its sweetness, that there is no point, no truth and no purpose. That it can't be faced. That all he has left to do is curl up in a ball and wait for the end to come. However many years it might take. And even though he knows that these emotions are only temporary, he is powerless to shift them. He can do nothing but sit back and let them wash over him. And that's what he does, he lies back there against the faux leather seats with his arms spread wide and feels the horror surge through him. Tastes that feeling of endless loneliness that comes on the end of it – knowing that he will never again see her like. And somewhere in the middle of this he realises that this is not true grief. It is some kind of pre-grief. It is a taste of what is to come. It is how it will feel at the end. And he knows that this will pass, but if and when that other thing happens, it will never pass, not for the rest of his life. And he knows this because there is another grief that still burns away beneath it, an older staler grief – but old and stale as it is, it is still there.

"Hold on. We'll get you there, son."

The cab makes a sharp turn and begins to bomb it down back roads. And everything drops away. Sam finds himself perched on the brink of his seat with his hands gripping it and his eyes wide, looking for that next sharp turn or any suspicion of traffic. He can almost feel the wind in his hair. There's a quickened rhythmic pulse through his chest. Adrenaline courses again. He is locked in, hurtling towards his destination. And there's a fear, a real fear there. A fear of what will happen when he gets there. When everything becomes real. And in one terrible moment, he knows that the fear is this: what if it is true? What if the policeman wasn't just making a stupid mistake? What if it was him that ran Nina over? And then with the clarity of a dream, he sees himself behind the wheel of a black BMW. Looking through Neil's eyes. The windscreen. A squirt of water and a swish of the wipers to clear it. The escalating hum of the engine as it accelerates. Then there she is, stepping into view in front of him. Nina. In all her beauty, lit up like a paragon, her dark hair whipping around her face in a sudden wind. She isn't seeing him, there's no recognition, she's looking the other way and something she sees brings a smile to her lips. She is carrying four shopping bags, three in the right hand, one in the left. And then the impact picks her up and before she hits the ground the vision fades, leaving the afterimage of her body floating in mid-air burned on Sam's retinas. And all he can think, sitting there in the back of the cab, is how did he know about the bags. Why was that detail so clear to him?

Sam doesn't hear what the cabbie says, but it is clear that he has been speaking for a while. He didn't notice the vehicle stop. And as he reaches into his wallet and passes the money across to the driver, Sam pictures Nina lying on the tarmac outside the supermarket. And the bags around her. Three bunched a little way from her, another several feet further on, smashed liquids pooling around it.

"Cheers mate," says the cabbie.

"Thank you," says Sam. And he looks into the man's eyes and is startled by how icy cool and clear the grey irises are and the cabbie frowns at Sam's elegiac expression and the way that his words seem not to be addressed to him but to someone else, someone far above and more powerful than either of them.

Sam bolts from the cab and comes to a sudden stop in front of the hospital doors. He stands there, stiff as a board. He picks up a trace scent of burning hair. And then his frame wilts and he droops forwards, clutching his chest, suddenly breathless. He staggers over to the wall beside the door and leans there, trying to breathe and hoping that his heart will slow before it uses itself up entirely. The colour gradually returns to him and he eases his weight away from the wall and onto his feet. His eyes connect with a man some twenty years his senior who is leaning against the wall at the other side of the door. The man looks at him with watery eyes and a sad smile that says, "I know how you feel". And Sam turns and pushes his way through the doors.

"Nina Trevanion," he says breathlessly, "How is she? How's she doing? Can I see her?"

The receptionist looks back at him with a level demeanour, clearly well-used to dealing with people in all kinds of states.

"Car accident?"

Sam nods like a dog on the back seat of a car.

"She's going to be fine. There was some surgery and she'll need a lot of rest."

"Can I see her?"

"Not quite yet, I'm afraid. Are you family?"

"I'm her boyfriend. Sam Peoples. Should I wait?"

"You can take a seat if you want, but it might be better if you went home for now. We can call you later."

"I... Do you know, if I came back later, what room she's in?"

"Yes. She's in the Doherty Ward, room 23"

"Thanks."

And Sam immediately heads in the direction of the wards.

"Mr. Peoples! Mr. Peoples! You can't go in yet!"

But Sam isn't hearing her.

When he reaches her room, a doctor and a nurse are just leaving her. They see him coming and move towards him, arms out blocking his way, telling him that he really just needs to let her rest and that she can't have any visitors right now. And he keeps saying, "You don't understand. It's okay. I'm her boyfriend. I need to see her." As if the more times he says it, the more likely they are to let him through. While they remonstrate, the receptionist arrives behind him with a male nurse in tow and between the four of them they manage to calm Sam and bring him to a standstill. He feels them relax and the moment they do, he surges towards the door, but these are professionals.

"We're all on the same side here. You'll have to take us at our word. It's really not a good idea right now."

The doctor's voice in his ear is soothing and he turns to the middle-aged man who is looking over his spectacles with an air of authority.

"You can look at her," the doctor says. "See. She's right there. She's doing fine."

And Sam stares into the room through the wire-reinforced glass. A swathe of dark hair swooped across a pillow and the blues and whites of hospital gowns and blankets and sheets. Her face is turned away from him. He picks up the gentle rise and fall of her chest and in spite of all the tubes he is reassured.

And then, for a moment, Sam is transported. He feels the suffocating warmth of another room closing around him. A darker, dustier room, not in a hospital but in a home and though the patient is the same, she's somehow different and at once she is not and she is and she is... not... and... A bolt of pain shoots through him, twisting from his kidney, around his heart, up through his chest and down his arm to the tip of his middle finger. He lets out the smallest of gasps and feels a hand on his arm. A concerned glance. But whatever it was, it is gone now and he turns to them and he says

"Open a window. Make sure she gets plenty of air. You hear me? It's important. It's really, really important."

"We should go now," says the doctor, "I don't want to run the risk of disturbing her."

And with a steady stream of gentle assurances, he escorts Sam back down the corridor towards reception.

He slumps onto the couch and in place of a need to act, or perhaps because of the frustration of not knowing how to, he sinks into a despond. And a bitter line of betrayal runs through it. Neil. How could he have done this to him? He thought they were friends. Kind of. And above all mitigations or logic or reasoning or trying to figure things out, this is all he is left with. *Him*? How could he have done this to *him*? Sam shrivels at the recognition of his own selfishness. Neil didn't do it to him. He did it to her. He did it to Nina. And that's the tragedy of it. Sam knows he's too far back in his own head to be able to do anything about any of this. He longs for guidance. For help. But there is none. Because deep down he knows what happens when he places his faith in another person. Sam draws his knees up to his chest and drops onto his side on the couch, staring blankly out at the window as nervous exhaustion overtakes him.

When he wakes up it is fully dark. The window is open a crack and a gentle breeze filters in, riffling the net curtain on its way. And for a moment he thinks he sees a figure standing there in front of it. Translucent. Blending with the net curtains, her gown is voluminous, too large, draped over her stick-like frame. And as he fixes on this figure, picking out her outline from the background, he notices two bright blue eyes, as solid and clear as if they were really there.

"Caroline!"

And the shock of it jolts him into wakefulness and he sits up, a hand groping the back of the couch, clinging at it as if he might otherwise fall off. He stares wide-eyed at the window. But the vision is gone. And steadily, he settles into a reasonable calm and comes back to earth. He stands, and as if he has moved through a layer of cloud, his head instantly feels clearer. He looks at the clock: almost ten. He's been asleep for a couple of hours. It surprises him that he hasn't been woken by the phone ringing. No call from the hospital yet. He dials them and is told that Nina won't be receiving visitors until tomorrow now, but she's doing just fine. He wasn't notified because he is not a relative. He hangs up without thanking the woman on the phone and tries to take stock, to contextualise everything. It feels like he is beginning to get a sense of Roberta's big picture. And the thought of it makes him shudder. Her whole roster of patients all turned against each other, utilised in a web of unhappiness designed to perpetuate their dependence on her. Could this really be true? Just thinking about it makes Sam's head swim. He goes to the fridge and retrieves a cold beer, which imparts some small comfort. But he needs to talk to someone. And before he knows it, he's walking barefoot down the corridor happily engaged in wiping the condensation off his beer with his thumb. And then he's knocking on Rosanna's door.

"Yeah and what do you want, twatface?"

"I'm just, I need a friend."

"Yeah, well I needed a lift."

"This is, something happened."

"Wanker allowance runs out in three, two..."

"Okay, okay. Look, I'm sorry about before. Look: I'm holding my hands up." And he is; beer in one, the other open like he's got a gun in his back. "I brought you a beer." He tilts it towards her.

She folds her arms and her face screws up,

"It's half-drunk."

"I could go get you one if you..."

"Give it." She snatches the bottle from his hand and, slurping, wanders off into her flat.

"Shit." The empty beer bottle dangles from Rosanna's fingers and she plops it down on the coffee table. "I can't believe that was just after you left me."

He nods at her, lips pressed together. A silence grows in the space between them. It's thick. It's dense. And it's distinctly uncomfortable.

"And Neil?"

"I'm not sure he even knew what he was doing."

"But why would Roberta target Nina?"

"Because without her I'd have been driven back to therapy, I guess."

"Do you think she knows that you know this?"

"I doubt it, otherwise what would be the point?"

"Have you spoken to Neil? Surely that's your first step."

"I don't know. I'm kind of a bit... scared?"

"Come on. Let's go."

And she gets up from her chair all bustley and businesslike.

"Isn't it a bit late?"

"Up. Come on. Let's go."

Rosanna jogs down the front steps of the block and walks at a clip down the dark street. Sam walks slower. His head is still in a fog of misapprehension and it feels as if it's physically dragging on him. His feet shuffle and slow to a stop. Across the road, the newsagent is collecting a bundle of newspapers. He pauses when he sees Sam. He's in his fifties, short, his face is lined and he's got something of a stoop. He's wearing jeans and a shiny green tracksuit jacket. He smiles and waves. Sam doesn't return either gesture. He just stands there with his arms hanging down at his sides, gawping at the guy. It feels good: being engaged in nothing but absorbed in the incidental details of his environment. The thoughts stop. The worries, the stress, the confusion. And all there is is that little man looking at him. Reacting to Sam's non-response, the newsagent first cocks his head, his brow creases and then he shrugs before bending down to pick up the bundle. Shuffling under its weight, he returns to the shop.

"Sam!"

Rosanna has her fists balled on her hips. Tight jeans tucked into tall brown boots; suede jacket with its sleeves scrunched back; the tight pony tail pulling back away from her face emphasising the sharp eyebrows and the shining pink lips pursed at the centre of her clenched jaw.

"What are you doing?"

He is too slow for her. He can see why most men might have trouble keeping up.

"I was, er, watching the man."

"What man?"

Sam extends a limp arm, his finger drooping in the direction of the newsagent's.

"What the hell are you on about?"

Rosanna takes her keys from her jacket pocket and points them over her shoulder. There is a beep and a double flash from a small sports car. She spins on her heel, holding a hand up and clicking her fingers like she's telling a dog to heel.

Sam sinks into the soft leather of the bucket seat. It's a cliché, the little sports car for the high-powered go-get-'em media girl. The only thing that differentiates the vehicle from the way it might have looked leaving the factory is a small flowerpot attached to the dashboard. The plastic pink sunflower in it has a smiley face. Sam can't help a little chuckle. Rosanna turns the key and the engine growls to life, suffusing the car with a low rumbling. Without indicating, Rosanna throws it out into the road, slams her foot down all the way and they rocket down the street.

She drives like there is nobody else on the road. And thankfully, there isn't. This time of night and North London is like a mausoleum. Still, Sam's hands grip the edges of his seat. He looks across at Rosanna. Her face is determined, predatory. He doesn't dare ask her if she'd think about slowing down.

In no time they are spinning down the narrow, winding street where Neil lives. With parked cars choking it on either side they'd be guaranteed to end up in the middle of a steaming pile of wrecked metal if anything was coming the other way. But nothing does. Sam can't help but let out a little gasp as the car jerks to the side and slams to a halt right outside Neil's block. His fingers uncurl from the seat leaving sweaty little impressions and he sits there, staring out of the windscreen at the back of a parked taxi only a few feet in front of him, just breathing.

"Well?" says Rosanna, with a big old toothy grin. "Let's go wake this fucker up."

Sam's body creaks as he grasps the doorframe to lever himself to his feet. She doesn't seem to have any trouble getting out of the bucket seat. Slides from it like a snake. Maybe it's practice, he thinks, or maybe this kind of vehicle is just built to suit the physicality of small ballsy women. By the time he's on his feet, she's already surging across the forecourt towards the block. The keys shoot up over her shoulder and there's a beep and a double flash.

She's waiting impatiently at the door when Sam gets there.

"Which number is it? I forget," she says.

Sam hits six, holding it down for a long, impertinent buzz. Rosanna lights a cigarette and sucks from it in a series of short, rapid drags. Her foot is wagging on the floor and the fingers of her unsmoking hand fidget with each other. Sam stares at the buzzer with his hands in his pockets. He puffs his cheeks out. Time unfolds in the absence of a response. It has a loose, baggy quality to it and Sam is not sure whether they have been waiting for seconds or minutes. He turns to look at Rosanna. Their eyes meet. She seems goosed up with adrenaline. It's like she's high on something. Just looking at her makes him feel tired. He raises his eyebrows in a facial shrug. She flashes him a tight, twitchy smile.

"Perhaps he's a–" Rosanna hits the buzzer "–sleep." She hits it again. And again. Holding it down for several seconds and then hitting it with a series of stabs. "Come on you fucker."

Sam grasps her wrist as she paddles on the button.

"Give it a moment. Wait for him to answer."

She nods.

"Are you okay?"

She shoots him an odd look,

"Yeah. Course."

"It's just you seem a little, I don't know, pumped."

"Yeah, I..." She looks down at the toe of her boot swivelling against the floor. Stops it. "I don't know. Maybe it's like, maybe it feels like we're close to something, you know? Like if you're right..." And she grins broadly. Grabs Sam by his lapels and looks him right in the eyes, her own dancing like an excited girl, "If you're right about all this, we could be so close to uncovering something really big, Sam. Our whole lives. You know? Our whole fucking lives."

"Yeah," he says.

And she throws her arms around him and hugs him. Squeezing him hard. And he can feel her heart rattling away inside her chest, tremoloing the muscles of her arms. And as abruptly as she grabbed him, she lets go and turns back to the buzzer.

"Come on, where is that fucker?" She pounds on it again. "Come on fucker. Wake the fuck up."

"What if he's not here?" Sam scans across the car park. It is full, but "I don't see his car anywhere."

"He could've parked on the road. Where else is he going to be at this time of night?"

And she walks over to the square of grass in the middle of the car park that is overlooked by Neil's kitchen window.

"The light's on."

She hastily scavenges a handful of pebbles from the flowerbeds.

"What are you doing?"

"He won't sleep through this."

"Rosanna, I don't think..."

But she's already chucking pebbles up at the window and she's shouting Neil's name, calling him out, demanding that he wakes up and comes to see them, saying she knows he's in there.

Lights flicker on. Not in Neil's flat. In others. And a couple of angry-faced residents appear in their nightclothes, staring out with their arms folded. A middle-aged man opens his window and shouts, "Do you know what time it is?"

But Rosanna's ignoring him and keeps throwing the stones and shouting. Sam looks up at the guy, embarrassed, holding up his hands and saying, "Sorry, sorry."

He takes Rosanna by the shoulders and tries to move her away but she digs her heels in and he's telling her, "Rosanna. Stop it. He's not here. We need to go. Come on."

He drags her more forcefully and she grunts in protest but shuffles away with him. And as she goes she throws one last stone as a parting shot.

And the window comes down like a sheet of ice.

They both freeze.

"Shit," simultaneously.

Rosanna runs. It takes Sam's flight response a moment longer to kick in. But then he's away, on her heels.

They hurtle down the dark suburban street, dodging wheelie bins and recycling boxes, ducking under overhanging fir branches. Sam catches up to Rosanna, running just behind her. And he can hear that as she runs, she's laughing. He calls out to her but she just keeps going and so he grabs her by the shoulders saying

"Rosanna, wait!"

She almost loses her footing, going over, but he catches her and she stands, bent over, panting and laughing with his arms around her and her hands clamp around his wrists and hold them. Then she spins round, dragging him by the arms and saying, "In here."

She pulls him down the side alley of another block of flats, past the brief stink of a communal bin and into the dank darkness of the passageway where she lets go of him and flattens herself against the wall, panting.

"We... we should wait here. In case they... call the... police or something."

He drops back against the wall beside her.

"What do we do now?"

"I don't know." Pant. Pant. "I don't know." Pant. Giggle. Breathless laugh.

"I'm glad you find this funny."

And she bends forward holding her stomach and clamps a hand over her mouth. When her laugh is stifled she says,

"I feel like a teenager again."

"Your teens sound a lot more exciting than mine."

She splurts out a laugh, "Of course they were. You're a geek."

"Maybe we should go to Roberta."

Rosanna stands up rigid.

"Confront her," he says.

Her eyes shoot round. Fixing him from their corners.

You are not your thoughts. He hears her voice. But her lips aren't moving.

You are not your past or your future, he thinks, without thinking.

A geometric shape floats up out of the black. Three sides of a square. Depth falls in and it's clearer now. A ceiling. A strip light across the middle. Magnolia walls dropping away on three sides. A television is on in one corner fixed to a bracket high up on the wall. The volume is barely audible. It takes her a few moments to recognise this as a hospital room. She thinks. Tries to think about what could have happened. What has put her here. But nothing much comes. The oscillating colours on the TV screen are grating. There is a throb at her temples and the back of her head. Her body hurts all over, particularly her left leg. She wonders whether and where and how she is hurt, but she has no urge to move any of her limbs and even lifting her head seems like too much of an effort. If it wasn't for the location, she might think that she was in the clutches of a really bad hangover. She closes her eyes, allowing darkness to slip over her again. Cosy, comfortable darkness. Hoping that with its soothing embrace will come a subsidence of pain. But it doesn't. She just throbs and throbs with it. And she doesn't notice when but at some point it all just slides away. And in the darkness behind her eyes images float up to her. That man, his hard eyes and acne-scarred face. A face that is so familiar, and yet she is sure she has never seen it before. And he's standing over her with a grim look like he's surveying something distinctly unimpressive. And she feels recognition coming but before it does, his face changes. Once again. Just like it did then. And just as he disappears she thinks of the commuter she tripped on the way home from work. The business clothes, the height, the haircut. But she can't be sure if it is the same man or not and all the elements that coincide are so generic. Or even whether she really saw this man when the thing, whatever it was that put her here, happened to her, or whether his face just floated to her at that moment out of some kind of guilt/fear cocktail. And she thinks of him standing outside the front door of her flat in the middle of the night jerking off into her letterbox. But as soon as that thought comes to her, he's gone. And in his place, Sam is standing over her with that same look of disdain. Those disconnected eyes hard, as if he had never met her. Sam. Standing over her. Like a bad angel.

And her eyes flicker open and even though the pain returns it seems as nothing to her. Because now she is shaking with fear and her eyes swivel to the extremes of their sockets. Seeing as far as she can without moving her head. Totally still, immobile. Trapped. And she tries to look at the door. To see who might be coming in. But she can't quite see it.

Red. And an overwhelming fury. Black and red. Flashes of red over the black. Ripped through it like slashes in a curtain and the force and violence of each slash cutting deep through. A feeling like a bursting of energy, like a surging. Blood and adrenaline pumping and curdling with rabid energy. Flashes of light. Ecstatic release. Everything inside wanting to come out. Muscles pulsing and about to rip and turn themselves inside out. The thundering sound of blood inside. Froth and spit and the feel of his own teeth grinding against each other, lips parted wide and the cold air freezing against the gums and then melting and dissolving as it meets the heat of the body through the teeth, inside the mouth and down the throat. Opposite, a visage reflecting all of these feelings, transformed by a frieze of equal rage. Eyes wild and dancing and senseless and full of blood. And a scream. A howl of anger or pain that comes from deep down within her body and forces itself out without the need for articulation.

Sam jolts up and back, whipping back into himself and almost stepping outside to see himself lying on top of her, his fist pulled back and high, its raw knuckles scraped red. And suddenly he's back. And Rosanna's right there underneath him, bucking and struggling against the weight of his body and shouting and howling and her clawed fingers shoot up at his face and he grabs them and jerks them down and away to the sides, holding them fast. She is barely recognisable. Her face is misshapen and wet with blood, her hair half-pulled out of its pony tail flies away from her and clings in slickened strands to her cheeks. One eye is swollen and closed. Her lips still shine, the blood forming into little bobbles there and running off the greasy lipgloss to let it shine out from the morass. Her teeth are clenched in a grimace reminiscent of her earlier adrenaline-pumped grin and they are outlined with a dark fluid that runs between them. And at first Sam is thinking who did this? Then, what happened? Then, how did we get like this? And then he knows as if waking from a dream that he has done this. And Rosanna is still writhing in a furious rage and Sam asks her all of these questions but she shouts and snaps her teeth at him with a hard cutting sound as they clip together and her head, the only unrestrained weapon jumps forward and the teeth close inches away from his nose and when he flinches backwards her knee shoots up and catches him in the groin and he rolls off her as the ache and nausea radiate from his balls and spread up through him. And then she's on top of him and her manicured nails, now split and ragged, rake at his face forcing him to rise above his discomfort and defend himself and he locks his arm around her head and pulls it into his shoulder. Her teeth bite ineffectually against his jacket. And he holds and chokes her and shouts her name into her ear saying, "Rest. Rest. Rosanna, rest."

Until she slows and the fight drains from her body and she lies there limp, clamped by his arms and his legs on the dirty floor of cracked side-passage tiles in the shadow of the large communal bin. And after her breathy panting eases he hears a small voice coming from his armpit.

"Sam. Sam, what's happening? It hurts, Sam."

And he loosens his grip and her wrecked face turns up to him with tears cleaning mud and muck and blood from around her eyes and the panels of her cheeks and she wipes her eyes and sees him and her expression transforms and she says, "What happened to you? Your face. Did I do that to you?"

Sam feels his face with his hand but his face does not feel his hand because it is mostly numb apart from when his fingers brush raised scratches that sting when he touches them.

"What's the last thing you remember?" He says.

She lifts an arm and it flops against the wall. And her lost eyes follow it to see her flaccid fingers groping damp brick.

"Here. Standing against the wall here."

"I said something. I think I said something."

He hears her sobbing and holds her and they lie there on the floor curled up in each other's arms.

It hadn't felt right to go home. Perhaps because of a wordless consensus that what had just happened seemed somehow illicit. But when they drove past their building they realised it was because it didn't feel safe. The lights in Rosanna's window were on. She didn't remember leaving them on. And so now Sam sits on the pristine white coverlet of a hotel bed while he listens to Rosanna in the shower. He looks down at where his hand rests. Lifts it to inspect his scoured palm and leaves an almost complete impression behind in dirt. Time is so slow and abstract that it seems barely to be moving at all. He lies back on the bed and listens to the sound of the water. And he knows that there are things to think about, things to figure out, but right now all he is capable of is non-thought. White ceiling. Water. He closes his eyes and lets the sound transport him.

"Your turn."

Rosanna is standing by the bathroom door. She has a towel wrapped around her and is fiddling with the fold, where it bunches at the top of her breast, making the shiny wet flesh swell. Her hair is loose and still wet and she wraps it into a coil and trails it over her shoulder. There is a yellowing bruise around her eye and her mouth seems puffy, but Sam's not sure whether this is down to him or the absence of lipgloss highlight to pique her lips to a point. An angry cross-hatch of graze glares out from her cheek, making the rest of her face seem sallow and colourless. Leaning up on his elbows, Sam watches her hobble over to the dressing table where she stops and turns to him. Their eyes meet. He gives her a sympathetic smile, his lips tucked in. She looks down.

"Are you alright?" he says.

"Just get in the shower so I can get dressed."

Sam locks the bathroom door behind him and crosses over to the mirror. The right side of his face from jaw to temple is caked in dirt and almost obscured. Where the skin on his face is visible, it is so blanched that it glares starkly from between the scunge and seems barely like skin at all. The left side of his forehead is rusty with dried blood and below it, on the white section, those ragged scratches rip across his cheeks and chin, around his mouth, cutting through all the different coloured surfaces and still shining and fresh and tattered. He looks. And he looks. He looks at himself. And the longer he looks, the less it seems that he is looking at himself. What looks back at him appears to be a tribal war mask. A vicious and artificial concatenation of elements designed to frighten the enemy. He almost wishes he could keep it. He might need it. But he knows that however much bravado he conjures internally, the mask is not him. It is not even an act that he can maintain. In the face of any challenge, it will melt away and at best he will just be ugly.

When he steps out of the shower, he feels clean but hardly refreshed. Instead, in the afterglow of the warm water, he feels stripped. Vulnerable to everything. No more war mask. He looks again at himself in the mirror. Naked. His impression is of something skinny and shrivelled and pale. His skin is blueing with goose bumps. The shadows and bruises and scratches seem to be an expression of the weakness of the whole. Everything that is underneath oozing out, the outer corrupted by the rotten inner. And the one thing that lingers with him is the notion that what he is looking at is not himself. It is a pulsating, revolting organ over which he has only partial control. That witnesses everything and stubbornly keeps secrets from him, harbouring something other that he is not allowed to see. There is a conspiracy of forces both internal and external which seem to have asserted a control over this entity and uses it in confidence. A confidence that eludes him.

"You are not your thoughts. You are not your past or your future. You are only your body and this moment right now."

Rosanna mutes the television as he emerges from the bathroom and turns in her chair to look at him.

"Something Roberta said to me once."

"Yes. She said the same thing to me."

"I think it is supposed to be reassuring." He sits down on the corner of the bed. "But right now it feels like the most disturbing thing I have ever heard."

"I don't know about reassuring. I think it's supposed to put you in control. But..."

"It makes an impossibility of control. It makes an impossibility of desire or ambition or planning or anything. It makes happiness impossible unless you happen to be happy."

"Ordinarily I'd argue with you."

Rosanna looks down at the floor. There is a sullen and deeply serious air about her.

"I should probably get dressed," says Sam.

"It's okay. I won't look."

And she stays exactly where she is, with her head down like that. Her hair hangs around her head like a ragged curtain. From there, theoretically, she could peep if she wanted to see Sam naked, but her statement has none of the playful challenge that could be implicit in it. Instead it is hung with a deadpan matter-of-factness. And Sam stands, loosens his towel and begins to pull on the clothes that are soiled and sticky with the filth of the evening.

"When I feel this fragile, I normally think the cure is a good fuck. A nice fuck."

Sam turns, half-dressed, raising an eyebrow. Her head is still down.

"But right now it's the last thing I want. The idea revolts me. In a way I feel like I've already been fucked. I want to be anywhere but in my body."

A shiver of resonance runs through Sam.

"No offence, that is. It's nothing to do with you, nothing personal I mean."

"No. I know what you mean."

"Are you dressed yet? My neck's getting sore."

"Yeah. Sorry. You can look."

And when she looks up, even though he is clothed he feels a flush of embarrassment as if his body is now under scrutiny. Only it goes as soon as he sees her eyes, which are dead and dull and show not the slightest interest.

The clock seems to have hung on five past three for the last half an hour. A beer grows warm between Sam's palms. They are turned away from each other, him with his eyes on the clock, Rosanna staring out of the window at the lifeless street outside. A tired-looking barman is drooping, his elbows resting on the spirits shelf behind him. There is a kind of corporate warmth about the otherwise deserted bar with its brass rails and glass and mirrors. A fruit machine flickers away noiselessly in the corner. The barman looks from one to the other. Their untouched drinks. Completely ignored, he raises his eyebrows and slinks away. A breeze wafts through from somewhere.

"Sam?" Rosanna says in a voice so weak it is barely there.

He turns on his stool just as she turns to him and he realises that they were waiting for the barman to leave.

"What do we do? I mean," and even though they are alone she hunches in and places her mouth against his ear, "we can't even trust ourselves."

"I know."

"What was that? Some pre-programmed self-destruct mechanism?"

He puts his arm around her waist and they sit there like lovers. She feels small and shivering.

"I don't... No. I do know. I think that's exactly what it was." He pulls away from her an inch or two and frames her face in his hands, looking her in the eye, "We're uniting against her. It's exactly the one thing she can't handle."

"This is insane."

And out of nowhere, a grin steals across his face and his eyes flicker with life again.

"You know, Rosanna, I think we've got this all wrong."

"What do you mean?"

"I think we're winning."

And he sees it infect her too. A fluttering smile that doesn't quite dare to remain on her lips.

"But if we can't trust ourselves, who can we trust?"

"Yeah," he sighs.

But there's a new light in her eyes, the cogs clunking into motion as she identifies a task that she can apply herself to.

"People that aren't under her influence."

Sam watches Rosanna sleep from the questionable comfort of an armchair. He sees her stir there in the bed and wonders if she is really asleep yet, or if she is lying there, aware of him watching her, thinking not about sleep but about something else. Deciding these are not the healthiest thoughts, he twists in the chair, tucks his legs under him and pulls the blanket up under his chin. He closes his eyes. But in spite of his physical exhaustion, he is far from tired and the closing of his eyes only makes his thoughts come awake. Alive and racing. He wonders what would really happen if he let himself sleep. And if he is in actual fact preventing himself from doing so. What would happen if he was to abandon his body – what subconscious impulse might rise to take over? Who might take control if he relinquishes it? And even if none of these fears came to fruition, what about the body now breathing quietly in the bed across the room. Who does that belong to? If Rosanna really sleeps, might it rise without her?

Sam opens his eyes and glances across at her. She has not moved and from her breathing it appears that she is now fast asleep. He turns his attention to the window. Beyond it the night still has hold of the city. A night that he might wander in forever, whose depths are eternal; and if the sun rises in a few hours, it may as well be an illusion. He shivers and closes his eyes thinking of the sun and daylight. And yet daylight will bring with it a need for action. That responsibility, the threat of it, weighs on him heavily and he enjoys the feeling of lightness in its absence.

Part Two:

Nina

Chapter Five

THE MIMIC ROUT

Birds twitter and the daylight makes a bright screen out of the blind. Like the projector is on but the film has either run out or is yet to roll. Nina lies in the hospital bed with her eyes wide open. She doesn't really know what else to do. Pain and confusion have receded somewhat, but in their place there is nothing. All she can do is lie here and wait.

There's a clunk and she looks round with a start. A jolly looking nurse beams at her, approaching the bed.

"Morning Nina. How are you feeling today?"

"I'm okay."

The nurse picks up Nina's chart and looks it over.

"There's a policeman outside who'd like to talk to you about your accident. Do you feel up to it?"

Nina turns towards the window into the corridor. She can see a uniform hovering at the edge; an arm and a shoulder. It is a heavy, muscular figure. The face is obscured. And something about its anonymity and the strange disembodiedness of the image gives her pause.

"Maybe," she licks her dry lips, "maybe later. If that's okay."

The Nurse smiles, "Of course. I'll tell him to come back this afternoon."

"I'm afraid I can't let you see her just yet."

Sam does his best to suppress his frustration, aware that the soft-faced middle-aged nurse and the system she is representing are primarily concerned with the welfare of their patients.

"Is she alright?"

"She's doing well. But I'm afraid only family are –"

"Have her family been?"

"Not yet, no."

"So she's seen no-one? Not a friendly face the whole time she's been in here?"

"I'm sorry sir but –"

"Why don't you ask her? Ask her if she wants to see me."

A hand falls on Sam's shoulder. He turns. The chest of an enormous police jacket fills his view.

"Is there a problem here?"

At first Sam is not sure where he recognises him from, but then it dawns on him that this is the same dim-witted police officer from the scene of the accident.

"Hello again Mr. Peoples. Been in the wars have we?"

"What's," Sam looks agitatedly from the cop to the nurse, both of whom wear forbidding expressions, "is there something going on here? Does someone want to tell me..."

"I'm afraid that until we have ascertained the truth about the accident we won't be able to let you see Miss Trevanion. For her own safety, you understand."

"For her own..."

The corridor extends away in the direction of Nina's room, so long that its walls close together into a vanishing point. The bobby sees Sam looking and places his other hand on his other arm.

"I wouldn't if I was you," he says, as if offering friendly advice rather than a threat. "I've been informed about your bursting-in yesterday. They say it could have been very detrimental to the young lady's position."

"Hold on, hold on," Rosanna inserts herself between the two of them, "are you saying you suspect Sam of running over his own girlfriend?"

"No suspect yet. It's just that reports have been a little bit confused so far and I've not yet been able to speak with the victim."

"What about Neil Allen? Have you spoken to him?"

"Mr. Allen has been unreachable."

"Great. That's just fucking great! And what about people at the scene? What did they have to say?"

"Like I said sir, reports are conflicting."

"Fucking..." The angry scratches on Sam's face bunch together. He storms off. And stops, breath rattling, to stare out through the glass front of the building, as if a solution might be out there somewhere.

"Okay, okay. Look PC–" Rosanna checks his name badge, "Frame, you have to understand my friend's frustration, but listen, I was with him when he drove off after Neil Allen and I can tell you that there was definitely something weird going on and Sam here was just going to check it out, that's all. It must have been Neil that ran Nina over."

"And did you see what happened?"

"No, I didn't go with them."

"Well then." He folds his arms. Stood in the opening of the

corridor like a sentry dog, he looks over her at Sam, who is now glaring at him, teeth grinding. Sam strides forward, brushing Rosanna as he passes her. His face thrusts up towards the bobby's dispassionate block of a chin, a whole head higher than his own.

"Right, I've got your number. 148SA. I'm having a word with your superiors. This isn't right."

Frame's upper lip curls with grim amusement. "Need a pen?"

Rosanna takes the proffered pen and scrawls the collar number on her palm. From high up on his perch Frame peers down at their battered and bruised faces. His eyes nearly disappear as his Neanderthal brow twitches down.

"You know," he says with a sniff, "speaking of Mr. Allen, I was informed that there was some trouble up at his flat last night. You two wouldn't know anything about it would you?"

Rosanna drops the pen. Mutters "shit" under her breath and bends to pick it up.

"What kind of trouble?" says Sam. But before Frame can respond, Rosanna pipes up,

"We, um, Sam, haven't we got to be at... I mean maybe we should go." She hands back the pen.

"Yes," hisses Frame, "maybe you should." And tucks it back into his breast pocket.

They scurry from the hospital like a pair of wet cats. Rosanna chases a juddering flame with the end of her cigarette.

"That's the fucking thing," Sam spits, "Nina would know what to do. She's smart, she's savvy. She knows about things. If they'd just let us talk to her we could get this mess cleared right up." He pauses, takes a breath, and a sad smile brushes his lips. "I wish you could meet her."

Rosanna takes a gasp of her cigarette like her life depends on it and blows a plume straight up at the sky. Squeaking pumps cross rapidly towards them and a voice calls "excuse me" from a distance.

"Can you think of anyone? Anyone you know. Someone who might believe us."

"Excuse me?" They both turn to see a diminutive male nurse with his face scrunched up and his hands on his hips. "There's no smoking in this area. You need to stand in the smokers' booth." And he points towards a tiny hut whose Perspex walls are stained yellow.

"We're outside, for fuck's sake." Rosanna flicks her cigarette at his feet and stomps off in the direction of her car. Sam catches her up and trots along beside her.

"That, that ex-boyfriend of yours. David was his name?"

She stops at the car and roots in her handbag for her keys.

Sam addresses her back, "Have you, um, spoken to him at all since it ended?"

"No, not really."

"I think you should."

She turns to him with a short-tempered sigh, folds her arms and leans back against the car.

"Why would I want to do that?"

"You still care about him. Maybe he still cares about you. Maybe he could help us – we just need someone, someone who's out of this."

"I'm sure he's forgotten all about me." She looks away, her jaw ticking, her shaking hand pulls a flyaway strand of hair from her face and tucks it behind her ear. And then her head whips back to him. And her lips are curled so he can see her gums and clenched teeth and her green eyes are fierce. "You almost got us nicked. And now you want me to go and see an ex that I'd sooner forget. How much shit, exactly, are you trying to get me in?"

"Don't you think we're already in it?"

A gust of wind picks up, howls across the sea of parked cars around them, and chills them both.

A winding road curves between bright fields and passes under an avenue of trees and then the hedges and fences give way and the front of the property opens up. An almost pre-fab bungalow that looks like it has maybe two bedrooms, but is set in plenty of space. Behind it a long and overgrown garden pours away down a hill. They pull into the driveway beside a muddy 4X4. Rosanna cuts the engine and they sit for a moment, staring at the building. She takes long, slow breaths; deep enough for Sam to hear and he looks across at her and it is clear that she is girding herself mentally.

"Shall we?"

"Just give me a moment."

Sam nods and opens the door and steps out of the vehicle, leaving her alone in there with her thoughts. He stretches his legs, places his fists on his hips, pulls his shoulders back and gives his spine a good click. He breathes deeply of the clean country air and surveys the surroundings. The road they are on cuts along the top of a hill. On the other side, a field stretches away, sinks, and more hills rise in the distance. A pastoral vision of beauty that suggests what the world might have been like before man came along. Sam turns back towards the cottage, where the hill falls away and plunges into more countryside. But then the countryside ends, dusting up in the distance into a blue mist surrounding the vast city that spreads out and fills the horizon. From here it looks beautiful.

Sam scrapes his foot on the dusty driveway, sending up a little cloud. There's a whine as Rosanna's window comes down and she says

"Go ahead, I'll be in in a sec."

Sam walks over to the house. He steps up a small ramp leading to a wooden porch, noting an accumulation of spider webs in the eaves of the canopy above his head. He looks for a doorbell, but finding none, he knocks. While he waits, he turns back to look at Rosanna sitting in her silver bullet of a car, expecting to meet her eyes and give her a reassuring smile – but her head is down and she is deep in thought. There's a kind of scraping noise from inside, like a table being dragged across the floor, only longer and more fluid. It moves right up to the door and then the door opens. Sam is about to say hello, but finds himself staring at thin air – and then he looks down: David Redmond is looking up at him from a wheelchair. He is sandy-haired, a strong-jawed angular face clogged by a little excess flab. A tight smile on his lips betrays a great deal of tension beneath the surface.

"Oh, I was expecting someone else," he says.

"I'm here with Rosanna."

"Oh. Oh, right," David's eyes drop.

And then he looks up and his face brightens, his eyes wide and sparkling. Sam turns to see Rosanna standing behind him at the bottom of the ramp. And her mouth is slack with shock.

"Oh my God. What happened to you?"

"It's good to see you," he says.

On a bright sunny day any interior is dark, but David's seems especially so. Sam understands it when he sees a home like this. A place where a man lives alone and can't be bothered to clean up. Although it does occur to him that when that man is in a wheelchair cleaning could take a little more effort. He and Rosanna sit in silence on separate couches while they wait for David. They glance at each other occasionally but for the most part they are lost in their own thoughts and disinclined to make conversation. A double door at the back of the lounge is open, framing the bright slope of the overgrown garden and the city glittering in the distance. They could almost be in a foreign country. It's one of those summer days where England doesn't seem like England at all.

David wheels back in with a jug of fresh lemonade and some glasses in his lap. He stops by the coffee table and places them there, leaving a damp patch on his trousers. Then he reverses into a space in the middle of the floor which had seemed strangely empty – and now that he occupies it, it is clear that it is normally the place where a single armchair might go, facing the two couches. He addresses Rosanna as if Sam wasn't even in the room.

"I knew you'd come back to me one day," he begins. Sam can see Rosanna balk inwardly, hiding her discomfort poorly beneath a swallow and a twitch of the jaw. "Don't worry. I'm under no illusions that you will ever love me again. I know you've moved on. What was there left for me to do but follow suit? It took time though..."

"David, please don't," she interrupts him, sitting forward slightly and then pauses, uncertain, looks down, reconsiders her words, "I mean you don't have to."

"You know, I'm not interested in your rolled eyes and your faux sympathy. So just shut up and listen will you? I know I don't have to. But you need to hear this."

He is sitting straight in his chair, eyes pinched and fierce. Content that he will not suffer any further interruptions, David continues.

"You never finished with me. Not properly. You never had the guts to tell me it was over. You waited for me to get better, get out of hospital and then you just stopped returning my phone calls. If I wasn't so blindly in love with you, I might have noticed your lack of enthusiasm, but I just assumed you were busy. Then you just sort of disappeared.

"Remember the last time I saw you, when I bumped into you in town? I made out like I was just passing. I'd been waiting for hours outside your work and then followed you until you got far enough away for it not to look like I was hovering around. You managed to fake a good game then, and I sort of swallowed it, thinking I'd see you at some point but slowly the truth began to unpeel in my mind. All of my friends were seeing it and I wasn't. And when I did, I felt like such a moron.

"And all I could think about was what could possibly have changed your mind. Because I'd had an accident? Because you were scared of what might happen to me? No, of course not – because to be fair to you, you actually did stick it out through the rough times. So what? I was mystified. And I still don't know."

"David I –"

"And I don't care."

He pauses, giving her a pointed look. Rosanna is frozen.

"I made contact with some of your friends. People that had started to become *our* friends – Jill and Ted, Robin, Deborah. They said you were doing fine and they had no idea why you'd left me, but all of them assured me that I shouldn't go after you. That it was pointless, that I'd be on a hiding to nothing and I'd only make myself feel bad and make things more difficult for you.

"But still, I couldn't just do nothing. Just let it slide. Not something as important as this. And so I sought out Roberta."

He takes a long slurp of lemonade. A listless breeze breathes in through the open double doors, barely stirring the curtains. Sam shifts in his seat. Rosanna's eyes are wide, glued to David. In a way it looks like she might be furious, but perhaps, thinks Sam, it's just all of the conflicting emotions forcing her eyes wide and making them bulge that way.

"I booked a session with her. I assumed that she hadn't realised who I was, because surely there would have been a conflict there – unless you weren't seeing her anymore, which I had no way of knowing of course – but then when I went into her office and sat down opposite her, she said, 'You know, I shouldn't really be seeing you. This can be our only session together. But I feel like it's the least I can do. Not that I can tell you much, but I hope that I can help you in some way.'

"Immediately it didn't seem right. Her motivation didn't add up and from what little I know about therapy, it seemed like she was close to the wind in ethical terms.

"Anyway, so for the most part she just reiterates all the shit that your friends had said and whenever I ask her something about you, about why this might have happened, she tells me she can't go there. And it's clear that she knows exactly why it's happened but she just won't say and she knows that every time she says 'I can't talk about that' it's driving me up the wall. And I'm sitting there huffing and puffing but she keeps this calm level tone. But there's something. There's a glint in her eye. I can tell she's enjoying it. And eventually I blow my top and I shout, 'Does it make you happy that I've lost Rosie and you've still got her?'

"And it's just a tiny thing. Just for a moment. But she looks sort of stunned. And then she shakes her head, sort of shakes it off and says she'd like to talk to me about strategies for moving on or some such bullshit and she says she can even recommend another therapist if I want. And I listen to her for a moment but then I'm like 'no, no, no, answer my question goddammit.'

"And she's trying to change the subject, to delay or distract me and I get really irate with her. I don't need therapy, I need my girl back! And before I know it I've really lost it and I'm on my feet and yelling at her. And then she's up out of her chair and she's trying to calm me but she can't get through to me and then I put my hands on her – not violent or anything but just a touch on her shoulders or a prod in the chest or something and the moment I do that she's screaming at me to get out of her office, screaming that she'll call the police. And I'm remonstrating with her and it's shocked me a bit that she's become this furious because you know these therapy people they're supposed to be all calm and level-headed and everything, but then she's shoving me, physically shoving me towards the door of the room. And by this point I'm just trying to apologise, saying I didn't mean to be threatening or anything and I can see my window closing and realise that I've fucked it and I'm never going to find out what I want to know and all of that's going round my head and I don't even notice when I'm outside the door and she slams it in my face. And I stand there for a moment, feeling like I'm hanging in mid air, leaning against a shelf of nothing, and I look back over my shoulder at the stairs descending from the attic.

"And the next thing I know, I'm lying at the bottom of them with both my legs broken."

"Shit," says Sam.

"She put you in that chair?" says Rosanna.

David looks at Sam and then Rosanna. And, slowly, he shakes his head.

"Oh, she did," he says. "But not then. A stay in hospital, some physio and I could have been on my feet again in a few months probably. But these babies," he slaps his dead legs and it sounds like steak on a butcher's counter, "they're like this forever.

"See I was lying there in that hospital bed. Don't know how long. And they had me on some kind of medication so I was pretty zonked. But every so often I would come to and as soon as I did I'd start shouting that I wanted to speak to the police. Or screaming to anyone who'd listen about how it was Roberta that did this to me. And of course they take this as meaning that I need to be further sedated. They say the pain is making me delirious, but that they'll have me speak to a police officer as soon as I'm ready. They even tell me there's police outside waiting to speak to me, but they're keeping it till they think I'm okay to speak to them. And I'm just like 'Now! Bring them in now!' but then it's – zupp!" And he mimes injecting himself in the arm. "And I'm off like a baby. And I don't know how long it's going on. I'm in and out and in and out like that for a while."

"Then one day I opened my eyes and the first thing I saw was this uniform. A policeman standing at the end of the bed. And I'm so relieved, I'm like: at last! But then I see his face and it looks kind of familiar and I've got this horrible sinking feeling as I try and puzzle out where I've seen him before. And he knows I recognise him and he's saying 'Don't you remember me?' or something and then I place it: this is one of the guys that mugged me and beat the shit out of me in the first place.

"And I feel sick. And I don't know what to do. He starts tapping the side of my face, trying to make sure that I'm awake, that I'm with it, that I'm listening. And then he warns me – he says I go near Roberta ever again or speak to you and I'll see him again. Just like that. That's all he says. 'You'll see me again.'

"Then he gives me an injection and the last thing I see is him reaching down towards my legs with a half-grin on his face and I feel the beginnings of an intense pain and then I'm out.

"When I woke up, the doctor told me that there have been complications and that my injuries are more severe than they had first thought. He tells me I'll never walk again. And that's pretty much that."

They all feel it. A weight on all their shoulders. A feeling as bitter and lumpen as a broken bone. Rosanna catches the reflection of the three of them in the glass of the open double doors, sitting in a despond so heavy that they cannot bring themselves to communicate any further. Bound by parallel emotion. Silent. Their heads slumped. She thinks of the four men sat in her lounge in the middle of the night. And the fact that Sam is one of them makes the correspondence of the images all the more cogent. It rattles in her. An intense buzzing frustration. A need to do something, to break out of it but with nothing to do and nothing tangible to break out of. And she shivers and jerks and before she knows it she has surged to her feet. The men look up at her and she lets out a sound. Something primal, right from her guts. It goes on for what seems like minutes, loud and powerful and purging, as if light was bursting from her mouth.

And then she stops. Her mouth slams shut and she hangs limply on her frame. Wrung out and swaying. And then, quietly, she begins to sob.

"It's okay, Rosie." There is a new softness in David's eyes. The kind of tender glance that passes only between people who have shared each other deeply. "Sit, calm down, breathe."

"I wish you could come over and hold me." She puts a hand to her mouth. "Sorry. Can I come and hold you?"

"No. Sit down."

"Okay," she whispers, and does.

And as the silence resettles, Sam notices something inside him. Something small but growing loud and urgent and surging like Rosanna's scream. Something that he couldn't hear before over all the noise.

"We have to go. We've got to get back to the hospital. She's in there now. There's a police officer there waiting to see her."

"Is he one of Roberta's? Jonathan Frame." Rosanna's voice is washed out, making her sound disinterested.

"There weren't any police officers in her notebooks at all, but she's told me herself she does loads of PTSD work."

"She does."

Sam leaps to his feet,

"Okay, so come on then what are we waiting for?"

"Er," David's head lifts and he eyes Sam with a squint, "We?"

"Don't do this to me David. We need you. Rosanna needs you. You have a clear mind. Roberta can't reach you. And you believe us."

"All of those things are true, but..."

"But what?"

"I don't know..." David turns away. His teeth play with his lips. His hands tighten and untighten on his wheels.

"You could have stopped this," says Sam. "Did you never think to say anything? To warn Rosanna? You left her at the mercy of the same woman that destroyed your life."

David exhales through his nose,

"Oh, I thought about it. I thought about warning her, but I knew I'd seem like some obsessive ex-boyfriend trying to get in with another chance. She'd never have believed me. Just thinking about it sent me into spirals of emotional bullshit. I had to make a break.

That was all I could do. Get away. Make a new life for myself. So I moved out here."

"And how's that working out for you?"

"Okay."

David blinks once. Twice.

"She had my number. She could call me if she needed to. And she did."

He nods to himself, satisfied with his explanation. Sam frowns, less so.

And then, unbidden, David expels a long sigh and says, "And I suppose in a sense I thought she didn't deserve my help. I had done my best and been treated with contempt. What else is there? I mean for all I know she could have been in on it. Christ, I'd already had one hell of a warning. What do you want me to say? I don't need to justify myself to you."

"No," says Sam, "I don't suppose you do."

He gets a smile from David in response.

"Look, I'm just glad to be talking to you now. It's so good to know that we're not a couple of nutjobs driving each other to further and further excesses. I... It's good. Thank you."

"Shit." David's eyes roll heavenwards and he blows air up to tease his fringe. He shrugs. "We should take my car. Rosie you can leave yours here if you like."

Something about the offer makes her smile.

The weather has turned. Skies darken as a storm rolls in. The rain lashing the window sends a rattling echo around the room that imparts a portion of the cold and wind that harries the world beyond the glass. Nina wonders when she is going to get out of here. She reaches for the bedside light and turns it on, her hands gathering in the bright pool it sheds, as if they could cup warmth from it.

Some sound. Movement outside the window into the corridor. The nurse is there with the policeman. They are looking in at her. It is the same burly fellow; he nods while the nurse says something inaudible to him. Then he notices Nina looking and he gives her what is supposed to be a friendly smile and waves. Something about the incongruity of the gesture with his physical makeup sends a shiver up Nina's spine. A sense of something inevitable. And then it comes.

The nurse turns towards the door and there's the little knock. The clunk and the tight squeak as the door opens a crack and her jolly face peers through.

"Hi Nina, everything okay?"

"A little cold."

"Oh, I'll get you another blanket." And then almost as an afterthought, "Do you think you're ready to speak to the officer yet?"

And the fact that he's right there, right over the nurse's shoulder makes Nina feel like she's run out of excuses.

"I suppose I could."

The nurse pushes the door wide and he steps in saying, "Hi Nina. How are you feeling?"

Didn't the nurse just ask her that?

"I'll go and see about that blanket."

"No. I mean, if you wouldn't mind, would you stay, just while I talk to officer..."

"Jonathan."

"I'm not a child. Name please. And I'll have your number while you're at it."

"148SA Frame. Jonathan Frame."

"While I talk to PC Frame."

"It's okay. Won't take me a moment. I'll be back real quick."

And the irksome smile and the Americanism make Nina suddenly glad to be rid of her. She disappears off and Frame steps into the centre of the room, filling it, as the door swings shut behind him.

"It's probably best that we talk alone," he says, his voice dropping to a low rumble.

"Why?"

"Because of what I have to say."

"What you have to say? I thought you were here to ask me questions."

"I am. But the way things are looking at the moment there might be some things I have to tell you too."

"Oh."

And he does a friendly little smile that again is not really comforting. It drops away immediately and never once touches his eyes.

"Do you mind if I take a seat?"

"Why would I mind?"

He sits and extracts his notepad from his shirt pocket. Flips it open. Pen poised. He looks up at her, sitting close, his face on a level with her and it feels inappropriately intimate. She can smell the sweet biscuits he's just eaten on his breath.

"Who ran you over?"

"I didn't," she shudders internally as images come back, "I didn't see."

He raises an eyebrow at the waver in her voice,

"But..."

"But what?"

"You have an idea."

Nina lets out a long sigh that shivers and trembles as it reaches its end.

"You know that your boyfriend was on the scene?"

"Yes."

"Do you think it could have been him?"

"No. No, of course not."

"Then what was he doing there?"

"Well how am I supposed to know?"

He looks at her with unwavering eyes, waiting for her to say something else. But she doesn't.

"We have our suspicions," he says.

And this provokes her to immediately supply, "There was another man there."

"Would this be Neil Allen?"

"I don't know. It wasn't someone I knew and I haven't heard that name before."

"But his presence there was significant because..."

"Someone has been following me recently. I thought it might be him. There was just something in his eyes, the way he looked at me."

"But it's not that you recognised him?"

"The person following me, they keep their distance. It's hard to tell. I only have details, not a whole picture."

"Could it have been Sam that was following you?"

"What makes you say that?"

And Frame shuffles in his seat, leans forward, the bedside lamp behind him throwing a bright ring around the edge of his close-cropped head. His eyes glint out at her from the shadow cast by his thick brow. The smell of sweet biscuits is strong.

"I am telling you this because I think you need to know. And I know that nothing is conclusive – we have not yet been able to confirm or deny the presence of Neil Allen or his car on the scene. But your man Sam – he has a record."

Nina's breath wells in her mouth and hangs there, flowing neither inwards or outwards.

"You know that he had a wife before? A wife who died."

The tiniest of nods.

"He killed her."

Nina can't move. She stares into the dark twinkles in the centre of Jonathan Frame's brow. Time freezes and slows and stops while they look at each other like that. Neither of them breathes.

There is a loud clunk and a squeaking swoosh of plastic against plastic as the door opens. Frame's hand shoots up, held open towards the nurse indicating for her to stop. She hangs there in the doorway with a blanket draped over her arm. Frame doesn't break eye contact. His biscuit breath grows hotter, closer.

"Was..." Nina's voice is the smallest weakest sound, a sound that would be drowned out in any space other than the noiseless vacuum that the room has become. Frame turns his ear to her. She swallows dryly and reiterates the question that she had just tried to ask. "Was he convicted?"

Frame answers without blinking.

"Not guilty. By reason of insanity."

Chapter Six

WITH THE RUSH OF A STORM

The country roads they took on the way out don't look familiar at all on the way back in. In a sense, they are the same, just roads that twist past, reflecting and refracting in the windscreen. And in another sense it is like they are venturing into a different country, and maybe they will return to a London that is completely changed – or to a different city entirely, a new place that none of them has ever seen before. Somewhere where the light is bright and palm trees shift in the wind. But for now the weather speaks only of rain and wind and darkness.

Rosanna's mascara is formed into big black panda smudges and there is a sniffle on her every third or fourth breath. Sam watches her watching the road, her concentration fighting the emotional squall inside of her. And he feels for her, he really does. He wishes he could help her but that is not in his power. All he can do is try to keep her functional, keep her focussed, make sure that he gets what he needs from her. What they all need. It seems like an unkind thought. But it is a time of necessity and necessity is the language that is required.

"I wish I could go back to how it was." Rosanna is speaking. It is not the language of necessity. Her voice has a cracked, wistful quality. "And it may be that Roberta was responsible for changing my mind, my personality. But regardless of whether it was my choice or if I was being manipulated, I am changed. And we – our minds, our feelings – they are what they are. We can't help that, we can't change them. We can only accept them."

"Sounds like exactly the kind of bullshit she would feed you," says Sam.

There's a period of silence in which he justifies his interjection to himself by thinking that he is trying to keep her on track. But after a while of no-one speaking he says, "Sorry."

And still there's no response or comment. Just silence and the humming of the car and the wheels rolling on the road.

And then there's another sound. A small sound. And he realises that Rosanna is crying again. Clearly he's not doing his job all too well.

"If that's the case," says David in a flat, even tone, "Then why does it upset you?"

"I don't know," she says, "I don't know. I wish I knew."

And she swallows, wipes her eyes and hunches over the steering wheel, concentrating on the road.

"I suppose," she says after a while, "I suppose I feel like I've been cheated."

Sam notices Rosanna checking the mirror two times, then a third, looking to see how David is reacting. He turns and looks: the man in the back sits in silence, his face illegible, his eyes meeting the reflection of Rosanna's in the rear-view mirror.

Sam turns back to the road.

Trees, road, trees.

A hand comes through the gap between the front seats and rests on Rosanna's shoulder, squeezing it gently.

"It's okay," says David, "You don't need to feel bad about it. Not for my sake."

She is quiet now, staring at the road, the sheen of the last tears still glistening around her eyes but no new ones.

"And if it's not for my sake," he continues, "then why else? For your own? For a past you? For a past me? Forget about it Rosie. What's gone is gone. And you know what, it's even good for us. We're apart. And you don't want me and I don't want you and from where I'm standing that's a painless position for both of us."

The hand stays there. She maintains her silence for a while and then she says in a low voice,

"Except you're not standing."

It almost feels like a joke, like they should laugh, but none of them does.

"And that's the one thing that's left," he says, "The sticking point. The thing we have to resolve. It's what we're doing now. We know where we are morally and that's what counts. If we stick to that then we'll always know we did the best we could."

"How can you... How can you be so..."

"It's okay sweetheart. It's okay. Say it with me – tell me it's okay."

And she does and she even manages a smile through the wet twitch of her panda eyes. A sniffle and she's sitting straight again, gaze clear, looking forward.

But it's not okay. It's not okay for her and whatever he says, it's not okay for David. And Sam knows this. And it's not okay for him either.

Frame sits above Nina. A moment ago, her eyes stopped looking at him. They switched to the ceiling and now they hang there, like she has been paused. As if her spirit has abandoned a body that has lost functionality; and the will to fight, following the physical ability, has departed to somewhere else. The blankets and the shoulders of her gown hang over her like an unpitched tent over a pile of sticks. But inside this almost lifeless figure, the cogs are whirring. Something is ticking over. Calculations upon calculations whirling around each other behind those dull eyes.

The nurse watches Frame hanging over Nina, like a dog before a lidded bowl, waiting for someone to uncover its contents. In contrast to her frail body, his large one looks dangerous and heavy as if, were he to lean any further forward, it might topple onto her and crush her. The nurse does not know why what Frame said caused her patient to shift into this strange kind of catalepsy, but she's fairly sure that something is not right. That what little she has caught of the conversation does not fit with the ordinary conduct of police officers trying to assemble the facts after a road accident. And in her three years on the job she has seen many such interactions. No. Everything about this seems wrong. From his posture to the look on his face, from Nina's expression and physicality to the emaciated sound of her voice and the contents of her question. In the time that Nina has been in here, the nurse has never heard her sound so washed-out, even in her delirious moments immediately following the crash. Something has hit her harder than a car could.

Everything in the room hangs. Grains of sand drifting, suspended in water.

A switch. Something moves. The nurse doesn't quite catch it but now she sees that Nina's eyes are fixed on Frame again. And before the nurse has time to quite register this

Nina jerks forward. Her head juts up at Frame as far as her limited movement allows. Their brows almost touch. If Frame flinches, it's so slight that the nurse cannot see it. Nina's chin comes to a sharp point, her face upturned. The lines in her throat strain and she becomes flushed with blood and her teeth grind together audibly. For a moment it seems as if she might be having some kind of a seizure and a wave of concern passes over the faces of both the policeman and the nurse.

"Get him out!" Nina barks the words, her teeth chopping together as if she is speaking without using her lips. "Out! Get this joker away from me!" And even though she is speaking to the nurse, her eyes never leave Frame "Now!" so that when she addresses him next, it is not entirely clear that the focus of her words has switched "I don't need you. How dare you come in here. You tell me he's a murderer when he wasn't even convicted."

Frame takes her abuse as if she was screaming at the sea.

"What? You think you're telling me this for my own good? Do you?"

He opens his mouth to answer but she ignores him,

"Then you get me the case files. Were you there? I want to see details! I don't care if this shabby bullshit fits some crackpot theory of yours. I've got your name and number, you hear me? And believe me, I will be having words with people."

And then she flops back onto the bed and breathes in and out hard like it is a real effort. And she stays there, having given it her all and with nothing else to say.

And the nurse looks at Frame and Frame looks at the nurse.

"I think you'd better leave," she says.

And Frame gives her a polite, curt nod, folds up his pad and gets up and leaves. After all, why wouldn't he? His work here is done.

No-one has said a word for the past fifteen minutes. The country roads are coming to an end. The trees are becoming thinner. More and more houses appear, winking past. The previous conversation feels like the end of an argument when two people say let's agree to disagree but both of them know that it is not resolved. The rain still patters on the windscreen but the storm is passing, the sun breaking through the clouds.

They turn onto a large roundabout where the trees no longer diffuse the daylight, making everything stark and bright. Sam feels that this is a world devoid of warmth. And can almost feel himself plunging into the cold depths of space as the vehicle spoons around a slip road and up onto the motorway. The three lanes of the M25 are not busy. They proceed around them with increasing speed and it feels like they are being drawn by a magnet towards some destination that he would really rather not reach. And he finds it increasingly easy not to think about it at all, just to lose himself to the journey. He wonders if his companions are doing the same. But does not look at their faces.

A thing nags at him. Something that does not allow him to remain in the safety of his reverie. And then he realises that his phone is ringing. He reaches for his trouser pocket but finds the material constricted by the position he is sitting in and has to twist to reach his thumb and forefinger in, using his other hand to force the phone upwards. The process is taking longer than he had first thought. And he begins to panic. What if it's Nina? His fingers fidget faster. He pries the phone loose, hits the button and brings it to his ear. And he hears a voice.

It is not Nina.

"What do you want?" Sam asks.

"I think we should talk." Roberta sounds collected and

professional as ever; giving her opinion as if it is unarguable, objective fact, "I think it has been too long since our last session. And, to tell the truth, when I don't hear from you I worry about you."

"Why are you calling me now?"

"As I said –"

"No," he cuts in over her. "I mean why are you calling me right now? At this moment." He looks aside to the others and mouths the therapist's name. Rosanna's eyes widen.

"Is it significant to you when or where I choose to telephone you?"

"Do you know where I am right now?"

"How could I possibly know that?"

Sam can't help but smile and shake his head,

"You've got to hear this," he says and puts the phone on speaker, holding it out in front of him. In the meantime, it seems that Roberta has taken his silence as a sign to continue: "I've been thinking about your dream," she says.

Sam rolls his eyes and makes a yapping mouth with his hand. Yadda yadda yadda. And the others stifle laughter. It is a childish moment but it draws them together. Grinning impishly, he humours her, "Which dream?"

"I think you know which dream."

His smile drops as an image enters his mind. He flicks the phone off speaker and brings it to his ear.

"About Caroline?"

"No. The other one."

"What other one?"

"The same dream you always have. You're in a car…"

moving down a dark road. It's so dark here that the only things he can see are the points of light, streetlights, cat's eyes, white lines, lines and lines flashing past. And the sound of the wind is furious. And then the car begins to slide violently to the left and to the right. He tries to regain control of the vehicle but the steering wheel keeps skipping out of his grasp. As he reaches for it something fights him out of the way, like branches flying in his face or hands grasping at his wrists. A terrible screaming wheels up out of the darkness in the vehicle around him; outside it, the orange glow of lights beckons him to the warm embrace of the darkness between them. The voices. Twin voices. A male and a female voice speaking as one. Screaming his name. Blows against his body, his head, his neck. The constricting embrace of hands around him. Cutting off his air. But all he knows is that he must stop this car. Stop it from drifting aimlessly into danger and death. On the road outside, caught in the lights, stands an emaciated female figure, a pale gown fluttering around it, whipped by the wind and plastered to the bony body by rain. A shrill voice. A figure so fragile and delicate that he knows that his only priority can be to protect it from harm and he tries to direct the car away from it. Anywhere. Anywhere but here. And other things loom out of the dark and come to prominence, threatening collision. An empty chair. A china ballerina, smashed. A baby's cot. An oversized stuffed-toy elephant, spattered with dark flecks. The vehicle becomes harder and harder to control. The steering wheel whips out of his hands, dragged by some unstoppable elemental current. His stomach sinks as he realises that it is not within his power to stop this inevitable descent. The lights outside spin. The vehicle is now somersaulting across the road with a series of violent thuds as metal meets tarmac. He's upside down, tumbling in the dark. He loses all sense of which way is up and which way is not. Then everything starts to fade and wobble. A heat haze. It becomes unbearably hot. Flames lick at the windows, melting the glass. The interior of the car is bathed in red and orange. There's red and orange and black, the deep endless black beyond the windows. He wrestles with his seatbelt, trying to get it off as the heat rises but it won't budge. It's stuck. He's stuck. And then he looks to his right. And sitting there, pinned into the seat, upside-down, there is another person. Her face is turned away from him and masked by a smeared mass of blonde hair. The car bucks, buffeted by a jet of flame bursting from beneath it like there is a volcanic vent beneath the chassis. There's a scraping and a bending and a shriek of metal and the woman's face tilts towards him, its hair hanging like wet shredded lace curtains only yellow and orange as another colour bleeds and mingles with it and as her head jolts and sways the curtains part and lifeless eyes tilt up in their sockets, pupils twisting in opposite directions, moved not by motor control but by the conflicting forces of gravity and impact. Equal and opposite reactions. The backs of the whites twist up to fill the sockets as the irises disappear. They are slick and pregnant and swollen and brown and bruised, as inhuman as sweetbreads. And her mouth stretches as if pulled over a rack and the teeth, stripped to the gums, reach together, straining to meet as the lips pull apart. A dark network of rivers closes over the face, descending through the mess of hair over the forehead and closing the face as they merge and swell in its pits and depressions. And Rosanna disappears, drowned and anonymous beneath a mud-slick of her own blood.

A cold wind whips through the vehicle. Light seeps and then bursts through an opening and in the space between a person dreaming and waking, night becomes day. At first all he is aware of is how bright and how cold it is and how the daylight does not bring warmth. It is a harsh bluey-white and it penetrates to his bones. The whole interior of the car is speckled with moisture, as if its surfaces were expressing a frigid sweat. As if the machine were in a fever. Rain comes in sporadic sprays, driven by cyclical gusts of wind, and each spray brings Sam closer to wakefulness and realisation like a slap on the face. He holds himself, fingers grasping at the damp arms of his shirt, and wonders how the rain can enter the vehicle with such violence, and why water has collected everywhere but on the windscreen. Only then does he notice the mosaic edges of shatterproof glass jutting from the edges of its frame. The windscreen is gone.

There is a sound like a perforated football being squeezed and repumped. Sam isn't sure where it's coming from. Beyond the shattered windscreen, a wet blackness extends upwards, its uniformity breaking down upon closer examination into tightly packed granules. Crystals cling to it as if glued to its surface. Below, blue-grey depths swirled through with white extend down through fathoms into infinity and Sam's stomach sinks and turns over as if he has woken to find himself in mid-skydive. But it is not depth. It is height. It is the sky. And the blackness above him is tarmac and the crystals are what is left of the windscreen. Where the tarmac disappears from view, blocked by the metal of the bonnet, there is a shoe with a sock and a leg extending from it. Realising he is upside down, held in place by his seatbelt, Sam panics; any movement might cause him to land on his head and result in further injury. He doesn't even know if he is injured, or what the extent of those injuries might be.

Metal creaks. Everything moves, the tarmac floats up and then settles back into position. Something whirs and then ticks, ticks, ticks. Sam turns towards the noise – and sees the wheel of David's wheelchair spinning in the boot. But in connecting the image with the sound, he can't shake the feeling that he has missed something. And then he remembers another object, something his eyes caught as his head turned, something bulky and strange and twisted in the seat beside him.

He turns back. A tangle of legs and hands and body. It heaves in short, fitting expansions and contractions that correlate with the punctured football noise. And there, pressed between the backs of her jeans and the steering wheel, Rosanna's face looks out at him. Her skin is drained of all colour and soapy, as if it might stick to his fingers were he to touch it. He has never seen a face so white before. Translucent, a bluey-white like the daylight. Lines of something almost black by comparison cut across the top of her forehead like gouges. Thick lines of blood. But she is still alive, still breathing. And this sends a wave of panic through Sam. He feels as if he is holding something small and fragile like a baby bird on the brink of death – like any movement could snuff out the life therein, but that a movement is necessary to save it. He is caught between action and indecision. Hanging there. Literally hanging.

He eases himself towards her. Drops. Hands fly out and he braces himself against the roof of the car, pushing up to prevent his neck being compressed by his own chest. He tilts forward to rest on the back of his shoulders. From this position he can barely see her. Just the side of her face. An eye and the corner of her lips – livid pink and purple against the white of her face. Where is her lipgloss now? If it has not been washed away it has been eclipsed by a rush of blood, or a loss of oxygen – or whatever it is that causes them to practically pop from her face. Sam tries to speak and finds a well of saliva clogging his throat. He coughs it out and a ropey glob ejects and splatters against the roof between them. And then he edges closer and says "Rosanna."

The eye he can see does not move. Nor do the lips. But he hears something like the ghost of a word.

"You"

And as he tries to figure out whether he can attribute the utterance to her, he notices that he can no longer hear the sound of her breathing. And now the knot of her body is no longer expanding and contracting. Something in it has changed. It has become a leaden mass. Sam reaches out to touch her and it is like touching a pair of shoes. His hand shoots back and he flies into a flurry of movement. His arms and legs grasp and kick and his body twists and he doesn't know how, but the next thing he knows, he finds himself outside the windscreen, crawling across the tarmac as gravity pivots around a 180-degree axis and the world rights itself with a nauseating swirl. Air swims into him, fresh and cold and spreads through his limbs and he pushes against the tarmac and then he's on his feet and he's staring at the underneath of the car, exposed to the sky. The roof is tipped up and away from him and he can see the thing that he knows is Rosanna bundled up inside, the back of her seat leaning drunkenly forward behind her, forcing her into an impossibly small space.

The crash barrier is bent and twisted for metres leading up to where the chassis rests against it. The traffic squeezes over into a single lane on the far side of the sprinkling of glass and debris around the wreck, the bunched-up line of cars extending away ad infinitum, buildings and the rest of the world rising behind them to fill the sky and disappearing away into a mass of everything. Inside the cars, faces press against the glass, each one queuing to pass the exhibit. They do not show fright or pity or horror. They are blank. Their eyes are glassy and vacant. The same as they would be if they were sitting at home staring at the television. And Sam notices that they are not looking at him, but at a spot several feet behind him. He turns.

David is lying face down. Thrown from the vehicle. Seeing him like this you would have no idea that those legs do not work. They look strong and healthy and no different from anybody else's. And this dislocation jars Sam's memory. He pictures the man sitting in his home, speaking dispassionately of the death of his passion. And then he remembers something else. His own hands grasping the steering wheel. Rosanna's wide mouth screaming in his face as she wrestles with him for control. The click and zip as David's seatbelt flies off and he lurches between the seats to try and pull Sam away from the wheel. The turning of the earth and the violent rotation of scenery beyond the windows. He remembers a phone call. A voice.

'The same dream you always have.'

And screaming back into the moment, Sam looks at the queuing cars and the hundreds of eyes gawping at him and somewhere in the distance the wail of sirens begins. A driver pulls over and opens his door. He is saying something but Sam can't hear it.

Sam's body moves without thinking, his mind sitting up top like a bemused old man. He vaults over the barrier and his feet slide down through shale and mud until he is running through rough scrub and bushes and damp grass. A screen of trees towers ahead of him. And he plunges into the welcome embrace of the shadows within.

Daylight dims into a blur of greens and browns, a swirling of leaves and swiping of twigs. He runs with abandon, his body working without input from his mind, his thoughts blank. Only the comfort that here no-one can see him. And that with every step he is putting distance between himself and that smashed car, that chaos of death and bodies and destruction and gawping passers-by and the inexorable approach of the authorities and questions that he cannot answer. It doesn't matter that it is damp here, or that twigs whip and rip at his skin and his face and his clothes. He doesn't notice them. He barely even feels them.

He has no idea how long he's been running when his legs collapse under him. They just stop going and the momentum carries his body forward and down until it collides with the pine-needled ground. His face presses into the cool wetness and he breathes in and out, watching the flutter of tiny plants stirred by his breath. The air is fresh and the scent of the trees and the mud is strong and wholesome. He feels his lungs stretching themselves out now that they are away from the choking fumes of the motorway, the compression of the interior of the overturned vehicle. And after some moments of just breathing, his breath slowing, becoming fuller as he recovers from the exertion of his sprint, a thought enters his mind. The first thought for some time:

Sit.

His arms drag his hands through the mulch. Elbows pull up and his palms press into the soft wetness. He peels up, the forest floor sticking to his face and his clothes. And he slides over to a tree trunk, leaning back against it and breathing in that fresh, fresh air, his face turned up towards the leafy canopy above him. Great branches outlined in black twist through the interposed layers of green in varying thicknesses and translucencies and, sporadically, drops fall and splash against his skin, each one washing him clean, one spot at a time.

And as he sits there, the warmth accumulated from his exertion begins to ebb and a seeping cold creeps into him. He becomes aware of the dampness in his clothes and the concomitant discomfort. His arms tighten around him and he begins to shiver. And with the shivering, with the return of the physical, calling him back to himself, back to the present, come the echoing thoughts in the background. Nattering away. Bidding for attention.

Something terrible has happened. He has done something terrible. He is responsible. But at the same time he is not. He knows that he was not acting according to his wishes. Roberta. How did she reach out and take hold of him from this distance? A phone call. One phone call was all it took to completely remove his conscious mind. To interpose a will not his own. How did she do it? How did she know? How could she possibly have been aware that at that moment three people had joined against her and were on course to take action, to do something, to bring her down and stop her? How did she know they were in the car? Is it even possible that she could have implanted this specific dream so long ago just to use it in this specific circumstance? Could she really be that prescient?

Sam's eyes drop from the wooded canopy and his chin rests on his wet knees. He is shivering more violently now. He hears a rattling close to him and realises that his teeth are chattering. If he just stays here, he thinks, the shivering and chattering might stop. His body might close down and accept the cold. Slow and keep pace with it and become part of it. There is so much life here, so how could the elements really threaten him? To be a tree, or a fungus, or a patch of grass would be so much simpler.

What if I am making all this up? What if I chose to do this? If for some deep fucked-up reason I decided to end the lives of these two people, to threaten my own. Just as I have decided to experience all that I have experienced. My life is my own, after all, is it not? I choose the path I walk down. It is not the things that happen to us that determine how things will be, but how we react to them.

Even now, he recognises Roberta's voice in his head. Her ideas. Her thoughts posing as his own.

Why would he choose to do something so contrary to his own desire?

This is the one thought that he must hold on to. The one thing that frees him from the spell. That makes it impossible for him to have done what he did without compulsion. He would never have made this choice. Never in a million years. Never.

The need for hard facts, reliable touchstones, is paramount.

Hard fact 1: There was a car crash.

Hard fact 2: Rosanna and David were both injured and are probably dead.

Hard fact 3: Everything was fine until Roberta called.

But he wavers. He doesn't feel strong in this. It's the problem with making lists. Lists like "what have I achieved in the past year" or "who are the people I love" – one element becomes uncertain and the rest starts to unpeel. The idea is that you just jot stuff down and then you have something solid, something to base action upon. But it's a series of things that you need to have some certainty about. And what if nothing is ever certain?

Did Roberta even call?

What has really happened to Rosanna and David?

But there was a crash wasn't there? And if the rest wasn't true, Sam thinks, then why did I run? And it seems right now that the only thing that he can be sure of is that he did run, that he is here right now in this wood sitting on a carpet of leaves and shivering and wet. He feels his pocket but finds it empty. His phone must have been lost in the crash. If he can get back there and retrieve it then he should be able to see if there was in fact a phone call. He can see the crash.

And dragging himself through the discomfort and the damp, he finds his feet and trudges through the trees in a direction that he hopes will take him back to the motorway.

Night is drawing in by the time he reaches the road. The traffic crawls past in a series of never-ending lights. It all looks so different. A dark river punctuated by infinite headlights floating away into a vague glow of artificial luminance. The landscape around the road has disappeared and been replaced by large dark shapes dusted in yet more lights. A vast mirror reflecting the stars. The crash is nowhere to be seen. Sam feels the horrible gnawing of doubt.

But then he notices a cluster of different coloured lights further down. Small, distant, but definitely there. Creating a knot in the traffic that bunches all the lights before it into a tight series, after which they expand and separate and flow more swiftly. He starts off towards the concentration, keeping to the darkness on the other side of the crash barrier. As he draws closer, the knot develops a bubble of its own light – lamps have been brought in and placed around the crashed vehicle. There are police cars, an ambulance and other official-looking vehicles clustered around the site. And there – in the middle of it – David's 4X4, upturned, exactly the way he left it. David no longer lies on the road. A stretcher is being wheeled into an ambulance, but Sam is unable to see who it contains. He inches closer – as close as he dares. Can almost smell the petrol, the exposed metal, the blood. And seeing those uniforms moving about, a tilted hat whispering busily into a radio, he realises why he ran. He can't explain it. Not even to himself. How he came away unscathed and, now, why he ran. He'd have no idea what to say when they asked him what caused the crash. And if he were to invent a story, he doubts he would be able to hold his nerve in the face of repeated questioning. In the face of officials with x-ray eyes looking for someone to blame.

Lurking here in the darkness, he feels invisible. Like he could just step over the barrier, walk up to the crashed car and retrieve his phone. To check it and know. But of course it wouldn't play like that. They'd see him and all their attention would switch on him. And then maybe he'd pick up his phone and say look, you see here, there was a call – and he could expose the whole thing to the police. How he was being controlled. But it would prove nothing. And if Roberta's police patients got wind of the investigation, began sticking their noses in, getting involved... For a moment, Sam feels like taking that risk. That way he could confirm things to himself. He finds the phone – if there was a call then at least it's a starting point. And if there wasn't then, well, he'd deserve everything he got.

No. He slinks back into the shadows. Seeing the crash is enough.

Hard fact 1: There was a car crash.

Hard fact 2: Rosanna and David were both injured and are probably dead.

And as for Hard fact 3, well, he'll just take it as read for now. What else can he trust if not his own mind? He can only try his best, act as he sees fit. And in any case, it occurs to him that there is another hard fact. A more important one.

Hard fact 4: Nina is in hospital.

And in the light of what happened to David, the threat to her may well not be over.

Sam walks away from the motorway into the deepening darkness, beginning his long trudge back to the city. Back to Nina.

Leaning all of her weight on the crutches digging into her underarms Nina scans the brightly-lit reception area: those sitting, those standing, waiting for attention or working. Alert for a face or a uniform. Someone waiting for her or someone watching: the policeman, Sam, her boyfriend, or the man who may or may not be Neil Allen. Three faces. And she doesn't want to see any one of them right now.

A face, right in front of her. The nurse with a smile so warm that it must require serious talent or experience. She says something to Nina about her being all right getting home. Nina nods curtly before continuing towards the hospital doors, beyond which the outside world twinkles in the night. Freedom. Release. Ordinary life. And so many other things. Some wonderful. Some she'd rather not think about. Not tonight. Not until she has been at home and drunk a glass of wine and had at least eight hours' sleep in her own bed.

The front door proves an unexpected problem. She wrestles to balance her crutches and pull the heavy handle towards her with one hand and wonders why tonight, of all nights, the automatic doors have to be broken. No-one rushes to her aid. She looks round for the smiling nurse but she is gone. And perhaps it is reassuring that she is already alone, anonymous. The cool air rushes in as soon as she gets it open a crack. It feels good on her face. She wedges her good foot in and pulls the door wide, keeping her back against it to hold it open as she goes through. And then she's out. The cab is waiting right there and she signals to it and the driver nods.

It takes a couple of moments for Nina to appreciate it, still panting from the difficult journey up the stairs, but there is something ghostly about her flat. Something Marie-Celeste-like. Her smart raincoat is still draped over a chair. A fat file sits on the coffee table next to a half-finished glass of wine. It's like someone else lives here; the version of her that existed before the accident. And Nina smiles to herself, feeling a nostalgic commonality with this other Nina. Like they're sisters.

She grabs the glass from the coffee table and tips out the remains of the other Nina's drink in the sink. She doesn't rinse it, just pops a new bottle and swills a drop of wine through and chucks that too. She then fills the glass to the brim, takes it over to the couch and lies back, feeling the silence. The emptiness. She gulps the first half of the glass and then takes regular sips from the remainder.

She wakes sometime later, stiff, still on the couch and curses herself for falling asleep there. Adjusting her neck, she looks down and notices the glass of wine on the floor, spilt. She has no urge to clean it up.

The phone starts ringing. Nina sits up straight, bristling with that unnerving feeling of prescience you have when you wake up just moments before someone calls you. She gropes for her crutches and hobbles over to the phone. The display shows a number she doesn't recognise, which only adds to her unease. And then she squints at the wall clock and sees that it is three in the morning.

"Who the fuck," she mutters. Even for Sam three a.m. is strange. And if it's not Sam calling, it's something even stranger. She decides not to answer and limps away from the phone, leaving it to ring out. By the time she gets to her room it has rung off. She shuts the door behind her and undresses with some difficulty. And falls back into the embrace of her sheets, which even though they probably need changing, feel crisp compared to the hospital bed.

Drifting off to sleep, she is dimly aware that the phone is ringing again, but it is not enough to wake her. An aeroplane crashing through the wall wouldn't be enough to wake her now.

Sam hangs up the payphone. The hospital told him that Nina was discharged and that she was okay at the time. And it makes sense that she wouldn't pick up now. But it feels urgent. It feels really urgent. Roberta's people are out there and they could do anything at any time. Frame has had free access to her in the intervening time since he was last at the hospital. He needs to speak to her. But he's not sure whether this need comes from a sense that she's actually in danger or from his own need for support. Although even if it is the latter, he really needs it now. Needs it enough to be waking her up at three in the morning the night after she's discharged from hospital. He's tired and confused and has no idea what to do. He rests his head against the plastic of the phone and places his palm on the perspiring glass of the box. Outside, the service station is empty, everything is quiet, there's not a soul about. It's so tempting just to pitch into the Travelodge and collapse into a rented bed. In the cold and lonely night, the lights of the building just over the road appear so inviting. But he needs to get back. And how hard can it be? Make one more phone call and then wait in the service station sipping a cup of coffee. He's run out of adrenaline. And now he's just plain knackered. It takes some degree of resolve to lift his heavy head and make that call.

The inside of the service station is almost noiseless, yet so brightly lit that it could be the middle of the day. Sam has a strange floating feeling while he sits drinking his machine-made coffee. Like he shouldn't be awake, or like he isn't. Like he's dreaming himself through the real world. As if his body and his brain have both switched off and everything around him is playing on a screen in the backs of his eyelids. The hot coffee doesn't taste good but it feels good. Just the warmth of it. The caffeine courses through his limbs and ignites his body, waking it up, but it doesn't really do anything for his awareness or for that floating sensation. It just makes it seem like the auto-pilot is having to deal with a lighter vehicle, one that responds a tiny bit better. And then the automatic doors hiss and there's a voice, "Minicab for Mr. Sam?"

And without any significant effort or even will on his part, his legs carry him towards where a shabby little man waits for him.

"Hello? Hello? Excuse me? Hello?"

Sam wakes to see the cabbie leaning over him, shaking his shoulder. A cold wind blows a spatter of rain in through the open door, disrupting the warm sanctuary of the one-person sleep-pod that the back of the cab has become.

Sam mumbles, "Yeah, yeah, yeah" and drags himself up and out onto the street, where he holds himself and shivers. He thanks the cabbie and walks towards his building.

"You need to pay me."

And Sam returns to him, digging in his pocket. He presses some notes into the man's palm and is about to tell him to keep the change but the guy turns and walks back to his cab without even saying thanks. The car pulls away leaving Sam standing squinty-eyed on the pavement, hands thrust into his pockets, arms and legs trembling out of tedium and cold, staring as the puddles on the rain-slicked tarmac coalesce and eclipse the trace of the cab's tyres. As the water settles and becomes still again, it reflects the lights of the windows in Sam's block. Most are invisible, dark, but a few are lighted – and Sam wonders who is still up at this time of night.

He finds his overworked mind drawn into a study of that reflection, trying to work out which window is which, playing a little game with himself. A car zips past, cutting the reflection into a chaos of dispersing water. Sam sighs. Shakes his head at the preposterous workings of his barely sensible brain.

Turning back towards the block is like peeking at the answers to a crossword. Flat 2, ground floor – a dopey stoner guy who does internet work from home. Flat 18, third floor – Bob and Natalie, no idea why they might be up. Flat 34, sixth floor – Marianne, divorced, probably up late watching weepies or something. And one more. Sam's flat. His very own. Why are the lights on? The window is so bright that it can't just be one light left on by accident. It's the main light in the lounge. Probably all the lights. He doesn't remember leaving them on. It was daytime when he left it – shit, it was only yesterday morning. His eyes track down to Rosanna's window. It's dark. Dead as a closed eye.

The sixth floor corridor is strange and alien now. There is nothing reassuring about returning home this night. It doesn't feel like his place. It is hostile. The walls are closing in, their paper sweating. He is awake now. The adrenaline has returned. He wonders if whatever gland pumps out that emergency chemical is capable of being drained, exhausted, broken. But now his consciousness is pressed right into the front of his face, his skin close, his eyes bulging and perspiration pricks the edges of his scalp producing an overwhelming desire to scratch. Only he daren't. All his movements must be controlled, cautious.

He stops at the front door. Takes a deep breath and reaches out to clutch the handle. Hand tightens around brass. He closes his eyes. Waits a beat. Waits for his heart to slow. Opens them. And twists.

The handle jolts to a standstill and the friction burns him slightly.

He stands back, panting. It's locked. That's a good sign. But if there is anyone in there waiting for him, they'll now know that he's here. He stands there for some moments, waiting for them to come to him. But they don't. Nobody does. Nothing happens. He looks up and down the corridor and it grows shorter and narrower. There's no-one there – or they're waiting him out. He reaches carefully into his pocket for his house keys. Places them in the lock. They jar, causing him to fumble and he hisses "Shit".

It's as if the keys don't know the lock. But then they slide in and he turns them as softly as he can manage. The door clicks. He presses his palm against it and eases it ajar.

The hallway is reassuringly still. Exactly the way it always is. Old scuffed wooden floor, chest of drawers, rack of hooks with a few coats. One is Nina's. Her short, smart purple jacket. Could it be that she's here? It brings a smile to his face. The thought of all this stress turning on its head. That it might be that she's here, waiting for him. A beautiful surprise after so much anxiety. And then the idea evaporates. She doesn't have a key.

Sam treads as softly as possible over the floorboards, lamenting the squeak and squelch of his damp trainers. If there was anyone here they would definitely be aware of his presence by now. So why bother being cautious at all? No. Caution. Caution is always important. With caution comes preparedness. He is ready to spring into action. A brash approach would allow him to relax too much, would reduce his awareness of the space around him. He stops. Through the half-open lounge door he can see one of the couches to the left, and the table to the right. He freezes for a second when he sees a glass and a bowl there, spoon poking up impertinently like a signal. And then he remembers that these are his own breakfast things.

One more step. Extending an arm, he slams the door all the way open, revealing most of the room beyond. Nothing. Nobody. He waits for a breath. Two. Then dashes into the middle of the room. His eyes jump to details: behind the door, the backs of the couches, the bedroom door, closed, the bathroom door, open a crack. A flash of a memory: a demonic face, an assailant, pain. He runs to the bathroom and throws the door open. Enters and spins in a circle. Sweeps the shower curtain aside, ripping a couple of its hooks loose. The smashed cabinet mirror, now cleared of shards, just a blank bit of plywood winking out from a ragged fringe of silvered glass. What about caution? Caution so quickly discarded. Impatient now, he trudges back through the lounge and shoves the bedroom door aside. The room is in darkness. He hits the light and sees it exactly as he left it – even the sheets rumpled in the same way. Not touched since the last time he slept here. It feels like an age has passed since then – but it has only been two days. Where did this start and when did everything change? How long ago was it that he was just seeing Nina and seeing Roberta and everything was fine? No. Seeing Nina and visiting Roberta. Dating Nina and seeing Roberta. Sam gives a grunt of frustration and ruffles his hands through his hair. Unable to look at that bed any longer, he closes the door.

In the middle of the lounge, he stands. And for the first time since he has returned, he takes in the room as a whole. Now that his attention is not so funnelled into the details, he can glean a more general impression. The room is saying something to him. It is saying here you are, wet and dirty and tired and wrung out and scraped and sore and exhausted – and yet here I am, untouched, unstirred. Whatever has changed, it is only you. It is not the rest of the world. Everyone and everything else carries on as normal while you rattle around in your own world destroying yourself. And there is something smug about the room. As if it is laughing at him. Sam's bile rises and a surge of anger courses through him. But, undirected, it simply expresses out through his pores and dissipates, becoming nothing. And in its absence the great wave of tiredness that has been waiting in the wings, held back by adrenaline, washes over him. His knees buckle. He almost falls. Grabs the back of a chair to steady himself and then shakes his head. His eyes slur across the room and the whole image slides, as if it was reflected in a tray of water being moved slowly in front of him. He needs to sit down. Before he falls down.

He drops so heavily onto the couch that for a moment all he can do is sit there. It doesn't even occur to him to lean sideways and collapse. And so he slumps forwards, his face rocking over his knees and caught by his hands. And it's there that she comes to him. Not the first woman, not the second. But Rosanna. In all her crackly spikiness. He remembers her at the doorstep of Neil's block. He sees the sharply-pulled-back hair, her twinkling little eyes and that whole ferret-like face that pulls together towards the glossed lips at its apex. He can almost hear the shuffling of her foot in the gravel. The impatience, the energy. Cigarettes sucked back like drinking straws. And then that unexpected moment where all of that transforms and a playfulness blooms. Her eyes sparkle and she cackles as she backs out into the street and throws stones at the window. Thinking of her then, he can see the little girl inside the embattled adult, sitting in there on a high chair with a soft cushion, controlling everything from behind a wall of grown up shit. And he wonders how much fun it would have been to spend more time with her. To play like that. Day in, day out. And for who knows how long they lived right beside each other, tormenting each other without even knowing it. And his memory falls back to the Rosanna he first met. In her flat, scared and vulnerable and empty. He had cracked through her usual façade without even knowing it. And inside he found a woman who called out for him, who just wanted to be told that everything is okay and was willing to take up any cause, any branch that was offered to her – even something as preposterous as what he had. Is that why she bought it? She came with him, trusted him. And Sam hears his own sob, a hollow intake of breath. And he thinks about what he didn't see. How lonely and desperate she must have been in those hours when she came in from work and shut the world out and was left only with herself.

Sam lifts his head. His palms are wet with tears. It angers him to see them shining and slick. To be this exhausted and still compelled to expend so much emotional energy on a useless expression of grief. He doesn't have the strength for this. He could strangle himself for making such a use of his emotional resources. Even the waste of fluid bothers him. He begrudges the use of those few drops of water, of less than a pinch of salt. He needs them. He needs it all. He needs everything he's got.

And then it happens. A stray movement to the side and gravity takes hold and he drops across the couch, a dead weight. And there's no time for recriminations. Sleep swallows him like the mouth of some huge creature.

When he stirs he does not remember falling asleep and it takes him a moment to remember where he is. But he is comfortable and feels no incentive to move. The flat is warm and though some of the lights are on, they are dim. He has no idea what time it is but there is no sign of daylight. He should go back to sleep. The only thing that troubles him, in inching increments, growing until it becomes a genuine question, is why he is awake. There is no apparent reason for him to have floated back into the land of the living and yet he feels that he would not have woken had he not needed to. And he hangs there, his eyes half-closed, on the boundary of surrendering to sleep. But he can't quite let himself go.

A distinct shuffling sound. Loud enough that he cannot ignore it. And he remembers with a sudden clarity the search around the flat before he fell asleep. The nagging sense that there was someone there. He lies on the couch, frozen, not quite daring to move. Listening out for another similar noise. An indication of movement, a presence.

But none comes. And yet he knows that he is not alone. Beneath the layers of fog, there is the knowledge that he should sit up, look around. That lying here like this he is vulnerable. His back is turned to the majority of the room. And if there is someone there all they need do is step towards him and reach down with hands or an implement and find his prone body soft and undefended.

But he can't move. For some unknown reason he is locked into that couch. His body vacuum-sealed to it. And he can't find sufficient impetus to rouse himself.

Something behind him slides across the floorboards. It's a soft sound. Almost imperceptible. And then his hearing sharpens with concentration and he hears a pad, pad, pad. Moving towards him. There is a light slap and then a subtle sucking noise – bare feet treading on the wooden floor. His body prickles. Someone is standing over him. He still can't see anything from where he lies. And his head refuses to turn to look up behind him. He screws his eyes tight like a child hoping that the cover of a duvet will protect them from a monster. And a faint, musty, mouldy smell fills his nostrils. And a flutter of fabric crosses his cheek before he feels a hand come down on his shoulder. A very thin hand, the feel of which against his flesh is almost sharp, ridged. And the hand is cold. The impressions of its five fingers, spread like leaves upon him, suck the warmth right out of him, even through his jacket and his shirt. It almost burns. And now he opens his eyes and sees it there. Grey, withered skin painted onto the bones, except for where it sags between the digits and in places rumples up into creases. Its wrist is draped in rotten cloth as thin as spider web. His head releases itself from the arm of the couch and twitches around to see a face leaning over at him. A face as wrinkled and rotten as the hand would suggest. The outline of the skull and jaw is fleshless. A deep flap of skin hangs from underneath the chin. The lips are barely more than the dry ends of the crease that could only just be defined as a mouth. The scalp catches the light beneath wispy hair. And in spite of the cadaverous appearance, Sam recognises her. As the only thing she could be. Caroline. The eyes stand out bulbous and large and yet somehow they are uncorrupted and pure. Clear blue circles inside large spotless whites. And the cracked lips part into something that could not really be called a smile, revealing perfect white teeth and they appear to be forming words, but all Sam can hear is an empty, breathless rasping, devoid of meaning or content.

As if he doesn't know.

And in that moment, Sam feels that he could die. And almost wishes he had.

But then he wakes. And daylight is streaming into the room. And he feels about as rested as if he had not slept at all, far from ready to face the day. He looks up at the clock – and with relief finds an excuse to take himself to bed and get some more sleep. It is still far too early.

Nina is up too early. She can see daylight cracking the edges of the curtains. And even before she moves, she feels the aching stiffness of her leg like an iron clamp is screwed to it. The clock beside her tells her that it is just after five. She could sleep. But there are things to be resolved. And there is no time like the present. And, of course, it's going to take her ten times longer than usual just to get out of bed, get showered and have her breakfast.

Her laptop has started up and is ready to go by the time she is halfway through her bowl of Coca Pops. Ordinarily, she has grapefruit and cottage cheese for breakfast, sometimes eggs on wholemeal, but she keeps the box of kids' cereal around in case of emergencies. Or hangovers. Times when she just can't be bothered being healthy. And today it feels like the most delightful of indulgences.

By the time she's scooping the brown milk out of the bottom of the bowl, she has already fired off a few emails, all of them on the same subject. As disconcerting as Frame's little prompt was, the presence of something objective in the amorphous mess of this situation is reassuring. And she is grasping for it with both hands.

She leaves her bowl on the table, not bothering to wash it up. Something she normally couldn't bear to do. Even now it irks her, but not enough to coax her to journey over to the sink and stand propped against the worktop washing up while the dull ache in her leg grows ever more savage. And so she sits there, thinking about what to do next according to the same considerations: how far will I have to walk, how long will I be on my feet for, will it hurt. And out of nowhere, the memory of the late night phone call pops into her brain. Logistics are no longer an issue. She needs to hear the message. How disappointing would it be if they hadn't left one.

But they had. He had. Nina sits on the couch as Sam's voice plays out of the machine, echoing around the empty flat with only the recorded hollowness and shitty little speakers to indicate that he is not, in fact, here. He sounds exhausted. His voice is reedy and mumbled. Great pauses yawn between words.

"Sorry it's so late. I just, I needed to talk to you. Some things have happened. Something – I can't even begin to go into it now but it's bad Nina. It's really bad. I... There's a... I think... That's why I'm calling so late, I mean. I think you might be in danger. It's Roberta. I've heard things, really bad things about her and I don't know what she's planning to do but I know she was behind what happened to you and I've met people and they've told me things. It's not just her. Her clients. She uses them. That police officer that was hanging around the hospital – Frame – I think he's one of her patients. And... stuff and... So please give me a call as soon as you can. And if you can't just, just try and be careful. Be really careful. I hope you're okay. I do hope you're okay. And... I love you Nina. I do."

"To hear the message again, press..."

Nina stays leaning on the arm of the couch while she listens to the instruction menu. She doesn't press any of the numbers. It stops all by itself. And when it is finished she stays like that for a moment longer. Then sits up and breathes a big ragged sigh. Emotions are crowding below her cheeks, threatening to break out. She wants to know what has happened to him. And as disturbing as the information about Frame is, she still needs to check her facts before she can proceed. Because Sam, the way he's talking, his actions, the late night phone call, none of it seems healthy. And whether it's out of exhaustion, concern for Sam, or desperation for her own situation, she drops her face into her hands and has a little cry. When it stops she should feel better, but all she feels is numbness. Detachment. Like she is watching herself. Like she is the real Nina, the Nina from before the accident, not the weak, emotional victim sitting on her couch with a plaster on her leg and red-ringed eyes. She is the Nina from before. The Nina that no longer exists.

By 9:30 a clerk has run round with the file. After a brief stop to enquire after her welfare – in which she tells him nothing – he leaves. It is not soon enough. The moment the folder is in her hands, Nina is itching to be alone.

And then she's sitting at the table with the folder in front of her. And her hands are so slick with sweat that the cardboard outer slips from her fingers when she tries to turn it. The label on the front reads The Crown v Sam Peoples.

Opening statement: We are here today to try Sam Peoples for the murder of his wife, Caroline Peoples, on Tuesday 6th June 2008. Mr. Peoples is charged with Murder in the first degree. Mr. Peoples how do you plead?

Mr. Peoples: Not guilty.

Cross Examination:

Q: How would you characterise your relationship with the victim, your wife, Caroline Peoples?

A: She was my wife. I loved her. We had been married for a year before she got ill and I looked after her during her increasingly debilitating illness for the past year. I did this because I loved her. I would do anything for her.

Q: And your wife had cancer? She was going to die?

A: Yes.

Q: How did you feel about that?

A: It was horrible. I was grief-stricken. Watching her get worse day by day. It's the worst thing I've ever seen.

Q: And how do you think she died?

A: I don't know.

Q: What do you mean you don't know?

A: I mean I can't remember what happened. The last thing I remember is standing in the room with her. And then she was dead. And it was the next day.

Q: Did you kill her?

A: I would never have done anything to harm her.

Q: Does that mean you did not kill her?

The defendant does not answer.

Q: Mr. Peoples, if you did not kill her then why did you tell the emergency services operator that you had?

The defendant collapses.

Coroner: The victim died of asphyxiation. In my opinion there can be no doubt about that. In addition there was some mild bruising around the nose and cheeks that seems to be consistent with her being smothered by a pillow. Although I could not say that this was definitely the method by which the victim's life was ended. What is certain is that her death was by no means natural. She could have lived for another two to six months had she continued under the level of care that she was receiving, which I am told was excellent.

A ringing drags Nina out of the black hole that has opened up in the pages. She stares at the phone. Each ring louder than the last. She doesn't know what she's going to say to him. Even the effort of reaching thc phone is terrifying. But there's a limit to how long she can put this off. She drags herself up and levers herself onto her crutches. And of course, before she can reach the handset, it rings off. She takes a deep breath. Closes her eyes. And calls him back.

"Nina, oh thank God, are you okay?"

"Well, I don't know about okay but..."

"And nothing, no-one's been... nothing's happened to you?"

Nina can't help a dry laugh, "Not today, no."

"I need to see you."

Words stick in her throat. Her mind empties of thought. She needs to know more. She isn't sure.

"Nina?"

"Sam, there's something I need to talk to you about –"

But he comes in over her: "Nina, something really bad has happened and I... Can I just come over and talk to you about it?"

"What? What is it? What happened?"

"I'd really rather tell you face to face."

"You can't say now?"

Background noise. If it wasn't for the sound of his breathing she might think the line had gone dead. And whether it is wrong or right she feels a swell of emotion, like she owes him this at least.

"Okay, come over."

She puts the phone down. A tightening begins in her chest. She clutches herself. Her breath shortens. Blooms of red and black flower in her vision. And for a moment she worries that she might stop breathing completely. But she takes control, tries to breathe in and out steadily and just focus on her breath. The panic subsides, but still, when she holds her hands up she notices that they are shaking. She is terrified. Every instinct tells her that Sam couldn't possibly be a danger to her but the weight of so many coincidences and ifs and buts and almosts and maybes is hard to dismiss. She considers taking some measures, some precautions. Wishes she had arranged their meeting in a public place. Thinks about calling the police but what is she going to say? My boyfriend's coming round and I think he might be out of his mind? She could call one of the clerks, ask him to come round as a kind of chaperone...

Nina shakes herself. Laughs at herself. She's being ridiculous. After all, what does the case file say? It says that Sam smothered his wife because he couldn't bear to watch her die a slow and painful death. And as a result of that he went a little bit crazy. Understandably. But he's been in therapy for years and now he's better. So. Fine. All good. This big dark secret seems hardly relevant. What bothers her most about it is that he hasn't ever told her. Although she can understand why he wouldn't want to talk about it. And anyway, he's coming round. She can ask him. Fine. All fine. In fact, when she thinks about it, the only mystery left is the question of who ran her over. And despite the lack of evidence in any direction, she's pretty sure it couldn't have been Sam. He doesn't have a shadow of a motive. Unlike some people. Unlike this stalking mass of question marks. This Neil Allen. And anything that the policeman Frame says is questionable. He has behaved inappropriately and unprofessionally. The idea that he's one of Roberta's patients doesn't seem all that far-fetched.

Because there's the thing. As long as Sam's beliefs about Roberta prove to be correct, then all they have to do is act. All she has to do is help him. As long as they are. But if they're not? If it's all one big fantasy? Does she even believe them herself?

She doesn't want to think about it. She stops herself, pinching the thought to stem its growth. After all, there's no point in thinking about it. He's coming round anyway.

The lift pings. Sam stops halfway down the corridor. There's no reason why its coincidental arrival should give him pause so, but something about it feels ominous. He waits for the doors to open and wonders why he should automatically think the worst about such a small thing. It could be a good omen: the lift arriving just as he arrives at it, a chariot easing his way, speeding up his departure from the building. And a Roberta-like thought pops into his head: maybe he doesn't really want to go, maybe he's scared of the confrontation that is bound to come, of what he must do, and maybe that's why this timely arrival has him nervous. He scowls. This kind of thinking flies in the face of everything sensible. After all he's been through there's only one thing he wants and it's here before him, about to yawn open and swallow him into a future of bright possibility.

The hiss of the lift doors. The gap widens, spreading its yellow light out into the hallway, and a figure is revealed within. Bit by bit. Black shoes buffed to a high polish. Pin-striped trouser leg fading underneath matching jacket. Brash lines of colour coruscating inwards through the spectrum of city shirt. Open collar revealing thin gold chain upon which Sam knows a wedding ring hangs out of sight. Head inclined with its sharp haircut and brow protruding over sunken eyes. A five o'clock shadow darkening the acne-scarred jaw.

"Hello Sam," says Neil. "Glad I caught you." His mouth curves into a cocky smile and he swaggers out of the lift, a hand extended. "Where you off to? Anywhere nice?"

But Sam doesn't take his hand. He couldn't if he wanted to; his arms are plastered to his sides.

"You being funny with me mate?"

And still, Sam says nothing.

"Look, I just wanted to come by. Been a bit worried about you. Heard a few things."

Sam stares at him, searching the man for some clue, looking for any signs. Is this the Neil that he hung out with, laughed and joked with, colluded with? Or is it Roberta's pawn, the body that drove the car that ran over his girlfriend? Is Neil, the real Neil, is he really there at all?

"Mate, are you, is there something up with us?"

A hiss of air escapes from between Sam's teeth, "Things. You heard things. Where did you hear them from? Roberta?"

"She's worried about you."

"She shouldn't have even been talking to you about me. Not that I give a shit. If I was to tell you the things that have happened in the last few days – the things I've seen. Shit, Neil, I don't even know what you'd..."

"You should go back to her. You should see her."

Sam stops for a moment, pulls himself out of the conversation. And he stands back and he looks at the man in front of him. He thinks about the morality of telling Neil what he saw him do while he was absent from his own body. This man is self-assured, he believes he knows who he is, and he has come all this way, out of the goodness of his heart, to try and help someone he believes to be his friend. It occurs to Sam that this Neil, the real Neil, may have no more proprietary right over himself than Roberta does. He wonders how long he spends as himself and how long his body is on loan. The other things that Roberta might do with him. Perhaps she uses him to earn her money in the city. He might be diverting funds towards her, making investments for her. And Sam can imagine this situation being the other way round if the circumstances were different. It makes it hard to blame Neil – almost as hard as it is not to.

Enough of this. He has somewhere to be. There is no time for this distraction. Without even making his excuses, Sam steps towards the lift.

An arm bars his path. An inch away from him, Neil's eyebrows are arched, head tilted. An expression so patronising, so disempowering that it riles Sam. And he is about snap something at him but then another thought clouds his mind, smothering the rage: the timing. Neil has turned up just as he is leaving to go to Nina's. It stinks of Roberta's reach. The way in their sessions she could always say what Sam was thinking at the exact moment he was about to start thinking it. He feels horribly powerless. She will always be one step ahead of him.

"Did she ask you to come here? Do you know where I'm going?"

"She's right to be worried about you, isn't she?"

"I really have to go."

But Neil doesn't budge.

"Why don't we go back into your place? Sit down. Talk. Hey, just half an hour, then you can go. Half an hour, yeah, that's all. What's the difference?"

Sam shudders to think about what could go on elsewhere in that half an hour, "Look, I really have to go."

He moves the arm out of his way. Neil sighs. His shoulders drop.

"Mate, I'm trying to help."

And Sam feels it's only right to muster a friendly smile, "We can walk and talk if you like, but I can't dawdle."

Sam hits the call button. Far below, he hears the cables start to churn and the carriage rising through its cavernous shaft. He doesn't feel the hands grabbing him.

Neil swings him around, throwing him against the wall. Thrusts his face towards him. The expression there is not aggressive. It is passive, balanced, the eyes clear and focussed. Is this the face of someone not in control? It could be. So disconnected from the action. Perhaps a switch has been flicked. But then, he's so present...

"Don't go," says Neil. "It can't go well. Not for either of you. Not now."

Sam glares back at him, seething. The lift pings and the doors slide open. He lurches towards them but Neil holds him fast, putting himself between Sam and the doors.

"What are you on about?" Sam pants.

"I think you know."

"Do you even know what you're talking about?" And now he's lost his rag. There's no holding back. Not for Neil's sake. And why should there be? This man has been an instrument of terror. "I've seen you do things. You've done terrible things and you don't even know it. Do you even remember when I last saw you?"

"Yeah. At my flat. With what's-her-face."

"Do you remember us leaving?"

"Yeah. Sorry. I think I..." He pauses, thinking back. "I kind of chucked you out, didn't I? I had some shit I had to take care of."

"Yeah. And what was that 'shit' you had to take care of?"

Neil wavers. The resolution crumbles from his face. He looks down at the floor, as if he might find pieces of it there. His hands fall away from Sam and he stands, lost in contemplation. From this angle it's difficult to see his expression but Sam gets a sense of cogs whirring inside, processing and analysing information.

"I know where you were. I followed you," says Sam.

Neil looks up at him, brow furrowed. And then the knot relaxes and an openness resides in his face. Perhaps relief that he is about to have his problem answered, the gap in his memory filled. It fills Sam with pity. Makes him feel the need to sugar-coat the pill,

"Neil, it's not just you. It's all of us. Me included. I've done awful things. Things that are perhaps worse. Definitely worse. You know," he takes several deep breaths, "Neil, you know Rosanna? I think I killed her."

Neil's head rolls from side to side, his open expression opening further and his eyes widening. He looks stoned. It could be a moment of profound revelation. The pieces slotting into place. Could be, because it's more like a parody of said moment. And then a low laughter gurgles deep in the trader's guts. It doesn't rise. It just stays there, rumbling, as his face returns to its familiar sneering set.

And he says, "Oh, and I suppose you're going to tell me now that you followed me and then I ran over your girlfriend and that it's all Roberta's doing, that she's been puppeting me into doing all sorts of heinous acts."

Sam is taken aback.

"Shame about that Rosanna," Neil adds with a dirty snigger, his eyes looking up to the spot in his brain where the images of her are filed. "Terrible waste of pussy. But I suppose it had to be one or the other of you. And you can't begrudge Roberta her favourites." His face splits into a lopsided moon of teeth. "After all, she fucked you, didn't she?"

"Neil..." Sam stares at him, incredulous. "Are you even there?"

"More there than you are."

"That... what? There's no way she could have chosen. The way it happened... We both should have died. It's sheer dumb chance that I got out."

"Nothing is dumb chance. She knows everything. Controls everything. Believe me, it always comes out the way she wants it."

Neil's cockiness and swagger have vanished. There is such

conviction in this statement that it makes everything else he says seem like he knows it's bullshit the moment he says it. And it terrifies Sam. He's facing a true believer.

"So you do work for her."

"I wouldn't call it that. But I let myself be her instrument, yes."

Sam's teeth grind together. He feels an urge to lash out, to destroy this man. There is an evil in him so deep he is only rottenness, black and spongy and foul-smelling beneath the skin. But he holds back. Because Neil is still talking. And there are things he wants to hear.

"I don't really believe Roberta cures people, Sam. Do you? But that doesn't matter to me. 'Cos she fills my life. You see, Roberta, she's a player of games. She shuffles us all about – intermingles our paths, gives a new richness and meaning to our lives. And by being awake to it, I get to see it all. Who knows what her motives are, why she does it, but before I started seeing her, my life was just go to work, come back, watch telly, rinse and repeat. Everything was dull and colourless and tasteless and boring. Every person, every relationship. But now, when she allows me a glimpse, I get to see beneath the skin like she does and, well, everything just kind of sparkles.

"You know how many ways she has of controlling you? It's not just hypnosis, not just suggestion. There's a whole world of stuff. She can populate your environment with people that do what she wants and they think they're doing it because it's what they want. I mean no-one really knows what they want. They want to be told what they want. We all do. Even me. Heh. Especially me."

Sam's gut churns.

"I've seen her turn whole families upside down." He shrugs, like he's talking about flipping pancakes. "There was one woman once who was a housewife. Tall, elegant, you know, the sort of cunt you just want to punishment fuck. She had this whole perfect life. Floating about like she was little miss fucking perfect. Kids, rich husband. Pillar of her social scene. Anyway, thing is, down beneath it all, she had these dark desires, right? Like she wanted to peel people's skin off and eat them. The sickest shit would come out in her sessions."

"How do you know what she said to Roberta in her sessions. Isn't it all supposed to be confidential?"

"Oh yeah, you reckon? Most the time I'm there with her, she's just telling me shit. All the crazy shit you retards come out with. But I guess there's confidence in a way – she'll only tell this to people in the network she can trust – and there's only a handful of us, a few of us that can do this awake, consenting. She loves us best of all."

He's glowing now, hands on hips, chest puffed out.

"The network?"

"That's what she calls it, yeah."

"And you... you're awake?"

"You could try it Sam. I know she'd love it if you wanted to go that way. I mean, come on, face it what else have you got to live for? Wake up. Become one of us."

He grins. Wiggles his head with his hands held up and his fingers crooked and says "one of us, one of us" like the whole thing's one big fucking joke.

"Anyway, so this bitch, yeah – the housewife – well, Roberta sees that all her dark shit's coming from the fact that actually she sees her life as one big prison. That really she just wants to run wild like some crazy teenager – which of course she never did when she was a teenager. So instead she gradually introduces her to a whole bunch of men in the network. And a few of us knew what was going on obviously, most didn't though, thought they were doing stuff 'cos they wanted to or weren't even aware of it – like they'd forget the next day and just wake up feeling strangely satisfied and can't stop smiling. 'Cos Roberta's got this cow fucking everyone. At first I think she had her do it under hypnosis and stuff, like she was sleep walking, heh, sleep-fucking, but once that seal was broken and it woke up that desire, she just can't stop – and so she'd do her rounds. And then she'd go back to her husband and pretend like everything's normal. And of course this produces a whole new set of complexes – guilt and shit, so really in her head she's just feeling worse and worse, probably worse than when she started therapy in the first place. But she doesn't know that Roberta's got shit-all to do with all of her fucking. And so she just keeps going and when she leaves each time maybe she feels a bit better, maybe she doesn't, but then of course she reckons it's helping her, like shit-tasting medicine or something."

Neil pauses for breath and tucks his chin into his chest for a self-satisfied chuckle. "And I tell you something," he says, "she was the best fuck on the planet. And the more fucked-up, the better she got."

"What happened to her?"

"Oh, it didn't end well," Neil says with a tiny smile that could almost be described as sad.

"What? Divorce? I mean that was obviously what needed to happen right? That was the problem?"

"You don't get it. It's not about problems."

"So?"

Neil draws his finger across his neck.

"She died? She..." Then he understands. "She killed herself?"

"Guess it all got too much for her."

That dark black laughter again, like oil in the depths of the earth. Only now it erupts into a broad cackle. And Sam can't stand it. The sound makes his brain fizz and spit like it is being fried.

He kicks Neil in the balls. Hard as he can. It's an impulse. He doesn't know where it comes from, it just happens automatically. Only this isn't anything to do with him being controlled. It's not some hypno-kick. This is deliberate; an uncensored physical expression of a subconscious need. And when Neil staggers back, Sam shoves him up against the opposite wall and his arm flies out and his fist connects with the man's face. There's a dull slap and Neil's head bumps back and dents the wall. Sam's other arm swings. And he swings and swings again and it's like he's not even doing it. He's never done this to anybody in his life. But he's in control there, sitting in the driver's seat. And he has the vague idea that the impacts should hurt his hands but he can't feel the contact. He just hears the sounds: the slapping of flesh, the cracking within it; the gurgles and the groans the impacts produce. And when Neil drops down to the floor he kicks him once, twice...

"You don't get it."

The words jerk Sam out of his red mist and he looks down at the battered man who, bizarrely, is smiling up out of the mess of his face and the tooth-cracked grin looks as incongruous there as bullion shining out through a heap of manure.

"Sam." He is somehow still coherent. His body is hurt but it hasn't dented him inside, like his ego is made of concrete, or not there at all. "I didn't come here to fuck with you. I like you. Honestly, I do," he spits blood onto the linoleum, "even now, I do. Heh. Look, if you go to Nina, shit is going to kick off. Shit in you. You don't even know all the things she's implanted in you. You could blow up, you're a fucking IED waiting to be stepped on. Get it? You can't trust yourself."

Sam narrows his eyes. He is so full of boiling, conflicting feelings that he can't respond, or even sort one thought out from the others. All he can do is stand and listen to Neil and smell the rankness of blood and sweat and salt in the air as the ache starts to creep into his knuckles and spread up through his hands.

"Or go. What do I care? I've done my best. I tried to get you to listen and you beat the shit out of me for it. Who gives a shit. I still like you though, Sam. Go on. Go to her. Go and explode. Hey, maybe then you'll be ready."

"Ready for what? To be," and the word sticks in his mouth like a hair in his food "'awake'?"

"Nah. You're already awake."

Chapter Seven

THE MUSIC OF THE SPHERES

Sam stands in the doorway to his block watching the street. It pops with bleached highlights as the sun bounces off cars and windows and billboards and it hurts his eyes to look at it all. There it sits. The world. Fresh air. Freedom. The path to Nina. All he needs to do is lift his foot over the threshold and take four easy steps down to the pavement. But it all seems too brash and loud and threatening. He feels like a subterranean creature when it unexpectedly breaks ground. If he was anxious before, now he has ten-times the reasons to be so. He tries to take that first step. But his foot won't move. A group of teenage boys and girls bounces past, their voices loud and obnoxious. "Such a fucking dick" one of them says and for a fraction of a second Sam mistakenly takes it as being aimed at him. Fucking, fucking, fucking. Every other word an expletive. Like punctuation. Sam tries to remember what it was like to be that age, but his memory won't go back past the last half an hour.

He observes that he is already distracting himself. Ruminating on irrelevancies. And yet still he hasn't taken that one step. It's no wonder Neil didn't physically stop him – and surely he could have, he's in much better shape than Sam is – he didn't need to. That wasn't what he came for. All he needed to do was plant enough in Sam's mind that he'd start second-guessing himself, analysing and reanalysing every move, every thought. Which is exactly what he is doing. This in itself is enough to produce the inertia necessary to prevent him from doing what he knows he needs to.

And he hates himself for stalling this way. He screws his eyes shut, swallows his nerves and lifts his foot an inch at a time, each one painful and frightening. And then he moves it forward. And he feels the outside air through his trouser leg, breezing past. And in the darkness, he brings his foot down, not even sure if it will find the step. It's a leap of faith. A necessary one.

He finds himself standing on the pavement. He knows, cognitively, how he got there, but those four steps between here and the ground – he can't really remember taking them. He turns and stares at them like they are strange, alien objects. There is a tiny gap in his memory. He could join the dots between A and B and go on and forget all about what is, ultimately, an insignificant detail – but it isn't there. It just isn't there. Sam lifts his hands in front of his face and sees that they are trembling. He honestly can't say if it's nerves or whether he's wired or scared or something else. But they are shaking – more vibrating.

The colours and sounds surround him now and he feels naked in front of them. He turns 360 degrees and sees that the street is busy. People to-ing and fro-ing, bustling past each other, each one's desire conflicting with all of the others, literally and physically manifested by the confusion that is created when they cross paths or collide. But there's more than that. Sam feels singular. Apart from them. And beneath all their hurrying it's like they can sense it. When he turns to see a mother with a pushchair, or a street cleaner, or a student hurrying with a record bag flapping over his shoulder, they look the other way the moment he looks at them.

It has to be all in his head. It has to be. But he can't help thinking that some of it might not be. He can almost sense Roberta's "network" running through the crowds, a web of tissue, microscopic and thin and connecting throughout the arteries of the city, covering every inch of it. What are the chances that someone there is her eyes or her ears, silently tracing his movements and passing them on with a quick text or a phone call the moment his back is turned?

Across the road the newsagent is standing outside the front of his shop, smoking a cigarette. His hand is folded into his armpit, shirt-sleeves rolled up, eyes sweeping the street, observing the human traffic in his mini-break. And then he notices Sam and their eyes connect, broken only by the blurs of cars moving between them over the asphalt gulf that separates them. Sam's gaze lingers on the man a moment too long. He needs to justify it. Not look weird. And so he proffers a succinct and wholly fake smile of the kind it is natural to give to sight-acquaintances. And with it a little wave. But the newsagent doesn't return it. Instead he drops his eyes with his cigarette to the pavement and crushes it out with his foot. Turns and disappears into the shop. What's he doing out there? Who is that guy? He's always around. All hours. Right across the road. Always watching. Staring with those jaundiced little eyes.

Sam shakes his head and chastises himself for being ridiculous. He puts the newsagent out of his mind. Despite the sunshine, a breeze whips up and cuts right through him. And all of a sudden he's desperate to move, to get away from this place. He can see his car. It's only metres away, just a handful of steps and he can duck into the sanctuary of his portable private space. Foot follows foot follows foot. He reaches into his pocket and hits the button and the car's indicators flash as he closes the last few feet.

He's there. Hand on the handle. Pulls it. The clunk of plastic and metal and the door is open a crack and he can smell the inside of the vehicle and he's about to step in. But he doesn't. The car is sending off great waves of anxiety. A sign flashing in front of his eyes. Warning. Warning. Warning. Bright red. Cars. Convenience of the modern age. Putting the power of accelerated travel at man's fingertips, and at the same time exposing him to dangers that are frequently overlooked. He becomes vulnerable to the slightest motion, the slightest miscalculation. A wrong impulse, a moment of self-destructive thought, and he can twist the wheel and send himself into oblivion. And twice Roberta has exploited this: once with him, once with Neil. Made them marionettes at a moment when they are at once vulnerable and deadly. What's to stop it happening again? It's an easy place for her to strike. All it takes is a push. How many others has she used in this way? How many cars have turned to weapons, operated by proxy, trigger pulled at a remove. How many road accidents, injuries, deaths can this woman be held responsible for? He decides not to give her the chance. And walks.

On the tube he finds a strange peace. Having chosen public exposure over the threat of auto-execution, he had expected to contend with the stares of strangers for the entirety of the journey. But thankfully it is not so. He has been rewarded for taking the path of caution. And he allows himself a little smile at this tiny victory.

With the entire carriage to himself, Sam leans back in the seat and stretches out his legs. The artificial lighting is less aggressive than the bright daylight outside. There is a comforting uniformity about this space, with its seats upon seats and its poles spaced at regular intervals. Wide Plexiglas panes stretch along in rows, like giant screens that turn trees and shabby trackside houses into a uniformity of motion. And the motion itself becomes so steady and solid that it barely feels like he is moving at all. The world is moving around him, perhaps, but he feels grounded. The one constant in the midst of all this transience. And it lulls him into a Zen-like space on the border of consciousness and his unconscious. A place where thoughts flow and come and go with ease. And in this space his mind begins to open and images, memories, isolated fragments disembodied from the flow of his personal history float up at him, where they begin to coalesce and new meanings become possible.

The car crash passes through his mind without emotional disturbance or interpretation. Roberta's phone call. The dream. "The one you always have." Roberta in her chair. Rosanna's blood-soaked face turns to him, matted around by a frame of hair. But it does not give rise to horror or revulsion. He just sees her. Sees her the way she looked in his mind's eye. Sees her the way she appeared in reality, trapped in a contortion by her seat. There are two Rosannas. One that he dreamt of. One that really lived and died. Their images are so similar and yet they are separate entities. And even as he brought about the death of one, he was seeing the other. Rosanna. Rosanna. Roberta. The similarity of their names. The closeness of the letters. Seven letters. Can letters alone hold a meaning other than their arrangements? Surely the cross-pollination should tell him something. Or maybe meaning isn't the important thing. Maybe it doesn't matter whether coincidence or design, divine or otherwise, is at work. Maybe all that matters is that the observation steers him in a certain direction. The collision of things. Of women. Of spaces. Of cars. Roberta riding above him, hungry, maternal, fleshy. Rosanna as desirable in death as Roberta is repulsive at her most alive. Repulsive and desirable at once. Tight jeans, lipgloss, smooth strong limbs. Bloated, soft flesh that consumes and envelops. One appeals to the eye. But the other appeals to the touch. And thinking about it, Sam notices that he is semi-hard and re-tucks himself, adjusting in his seat for comfort. And he has no idea which memory has engorged him. Nor does he care. He tries to think of Nina, but none of those memories come to him. Trying to think seems to be something he is not capable of now. He can only observe his thoughts. And Nina is not there. Not now. *The one he always has*. When was the first time he had this dream? Did he ever dream of Roberta in that way? Had she entered the realm of sexual fantasy before she entered sexual reality. He is not sure. But he finds it hard to believe that a woman like that, who figures so large in his life and is so proportioned could not have crossed his mind in that way. For as much as she is unattractive to him, her ballooning curves are undeniably sensual. Her very form speaks of sensuality. A sensuality that it appears commonly eludes her. And when did he first have that dream? It feels like it has belonged to him forever. Since before he ever met Roberta. And yet he knows it hasn't. He knows that it only entered his mind when it was "discovered". And something slides out of the shadows and emerges into the light, rearing up huge and obvious. And it is almost a glorious thing. Rosanna. He has had no congress with her. All of his sexual thoughts about her belonged exclusively to his imagination. But now he pictures, almost feels, a tangle of limbs. An intertwining. It was not a sexual act, it was an act of mutual violence, of their bodies upon each other, their bodies stolen from them and used against each other. And still, they were in there. And it was congress. He was on top of her. Their arms and legs clawed and pulled each other close. As close as lovers. Closer even. An act engineered at some time unknown to them both.

Sam is in a lounge chair. An armchair. On a couch. He sits in the stillness and darkness of a room. Others are there with him. And he is as an empty vessel. Thoughts pour through him then as they do now, without stopping, without latching on, without meaning or consequence or the need for action. He sees himself at a remove. As an astral projection. A sixth body in that room, standing in the corner and watching the others sit in silent communion. He can see the flow of shared thought between them – a ring of ideas that pour from one mind to another to another to another to another to another and back again. Rosanna in her pyjamas. Four dark men brooding in dark clothes, their shoes heavy and wet, the carpet marked by their footprints. Footprints. She never mentioned the footprints. There are things we see and do not see. And the peace in the room is an intense peace. Is it that thoughts are flowing wordlessly between the minds of the sitters, or is it simply that their minds contain the same thoughts? That they know they contain the same thoughts. Is that enough? To sit with thoughts in perfect synchrony? Thoughts that are not their own but have been programmed. And a unique sense of fulfilment comes from that. Like singing in a choir. Hearing one's own voice in harmony with others'.

Rosanna she did not see the footprints. What else did she not see? What did he not see? In his pocket his hand plays with his keys, separating them out and feeling them one at a time. He can picture the bunch of keys but to his blind fingers it appears that there are more than he would have thought. If he was asked to name all the keys on his key ring, could he? If he drew a picture and compared them, would that picture be complete? How did he get into Rosanna's flat all those nights. How did she get into his? Or did they let each other in? Is it possible that the senses lie – or can be fooled? Eminently possible, it seems. And he would agree with that statement even under normal circumstances. What else have they done that they have not seen? How many actions have been performed in the grey shadows beyond awareness?

And he is sitting in Roberta's chair.

He is sitting in Roberta's chair. And she asks him what he dreams of. She intones it in a low tone and her words slip and are liquid and do not hold up to any examination or substance or reality. They are ideas that split like mercury and separate into tiny balls, running away into the grooves and gutters and grey shadows in the corners of the room. Sam sinks into the chair, listening to her, his eyes burning bright and keen from his face, which blurs and becomes a blank mask marked only by two shining buttons.

She speaks of progress and recovery and Sam feels warm and held. She joins his mind and speaks of a journey across a landscape that is dark and how the destination is not important, only the journey. There is no destination, no light at the end of the tunnel. But there will be light. You will travel and the light will come. Night will give way to morning and the road will become bright. So bright that it blinds you. And in some ways the darkness is safe but the sun will always rise just as it will always set, the only question is whether you keep on moving and it is up to you whether you do that. Whether you move or stand still. There will be others that will carry you with their momentum but the journey is yours, to stop at any time. Because not everybody stops to see the sights. And the sights you want to linger on may be different to the sights that other people consider relevant. The power is always yours. You can exist in peace or in chaos and neither one is good or bad, it is for you to choose what you need at what time.

And the daylight disappears, sucked into blackness as the screens go blank. Instead, the inside of a tunnel. The occasional light shooting past – each one switching a new screen on and off. A new image. Sam sees himself. Himself in the space, in the empty tube carriage. The edge of the window cuts off his head. He is only a body, arms and legs and a trunk. And he lowers his head, adjusting his perspective and his own eyes come into view. And they flicker like screens – as if the tube windows have inhabited them. And contained in their reflections the reflection of a reflection. He sees himself in the space, the space in himself, reflected and swapped to an infinite degree. Always watching and watching himself. How many iterations are there? As many as there are small words that connect and coalesce to create greater pictures when they become a whole. Little words planted by Roberta, not just under hypnosis, but right there in front of his mind. You will visit other lives but you will always come back to your own.

The first time he steps into that room. Sits in that chair. We will take a journey together. If we are to complete this journey, you must trust me absolutely. This is a safe space. A safe space. She tells stories, parables to illustrate. Names that he will not remember. Let's call her Rosanna. Let's call him Neil. Or Jonathan. She has a need for acceptance. He has desire. They are empty. They find things buried in the world, in the lives of others.

And Sam slams up from his seat, jerking to his feet and staggering wildly, completely unbalanced, the train throwing him half across the carriage as it pulls to a halt. Sam grabs a pole to stop himself from falling. And he sees himself white-faced in the reflection. It is only instinct that has stopped him falling. His body has acted on its own to save him. Because his mind is occupied. The pattern of instructions and images. And certain things are so painfully clear now. The placing of a dream through suggestion. Wrest the wheel from your co-travellers. The woman beside you is driving the car. But only if you let her. Who is that woman? Is it Caroline? Or is it someone else? If a blaze of glory is what you want then you must take it. Her way is not your way. Her life is not your life. Your life is your own.

The name of the station fades through Sam's reflection. He is here. He has arrived. It is time to get off the train. Time for Nina. Time to save her. To save them both.

Nina's leg is trembling in its cast. The inside of the plaster sucks at her skin with a million little kisses. The knock comes a second time. And even though she has already buzzed him in she says, "Who is it?" whether as some kind of nervous tick, or super-caution she does not know. The tension in her is unbearable and she longs to be out of this moment. Give me the next second or the one after that, she thinks, because the one that I occupy now is untenable.

Sam identifies himself and her heart leaps. Her hand leaps to the doorknob and twists and the door is disappeared like a curtain drawn aside and in its place there stands her Sam.

But is he hers? He doesn't quite look like her Sam. He looks similar, but somehow changed. She doesn't know what it is; if she had to specify, she couldn't say. She could say that it is everything. Or she could say that it is nothing. He hangs loosely on his frame. Like a sheet on a pole. A ghost in the trees. Perhaps he is just tired. Exhausted. His skin looks paler, not like the tone has really changed, but it has a translucency about it. And inside it something burns. If his outside appears more fragile, it seems that there is something stronger on the inside. He stands crooked in the doorway, his bony shoulders held at an angle that conflicts with the regularity of the doorframe and sets the space between him and it into an uncomfortable opposition. His face is like a shadow moving across an uneven gravel floor. Every tilt and movement provokes new shades and expressions so that it becomes impossible to read him. Even the smile, so full of gladness and love, tells her nothing.

And when he steps forward his upper carriage shambles, languid arms swaying, unfixed. And with proximity, she cannot help but be moved and love swells inside her. His arms throw themselves around her and she presses herself into the crook of his shoulder and a smile spreads shamelessly across her face. Inside the familiarity of his scent there lurks something else, something sour, tangy. Off-milk shot through with citrus. Infecting her, it mingles with her gladness, producing a bottom note of anxiety.

And when their eyes meet his gaze wobbles, jittering on the boundary of looking away. Every part of him is fluttering, his heartbeat irregular and febrile. There is a wariness, something giving him first-date nerves. As if he doesn't trust or believe in his own instincts. And in turn, this mistrust, this uncertainty manifests in her and her smile shakes and gives way, causing her to refresh it constantly. Like a flickering screen threatening collapse. It might disappear in a pop of static.

"Where have you been?" she asks. "What have you done?"

And he looks to the floor. And when their eyes meet again, his are more constant.

"I want to kiss you," he says. "I will. But not now. I just want you to know that I want to. But now I have to sit."

He shambles towards the couch, fingers trailing through hers until they slip away and his arm swings loosely to join the rest of his body. Reaching the couch he does not flop, as she expects, but sits, straight-backed. And his eyes move across the floor and up along the wall until they stop, staring at some other space not visible to her. The translucency of his skin warms and becomes more solid looking. Like he is recollecting his humanity. Building himself back up. In this strange moment of suspension, the flat becomes entirely quiet and all Nina can hear is the sound of his breath: slowing, becoming more steady, the ins and outs elongating until the shaking of the air in his system is entirely eliminated. And then it seems he is at peace. Still.

"Would you," she is unsure whether it is wise to break the silence, "like a cup of tea, or..."

Why is she so unsure of herself? This is not like her at all. Sam is unresponsive. Just sitting and breathing. She starts towards the kitchen anyway. Freezes as a sudden movement of his head brings his focus back to her.

He smiles. "That would be nice."

The teaspoon jangles against the side of the teacup. Nina tries to still her hand. But all she can think is "Oh God, this is so fucking weird". The crutches dig into her underarms and she adjusts herself on them. Reaches for the cup, not quite sure yet how she's going to carry it, and the stray twitch of a nerve sends it spinning out of her fingers. Sam hears the cup smash in the next room. But it is as nothing to him. As incidental as the sound of a car outside. The honking of a stranger's horn somewhere far away. She has to call several times before he comes to help her.

"Sorry, had a little accident," she says with a nervous smile.

"It must be difficult," he says, from behind her shoulder.

"Yes, it is."

She perches on the arm of an armchair rather than taking the open space on the couch beside him. Sam lifts the mug to his lips. He blows on the tea to cool it and, peering over its edge at the wall, still not looking at her, he says, "We need to be careful."

"Of..."

"I don't want you to be alarmed," and now he looks at her and his eyes are wide and intense, "but I may not be myself." His mouth creases with a hint of a smile. "Although I am probably at less risk of not being myself than I have been."

"What exactly are you saying?"

"I'm saying that we need to proceed with caution. There is much to do, even more to talk about, but you need to understand that there are certain things that could act as, well, triggers, and that if I sense that we should skirt around something or suddenly change tack then it is important to take notice and follow suit."

He is so uncharacteristically in charge that she cannot help but listen attentively. She has never seen him like this. She didn't really think he was capable of it. It is something that might have ended their relationship one day had everything proceeded along its natural course. It makes him more attractive to her than he has ever been. And yet there is something deeply unsettling in that. Like finding that the pet she was holding is actually a lion. It might devour her. But it is a much cooler pet.

"If you notice any change in me," he continues, "sudden or otherwise. If I don't seem like myself. It might be good to get away from me. I'll contact you afterwards, when I am myself again."

"Right." Her jaw ticks. "Right Sam. Right. Are you trying to tell me that you now believe not only that Roberta is interfering in your life – our lives – making things happen *to* us, but that she is also controlling you?"

"Yes."

"Jesus." Her eyes pierce Sam for a second before they find the ceiling.

"I know it's a lot to swallow."

"A lot to..." Her breath hisses out between her teeth. "If. If what you believe is true, do you know how utterly shittingly terrifying that is? I've lain in that hospital bed hoping, praying that whoever ran me over was someone other than you. I very nearly, almost, you know, wasn't even going to see you. Not until I had this sorted in my head, but you know what? I gave you the benefit of the doubt. And now here you are telling me that you're not in control, that..."

And it's too much. She gives way. The floodgates open. An audible sob escapes her and her shoulders hunch and shake. She watches her fingers tying each other in knots and retying themselves. The floral pattern of her skirt below them. Blue and yellow petals on a background of white. And extending from under the hem one normal leg, foot unshod, and another, thick, heavy, off-white. Plaster cast.

She doesn't notice his shadow fall across her. And she jumps as his arms close around her. She looks up at him, her face all red and creased and wet-cheeked. And a thumb brushes her cheek to wipe a tear away and he touches it to his lips, before leaning in for a tighter hug.

Her body stiffens. She sits back. Her hand is on his chest, pushing him away.

"A," Nina sniffles, collects herself and begins the sentence again. "A policeman came to see me when I was in the hospital."

He returns to the couch. "Jonathan Frame?"

Nina nods.

"Don't believe anything he says. He's one of hers."

She sighs. Must everything she says be measured against his doctrine?

"Who ran me over? Was it you?"

"No. Of course not. I..."

"You said you're not always in control. You said... You said on the phone that you've done terrible things. And Frame, whoever he is, whether you can trust him or not, he seems pretty sure that you..."

"He doesn't know what he thinks!" Sam's façade gives way. A wave of anger directed not at Nina but at the orchestrator. "I couldn't do anything to hurt you. Not ever. That I'm sure about. That's why, don't you see, that's why she had to bring in someone else."

"Neil Allen."

"Nina I'm so sorry."

"You don't need to be sorry," she says in a ghostly monotone, "you didn't do it, did you?"

He doesn't know what to say.

"Frame told me something else," she continues, still in that thin and spectral tone. It's like she's only half there. And maybe she is. Maybe she's had to push herself away so that she can say what she needs to say: "He told me that you killed your wife."

"Caroline." He intones the word with a special reverence.

"He said you killed her, Sam."

"I told you, you can't believe anything he says."

"And I don't! I don't, Sam. I knew he was dodgy as soon as he started telling me these things. It's not how a police officer's supposed to act. He was for sure, definitely, a hundred percent trying to put ideas in my head. And I agree with you there. See, I agree. You're right. You're totally right." She pauses to get her breath. “But I had to follow it up, didn’t I? If there was a trial, if there was concrete evidence, then I had to look into it, right? You see where I’m coming from?”

“What trial?”

“What?” Her eyes are wide with amazement. “Did you... Sam, there was a trial. You gave testimony. You...”

His head shakes. Minute, tense little shakes. Nina hobbles over to the table and picks up the file. She clunks back towards Sam and thrusts it in front of his face.

“Look at it.”

But he doesn’t.

“Sam if you don’t turn round and look at this I’m going to wrap it round your head!”

She is beginning to ache from standing in this awkward position bent forward with one arm extended, holding the heavy file.

“Take it. Take. It.”

His fingers pry it from her as if he is being handed a bag full of dog shit. He drops it into his lap and shrugs: “What now?”

“You’re going to read it.”

And she hobbles back to her seat. He sits there with the file on his lap, ignoring it, watching her. Now there is uncertainty. Now he looks challenged. She glares pointedly at it. And he opens the front cover.

He flicks from sheet to sheet. Different documents, records, solicitors’ notes. His mouth curls like he’s chewing something disgusting. The sweat on his brow is not the kind that you get from physical exertion, not the healthy sheen of the pores expunging toxins. It doesn’t run. It beads and hangs there. She can see his back losing its straightness, and his upper body begins to sway. His eyes half-close, becoming lidded as if he has no energy and might fall asleep. But he doesn't. He keeps reading. And watching him is a kind of agony for her.

She has a constant urge to leap to her feet, swipe the file from his lap and send it flying out of the window, its leaves fluttering across the street below to be lost in rainy gutters and soaked into pavements. But they have to do this. It has to be brought out in the open.

And she recalls Sam's frustration at Roberta pressing him to rake over his past. At the time it seemed like she was trying to force something upon him that wasn't necessary. And it makes her think – even though she knows she shouldn't, won't, can't think it – that, far from trying to coerce him to stay in therapy, Roberta could have been onto something. Her expertise was telling her that there was something major still untouched, that Sam could not be cured – not as long as he still held this secret from himself. And just thinking this commutes Sam's nausea to Nina. Her stomach churns. The most horrible possibility rearing its head: that all of this has been a product of Sam's imagination, his mind throwing up an elaborate fantasy to prevent himself from engaging with the truth of his past.

And the ramifications: that all of the things he has done, everything, it has all been because of him, because of his sickness and ultimately it must have been Sam, her boyfriend, the man that she thinks she loves, that mowed her down with his car in broad daylight. When she looks at it like this it all seems so simple. Simple. Yes. It seems like the most simple and best explanation. Ockham's razor. And to her horror, she thinks not of calling the police or running away, but of how she can help him, what she might be able to do to make him get better so they can carry on and live a normal life together. Even after all the pain he has caused her.

No. No. Might have caused her. Might.

Because it's not, is it? It's not the simplest and best explanation. It leaves so many questions unanswered. So many loose ends. Why was Frame behaving the way he did? What about her stalker? What about Neil Allen? What about the coincidence that all of these things and people seem to be intimately connected to Roberta. That it all leads back to her. But as soon as these questions are posed, Nina finds her mind locating answers for them all. Isn't that the way policeman sometimes behave, trying to put ideas in witnesses' minds in order to secure a conviction? Etcetera. And she stops herself. And with this slamming-to-a-halt of her thought process comes a swooning sensation and the churning in her stomach migrates up through her chest and into her head.

Sam is engrossed. He has committed himself to his ordeal. So she heaves herself to her feet and hobbles as fast as she can to the bathroom. In the solitude of the white-tiled room, she hangs there with her head over the sink, waiting for the nausea to complete. But it doesn't. Whatever is stuck inside of her refuses to come out. And all she can do is splash her face with water and wait for the sensation to ease.

When she returns Sam is nearly at the end of the file. She takes her seat on the edge of the armchair and after a few minutes he closes the back page of the folder and looks up at her.

"Where did you get this from?" he says.

"What? You think it was planted? That it's a fake? That it's all part of Roberta's great master plan?"

He doesn't rise to it.

"It's an official court document, Sam. I got it from the hall of records."

His mouth twitches like he's trying to get rid of a tiny fly. But there's something coming over him. A change in his face. It's sinking. His eyes become moist. And when he speaks it is with a cracked voice, "It was like reading about somebody else."

"Sam, I, look, this is really important: I'm not judging you. Even if you did... Whatever you did, I understand. Hell, the court understood didn't they. They were compassionate. They commuted your sentence. It was a really desperately sad thing and even if the law wasn't on your side then the moral weight was – they saw that then and what kind of lover, loved-one, fuck it, what kind of person would I be if I couldn't give you that? Anyone can understand why –"

"I didn't do anything!" He's on his feet, leaning towards her and his fingers jab aggressively at his own temple, "It's not in here. Don't you get that?"

Blood pumps through her arms and legs as his ferocity brings on her fight-or-flight reaction like a train. But she holds her ground.

"And that's the fucking problem, Sam. It's not that I'm worried that you're a murderer, or that you've got blood on your hands or... it's just... if you deny your own truth, if you can't even see it yourself, then how am I supposed to believe any of the things you've told me? Because if you're not in touch with reality, then, then what? I don't have any proof of anything. Not one thing. None of the things you've told me about, the things you say have happened. I haven't seen any of them. I haven't seen any evidence. Nobody else has corroborated anything you say. Shit, I haven't even met half of the people you talk about. The only one in this whole big old story I've met is Roberta – and you know what? She was right. She was on to you. She knew you had something you were hiding from."

"Yeah, and how do you think she knew?"

Nina's mouth hangs slack for a moment. "She was there. That's where you met her. The Ross and Waverly Clinic. So she knew exactly what you were hiding from. That, well, that makes her right. Doesn't it?"

Sam peels away, whirling in a circle. His arms fly out loose and wild. "No way! That's how she got her hooks in me. No way are you... You're not siding with her! You're..."

"I'm not siding with anyone."

And when he looks at her there's hurt and spite and anger in his face and his cheeks are burning red.

"I'm not. It's not about siding. I'd love it if you were right, but for my own sake I have to establish what's really going on here. Give me some proof. Give me anything."

"What, and my word's no good?"

"No." And now she makes the effort of lifting herself from the arm of the chair and propping herself up on her crutches, "Because your words, both in that courtroom and right here in my flat, right in front of me today, were that you loved Caroline more than anything in the world and you could never hurt her. But if you did..." and she's leaning close to him, her eyes clear and wide.

"If I could hurt her, what's to say I wouldn't hurt you?"

Nina's face crumples. She gives a tiny nod and rests her forehead against his. And she stays there like that and he just keeps whispering: "I wouldn't. I wouldn't. I promise I wouldn't hurt you."

"Is there anything you can show me?" she sniffles.

He places his hands either side of her head and looks directly into her eyes: "Yes."

Sam reaches into his pocket. He produces his keys, weighing them heavily in his hand like a bunch of grapes. He turns his hand over, sliding his finger through the ring and extends it, jangling them in front of her, as one might entertain a baby.

"What?"

"Take them."

She does. "Okay. They're keys."

"Hold them away. Count them."

Sam turns his head away.

"One, two, three,"

"Not aloud. To yourself."

"Sam, what the hell is this? You think this is the time for some stupid game?"

"It's not a game. Count. In your head."

And he walks away. Nina sits down and stares at his back. He is slumped, his shoulders rounded. She experiences a pervasive feeling of disappointment. It was always part of the deal that she would accept that he was a damaged person, a fragile soul on the precipice of recovery, but she had hoped that when occasion came, he would rise to it. The length and difficulty of his recovery had made her think that a strong man was waiting for her on the inside, ready to come out one day. And now she has the distinct impression that that strength was nothing more than a projection on her part. She is watching him trying to fight what is perhaps the hardest thing in his life, but none of it seems to her like a sign of strength. Because she is pretty damn well sure that he's just running away. That this effort is all in service of avoidance. And however much he pits himself against it, that's not strength, that's cowardice.

When she has finished counting the keys she says, "Done" with a washed-out sound to her voice.

"Okay. Do you know how many there are now? You've got the number in your head? Don't! Don't say it yet..."

His frown of concentration; the hands leaving his hips and rubbing together. He looks to her like a cheap stage magician about to perform a trick. All he's missing is the spangly jacket, the glamorous assistant. Oh, no, wait...

"I know, I know. You don't see the point yet but... Look, I counted them earlier, right. I counted eight. How many did you get?"

"There's fourteen keys here, Sam."

His eyes widen. If he's feigning surprise he's doing a bloody good job of it.

"What? Really?"

"Mm-hmm."

She throws them over to him. He counts them one by one, aloud. But his fingers skip some. Wilfully dropping stitches.

"Oh come on, Sam, you're not even doing it properly. Look, I've had enough of this fucking around..."

"No. No. Wait." He dashes across to her and crouches down to her level. She shrinks back as he touches her elbow. "I promise you, I'm counting eight. I can see it right here. Eight keys."

She's trying. She's really trying to engage with him but he's got this strange hyper manner about him and it's all a bit loopy.

"Come to the table. Come on." And he starts to lift her by the elbows. She hisses in discomfort.

"Wait, wait, wait." She places a hand on his chest, establishing a distance between them. "Hand me my crutch."

"It's okay, you can lean on me." And then he catches her offish squint. "You don't want to?"

"I'm sorry, I, look, it's just if I don't have my crutches then I feel like I can't get up when I want to. It makes me feel trapped. You know, like claustrophobia."

"Uh. Okay."

They settle opposite each other. He asks her to take all the keys off the ring and place them in a line across the table. She's not quite sure why she's still playing along with this charade. It's gone from annoying to tedious now and the sound of his voice is making her feel sleepy. As he instructs her to hold them up one by one, saying a number each time, she drops her head forward and pinches her eyes.

"Please bear with me, Nina."

She looks up at him and there's need in there, but there's also sincerity. Despite herself, she wants to see all this through to its conclusion as much as he does. Either way she wins. If he's right, he's right and there are things that they can do. If he's a basket case loser then she's got a licence to extract herself in one way or another. That Paul Simon song goes through her head. *Fifty ways to leave your lover*. She only needs one.

Nina's breath hisses backwards through her teeth. She hates thinking like this. She hates feeling like this.

"Alright, alright," she says, wriggling her shoulders to shake it all off, "Let's do this."

And she picks up the first key. "One."

"My flat. Front door. Chubb lock."

"Two."

"Car."

"Three."

He stares at her fingers. The hand inverted. The tips curving up and pinching together as if holding something.

"There's nothing there."

"Don't bullshit me, Sam."

"No. I really can't see it."

She frowns and turns the key towards her, peering at it as if it is something other than it is. But it isn't. It's just a key. And it's right there in her hand. She holds it out to him, "Take it."

And he reaches across the table. His hand stops an inch away from the key. He frowns in concentration but it sticks there. Like he is pressing against an invisible barrier.

"I... can't..."

"What do you mean, you can't?"

He's testing her patience now.

"I can't move any closer. I mean..." He grasps his wrist with his other hand and tries to move it but it won't go. "I can't see it but I can see your hand there, I can see where it should be but my hand, I don't know how to describe it, it just won't move."

"What do you see?"

"Nothing. I see nothing. Just your hand. Your fingers pinched together but there's nothing in it."

"And when you look at the table here?"

"A row of keys."

"Evenly spaced?"

"No. There are gaps."

She releases an audible sigh, almost a laugh. It's all too ridiculous. And unable to help the smile on her lips, she says, "Okay, turn your hand over. Hold it out flat."

He does.

"Right. I'm putting the key in your hand now. Do you feel it?"

He shakes his head. Now this is weird.

"Try. Just try and hold it in your fingers. Hold it up. Like I was."

He tilts his palm forward to slide it into his grip, then brings his thumb and fingers together as he twists his hand round. He's frowning in concentration, she can see that. But he misses the key. It clatters to the table, the sound jagged over the silence of their held breaths. It spins once and then comes to a rest. And Nina's eyes move up to Sam's hand, which is upright, the fingers pressed together.

"Am I holding it?"

"You didn't hear that? You didn't hear it hit the table?"

He shakes his head. She reaches for the key.

"Okay, let's try again."

She holds it out to him but he removes his hand, folding it into his other one on the table in front of them. The bare wood yawns between them.

"No. Try another one."

"Sure." She is about to add 'whatever' but catches herself and realises that she is getting caught up in the curiosity of this magic show. And that's a good thing. She's glad that the fog of antipathy is dispersing – and it doesn't really matter to her what is making that happen. She's just glad it's happening.

She places the key back in the line and reaches for the next one: "Four."

A nostalgic smile flourishes. His eyes look far away.

"My mother's house. I sold it but I keep the key."

A swell of warm feeling within her. The emotion plays pinkly on her cheeks. Next: "Five."

"Nope." He's staring blankly at her, like a blind man looking in the direction of a sound to affect normality.

"What am I supposed to do with this, Sam?" she says, putting down the key and taking up the next. "Okay, so we've seen the party trick. Now what? You just want to keep doing this for the sake of it. So we know what we know. You'll see eight keys, you won't see six of them. Amen. The end. Whoopdeedoo."

"No, just, just keep going."

"Fine."

She holds up the next key.

"Six."

Sam shakes his head.

"I thought this was supposed to be proof. Evidence of something. You told me you could give me something solid."

She is about to put it down but he indicates for her to keep it there. And she lifts it higher, so that it is in front of her face. She sees the key obscuring the band of skin between his eyes, her fingers covering his nose, her hand blocking out the bottom half of his face. She shifts her focus back to the key and his face becomes a fleshy blur. Shifts her focus back to his face and the key becomes a blur, then a thin line, disappearing into the dead space in the middle of her vision. She imagines the same thing from his point of view. Only he can't see the key. There should be nothing to focus on. He should be looking right into her eyes. Either that or down slightly, at her fingers. But he's not. His eyes are level opposite hers, but not meeting them. They are fixed on a point. A point slightly above her fingers and half a foot in front of her face. There's something there that he's focusing on. Something that he must be able to see.

Sam's attention is trained on the space where the key should be. But as hard as he stares, he sees nothing.

His mind begins to idle, freewheel, abandoned in the space left when all of his concentration is elsewhere. He can't see anything, but there is a definite sense of something. As if the air there is tingling. Thoughts come unbidden out of his subconscious. He finds himself meditating on the idea of the key as a metaphor. A symbol of opening, of access. An object that has both a literal and metaphoric existence. Just as now he is trying to open a door in his mind, to gain access to a space that has been locked away, and consequently to gain access to that space in reality. A space he remembers nothing about. Except he has been there. And he has access. Because he has the key. And he knows he must have it for a reason.

Nina's hand drops. His concentration breaks. He sits up with a gasp, "Don't! Keep it there."

"Sorry."

And she replaces her hand, re-entering the fixed oval of his concentration. And there, between and above her fingers, the air now has a different quality. A subtle blurring of the space behind it. Like a heat haze.

Sam takes a long, slow breath.

And the air coalesces. A silver shape begins to materialise.

"Rosanna." His voice has an airy, trance-like quality.

"Rosanna? The one who lives in your block?"

The air is sucked out of Sam's lungs. His body stiffens and braces and the muscles of his arms and chest begin to quake. He identifies the sensation as fear, but this doesn't help him control it. The pull on his lungs is inescapable. He feels that he might suffocate right there and then.

And then a pop. He jolts backwards. His back slapping the back of the chair and he takes a huge breath in.

"Each of these," his voice tremulous now, filled with a far-off awe, "holds an answer. This is the easiest one." His eyes find Nina again, and fix her with a clarity that pins her in her seat. "I am... waking up."

"What do you mean, waking up?"

"I'm awake. It's something Neil said."

"Neil Allen? You've spoken to him?"

"He came to see me just as I was leaving. I beat the shit out of him." Sam plucks the key from her hand. "This is the key to Rosanna's flat."

"Rosanna, of course. She was going to help you, right? So why isn't she here? She can corroborate everything." Nina brightens. An intake of breath that is almost a laugh. "Shit Sam, we wouldn't even be having this conversation if she'd..."

But Sam isn't sharing the levity; he is looking at her with a solemnity that takes the wind out of her sails in three clear beats. One, two –

"What?"

"Rosanna is dead."

Nina's jaw drops.

"You met her, you became friends and now she's dead. And all this in the space of, what, three days?"

"I mean she's probably dead."

"What? You don't know?"

"I can explain."

"This is what you're not telling me. This is the whole... why you look so different, so traumatised, so, you're like fucking Moses when he came down the mountain. There's this big cloud hanging over you, some vast and huge change and you're only telling me now? After we've played your stupid key game and that was the key that came out in your mind and so now you have to explain it. Would you have even said anything if it wasn't for the key? Shit, this whole thing's like some stupid cardboard cut-out of a therapy session, like I'm your therapist and I have to dig up all your shit – you'll only say stuff if I force you there by prodding in the right direction, right, by forcing stuff to the surface?"

"Calm down."

"Is that the case, Sam? What else have you not been telling me? Have you had an affair? Have you got ten children? Are you Josef Stalin? What the fuck Sam?"

"Nina. Calm. Down."

And whether it's because she listens to him or she's just run out of steam, she does.

"I will tell you everything. Everything I know. But you have to realise that there are things I have done that are not me. It is not me. And you can hold them against me if you want, but I'm telling you, it's Roberta."

"I'm just... Do you know how scary that is?"

"Yes. That's why I need to be careful what I tell you when. Let's go to Rosanna's. Let me show you that this is the key. Let me prove it. And then I'll tell you everything. And even then," he reaches across the table and takes hold of her hand. Her heart jumps with fear, but she lets him hold it. Because this Sam is so clear and strong – this Sam that she hasn't seen before today – that she wants him to be right. Desperately wants him to be right. "Even if you believe me, there's no obligation. You can walk away at any time. I promise I won't blame you if you need to. I don't know, maybe that's even the safest thing."

And her breath catches in her throat. The most unnerving thing is not how quickly he can change – from vulnerable and pathetic to powerful and resolved – but how malleable her own feelings are. A moment ago she wanted to be as far away from him as possible. Now that she is being given permission to walk away, she wants to do anything but. She feels like a small child, turned on a finger and a thumb by the simplest reverse psychology. But there's nothing she can do to help it.

"Okay," her voice has become a hoarse whisper. "Let me get my keys."

"No," Sam says. "No cars."

They watch the other travellers, watch the people they pass, the blurred landscapes that flicker outside the windows. Looking at anything but each other. As if they don't even know each other. They appear as any other tube denizens: no personal contact, no risk of mutual acknowledgement. Nina recalls a trip to Japan – being handed a magazine by her host before they got the train and told that in Japan they DO NOT talk on the metro. It's a hard and fast rule. Here it's more casual. For Londoners, not talking on the tube is more of a fashion, it's the way it is because most people simply prefer it to be. There is little that would indicate to the casual observer that these two people sitting next to each other are a couple. They are not holding hands. There is no commonality of style of dress. Nothing mutual. The only thing, if one was to look particularly closely, is that they share the same slightly haunted look. The hollow cheekbones, the wide, unfixed eyes. On the streets, the effect is more noticeable. They do not walk together. Sam is slightly ahead of Nina, as she hobbles with her crutches and her cumbersome plaster cast. The expression is still there and it is also legible in the way they walk. For although their gates are different on account of her handicap, their heads are fixed in the same way: slightly in front of their shoulders, alert to something, always watching and their limbs move languidly and freely as if propelled by a separate intelligence to that which resides in their cautiously-set heads, behind their restless and watchful eyes. They are neither blissfully clueless ambling prey, nor avid purposeful predators. They are both.

"Weird," says Nina. "It's just like your floor, only different."

"Yes, it's colder isn't it? It feels slightly colder."

And Nina rubs her arms as if in agreement. There are sounds: voices, a couple arguing, a loud TV, children.

"You know, I've never been to any of the other floors in my building."

"Well why would you?"

"I know. Maybe it's something that we're not supposed to see. Like a parallel reality."

Sam looks at Nina, raising an eyebrow. She catches the implication and sublimates her joy at the shared thought, pushing it down under a business-like frown. It is so easy for them to lapse into commonality and enjoy being together as a couple. But she can't let herself. Not yet. Soon, though. Nearly there.

Number six.

"Here we are." Sam stops at the door and rummages in his pocket for his reassembled key ring.

As he thumbs through the keys to find the right one, Nina feels a horrible, weighty suspense. He locates the key with no problem now – none of the same games, the seeing it or not seeing it – the key has become an accepted fact. And it is clear from the movement of his hands that Sam is not feeling any of the same suspense. His carriage is light, almost nonchalant. He places the key in the lock like he is opening the door of his own flat. The action is practiced and familiar, as if he has opened this same door many times before.

But the key sticks in the lock. Sam frowns. He pulls it out and reinserts it. It goes in all the way but when he tries it doesn't turn at all. There is no give. Nothing.

"Definitely the right one..." he mumbles to himself. And he places his hand against the door with a thump and leans into the lock, trying to get leverage and twisting.

Nina feels ill.

A clunk. The door swings inward. It takes Sam off-guard and he loses his balance, recovering only just in time to brace himself against the doorframe and stop himself falling flat on his face.

"Who are you and what are you doing?"

The voice is indignant and proprietary. It belongs to a short, plump young woman with a busy mass of brown curls and small rimless glasses. She holds a goggle-eyed infant in her arms.

"I'm guessing this isn't Rosanna?"

Sam shakes his head.

"Er, hello?" says the woman with the baby, "Why are you trying to open my front door?"

"I'm a friend of Rosanna's," Sam garbles. "She gave me her key. I came to get... some stuff."

"Well there's no Rosanna here."

But Sam is not engaging with the woman, instead he's trying to look around her into the flat. He can see the hallway – in it some boxes – and the door behind is open showing a lounge that looks completely different. There is no tattered, ruined furniture. No sign of distress or damage or an insular, lonely life. The carpets are pale and spotless, the walls papered in pastel patterns, Ikea furniture placed minimally around the room.

"Excuse me!" The woman shouts, breaking his concentration. She sidesteps to block his view. "Do you mind? That's my home you're sticking your nose in."

"How long have you been here?" Sam says, ignoring her protest.

"There a problem, babe?" A tall man in a tight white muscle top appears behind the red-faced mother. "What do you want, eh?" he says with an unnecessary click of his neck. "You want to ask yourself if it's worth upsetting my wife over?"

Nina can see that Sam, far from feeling threatened by the arrival of this alpha male, is bristling with frustration. She steps into the space between him and the couple.

"Rosanna was the previous tenant," she interjects in a pacifying tone. "She was a friend of ours. Do you know her at all?"

"Nah," comes the man's reply. He's backing down but still terse. With the boundaries now established his wife enters into civil female discourse, dropping the information she was holding so closely to her chest a moment ago.

"We just moved in yesterday," she says to Nina.

"What, and you've already redone the carpet and all the furniture? Rosanna was living here three days ago and as far as I know she had no plans to move out."

"No, this was like it when we got here. We're still moving our stuff in."

A glance passes between Nina and Sam.

He turns back to the couple, "You don't have the landlord's number do you?"

"Uh, yeah. Got a card for the estate agent, I think."

The man disappears momentarily. Nina and Sam stand opposite the woman and her child, exchanging false smiles. They look at each other again. His face is pinking. Upon meeting his eyes she is nearly brought to tears and has to look away at the floor.

The man returns and hands the card to Sam.

"Er, thanks." Sam takes it. The man reaches over his wife's head to close the door. Sam places his fingers against the wood,

"Er, one more thing," he says. "Neither of you are in therapy are you?"

"Fuck off!" The woman slams the door in their faces.

"I know, I know, I know what you're thinking." The justifications have begun before they even reach the lift. "But it's obvious what's happened. She's covering up, isn't she? She knows that if she can make you think I've lost it then you're going to leave me. That's the game, don't you see? Either way she wants you out of the picture so she can have me to herself."

"Either way? What do you mean either way?" Nina stops halfway down the corridor.

"I'm sorry, I didn't mean..." Sam looks away, blows a breath up towards his fringe, then turns back. "No, look Nina, I can't sugar coat it for you. That's what we're dealing with here, okay? That's what she wants. Do I need to spell it out? I'm not the one that got run over in a supermarket car park."

"So what? They just changed the decor in five minutes flat while Rosanna stepped out?"

"We'll speak to the estate agent."

"Oh yeah, and if he says no, the flat's been on the market for six months I suppose you're just going to say he's in on it too."

"Well if he says that..."

"Fucking hell!" She clunks off to the lift. Hits the button. Stands with her back to him.

He walks up behind her. Reaches out towards the shoulder blades bunching up the back of her jacket. She shrugs his hand away without looking at him.

"Nina, we can't expect this to be easy."

He hears a blast of air from her nostrils. Sees the back of her head tip forward and shake. The lift arrives and she steps in. Turns to face him and hits the button for his floor pointedly, eyebrows arched, head cocked.

"She planted it. And all she had to say was "I was thinking about that dream: the one you always have," and there I was: in it. And the next thing I knew the car had crashed. I did it, Nina. It was me. I killed Rosanna. And David. I killed him too."

Sam recounts the events of the crash in a matter-of-fact tone. When he is finished Nina looks at him for a long while without saying anything. Her eyes are wide, unblinking, her lips pouted in a pose that suggests that she is caught on the cusp of a thought. Sam feels the need to fidget, but he controls it. Watching her sitting there, pensive like this is like being eaten alive by midges and not being able to swat them away.

"We should do something," she says, finally.

Sam sighs with relief. He rubs his eyes. Then looks back at her: she is still as a praying mantis, her fingers arched together. The tension that had momentarily left him is still there in her.

"This," he begins. And then pauses to choose his words more cautiously, "This is what I meant when I talked about being careful. There was one point where me and Rosanna decided to go and confront her. And there wasn't any phone call then, the decision just flicked a switch in us and we attacked each other – as if it was an in-built program, as if she had made the very idea of taking action against her anathema to our sub-consciouses."

Nina's head drops with a groan.

"I know, I know, it's frustrating. That's why we had to get David involved, but then look how that went. I feel like if anything needs to happen it needs to happen without my knowing."

"And it can't involve the police because you don't trust them and it's..." she looks up at him, her eyes flaring, "but that's not what's frustrating me, Sam. That isn't the issue. Yes, there are things I could do, there are people I could call. You see, unlike you, I'm a resourceful person who knows how to help themselves." Ow. That hurts. "It's just that my will to continue with this is in imminent risk of being depleted. When I said 'We should do something' it was an olive branch. I was saying, okay, let's go somewhere with this. Yes, I'm freaked out and fucking disturbed by what you just told me and it all sounds increasingly insane but I'm willing to give you the benefit of the – no – I'm willing to humour you. But even to that, you say "oh, er, no wait, hang on a second" because something tells me that you don't want to resolve this. That the most important thing to you here is this fantasy. The idea of being persecuted."

Silence falls on the room like an anvil. Nina isn't sure why she said what she just said or where it came from; it just came out. Sam looks like she's punched him between the eyes.

The buzzer goes. An incongruous sound, so far removed from the vacuum that has sealed up around them. The world outside feels like something that has never existed at all. All either of them can do is sit there and stare at each other.

Then after a while Nina says: "Aren't you going to get it?"

And Sam pushes himself up out of his seat. His body feels strange and weightless. As he walks to the intercom his steps feel spongy like his feet are indenting into the floor and then springing out again.

In the hallway, he picks up the intercom phone, "Hello?" His voice sounds foreign and far away, like it doesn't really belong to him.

"Hi Sam, it's –"

Sam comes hurtling back into the lounge and slams the door behind him. He leans against the wall with his hands over his ears and he is panting and sweating and all of the colour has drained out of his face.

"Sam, what's going on?"

"It's her. I know it's her. I know that voice anywhere. I can't hear it. I don't know what it'll make me do, I..."

"Roberta's outside right now?"

The buzzer sounds again.

Sam nods feverishly.

"Well what are you going to do?"

"I don't know," says Sam. And he sinks down to the floor and makes himself into a small ball. He's shivering and his face is buried between his knees. He doesn't say anything else, or if he does it's incoherent mutterings that are lost and muffled. Nina watches him with her hands on her hips. It's all swings and roundabouts. He's about as stable as caesium. She doesn't even know whether he can be trusted – it could just be some kind of gambit.

Nina stumps over to the window. And she suddenly feels incredibly guilty for the thought that propelled her there. Roberta is standing on the street below, her hand shading her eyes as she looks up at the building. From here she is a little pudding of a thing, the perspective compressing her into a purple ball with a head. A chubby arm waves at her. And Roberta is smiling.

"I'm going to go and talk to her."

"No, don't!" Sam barks.

"Why? What's she going to do to me? She's in your head, Sam. She's never been anywhere near mine."

"No, I... Nina, you..."

"Just stay put, okay. Try and relax. I won't be long. And when I get back I want you with your head screwed on, okay?"

And all Sam can do is stare after her as she disappears into the hallway. He hears the front door slam.

"Oh dear, what happened to you?"

Roberta is still shading her eyes. She is wearing a floaty short-sleeved purple dress and her copper curls are glossy and bouncy in the bright sunlight. Nina hobbles down the steps to the street. She notes that the therapist doesn't make any attempt to assist her. Settling herself against the iron fence at the bottom she shrugs, "I was in a car accident."

"Oh how terrible."

Roberta's eyes have a glacial stillness, her face affecting an unquestionably grave look of concern. Nina squints at her, trying to see past it, but it's flawless – impossible to find any note of insincerity. And this in itself makes Nina uncomfortable. If this had been the other way round, if she herself was talking to a vague acquaintance, although she would no doubt feel genuine pity upon hearing such news, she would not be able to so readily produce the same level of feeling that she might were it an intimate – there would always be a slight undercurrent of disinterest.

"You didn't hear about it?"

Roberta frowns, "I haven't seen Sam in weeks."

"Oh don't tell me you didn't know."

Nina regrets her riposte the moment it comes out of her mouth. A tactical blunder. She's given the game away. But if Roberta takes any pleasure in this, she hides it beneath a small smile that connotes the deepest sympathy and understanding,

"Look, Nina, I don't know what Sam has been saying to you but I'm really worried about him. That's why I'm here."

"Your timing's pretty good, isn't it?"

"Why? What's going on?"

Nina snorts a laugh and looks down at her plaster cast, then looks back up at Roberta, "Nothing," she says.

Traffic moves lazily past them, exhausts shimmering in the heat, radios playing tinny voices that come muffled through closed windows, bass thumping through open ones. The tinkling of an ice cream van. Frère Jacques.

"Nina, listen. You already know that Sam and I go back a long way. So as you can imagine, I know him pretty well. Arguably better than anyone."

Nina's hackles rise, but as close as she is to Sam, she has to admit that, technically, Roberta is probably right.

"In the four years since I started working with him at Ross and Waverly, there hasn't been a week that has gone by without us having some sort of contact. Until now."

"He told me what happened. What put him in that place."

"He did? Oh my, that's... That's a real breakthrough. I..." and she's actually choking up, "I'm almost jealous. You know, that I wasn't there. Oh, I knew you'd be good for him Nina." And thrown away as an afterthought, "He tell you that himself, did he?"

Nina can't hide the wince, but her mouth stays firmly shut. A smile dies on Roberta's lips and her eyes fill with pity. Nina balks inwardly. Despite her indecision regarding the situation in general, she has an intense dislike of this holier-than-thou, butter-wouldn't-melt sow. Of course, she knows she's bound to feel like that, that she can't help but take Sam's side. But even if her boyfriend is completely stone-cold crazy, she'd still like to give the hag a big old kick in the vagina. And if he isn't... Nina tries Roberta at her own game, folding her lips in an expression of faux sympathy that she is sure is nowhere near as effective as the witch's masterful facial subterfuges, and meanwhile at the back of her eyes, right behind the smile she's thinking: I will end you.

"Roberta, can I throw a few names at you?"

"Of course."

"Neil Allen, Jonathan Frame, Rosanna Harding. Ring any bells?"

Roberta narrows her eyes, "If... You're asking me about other clients. I'm afraid I can't talk about..."

"That's okay. Let me tell you what I know about them. Neil Allen drives a black BMW and several days ago he drove it into me, since when he seems to have disappeared except to show up out of nowhere at Sam's apartment to try and keep him away from me. And Rosanna, well, it just so happens she lives right here in this block. And, oh yes, now she's dead."

"I..." Roberta looks at Nina like she's just said she's from Mars. "Really?" Sighs and shakes her head. "Look, I can't tell you much about Rosanna but what I can tell you is that she doesn't live in this block and I'm pretty sure she is alive and well. At least she was when I saw her for her appointment yesterday."

The iron fence digs into Nina's back. She shifts her weight against it.

"Why don't you give me her phone number? I'll give her a call and ask her myself. Wait, don't say it, you can't do that."

"I could ask her if she's willing to speak to you and then pass on your number to her if that would be agreeable to you?"

She stares at Roberta, trying to peek beneath that well-worn care, that sincerity.

"You know what, forget about it," she says.

"Nina, all this is very concerning indeed. Do you think, maybe, I could come up and have a talk with Sam?"

Nina blinks twice. Three times.

"And what are you going to charge him for that?"

"Sorry?"

"You know, emergency disaster prevention therapy."

"Nina, I don't know what he's led you to think of me, but..."

"I know what you're up to Roberta."

The innocent confusion on the therapist's face is immaculate.

"So why don't you just fuck off."

Roberta's mouth drops open.

"Yeah, don't make out like I'm shocking you. Look, I'm getting a restraining order against you and if I see you round here again, I'll have the police round like that" clicks her fingers.

Roberta holds up a hand and closes her eyes. She makes a sniffling sound like she's holding back tears.

"We're coming for you, Roberta. Best batten down the hatches."

The therapist opens her eyes, wells of tears collecting in her lashes. "Look," she sniffles, "it's clear that there's not much I can do for you at this point. Although I am mystified as to..." she sniffs and wipes her eyes, recovering her poise, "Look, you know where to find me if you need me. My door is always open to you. Both of you."

And with that, Roberta turns and waddles off down the street. Nina watches her go, allowing her face at last to cloud with the thunder that she has been holding back. She can't help but admire the woman. It was one hell of a performance.

Nina pauses in the lobby, leaning against the wall. Her breath comes in short gasps and she can feel her heartbeat right through her arms and down into her fingers. The woman is either a formidable and sociopathic adversary, or else her boyfriend is completely out of his mind. Either contingency is terrifying. The lobby wheels around her as her head lolls backwards and forwards, reeling from the enormity of the situation. The world suddenly seems like an incredibly bleak place. Bleak is the common denominator. Whether it's one awful permutation or another. At least one of them offers some hope. Nina feels a shiver, her head becoming still. That's why she is so inclined to disbelieve Roberta, why she can't just abandon Sam to his own psychoses and get well shot of him: because the scenario in which Roberta is the villain at least offers some hope. Nina's heart sinks as she sees that every decision she has made up to this point has been based not upon rationality but upon a preference of outcome. She hasn't been weighing things up evenly, she has been trying to make herself feel right about choosing to believe what is more comforting to her. And there's a horribleness about the coming-unstuck of that reality, seeing it for the sham that it is.

She shakes herself, pulls her emotional socks up, forcing herself to stand, leaning heavily on the crutches. Pragmatism, practical steps, action, that's what's needed here. There is no value to be found in wallowing in self-indulgent reflection. She moves the crutches in the direction of the lift. Takes a step. Moves the crutches. Stops.

Returning to practical concerns brings a ringing alarm bell to the front of her thoughts. What has she done? What has she done? She made an enemy of Roberta, let her know exactly where she stood and signalled her intentions to her. The whole thing was ill-advised. Sam was right. Even when it comes to a person who is not under her thrall, Roberta has power. She exploited the situation to gain a secondary objective – and Nina gave her the update she was after. Handed it to her on a plate. All of that information, which Roberta can now go away and begin to act upon. Why would she have done that? Was it some mind game that Roberta played with her, some form of instant hypnosis, or the power of suggestion, neuro-linguistics seeded into the conversation, into words into hand gestures?

No. Nina chastises herself. And in that instant she understands how very easy it can be to find external explanations for one's own behaviour. It's seductive, this whole Roberta narrative. Whether she believes it or not, it's clearly the kind of thing that makes you want to believe it. But no. It all came from her. She is responsible. From the moment she saw Roberta in the window she was looking to pick a fight, and she went out there with her fists up. It's her own fault. But it's irrelevant. Things are what they are.

The lift opens on the sixth floor. Nina sighs. She's never noticed how long the corridor is. When every step is an effort, when you measure them one at a time you become painfully aware of just how many of these small repetitive movements are involved in everyday life. She spends so long contemplating the distance that the doors begin to shut automatically on her. She inserts a crutch between them and they bounce back open. And she pushes herself up and begins to hobble down the corridor. After all that walking earlier, following Sam's insistence on taking public transport, just the journey down to meet Roberta and back up again has left her feeling exhausted. It's around thirty-five steps. She counted them before. And now she counts them again, as if picking up breadcrumbs. She smiles as an image comes to her of herself as a little Pac-Man, eating up pills one by one as she goes (and surrounded by hostile ghosts).

As she nears Sam's apartment, she becomes aware of thunking and clunking noises. She stops to listen. Thunking and clunking. And then a smash. In a moment of panic she hobbles as fast as she can towards the door, forgetting all about counting her steps. She loses her balance when she reaches it and has to lurch to the side to fall against the wall. The door is still on the latch. She pushes it open, a crutch feeling the ground in front of her like an antenna.

Sam is nowhere to be seen. In the short time that she has been away, the flat has been turned upside down. An armchair lies on its side, the seat cushions are all off the couch and scattered. Every flowerpot has been smashed, little explosions of soil bursting over the floorboards. The TV lies on its front in the middle of the room. The door to the bedroom is ajar and the sounds of objects being tossed about emanate from within. In between them she can hear Sam swearing and cursing. She moves towards the door and cranes her head, trying to get a glimpse of what is going on inside. The bed linen has been thrown in a pile at the foot of the bed, but Sam is out of sight. Although by the sounds of it, he is alone. She calls out his name in a quiet, nervous voice. But the chaos continues unabated. She is about to call out louder when he comes stomping out of the bedroom, his face in a thunderous scowl. Instead, his name comes out as a question: "Sam?"

And as if he hadn't even noticed she was there, he turns towards her with a "Huh?"

"What are you doing?"

Sam's eyes sweep the room. His arms are extended at his sides, lifting up and down uselessly as he ranges around.

"I don't get it," he says.

"You don't get what?"

"I've looked everywhere and I can't find anything. Not a damned thing."

Nina's not even sure if it is worth questioning him any further. Whatever random impulse has claimed him this time, there's nothing she can say that is going to make any difference. He walks over to one side of the room as if with a purpose but then stops suddenly. He pulls his shoes off and looks inside them, pulling out the insoles and feeling around inside them. Not satisfied with that, he starts trying to pry the soles from the bottom of the shoe, feeling around the heels as if expecting them to somehow detach. Then he throws them to the floor. His head whips round towards Nina. His eyes are wide and staring, sweat standing out on his forehead and along the pronounced veins in his neck.

"Gimme your shoe," he barks and walks towards her. "Come on, hand it over."

"What? Why? No, Sam, what do you want with my shoe?"

He stops in front of her, glaring and puffing out his cheeks, "The way she showed up here. It's obvious she's got the place bugged. She must have. There's no other way around it. But I, but..."

"You haven't found anything."

Sam hangs his head, jaw clenched and ticking.

"I suppose I also thought that, that if I could find something then, well, you'd have your proof."

And when his eyes find her, there is a desperation in them. It's clear that he can't live with the idea that she might not believe him. Hates the very notion. It's a wedge between them – and the longer it persists the further it will sink, widening the gap until it splits them apart.

It's that same thing, Nina thinks. The same thought she had earlier about herself. His actions are being directed by the need to show himself that he is right – the truth is an irrelevance – being right is the only thing he cares about. And she can't help but feel sympathy for that desire, as wrong-headed and destructive as it might be.

She is about to say something but then stops herself. Her mouth hangs open. She shuts it again. She puts herself in his shoes for a moment: from his point of view, all of Sam's actions are entirely rational. She is giving him too little credit.

"What?" he asks.

"Nothing," but her gaze is far away, caught up in a thought.

She returns to the present.

"Sam, you don't need to worry about proving anything to me."

He looks confused.

"You know what you need to do. Whatever *reality* is, it'll all come out in due course."

"I *wish* I knew what to do."

"Come here." She holds out an arm. He steps towards her and she folds him into both of them. Her crutches drop to the floor. She feels his face nestled into her shoulder. Smoothes her fingers through the sweat on the back of his neck. Listens to the sound of his breathing growing calmer against her blouse. "Well think about what you do know. What leads do you have?"

The estate agents are of little help. They promise to pass a message on for Rosanna's landlord to contact them. Their reticence to provide any name or contact details gives Sam hope that there may be something to be dug up in that direction. But as he hangs up the phone it feels more like a sword hanging over his head. An effective cover up might be enough to persuade Nina once and for all that he is nothing but a disturbed fantasist. He tries to contact Neil, hoping he can coax him into letting Nina in on what he knows about the network, but he doesn't answer. He calls Neil's work. He hasn't been in all week and nobody knows why. And so, with little other recourse, they find themselves outside his flat, Sam lending Nina his arm as he helps her out of the cab.

"See? Isn't that better?" she says, praising Sam's reluctant consenting to take a taxi rather than public transport. Certainly, she feels the better for it. She takes up her crutches with a renewed energy.

The cab waits while they approach the block. It looks quiet – most of the occupants are probably still at work.

"They fixed the window," says Sam. The new glass gleams darkly with reflected sky, as if it had never been broken and that night with Rosanna had never happened. They ring the bell. They wait. They ring the bell. They wait. They shrug. It's what they expected.

"Shall I get the basket?"

Nina looks at the well-kept grassy area at the front of the block, fringed with conifers and colourful flowerbeds.

"Yeah."

Their eyes meet, alive with playfulness. Sam collects a wicker picnic basket from the cab and lets the driver go.

When they are finished eating, they lie back and stare up at the clouds, twilight beginning to shade the space between them. Sam turns to look at Nina and she turns to look at him. They are both happy to be lost in the wordlessness of each other's company. In spite of everything, in the midst of all of this chaos, they have managed to find an oasis of calm. A few meters of grass in a car park in the middle of an ugly suburb, but to them it could be a rolling meadow. It feels like an enormous achievement. Or a small victory. The only one of its kind in the entire campaign.

"We should probably sit up," says Sam. "In case he comes. We want to see him before he sees us."

"Let's just lie here. Just a little bit longer."

It's a request that's impossible to refuse. Sam reaches out and pulls her towards him. They kiss for a while. Soft, tender kisses. And then they part and she snuggles into the curve of his body.

"Do you ever think about where we would be now if it hadn't been for all this?"

"Honestly? No, not really. I suppose there just isn't ever really a time when it stops for long enough for me to think about anything."

Nina tucks her chin into his arms.

"Except for now."

"Yeah, except for now."

And they drift into silence once again, enjoying the closeness and the comfort and the fresh breeze that sighs through the screen of trees.

"Or maybe," he says after a while, "Maybe it's so much a part of me that I can't really imagine things being any other way."

Nina squeezes her eyes shut and suppresses an uncomfortable feeling that threatens to mar her bliss.

"We could be on a beach somewhere," she says, "on an island somewhere hot, with stupid-looking drinks served in coconuts with umbrellas and curly straws. People would bring them to us, young men in crisp white shorts and T-shirts. And there would be other people, women in bikinis playing in the surf. I'd see you looking at them and get jealous, maybe tell you off. You'd say you weren't looking and I'd say you were and then you'd say something stupidly romantic about how you could never look at anyone else when you were lying next to me and I'd forgive you and we'd lie back and there would be sweat on our bodies and when it gets too hot we'd retreat into an air-conditioned hotel room where there would be a bucket of champagne waiting for us."

Nina feels Sam make a sharp movement. She looks around to see that he is sitting up. At this angle it's difficult to see his face properly, but his mouth is firm and fixed and he is definitely looking at something. She follows his gaze to the road. Beyond the border of conifers, the narrow street is crammed with houses that have been split into flats, and lined on both sides by parked cars, allowing just about enough space for one car to get through. Occupying that space is a stationary car with its engine running. But from where Nina is lying it is obscured by the other vehicles.

"You see that?" Sam's voice is hushed. Nina feels a flutter of adrenaline and sits up.

"A police car," she says.

Sam nods.

"Who's the driver? Is it Frame?"

"I can't see from here."

"Well either it's him or it isn't. If it's not, what have we got to worry about?"

"There are others," he says.

"Yeah, but what are they going to do? Go back to Roberta and tell her that we're having a picnic. Big wow."

"Look at the way he's sitting there." Sam's arms are locked rigid, supporting him. "Just sitting there."

The shape of the driver in the interior is nothing more than a blob in the fading light. The features are indistinguishable – only the white of the police shirt and the orientation of the head, which is turned towards them.

"So? Why don't you go and say hello," she says, "see who it is. What harm can it do?"

"Maybe we should go home. It'll be dark soon."

"What about Neil?"

Sam's eyes switch to her and he pauses, thinking about his response. He looks back at the police car.

"It's not looking likely is it? I mean it was nice sitting here and everything, but Frame told me they haven't been able to find Neil and he hasn't shown up at work all week, so what do you reckon? She's probably got him stashed away somewhere till everything dies down."

Nina places a hand on Sam's chin and turns his face towards her. "But it's not going to die down, is it?"

Sam doesn't say anything. He offers a smile. A weak one.

"Look, if you're not going to go over there I am." But she can feel him trembling. He's not going anywhere. Nina sighs and begins the arduous task of getting up from the floor. She grabs a crutch and then pushes up with her good leg and a hand. It's not graceful, but after a strenuous few moments she is on her feet.

She hobbles towards the car. Reaches the pavement. Peers into the window. The driver is a woman. But Nina is not going to let it go. She steps to the edge of the pavement. Reaches out to knock on the window. A roar. The car accelerates away. She stands leaning on her crutches and watches it pursuit-drive down the winding road, negotiating each obstacle and bend in the cramped street with ease.

She turns back. Crowded with rubbish and leftovers from their dinner, the picnic basket looks a bit shabby. Sam is sitting on the blanket with his legs crossed, like a child.

"See?" she shouts across to him, gesturing large with a crutch, "They're pussies! What are they going to do? Their whole operation is beneath the surface – they can't deal with open confrontation."

But Sam doesn't seem reassured by this. He doesn't even nod. Nina hobbles back over to him. Standing above him he seems so small that she almost feels bad for shouting too loud. But something's got to snap him out of this,

"Sam, look at me. If we're going to beat them we've got to take the fight to them. You understand?"

He claps his hands over his ears and squeezes his eyes shut. Shit, thinks Nina, what now?

"You can't say those things to me," Sam says, still sealed up, "it's too dangerous."

"Oh, for fuck's –"

Sam looks up at her and he's so serious that it cuts her off.

"Whatever you've got in mind, don't tell me about it. Not until you absolutely have to."

She gives a huge sigh, "Well maybe I should go back to mine and you should go back to yours. That way there's no danger of –"

"No. I don't think either of us should be alone."

He gets up.

"Shit."

Nina stands there in shock. The place looks like it has been turned over in their absence.

"What?" says Sam.

And she remembers him making the mess earlier.

"We should really get this tidied up."

And when she says "we" she's thinking Sam, as she's hardly in a state to start schlepping things about herself. But Sam has wandered off into the middle of the room. He's searching around for something again, like a dementia patient trying to find the glasses on top of their head, finding them and then looking for them again a moment later.

"We need to go about this differently," he says, as if he hasn't heard a word, "we're doing this all wrong."

Nina looks around at the place. What she had always thought of as "character" now looks entirely dingy. There is nothing appealing about it. The room seems smaller, shabbier, dirtier. She notices streaks in the paint on the walls, the scuffed floorboards, grubby finger marks around the light switches.

"You've got that right," she says.

"We need to, we need to..." Sam is almost stammering. It's like he's on speed, ranging about the place full of nervous energy. "Where are the keys? The rest of the keys, where are they?"

Nina raises an eyebrow and nods towards the table, where the unrecognised keys are sitting in a pile.

"Where? I can't see them?"

This again. Nina scrapes across the room and drops heavily into a chair. She takes a pad of small yellow notelets and writes out the numbers one to five on separate notes. She places a key on each one and then spreads her hands above them in a fan. "There you go."

Sam moves to the table like a homing missile. He sits down and pulls the notes closer to him. The change that comes over him when he has a purpose and a direction, something to do, it's really striking.

"Wait," she says, "Before you start that, why don't you give the place a bit of a tidy? You never know, it might be good for you, might help you think."

"I'm sorry." A conciliatory smile. He covers her hand with his own. "Sorry."

Nina takes the pen and traces the outline of each key onto the note it sits upon. Sam pauses in his tidying.

"Genius."

"I thought so too."

When he is done she leaves him counting keys and goes into the bedroom.

With the door closed she is sealed off from all the craziness whirling around Sam and there's something liberating about that. At last she has her own space to think. To bring her considerable powers to bear. The tall windows let plenty of light in during the day, but now that it is dark outside they are just shiny panels of blackness. Condensation gathers at their corners, creeping up their length. Nina tugs at the neck of her blouse. Looking at the bed where they have slept and made love so many times her mind is filled with images of their bodies twisting amongst the sheets on hot sweaty evenings like this, when the humidity is high and there's a storm threatening. Thunder and lightning bring release, ecstasy as the pressure of the world drops. But there is no such release now. There is only pressure and humidity.

It is only when she reaches the window that she realises she'll need two hands to get it open. She looks around, calculating her movements in advance, finding a place to prop up her crutches within reach. She sees the sealed door, the crowded desk full of papers, the sweating windows and the bed which generates a heat all of its own and suddenly the room seems so much smaller. Turning back to the window she is confronted by a reflected image of herself in the space; tall, ungainly and winged, she looks too large for it. She gets the window open and cool night air blasts in and she stands, one leg crooked, letting it blast and blow around her. The pressure is gone, but something of that stuffiness remains with her as she takes a seat at the desk.

It is now almost nine: she has an hour and a half at most to call people before it becomes unsociable. But then it is an extraordinary circumstance and if she needs to get someone out of bed it is thoroughly justified. Whether she'll be able to convey that to a grumpy friend or colleague who has just been jerked out of bed and probably had his or her kid woken up is another matter. Well, there's always tomorrow. It all feels so urgent. This makes her stop and think for a second: why is that?

She pages through her address book. Stewart Worth. Her finger hovers over the button. It has been a long time since she's spoken to him. He's definitely high on her list, but he's a night-bird. She can probably call him into the small hours, and anyway he'd take a call from her even if he was asleep.

She makes another call: "Hi Sandy, it's Nina, how you doing?"

Sandra Patel is a solicitor who specialises in domestic abuse. They were at university together and have remained good friends ever since. Over the years the intervals between seeing each other have grown greater but Nina still considers her a close friend.

"So what's news?" Sandra asks. "Are you still seeing that guy – Sam, was it?"

"Yeah. Yes. Um, look Sandra I know we haven't spoken for a while but this isn't really a social call and I'm afraid I don't have much time to chat. I need to ask you a favour."

"Oh, okay."

"I need to seek a temporary restraining order against someone on Sam's behalf. But there isn't really much in the way of evidence. I mean I think I can give testimony that might be enough but I'm not really sure. It's all, well, it's a little bit strange... Shit, I don't even know how to start explaining it to you, let alone to a judge."

"Hey. Nina. It's okay, just talk it through calmly from the beginning. I'm sure we'll be able to work something out."

Nina is reassured by Sandra's confidence. Her pride is pricked a little as she realises that this must be exactly the way that Sandra deals with terrified battered wives who know nothing about the law, but at the same time she's relieved to be in good, competent hands. She goes through the story from the beginning, trying to stick to Sam's side of it and leaving out any of her own doubts. In doing so, she feels that his case is stronger and it seems to reinforce itself in her mind. Even though she skirts around some of the crazier details, and leaves out the things that Sam has "done" altogether, there are parts where Sandra seems taken aback by the outlandishness of her claims.

"Look," says Sandra, "The main thing is that we need to say that Sam has been caused harassment, alarm or distress by his therapist since he tried to end his treatment. I think we should be able to make it stick – certainly for a temporary order anyway. The most important thing is that we break the cycle of control. Roberta is doing what many abusers do, which is to surround their victim, making their world feel smaller, so they feel like they're isolated and have no-one to run to."

When Nina ends the phone call she feels much better. They aren't alone anymore. And that's exactly what she'll do. She'll break the cycle. She is breaking it. Right now.

Then the head clerk. She asks about the private investigators the chambers uses, specifying that she needs the best one. He gives her the details of a Mr. Furst and she thanks him. She is about to hang up when he says,

"Is everything okay?"

"Yes, it's fine. Thank you for asking, William."

Is she fine though? Is she really? She hangs up and notices that the phone has become hot in her hand. A thin line of sweat rolls from her temple to her cheek. She dials the number scrawled on the pad on the desk. She is sure the phone is about to ring off when a gruff voice growls,

"Yeah what?" in a blunt barrow-boy accent. His phone manner

doesn't inspire a terrible amount of confidence. And for a moment she questions William's judgement – but he's the head clerk, possibly the most reliable and effective person she has ever known.

"Good evening, this is Nina Trevanion from 3 Inner Temple. I apologise for the hour. I hope it's not too late to call."

"Nah, luv, 's fine. I'm still at the office. What can I do for you?"

"I need you to find out everything you can about a therapist by the name of Roberta Klein. I need details of any legal proceedings against her. Any claims filed, any professional misconduct, as well as names and contact details of present or former clients who have had any grievances. Criminal record, of course, if there is one. Anything you can find on her, any wrongdoing, dodgy people she might associate with. Whatever. I'm sure you'll know better than I if you find something you think might be able to be used against a person."

"Dunno about that. You're the expert." An emphysemic chuckle.

"We're not just talking about legal avenues – I mean literally anything."

"Anything? You sure about that?"

"Anything."

"Gotcha."

"Can you make this your highest priority? I need information fast. I'll pay double."

"I'll get on it right now."

"When do you sleep?"

That phlegmy laughter again, echoing in the earpiece. Nina hangs up with a wry smile and says aloud, "Sorry I ever doubted you, William."

By now it is pushing eleven o'clock. There is one more call Nina has to make. She flicks through her address book until she arrives at the name again. And it is only when she sees it that the nerves come back. This is going to be awkward, she knows it. But it's for Sam.

"Hi Stewart. It's Nina."

"I know. Long time."

"Yeah, I know. I'm sorry."

"You don't need to apologise." His being nice only makes it more awkward. But then he was always nice. "How have you been? What have you been up to?"

Already she can detect that hopeful tone in his voice, like she might be calling him to say that she wants to get back together, or even just meet him for a drink and let him pretend for an evening. And she feels bad just thinking about it. Because he has a right to hope for that – in the past, before Sam, when she felt low, she would do just that. And she'd always come home feeling thankful that those goo-goo eyes put her off before she ended up sleeping with him, and promising herself that she wasn't going to use him that way again. It wasn't fair on either of them.

"I need your help, Stewart. It's..." She hangs there, wondering whether she should say it, imagining the twinge he'll feel when she uses the word, worried that when she says it he might just hang up and not help her at all. "It's for my boyfriend. He needs your help. We need it. Both of us need it."

She can hear him breathing.

"Sure," he says after a while, managing to sound upbeat. "Whatever you guys need."

Maybe he's over her, maybe he's got a girlfriend or is married. Maybe he has kids. But she doesn't want to ask him any of these questions.

"Do you know someone in the force called Jonathan Frame?"

"No. But I'm sure I can find him. Do you know where he's stationed?"

"How about a therapist. Roberta Klein. Does some PTSD work."

"Again, I don't but I can check it out."

"You need to be discreet," she warns. "I need to know exactly who she sees. Names of officers. How much work she does."

She hears him hiss through his teeth,

"Nina, you know this is some dodgy ground you're asking me about. I'm not even sure if I can really... Look, why don't you tell me what this is about?"

"Okay, well, um, some of this is going to be hard to swallow, but you've got to trust me. Do you promise you'll believe me?"

"I'd never doubt you Nina. Just tell me. I said I'll help you in any way I can and I will."

And she explains about Roberta, about her attempts to get Sam back into therapy. When she gets to the hallucinations, the spiking and the involvement of the other patients, the phone grows hot again and she feels sweat emerging behind her ear. She keeps expecting Stewart to call bullshit, to come out and say that he doesn't believe her but he never does.

"So this woman's somehow harassing you and Sam and she's using her patients to help her do this?"

"Something like that. Yes. I know, I know, it sounds mad, like a mad conspiracy, but I think, I think it's really happening."

"Has she done anything to hurt you?"

Nina holds her breath. Every bit of information she passes on to someone not involved feels like stepping over a line. The more she tells Stewart about this the more real it becomes. It's so much harder than just asking a private eye to do some digging. It is not furtive. It is exposed.

"She had one of her patients run me over."

"What the fuck!" His indignation is so forceful that Nina has to hold the phone away from her ear. "What, how, do you know who this guy was?"

She considers communicating her doubt. It might be advantageous to have someone in her corner who is looking out for her interests, not just hers and Sam's as a unit. But there's no need to tell him that now – it might funnel his concerns in the wrong direction. The tone of his voice when she hinted at the things Sam might have done was already a little bit suspicious – he's already halfway towards wanting to paint Sam as a villain and protect her against him, and she doesn't want to feed that inclination. So she tells him about Neil Allen, his disappearance and Jonathan Frame's attempt to cover it up, omitting the suspicion cast over Sam.

"It all sounds really fishy. But I can see why you're being wary. And it's not like there's really anything solid to connect to her that could justify any sort of investigation. Wow. That's really frustrating. Difficult."

"I know."

"I'll see what I can do." And he pauses and she thinks he's finished and says,

"Thank –"

"And what about Sam? Is he also under her influence in this way? Are you sure you're safe with him?"

"Yes. Yes, of course."

"Sorry. Had to ask."

"I understand."

And she's kind of glad that he did ask. She feels that, much as she hates to think about it, but just in case, *just in case*, she's got an ace up her sleeve. She wonders if this is the real reason she called, but then quashes the notion. There's very real, practical reasons for seeking his help that have nothing to do with any horrible thoughts of that nature.

"Thank you so much, Stewart. It's really... I feel so much better having you helping out. I really do."

"Anything you need."

Nina puts the phone down and leans back in the chair, taking in a huge breath. She stretches her arms and legs and spins in a slow circle, scanning the room like she is a camera being moved through 360 degrees. This room. Her space for now. She luxuriates in the solitude and silence of it. With her duties executed she feels an enormous weight lifted. Birds are flying on their own now, all she has to do is wait for them to come back to her. Outside that door, Sam is sitting at a table staring at keys, his confusing thoughts hanging around him like a cloud, filling the room. But here they do not penetrate. Nina has done what she can to help him. And it feels good to keep his stratagems and confabulations at arm's length for now.

Sam listens to the inane music of his brain. It comes in cycles. Every so often. Like an annoying tune that he can't get out of his head. He takes one square of notepaper and slides it towards him. Stares at it – at the shape of the key traced there, at the number. One two three four or five. The yellow of the paper fills his head until the blue ballpoint outline becomes nothing but an incomprehensible shape and disappears into the yellowness of its background as his eyes defocus. He is looking at nothing. He might as well have his eyes closed. There is only unfocussed yellow shifting in front of him. And at first he tries consciously to think of things. Places. Rooms and corridors come to him from the abstract image bank of his life. And he'll find a particular one coming to his attention. A stark corridor, the echoes of voices and feet. A room off of it, empty, full of tables and chairs. And the room feels familiar and he enters it and walks around and tries to let it all come back to him, to let the image of the room and the corresponding key coalesce in his mind's eye and before his eyes respectively. And then he'll realise that he is picturing his secondary school and slowly his fellow pupils will drift into the room, some of their faces coming to him, the smell of adolescent boys, farts and bodily odour. And he'll scatter the image from his mind, sweeping the table of his memory clean, all the fragments drifting off onto the floor. And in the absence as he waits for it to fill with another image, the music will come, a combination of words and phrases and images unifying into a mental routine that holds nothing of use. Where's your homework, milk, toilet paper and bread, fragments of a shopping list, the waitress in the cafe near Roberta's asking do you need anything else? And these things go round and round and Sam wrestles and writhes to be free of them, but as soon as he tries to direct his concentration to something new these things crowd back in, rising slowly from the background. The inane music of his brain. Until a fresher, more potent image rises. Nina, her head lying back on the pillow tilted back in ecstasy, her body arcing towards him, breasts pointing to the ceiling as her arm reaches down and her fingers find their way into his hair and spread through it. He can almost feel it. He becomes lost in the image and finds his body beginning to respond to it. And then he's somewhere else, walking down a dark street, his hands thrust into his jacket and there's a light spattering of rain on his shoulders, prickling his scalp and spraying a refreshing mist across his forehead. The smell of spoiled rubbish. Rosanna's flat drifts in and out and through his mind. The five of them in silent communion. From outside of himself he watches himself, Neil, Rosanna and two other men whose faces are not clear. One, he thinks, is Frame. Who is the fourth? A face begins to materialise. A leather jacket. A semi-bald head with strands of hair scraping back over it, the back of his head, long and wild and curling. Who is this man? Does the name matter? He has seen him before. A fourth man. Do they know each other? Have they spoken? Where does he live? Has Sam been there before? But then the image passes and his outer body floats up through the window and outside it five yellow squares emerge and Sam is back at the table and he is staring at yellow notes with the outlines of keys on them. And his eyes return to the one that he has pulled forward. The number two. And he thinks about moving back into it, wondering if he has built something and whether he should stay with it but it seems he has nothing really, nothing tangible and the other notes are calling to him more strongly. So he slides the paper back over the MDF of the table top and he hears the smooth papery sound and it is back in line and he slides another forward. A sigh leaves his lips. Square One. It begins again. All the frustration, all the searching, to reach that place where images come unbidden takes work and time. Sam's body squirms and he wriggles; stands to try and shake off some of the tension that has built up in his muscles while his concentration has been so uniquely focused. And he stands. Walks around the room. Looks at the clock. It is past eleven. He sits again. Breathes deeply and forces himself past the malaise and the horrible feeling that he is achieving nothing. And he sits. And he stares. He sighs and looks up. Nina stands in the doorway to the bedroom, watching him. She gives him a small smile. She doesn't ask him how it is going. She doesn't want to disturb him. Perhaps she knows how frustrating it must be already without somebody coming and asking him how it's going. A good girlfriend, he thinks, and smiles back and then returns to the square of paper. It looms up at him, offering him nothing. In the background he can hear the sound of water running in the kitchen. Nina returns to the lounge, passes Sam and heads towards the bedroom without interrupting him. The sound of her bare foot padding across the floorboards and the rhythmic knock of her crutches grow louder in his mind and she approaches closer to the front of his perception, like her feet are padding across the notepaper itself. Sam looks up and she is standing in the doorway to the bedroom again and now she has a bottle of water in her hand. Their eyes meet and Sam holds her gaze, his face lifting out of its crease of concentration indicating to her that it's okay, she's not disturbing him now.

"I'm going to bed," she says. And he looks at her there, raven hair tied back in a ponytail, her thin white blouse ending just below her hips, her long legs bare, one ending in that thick white sock of plaster. The shadow of her bra beneath silk. The angular crutches propping up her willowy frame. She takes a sip of water. He can hear the sound of it slipping down her throat.

"Will you do something for me?" he asks her.

"Of course," she smiles, the wetness of the water glistening on her lips.

"Can you undress for me? Just there. Right there in the doorway."

Her smile spreads wider. She props one crutch against the doorframe, bends down and places the bottle on the floor and when she stands, the smile is gone and instead her face is set in a very direct stare, her grey eyes fixed on him, almond-shaped and wide. Her lips part, her tongue pink and wet behind them. She reaches up and unties her hair, shaking it loose in a glossy black fan across her shoulders framing her face, making its oval outline more defined, sending shadows up along her cheekbones. Her eyes never leaving him, her fingers find their way up the line of buttons between her breasts to the top one. They twist and the white silk parts by an inch. The delicate fingers descend to the next button and then the next and her blouse opens up a strip of skin from her knickers to her collarbone that glows olive next to the whiteness of the silk. She shrugs her shoulders and the blouse slides off, revealing the hard lines of her collarbone and the gentle undulation of her shoulders. It peels off one arm and catches on the other where it rests over the crutch. Maintaining a gracefulness of motion, she reaches across to hold the crutch while she raises her arm and lets the fabric drop to the floor. She stands there then, her underwear black strips across her body, the crutch scaffolding on a statue. She unclips her bra and rolls her shoulders forward. Her small breasts stand proud, the dark nipples erect. The bra catches on the crutch but she doesn't release it. It just hangs there like a flag. She draws her hand across her breast, grazing the nipple and then finds a perch for it on her hip.

"Good?" she says. Sam looks at her, her length, her curves, the unadulterated glory of her skin and he feels a longing to go over and place his hands on it. But he doesn't. He must stay put in his chair, despite the growing physical urge to be close to her. And in the shadow of his arousal there lurks a faint sadness. He can't quite pin it down at first, but he finds he is storing the image, engraving it on the wall of his mind. And then it hits him. He doesn't know why, but he feels like he is seeing her this way for the last time.

Nina bends forward to take her bottle and return to the bedroom.

"Wait," Sam says. And she stops. "And the rest."

He needs it all.

Nina slides her hand along her thigh and he can hear the sigh of skin against skin. The stretch of fabric as her fingers breach the elastic at the edge of her knickers, the inside plane of her hip becomes visible and then the shadow beneath them. Her thumb hooks the edge of the elastic and tugs it down and it slips away, exposing her. The tangle of curls that ends in the plump fold beneath. She lets go of the knickers with a snap and they drop to her ankles. She has to bend down to lift them over the plaster cast, her breasts falling forward into rounder curves. She releases them and then stands, flinging the garment across the room with a flick of her foot.

Sam forgets to breathe.

"Goodnight."

The word whispers across the room. He doesn't see her lips move. She turns and he watches the omnipotence of her naked body, its movements hovering between sensuous and lurching as the crutch swings her a step into the bedroom, the heavy white sock like the last remnant of a shell that has been chiselled away. She turns towards him, the profile of her body, proud breast, badge of pubic hair, curve of hip and buttock. She blows him a kiss. Takes the other crutch. And closes the door.

It comes to him immediately. His eyes switching straight to number one, ignoring the paper that had his attention before. A space. Another space. A space other than this. He can feel it around him. All he sees is the lounge, familiar and safe, but the sensation of it is lost, has been replaced and it is like he is lifting up out of it, disconnected from its air and smells and the feelings imparted by the orientation of its furniture. Instead he feels a coldness, a wetness, night air and rain. And then, as his hand moves to the paper and takes hold of a key that he cannot yet see, a door appears and the room around him begins to fade, a brick wall around the door, picked out in the glow of a security light, the rest of it falling into darkness outside the illuminated circle. The whole image is brighter and more present than the reality of his flat, like it is stage-lit. And he reaches out and he turns the key and as his eyes close his mind takes a step forward.

The corridor that closes around him is dark and damp. Bare bricks enclose him on either side, cobwebs, spiders scuttling in the rough hollows of the ceiling just above his head. He descends a set of concrete steps. The echo of his footsteps is shortened by the compact space so that they slap back at him. There is a musty smell. He comes to the bottom of the stairs and turns a corner into a basement space that collects all the moisture of the building above it; moisture from breath and people and rain and condensation that seeps down through brick and carpets and floors until it appears here, hanging in tiny droplets from wide patches in the ceiling. The floor is cement and the walls are bricks flaking with the grey remains of paint that may once have been white, maybe fifty years ago. At the top of the wall a small barred window lets in residual light from the street outside. There is no other light. There is the smell of earth, and the sensation of pressure, of being in the earth. And there is also a warmth here, a close warmth. A warmth that comes from the bodies. In this small room it is hard to count them. Maybe twenty, maybe more. They are standing close together and Sam picks his way through, brushing up against them as he works his way to the centre of the room. It is so close and packed that it is uncomfortable to breathe. It is an organic space. It has the claustrophobia of a womb.

He pushes into the centre and a space opens up. The heat and closeness of the air drop and the natural cool damp of the room is allowed to circulate. Sam feels he can breathe a little. He looks around at all of the people gathered there. For the most part it is too dark to make out any details, except for a small section opposite the window whose faces are dimly lit, hollow and ghostly. He does not recognise any of them but he feels like he knows them. One of them, a woman with short hair and angular features, a head that is almost oblong in shape and a face that is flat, she seems particularly familiar, like he could almost put a name to her, like it's on the tip of his tongue. But he can't. The woman has her eyes closed, her head tilted forward. The others in the light beside her all share the same pose. Eyes closed. Standing straight. Heads tipped slightly forward as if they are looking at their feet. Looking around at the others, the many others, he recognises from their silhouettes that they are standing in the same way. As if they are asleep on their feet.

Turning then, he notices four figures in the middle of the circle. These are not sleepers. They are awake. He approaches them and even though their eyes are open, scanning the room with a cool indifference, they do not see Sam. They have their hands clasped in front of them or in their pockets. They are calm. Sam walks towards them, right up close and he peers at the nearest one. It is a woman that he does not recognise. Her tangled curly hair is tied back behind her head and long earrings dangle from her earlobes. It is too dark to really tell how old she is. Standing next to her is a man that he recognises after a moment as Neil. And beside him is another man, a large man. Jonathan Frame. Not in police uniform but in some sort of hooded top, in his civvies. At the end is a third man, this one in a leather jacket, bald on top with wild curls at the back of his head, a relaxed manner to his stance. Sam recognises him from a foreign thought, a thought that he had just a moment ago, but that belonged to a completely different space, another mental process. And it comes to him. The other man from

Rosanna's flat. This is William Ross, the entrepreneur. Sam has watched him going into Roberta's for his appointment.

These four. They are awake in a room full of sleepers. Neil Allen, William Ross, Jonathan Frame and an unknown woman. Roberta's inner circle. He sees them now as clearly as if he really was standing right there in front of them. But he knows he is not. And the room begins to fade and Sam clutches at the memory, not wanting to leave it, but it grows lighter and lighter and the room becomes indistinct. And then, just before he is gone, when the walls and the people have become translucent and he can see the walls of his flat, his furniture behind them, the table in front of him, the five yellow notelets, he begins to hear a low humming, a vibration, coming from the assembled people, a common sound, linking them like the identical matching of their thoughts. And he turns and he sees, in a flicker, for a moment before he disappears, he sees her. He is standing behind her. She sits on a low chair in the middle of the room. Her hands are rising and as they rise the sound of the hum grows as if she is the conductor of an orchestra. He wants to walk forward, to turn her round and look her in the eye but as he steps, in the time it takes for his foot to rise and fall again, the image disappears.

And instead he has stepped back into his flat, into his chair, where he now sits staring at five yellow notelets arranged on the table before him. The silence of the room is so loud in the absence of that humming. He can hear the buzzing of the fridge in the kitchen, the low sounds of the city coming through the closed windows. Nina's light snoring from the next room. He thinks about joining her there, about curling up next to her warm body in that cosy bed and burying his face in the back of her neck and closing his eyes and drifting away into a sleep where, if he is lucky, he might forget the frightening realities that are emerging, that feel so large and complex and unassailable that all he wants to do is run away. But he can't sleep now. His mind is buzzing. He is awake.

And as if a hand has come to rest on the back of his head and pushed it forward, his eyes drop to the table. He reaches out to key number one, which now lies fully revealed on its yellow notelet, sitting neatly within the outline that Nina drew. And he passes his hand over the key, not quite daring to touch it, as if sensing some kind of energy pouring out of it. His hand moves across to the next yellow square. And as it passes over, the space inside the shape of the key begins to shimmer, the yellow paper within starting to change in colour. Sam shudders. His heart starts to pump faster. And now he notices that all of the remaining notes are tingling like that, little patches of heat haze rising above the inky outlines of the shapes. He continues to move his hand across, hovering over them and all at once, the yellow inside their shape changes and takes on a metallic sheen. A silver or a coppery brown. And with the keys, images begin to come to him, flooding in all at once. Sam is slammed back into his chair, his eyes and mouth wide open as he stares at a fixed point that represents no actual thing or space in this room. And images, flickering and firing, come pouring into him, blending and confused and massive and terrible and overpowering as the room around him disappears and once again he feels himself lifted into another space. But now it is not one space, it is multiple spaces. All of them combined, their features confused and jumbled. He cannot separate them out; all he can do is sit there and let them flow into him, a conduit for stray images that feel like they are always hovering around in the ether, hovering around all of us, ready to be seen, but remaining unseen until someone is opened. The ferocity of it brings a heat, a friction, his brain is overheating, being overworked, cranked up to the maximum. And his head feels like it might ignite into flames at any point, his hair incinerating and a wreath of fire ringing his scalp and his face. But there is nothing he can do. Because he is not here. He is somewhere else. And if he ever comes back down to earth, back to that room, to his room, he does not know what, if anything, will be left.

Part Three:

Caroline

Chapter Eight

UPRISING, UNVEILING, AFFIRM

Nina wakes with a start. She blinks in the darkness, seeing nothing. Her heart is racing, her sweaty limbs twisting under the duvet. The fear is an anonymous one. A vague notion that she is not safe. That here she lies, still paralysed by the heaviness of sleep and yet she is exposed to something. The whole world could come into her chamber and do with her as they wish. There are people out there, people with craven desires. They are feeling their way through a cold, empty world in the gloom. And all they are looking for is an open door to a warm room. They are hungry. And her door is unlocked. They haven't found it yet, but as their blind hands fumble across every inch of every surface of the benighted world, they are bound to find it. Their coming has not happened yet. But it will. It is inevitable.

Nina looks around in the darkness for the people, for the door, for the opening through which those who wish to do her harm might come. And her eyes find a square outlined in sharp bright lines. It is the door, the closed door to her room and beyond it the world is bright. Beyond it. Beyond...

Her senses begin to come back to her. Shapes coalesce. She recognises the door. The shadowy shapes of its panels. And she realises where she is. She is in Sam's flat. She does not know what time it is, only that it must still be night. The still depths of night. And though she is still paralysed by sleep, trapped in a body that is unwilling to move, she breathes a sigh of relief and acknowledges that the thoughts clinging to her from the dream she must have been having are only that: thoughts. And now they are gone.

Yet, as she stirs and comes back to herself the unease remains. The room comes into focus. There's the bedside table beside her. The curtains over the windows, no longer black but now backed by the faint light of the city and the streetlights outside. She is in Sam's bedroom, it is the middle of the night, and everything is fine. Except that she still feels distinctly unsafe. And she doesn't know why. She has the urge to sit. To get up. To check something. To go and see. But she doesn't know what. The sense that the world may be in some way broken, perhaps, and maybe there's a hole, a gaping tear in the next room, an opening to something that shouldn't be there. Like a hole in the side of an aeroplane. Except that this hole is not sucking things out of the room. It is blowing things in. A vortex through which large and dangerous ideas can enter. Ideas that can tear the world apart. She doesn't know if the hole is really there. Everything is probably alright, probably okay. But she feels like she should go and check.

And then as she slides her elbow back, about to push herself up to a sitting position, the impulse leaves her. She doesn't need to check anything. She is just half-awake and she is panicking about something. Her body is still in that excited state, adrenaline pumping blindly and pointlessly around her body. That feeling of emptiness in her stomach as the blood is directed away from it towards the limbs, ready to fight or flee. All of this in response to some fleeting yet terrifying image that came to her in the midst of sleep.

And although she cannot recall what that image was, she has the lurking sense that she knows where it came from. Staring at the bright lines that mark the outline of the door, it seems to swell and fill her perception. Sam is out there, most likely still staring at those stupid squares of paper. And while she has slept, he has been awake trying to delve into the recesses of his subconscious. Who knows what he might dredge up, what could happen while she lies here, vulnerable and defenceless. She chastises herself, appalled at the idea that she might fear Sam, the idea of betraying him, even if it is only on the level of thought. But then she knows that he would not be appalled. He would say that she might be right to fear him because he doesn't know what he is capable of. And despite all his assurances that he could never hurt her, he is still holding her at arm's length, keeping her away from parts of himself that he doesn't trust. Because he does not really know what could be unleashed.

It is the thought that has never gone away. And she feels a chill and now she does sit up and she pulls the duvet tight around herself as if to fend off this horrible idea. But it is there and it always will be no matter what she does. And if it is there, she knows it must be there for a reason. Because that is what she really fears, that indeed she may be doing the wrong thing. She could be putting herself in danger. And the scariest part of all of this is that she will one day have to face that unpleasant reality. All the horrors of the world do not compare to the horror that she might be alone again. Is that it? Is it about being without Sam – or is it just about being alone? Does she cling to him because he is who he is or just because she needs someone to cling to?

Nina buries her head in the pillow. She is sick of these amorphous nocturnal thoughts that supplant reality in the darkness. The only thing worth thinking about is what is actually happening. Realities. Things that she can see and touch and feel. She screws her eyes shut and defiantly tries to find sleep, hoping that this time she can find a room with nothing in it where she can just close the door and rest and keep all of those harmful thoughts on the outside.

She wakes to the golden glow of daylight filtering through the curtains. The sounds of life from the street outside tell her that the world has already got going. The traffic noise throbs with all its instruments, the low growls, the high whines and the squawking of horns. In the distance a police car howls its way across the city. Voices, too. Chatter, shouts, the screaming of a disgruntled infant. It must already be well into the morning, way past the hour that Nina normally gets up. Whether it is the stress of recent events or just being off work, something is making her lazy. Ordinarily, even on a hung-over Sunday she's up at seven on autopilot. She sits up rubbing her eyes and swings her legs out of the bed.

Clunk. Her plaster hits the floor and it sends a painful shudder through her leg. She's still not used to this. Already it has put a kink in her day. She hisses through her teeth and reaches for a crutch. Lifts herself up in strenuous, lurching stages and then, standing at her full height, she stretches. Not all at once the way she normally does – arms in the air, pulling the body from her fingertips to the balls of her feet – but each limb separately. Everything requires thought. Even this automatic process now has to be taken one careful step at a time. She looks around the room, scolding herself for leaving her clothes scattered about the floor. She is about to start picking them up when she turns back to the bed. It is empty.

She opens the bedroom door. Sam is slumped over the table, face first. His arms are splayed out in front of him and in his sleep, or in the act of falling asleep, he has disturbed the keys, separating them from their notelets and scattering the five metal objects and the five yellow squares all over the tabletop. She wonders whether this was an accident or perhaps a fit of pique that presaged mental and physical exhaustion. She considers waking him. It doesn't seem like he could be getting any decent sleep sitting there the way he is. The very least she can do is wake him up and get him to move into the bedroom.

She stops beside him and runs her hand over his shoulders, feeling their broadness. He is not a muscular man, but they feel solid through his shirt. Her hand moves up the back of his neck and an affectionate smile creeps onto her face as her fingers play with his hair where it begins on his nape. She can almost picture him as a sleeping child. She cranes to look at his face where it rests against the table. His mouth and nose are smooshed and funny-looking but still he seems so peaceful in repose, so benign.

"Sam," she whispers as she moves her hand through his hair, her fingers tracing lines up to his head. She leans in and places her lips against his ear. "Sam," softer, gently shaking his shoulder.

Sam's head whips up with a ragged roar-like in-breath. And he's bolt upright, his eyes wild and staring. Nina totters and almost loses her balance. Correcting herself on the crutch, a tiny laugh escapes her.

"Are you alright?"

He gawps around as if he has woken to find himself in the middle of a warzone.

"Who..."

Nina smiles and replaces her hand on his shoulder,

"It's me. It's Nina, honey." She smoothes her hand along to the other shoulder until her arm wraps around him. All bed-headed, he looks freshly minted, like a newborn. He blinks twice at her and then his face eases into a gentle smile.

"Oh," he says, his lips still sticky with sleep.

"Good morning you." And she places a soft kiss on his lips. "Long night, was it?"

"Uh, I dunno."

His arms sweep across the table, ranging, searching blindly for something.

"You made a bit of a mess here. Do you want me to," and she reaches to pick up one of the keys, to replace it on its notelet.

His hand gets there first. He holds the key up between them, looking at it as if it was an alien artefact. Nina's jaw goes slack,

"Wow. Okay."

Sam picks up three more keys. Looking around for the fifth and final one, he dips under the table and retrieves it from the floor.

"Okay," Nina says again. "How about a coffee?"

Sam weighs the keys in one hand, jangling them together, and wipes his eyes with the other.

"Mm-hmm."

The fresh bitter smell works a magic all of its own, heralding the dawn of a world of wakefulness and activity. The keys are ranged out on the table in between Nina and Sam. No need for the yellow notes anymore. Sam takes a sip of his coffee and blinks at them, stretching out his eyes and taking a deep lungful of the air that blows in through the open windows. Nina clasps her mug in both hands, waiting for him to speak of his discoveries.

"So much..." his words trail off as the thought continues in his head. A shadow passes across his features and he looks down into his coffee. His eyes twist up to her, hooded.

"I have been to places," he says, "five places. But those places, they, each of them, they contain so many things. So many moments and events. Terrible and wonderful things. Mostly terrible. I... I don't even know where to start. It feels like I've spent half my life in these places."

"Start," she reaches out, a finger extended, and rests it upon the rightmost key, her left, "here."

"Okay. Sure. Um. No. Not that one. Not yet. Maybe this is a better place to start."

And he wipes his brow as if clearing sweat from it. Nina can see that he is interceding, cautiously organising thoughts and information to make it palatable for her. Already. But she is willing to allow him this. If he's going to give her everything then he'll get to it, why not let him do it in his own time?

Sam's hand rests on the middle key, a large grey Mortis.

"This is the key to a basement. I don't know where it is. Not exactly. Not yet." He takes a deep breath in and lets it out slowly. "I've only been there at night. Maybe the specific place will come to me. I don't know. Maybe if I wandered the streets or..."

"It doesn't matter where it is. Just tell me what you know."

It seems like he is stalling. And for a moment she doubts whether he could have actually found anything new just from sitting at this table all night. But before this train of thought has time to develop, he breaks it: "The door is in an alleyway at the back of a building.

It's a commercial building I think. A restaurant or some shops or a small office building, something like that. Anyway, the door leads down to this basement. And it's a place where Roberta brings us all, at night, without our knowledge. And she does some kind of, I don't know what it is, like a ritual, a communion. It somehow seems to bind us together and it allows her to give us instruction. Keeps us conditioned and malleable. Sometimes everyone is there and sometimes it's just a few of us. And she tells us things, things to do. I suppose it's a command centre in a way. When," he pauses, swallows, "When we're in there, none of us are aware of being in there. We're all in some kind of a trance. Like we're asleep. If any of us remember it, it is as if it's some strange dream, some otherworldly place. And it mixes with the complex images. Things she shows us down there. The dreams and memories she creates in our minds. All of her secrets are down there, I think. I don't know if there's maybe a store room or something, if we could find it maybe there'd be some evidence or... Anyway, the only people who are awake in there apart from Roberta are these four people. They're awake. As in "Awake", you know, like the way Neil used it. Like the way I am now."

"What does that mean? Why are they awake?"

"Well, not like me. I mean not like me at all – but they know what's going on. Like I do now. It means that they are willing participants. They're her inner circle, like her lieutenants."

"You mean that they know what they're doing? Accomplices? Why would anyone do that?"

"I suppose they all have their reasons."

"Who are they?"

"Well, Neil's one, obviously. Then there's Jonathan Frame, who you've also met. There's a guy called William Ross. I haven't met him. Not properly. But I've seen him going into Roberta's house. And then the fourth is a woman, but I don't know who she is. I've never seen her before. Well, not consciously anyway.

"Ross is a very rich, powerful character. I'm guessing from his notes that Roberta's given him so much, you know, legitimately as a therapist, that he sees her work as a good cause or something and that's why he gets involved. I suppose if you think everything's in service of something good then you don't question what is involved so much."

Nina's eyebrows are raised. She folds her arms and blows a thin line of air out in front of her.

"Not *the* William Ross?"

Sam frowns, "You know him?"

"Well, if it's the same William Ross you're talking about, and it sounds like it is, then yes. And you should know him too. He tried to buy Blue Mountain after you sold it but the board of directors wouldn't play ball. He's trying to sue them as we speak. I'm working on the case myself."

"No way."

"Mm-hmm. Do you reckon we should speak to him?"

Sam almost laughs. He shrugs and shakes his head.

"Look, I have no idea whether he's in with Roberta for his business interests or whether he's just a sick, sadistic bastard who gets his jollies fucking with people, but either way I can't imagine him being very sympathetic."

Nina frowns.

"On the other hand I don't really see what harm it could do."

"A sick, sadistic bastard. That's Neil, isn't it? He just does it for the kicks."

"Well, that's what he says. I'm not sure if I believe him. All of this, it's... People have motivations behind motivations. There's always a human reason for everything. No-one's a monster."

"The man tried to kill me."

"Okay, he's a monster. I don't suppose it hurts to say that."

Nina doesn't look especially comforted by the words. Her arms still folded, she's looking down at the table.

"I got him good for you though," says Sam and she can't help but crack a smile.

"But these awake ones, they're maybe people we could speak to. See if we can turn them against her – or at least get them to help in some way?"

"Just because they're awake doesn't mean they're not programmed. There are some things that it's still better that they do when they're not with it. If anything I guess they're more willing – more likely to carry through instructions that go against what they would do if they were conscious. They're her zealots."

"So we'd be better off trying to wake some of the sleepers?"

"I don't know what to tell you, Nina. I'm not at a place where I can make any practical decisions yet. And neither are you. Not until you've heard the rest."

"Sure. Go on. Next key."

Sam is absorbed in the keys for a minute or so. About to open his mouth to speak when the ringing of Nina's phone cuts him off.

"Sorry, could you..."

"Oh, yeah. Yes of course."

He gets up and retrieves her phone from the bedroom. She takes the call.

"Hello?" Listens. "Sorry, could you hold on a sec?" She holds her hand over the phone and looks at Sam. It is a strange look.

There's something furtive in it, something guilty, but he interprets it correctly – this is not for his ears.

"Another coffee?" he says.

When he has left the room she uncovers the mouthpiece and says, "Mr. Furst. Sorry about that."

"'s alright," mutters the gruff cockney voice. It sounds like he's been up all night. It sounds like he's probably been drinking. It sounds exactly the way it did when she spoke to him late last night.

"Preliminary investigation," he says without pleasantries, "Nothing on her in a criminal sense. She's squeaky clean. No record. Court actions same. No-one's sued her or nothing. No malpractice. Professional associations are all happy as Larry. Matter of fact she's affiliated with six different organisations. She's even on the governing board of one, the British Society of Psychologists and Psychotherapists."

"Sounds important."

"I dunno. There's a lot of these societies of this and whatnot of psychobabble. Who knows which ones are actually, you know, something, and which ones is just three old biddies meeting every other Thursday for tea and cake and sending out a newsletter. This one seems pretty reputable though. The other board members all got plenty of letters after their names."

"Can you give me a list of them?"

"Might as well just check out their website – BSoPP.co.uk – it's all there."

"Thanks," Nina says as she quickly scribbles down the web address. She puts the pen down and sighs. "Shame, I thought there might be something, but she seems like a model citizen."

"Oh, that she is," Furst grumbles. "Even her clients are squeaky clean. Reputable. Pillars of the community. Lots of coppers."

"Yeah, I know."

"There is one thing, though."

"Oh?" Nina sits up.

"Dunno what's usual for this sort of thing, but considering her types that she sees, it seems a bit fucking fishy, if you'll pardon my French." Nina can hear papers being shuffled about on the other end of the phone. "Here it is. See, BSoPP keeps a confidential list of all its members' clients. It's a kind of insurance thing, I think, in case of malpractice or anything funny happening. Fortunately for us, whoever deals with their server security is a bit of a dunce. Password's BSoPP1234." Forty Rothmans-a-day laugh. Nina grimaces, wishing he hadn't told her how he obtained the information. "Anyway, so in the past ten years, she's lost eighteen clients due to their dying."

"They died?"

"Yeah. Eighteen."

"That's almost two a year."

"Yeah. Most part though, they seem to have increased as time goes on. In the first five years she only lost six. Later, there's more."

"Jesus. How did they..."

"Lot of suicides." A cold feeling works its way through Nina's fingertips, up through her arms and into her chest. "I mean, you'd have thought a shrink that clocks up a suicide a year's probably no good and should be struck off, wouldn't you?"

"I don't know. Not if they're working with generally suicidal patients."

"But she's not, is she?"

Nina nods, as if he could hear her assent.

"Other thing is car crashes. Lot of them. She's had nine suicides. Seven car crashes."

"And the other two."

"Murdered. One was a botched mugging, other was killed by his wife."

"Shit, what do we... I don't know what to make of this."

"Ask me, I think you definitely got something worth looking at here. Leave it with me. I'll see what else I can get."

"If it's of any use to you, I've got a copy of her patient notes typed up. I could email them over to you if you want."

"Yeah, that'd be grand."

When she hangs up all she can do is stare into space. This is something she really hadn't been expecting, and all of a sudden their situation seems significantly more perilous.

Sam returns to the lounge holding two cups of coffee, which by now are lukewarm. Nina is looking out of the window and her face has a drained look on it. The phone is still in her hand.

"Is everything alright?" he asks her.

"Er..." she looks down, rubbing her eyes. Takes a couple of breaths. When she looks up she is smiling, a little colour back in her cheeks. But it's a fragile pretence and it's obvious to both of them. "Yeah, yeah, I'm fine."

Sam places a hand on her arm, "If you..."

"Can we talk about this later? Why don't we just carry on for now, okay?"

"Sure, sure. Whatever you want."

Next key.

"It's someone's house. A suburban semi in a quiet cul-de-sac. Whenever I've been there it's night time. I don't know who lives there but when I open the door no-one else is there. I leave it open and others come in. We do not speak. There is no conversation, no casual chitchat. Some of them I recognise, but each time the people who are there changes a bit. We sit in a circle. Ross is there. I think he's in charge. Everyone is silent except for the person who is talking. It's some kind of sharing group. We all go around the circle and we talk about the things we have been doing in our lives.

"When we have all finished, a silence falls over the room and everyone's heads drop and we sit there with our eyes closed until Ross speaks. He asks us if anyone has anything to say to a particular person. That person will stay sitting with their head down, as if asleep. The others will sit up. And one by one they will begin to say things. And, Nina, the things they say," he takes a deep breath. His eyeballs ricochet beneath his closed lids. Reading something off of them. "It's like this: on a number of occasions I saw Rosanna sitting there. She would talk about the things that she had been doing, what had been happening to her. She would often talk about how lonely she was feeling. Sometimes there were accounts of dates or short-term boyfriends. Or stuff from work, like that she'd been doing well or she got a promotion or she got in trouble 'cos she'd dropped the ball on something and her boss told her off. You know, the kind of thing you expect people to share. And she'd go into her deep feelings about that, the way she thought her loneliness related to such and such feeling of a lack of self-worth or something.

"And then someone would stand up. And I swear, listening to it now, last night when I saw it, it was the most horrible thing. Like they were picking apart her life, her aspirations, her whole personality." His eyes open. Wide and electric and staring right through her, "They would say, 'You deserve to be alone. Nobody could love you. That guy was right not to call you because all he would have gotten off you is a load of shit. Why would any man want to be encumbered by that?' Then another one'll get up and he'll say, 'Of course your mother never loved you. When she left you at the supermarket as a child it was because she was trying to get rid of you.' And another, a woman, she says, 'You dress like shit. You look like a horrible desperate tart. The way you wear your hair that's disgusting. It looks all greasy and covered in shit. You'd probably be better off if you just stayed at home as much as you can eating ice cream and running down the batteries on your vibrator.'"

His head switches to the left, to the right as the interchanging voices inhabit him, the pace and ferocity of his language picking up, spit flecking his lips, teeth fizzing on sibilants.

"'You use a vibrator?' says a man, an older one. 'That's disgraceful. It's bad enough that you spend time furtively masturbating in your filthy little flat but the fact that you've actually gone so far as to buy a vibrator, to spend actual money on pleasuring your slimy cunt. And I bet you bought it mail order didn't you? You wouldn't have the guts to go into one of those grim Soho shops to buy one. No, of course not. Because it would remind you of how sordid you really are and where you belong. And because you know. You know deep down what everybody would say about you if they knew.'

"And then I saw myself standing and heard the words coming out of my own mouth in my own voice and I was saying 'The only reason you got promoted is because your boss wants to fuck you. You know it's nothing to do with your own abilities. You have no special talents or skills. Not that you even need them in your line of work. You pedal bullshit, it's just white wine, high heels and handbags and the only thing that matters is who's the biggest slut. So it's no wonder that guy gave you a promotion, but remember, he's just going to get his dick wet in you and then discard you like the rest. I mean, if you were good looking enough then maybe you'd get somewhere but you know ultimately this is as far as you're going because you're not. And you can put it about as much as you want but all you're going to get for it is a mouth full of semen. Is that what you want? To taste as many different loads as you can? 'Cos I'm telling you, you can't expect more than that.'"

Sam slams to a halt. His face is red. His eyes snap back into focus and he sees Nina. Shudders. Shrivels in his seat. He was at least going to try and sugar coat it or dispense with some of the language, but the retelling just snowballed and took on a life of its own. His face feels cold. Hers is fierce with outrage and disgust.

"I know, I know," he says. "I can't believe I actually said those things. That any of us said those things. It was really horrible. Like we were trying to break her down. Assassinate her character. And the whole time she'd just be sitting there with her head down taking it all in. Our voices planting things like seeds in her subconscious."

Nina looks away, holding a hand up to her mouth as the edges of it curve down involuntarily. She looks nauseous for a second. And then she splutters a hiccup of laughter into her balled fist. Smothers a snort.

"You know it's almost funny," she says. "It's like a reverse therapy group. I mean do you think that shit actually works?"

And she looks at Sam with the question.

He is thrown by her amusement, "I have no idea."

"Sorry, I didn't mean to make light. It's just, ugh." She flaps her arms as if shaking off filth. "And it wasn't just Rosanna – everyone goes through this, this kind of gauntlet, right?"

Sam nods, "We all did."

"And you were the keyholder, right? What does that mean?"

"I suppose because I've been a client for such a long time. This is what's really bothering me now, it's that I thought that I was just another pawn, or that I'd just been a little bit involved, but it seems that I was in really deep. Was? Am."

"Sam." She takes hold of his hand and looks into his eyes. "It makes sense. It all makes sense, okay. If you weren't in deep why would it be such a problem to get you out?"

"Shhh!" Sam yanks his hand away from her.

"I..."

He silences her with a further glare. She looks away and tucks a strand of hair behind her ear.

"Can we, can we just not talk like that, okay? I mean, we need to, but we can't just, you know, casually. When we come to that we'll do it, but it needs to be focussed, purposeful."

She smiles tightly and nods, folding her arms, "Okay. Fine. What's next?"

"It doesn't get better."

"Sam, I want to hear it how it is, okay. I'm not judging you. Don't worry about me."

"Thank you."

He holds up a coppery Yale key.

"I unlock the door. It's a central London terrace. You know, bigger on the inside than it is on the outside. It's huge. The hallway is marble-floored and there is a wide carpeted staircase leading up to the next floor. It is the middle of the day and there's nobody about. The place is opulent. Ridiculous. Everything in it is hideously expensive. In the hallway there are antique glass-fronted cabinets. Inside them there are many small ornaments. I don't know what they are made of but they are all intricately carved. They're Chinese looking. Sometimes all I do is open one of these cabinets and move some of the artefacts around. Swap them over, so that they're standing in the wrong places. And then after doing that I go and leave and within ten minutes I'm walking around central London going to the shops with no idea that I have been to this place.

Other times I will go up the stairs. There's a large landing there with lots of old original paintings. Some large portraits, smaller landscapes. I walk towards a picture about the size of an A4 piece of paper in a gilt frame. It is a pastoral scene, a farmer, a horse and cart, rolling hills. I take it down from the wall and without even really looking at it, I turn it upside down. Then I go back down the stairs and leave. The next time I visit I go up to the third floor. Here it is darker. A thick blue carpet runs between the doors to several bedrooms. I enter one. An enormous bed occupies the centre of the room. It has a large padded leather headboard. The curtains are closed. The place is immaculate. Clothes are folded on a chest at the front of the bed. A pair of slippers sits on the floor next to the bed. I go into an en suite bathroom. It is the biggest bathroom I have ever seen. The floor is marble and one wall is entirely taken up by a mirror above a big round bath. I look at myself. It is like I am looking at another person. His expression is flat and without any sign of emotion. His eyes are dead. I cock my head. He cocks his head. And then without giving this reflected person any further thought, I turn and walk over to the sink. There, I find an electric toothbrush and a shaving kit. I swap their places. I return to the bedroom and I swap the slippers over so that they are the wrong way round, their insteps facing outwards. Then I take the pile of clothes, I open the chest and I put them inside.

"I leave the room and I walk back down the blue carpeted corridor. I descend a flight of stairs along which there are many small paintings. I do not see them because I do not stop to look at them. I move across the next landing and despite all the finery I do not linger, I move with steady, regular steps towards the staircase. Then I descend towards the main hallway. As I reach the bottom step the front door opens. An elderly man enters, walking with a stick. He does not look well. His face is gaunt and haggard and his wispy white hair is kinked and frizzy. His clothes are immaculate. I do not greet this man, nor does his entrance cause any change in my behaviour. I keep walking towards the front door. He tries to block my path and he is shouting at me. He threatens to call the police. I keep walking. He begins to hit me with his stick, but his arm is weak and it does not really hurt. On the threshold, I stop and turn and I tell him in plain simple words that he has seen nothing. The man turns away from me and looks up at the stairs behind him. I close the door and leave him. Within ten minutes I am shopping on Oxford Street. I feel completely normal and I have no memory of this event. I have gone there because I feel like taking in the atmosphere in central London. I buy myself a cheap domestic camera at an expensive price from an electronics shop. I still have the camera. I have never used it."

Sam's words stop. There is no flourish or sense of conclusion. The whole telling has been in a monotone and it ends in that way, as if it could just continue on. A strange silence fills the room. The kind of silence that follows a persistent tone that has been present for some time before it abruptly breaks off. The kind of silence you can hear. Sam puts the key down on the table. His eyes are still fixed on Nina and they do not deviate. Nor does he speak. Nina can't take the silence any more and so she coughs. And then she speaks, "What do you think that was all about?"

"I have no idea. I just see these moments. Remember them. I can't interpret them beyond any obvious explanation."

"It's so odd." Nina looks out of the window, as if a plane might fly past trailing a banner with the answer written on it. She sees clear skies, the occasional white cloud, the tops of buildings. But no plane. "I suppose it's just fragments of a life. You've got three pieces out of a thousand-piece puzzle."

"Fragments of a life," Sam echoes. "It makes me think of Rosanna. The way we would wreck her flat and then she would be made to think that she'd done it to herself."

"She's trying to drive you all nuts. Anything to keep you in therapy. Whatever push it is that you need."

"Right."

"Are you ready to continue? Do you need a break?"

"No. It's fine. I can go on."

Sam looks down at the keys. He licks his lips as he studies them. He reaches out for one, but hesitates. Pulls back his hand. Then he reaches in and takes it and Nina can see that his hand is shaking. A silver Yale.

"It's the lounge in a house somewhere in a big suburban sprawl. Like Borehamwood maybe. The house is bland as hell. All Ikea furniture and you can see out into the garden and it's just a strip of concrete with a small patch of grass and a fence so high it screens out everything but rows and rows of identical roofs. I'm sitting with a man. A small guy with a funny face, he's not ugly, just distinctive. He's got a large round nose and thick eyebrows and his brow is quite pronounced, so it looks like he's squinting all the time. And he's looking at me. Right at me. Right in my eyes. And there are tears in his eyes. The rest of his face isn't really moving. It's like a mask. But his eyes are crying and the tears are leaking all down his face, completely uncontrolled. But he doesn't reach up a hand to wipe them. And part of me somewhere wants to hand him a tissue. The longer it goes on the more I feel I should just reach over and wipe them myself. But that part of me is locked away inside. It's like hearing someone faintly calling from a long way away. Someone in a room underground. Someone you couldn't see even if you looked. And he doesn't move at all. And neither do I. I'm just looking at him.

"And from upstairs there's a sound. It goes on and on and on. A creaking. And it gets louder and louder. And then you can hear a thumping coming through the floor. And I know what the sound is and I know why he's crying.

"After what feels like a long time, the creaking stops. And then I can hear muffled voices from upstairs. But they're too indistinct and I can't make out what they're saying. Then there's footsteps on the stairs and a man comes down into the room. It is Neil. He's completely with it. He's not walking in a trance. He's got a spring in his step. He stops to look at us. And a sneering smile creeps onto his face and he gives a little chuckle when he looks at the other man. And then he walks out of the room and I hear the front door close.

I now know the man I am sitting with. His name is Jeremy Vickers. I have seen him at Roberta's.

"Then another man walks in from the hallway. I do not recognise him. He is in his late twenties and has long dreadlocked hair, loose-fitting, hippy clothes. He goes up the stairs. And then I hear a door shut and the creaking. But the whole time I am not really concerned with any of these things. I am just looking at Jeremy and Jeremy is looking at me and he is crying without emotion.

"Another sound. It is a baby crying. Also coming from upstairs. I do not feel anything. It does not mean anything to me. I get up from my couch and I walk towards the stairs. Jeremy follows after me. We go up the stairs. There is cream carpet on the stairs. The floor of the landing is that kind of shiny fake wood floorboards. The walls are a neutral shade. The only picture is a bad print of a blue flower next to the bathroom door. I stop next to a door and open it. Inside there is a cot and the baby is inside it. Jeremy walks inside. I close the door after him and then stand with my back to it.

"The creaking is much louder up here. And I can hear panting; breaths. I see – but without looking at it – notice without noticing – that the door to another bedroom is slightly open. And inside it I recognise a woman lying on the bed. She is Mandy Vickers. His wife. The same oblong-headed woman that I have seen in the basement. She is half-naked. And the dreadlocked man is on top of her. They are having sex. Her head hangs off the end of the bed while he has sex with her. Her face has no expression. It is flat. As if she is waiting for a bus.

"When the baby is quiet, Jeremy comes out of the room and I take him back downstairs into the lounge."

Sam puts down the key. There are tears at the corners of Nina's eyes. But she doesn't wipe them away. They are stinging her but she does not blink. She stares at Sam and Sam stares back at her and he is blank. But she knows that it is not an unfeeling expression: it is masking great pain. The things he has seen. So many painful images stored away in the backrooms of his mind. She wonders if it is right or even healthy for him to be doing this to himself, and for her to be aiding him in it.

"Is this even real?"

"I think so."

"But, if, just think," her hands play pat-a-cake on the table, leaving clammy imprints every time they move. "You have these keys, right. And some of them are for general things – the basement and the group house. But these last two, they're specific actions, so, and, what I'm trying to say is that it only needs one of you to have the key to go into people's houses when they're not there or "asleep" or whatever. So surely there must be other things that you've been involved in where you didn't have the key, right? Where someone else did."

Sam nods, "These are just two. They're just," his forehead creases, dark things rippling beneath his skin, "a glimmer."

Nina holds her hand to her mouth and bites her finger as if to still its shaking. She fumbles for words. Her lips move behind her hand. Then she moves it away. She opens her mouth to speak.

A shudder goes through the flat. The whole building shakes. And there is a noise from outside like the tearing of concrete and a smashing and a sound like heavy gravel being thrown on the floor. Nina and Sam sit rigid in their seats. Sam's first thought is that something is happening to him, and he has to ask Nina, "Did you feel that?"

She nods rapidly. And then they're both on their feet and they're at the window.

"Car crash."

They say it simultaneously. The coincidence of speech provokes them to look at each other. It is a strange, dislocated look, and in that look the significance of what the words are describing is emphasised.

In the street below, there is a rust red Volkswagen Golf. It is an old model. The bonnet of the boxy little car is embedded in the front of the newsagent's. Most of the plate glass frontage has fallen away around it and bright fluorescent lights burn inside the hole that it has created. Smoke and dust swirl in the opening. Loose newspapers flutter up and around the vehicle. Vegetables and canned foods have spilled out. Glossy magazines overlap in a heap, forming a collage of tiny images, a scaled effect that shines like the skin of a fish. On the road either side of the accident the traffic has ground to a halt. And Nina wonders how, on this street, a car could have gotten up the speed and been able to turn so sharply to collide with the window. It must have been a handbrake turn. As they watch, a figure covered in white-grey dust stumbles out of the opening, his feet slurring through the spilled contents of the shop. He is walking with his head leaning forward and his back slumped, his arms hanging loose and low to the ground. He reaches the edge of the pavement and sits down on the curb. Even though his face is downturned and his clothing is obscured by dust, Sam recognises him as the newsagent.

The traffic stays still for some time but no-one gets out. They are gawping at the scene, as if unaware that they could leave their individual automotive bubbles and interact with it – or perhaps just waiting patiently for the obstruction to be cleared. After a few minutes horns begin to honk, obstreperous yelps from drivers who are too far away to see what has happened. Then, to the left of the accident, on the side that is blocked by the jutting back-half of the Volkswagen, the car nearest to it swerves around it into the opposite lane and accelerates into the gap between the accident and the stalled oncoming traffic, taking advantage of the moment to get away and get on with its day. The street holds its breath, as if in shock at this bold and heartless manoeuvre. And then the car behind it attempts to follow suit. A mutual blaring of horns as the vehicle going the other way decides to move forward, obstructing its passage and nearly colliding with it. Both cars stop. The follower is forced to reverse to the safety of his own side of the road. The obstructer continues on his way and the traffic behind him begins to flow again.

"I don't believe it," says Nina. "People in this city." She turns to Sam but his eyes are glued to the scene. She turns back. A man on the blocked side of the road gets out of his car and approaches the crashed vehicle. He bends down next to the window and peers inside. Then he opens the door and he seems to be speaking with the driver. He takes out his phone and dials. Nina hears a sharp intake of breath from Sam. There is a new tension in his forehead, his eyes narrowed. A couple of other members of the public arrive next to the newsagent. One stands talking to him, the other crouches beside him, rubbing his back. Maybe they're not all bastards, thinks Nina.

Sam has both his hands on the windowsill. His feet are pushing up onto their toes and his forehead is pressed against the glass. His face is contorting. The skin has tightened and now it is pulling his mouth upwards in an uneven way that exposes clenched-together teeth.

"Sam?"

His head whips towards her.

"Are you okay?"

"I know you're going to think this is just coincidence," he says, "but..."

"I know," Nina says.

"You know what? You don't think it's a coincidence?"

"I'm not sure. There's something that I heard."

"What do you mean?"

"I'll agree with you that it's pretty fucking disturbing."

"What did you hear? What..."

A high-pitched pinging cuts them off. It is Nina's phone ringing and they both look down at the table, where its vibrations are causing it to rotate in a lackadaisical swirl, like a canoe with no oars.

Nina picks it up, "Hello Stewart."

"Nina, I've got that information for you. Needless to say, it is absolutely for your ears only. You don't share this with anyone okay and you certainly don't tell anyone where you got it. It could cost me my job. Or worse."

"I understand."

"Okay, have you got a pen and paper?"

Sam watches Nina listen with a series of nods and mm-hmms. She is on her third notelet by the time she stops scribbling and thanks whoever is on the other end of the phone profusely.

"Who was that?"

Nina's face hardens. Her grey eyes become steely and they search Sam's.

"Are you sure you want to know?"

Sam drums his fingers on the windowsill. He looks at the evolving scene outside. There are more people gathered around the accident. A crowd of onlookers has begun to assemble on the near side of the street below his window.

"It's difficult," he says after a while. "I know you've been doing something. And I'm grateful for that. But I can't tell if making me aware of it is a good thing or a bad thing."

Nina sighs. He's being so woolly about every little decision.

"Well, how about this? What if we take it a little bit at a time? And if anything seems somehow dangerous to you then we can stop."

"Sounds sensible."

"Why don't we sit down and I'll go through it slowly, okay?"

A tentative nod. They take their seats at the table, facing each other. Sirens sound in the distance, growing closer. Nina opens her mouth to speak.

"But," says Sam.

"But what?"

"What if it's not at the moment of you telling me something that's the problem? What if there's an accumulation of factors? What if something happens later and then it's because I know that you've done such and such that it makes me..."

"What if, what if, what if! Sam, we have to take some action. We have to do something. Don't make me be alone in this. Don't you see, if we're isolated from each other, scared of every move, then we're playing right into her hands."

"Sorry. You're right." He folds his arms and tries to smile, but it's a tight, stretched kind of expression.

"I have a contact in the police. His name is Stewart Worth. He's an – we used to be very close." She looks down to see that her fingers are tying each other in knots.

"Close how?"

She takes a deep breath, "He asked me to marry him. I said no."

"Oh."

The silence is uncomfortable. Sam is not sure if to ask any more would be prying. Nina is not sure whether further explanation would make the awkwardness of the moment better or worse.

"These names here," she pushes the notes towards him. "They're all police officers. As far as Stewart could tell, it's every PTSD client she's ever had from the force. Do you recognise any of them?"

Sam scans the notes. There must be some fifteen names there.

"Jonathan Frame." Their eyes meet. Nina nods. "The others I've never heard of before." He smiles at her. "It's good though. Well done. Thank you."

"Whatever it takes." She holds his gaze. "There's something else," she says. And, choosing her words carefully, she tells him about Furst and his findings. A shiver passes from her to Sam. Neither of them dares look at what is happening outside the window.

"But that's not all, is it?" says Sam. "It's not all suicides and car crashes."

"No..." The hairs on the back of her arms are pricking up. Something is moving in. A dark cloud. A storm. "Two of them were murdered."

"I know."

And his hand moves towards the fifth key. Nina's throat sticks together when she tries to swallow. Sam is looking through the key, his eyes are unfocused. His breathing becomes slow and steady and a trance-like pall falls over him. He holds the key up. A green-gold Chubb.

"We're standing in the back garden. It's a horrible night. The rain is coming down heavy. But we don't shrink from it. No-one covers their head for shelter. We just stand there, five figures amongst the black shapes of shrubbery. All straight. Rigid. Soaked to the skin. The grass is so wet that water is seeping through my shoes. But I don't care. There are five of us. Me, Neil, Frame, Ross and a woman. In this light I cannot make out her face. Not yet.

"One by one, the lights in the house go out. And then I hear the opening and closing of the front door. Voices. A man's. Children. The man is coaxing them on and I hear their footsteps and their voices growing fainter. And I see them emerge onto the road at the front of the house and they are walking off down the street. They each have backpacks on. The small boy has a red one and the slightly taller girl has a pink one and holds an umbrella. The man is holding their hands. He has a large pack, the type you might take on a round the world trip. He is walking as quickly as he can, but the young boy is dragging on his arm, holding him up. Every so often he stops and turns to the boy, telling him to hurry up, then jerking his arm impatiently as he continues.

"When we can no longer make out the sound of their voices, we move towards the back of the house. Frame and Ross are in front, with the other three of us walking in a line behind them, our feet falling on the wet grass and squelching in unison. I can tell from the even, lifeless way that they walk that Neil and Frame and Ross are all also asleep at this point. Just like me and the woman. We reach the back door and the others part and I walk to the front. I produce this key and I unlock the door. I hold it open for the others to enter.

"We move in single file down a side passage. In the dark I cannot see much, but I can tell it is some sort of utility corridor. It has a glass roof and the sound of the rain falling on it is loud in this narrow, brick-walled space. We reach another door and Neil produces a key and unlocks it and we file inside one by one.

"It is a large house. Old. We move through its rooms in darkness. A kitchen. Then a hallway where the floors are wooden and a large staircase rises to the upper floor. Then we go into the front room. Neil shuts the door behind us and we assemble into a circle in the middle of the room, around the coffee table. And we stand there with our backs straight and our arms by our sides and our faces turned down towards the floor. We stay like that in the darkness for some time. No-one looks at each other. No-one speaks. There is only the darkness and the slow ticking of a clock and the sound of our breaths.

"A light outside illuminates the curtains. It is a car moving along the road. It throws some of the others' silhouettes into sharp relief. And I recognise them. And I realise that I had no awareness of who was standing in what order until this moment. Neil is beside me to my left, Ross is next to him. Next to him directly opposite me I can see the silhouetted pony tail of the woman sticking up at the back of her bowed head. Then on the other side of her is the large shape of Jonathan Frame. The outline of epaulettes on his shoulders tells me that he is wearing his uniform.

"The lights on the window concentrate as the car pulls into the driveway. The engine shuts off and doors clunk. Faint voices are coming through the window. A man is remonstrating, his voice high and wild, while two other men speak in lower tones, calmer, but with an air of force and authority. I hear the front door open and the voices are clear now. The light comes on in the hallway, shining under the door. The man is begging, pleading with the others not to leave him here. They are reassuring him. They tell him that he's going to be okay, that nothing is going to happen to him. He asks what is going to happen to his children. They do not answer. And then he goes quiet. The front door opens and closes again.

"Neil goes first. He opens the lounge door and we follow him into the hallway. We are walking slowly, our feet padding quietly over the floor. I see the man. It is the same man that I had seen earlier leaving with the children. And now I recognise him. His name is Scott March. He is standing beside the front door, looking through a window at a police car reversing out of the drive. He turns when he notices us and immediately bolts for the door. But

Neil gets there before him, blocking his way. Frame grabs and restrains him, pushing him to the floor. Scott is begging us to let him go, but his pleas are useless. We stand around him in a circle, our lifeless eyes turned in his direction but not looking at him, not directly, not really.

"And then the woman steps into the circle. This is the first time I can see her clearly. It's Lorraine, his wife. She is wearing a pin-striped business suit with a skirt and her hair is scraped back neatly from her face. She is a good-looking woman, her eyes and lips are picked out by carefully applied makeup. As soon as Scott sees her he begins to scream. These screams are not the same as the shouting and pleading that we heard from him a moment ago. They are high pitched, ragged and uncontrolled. He stumbles backwards onto his feet and spins around, running again for the door. He collides with Frame, who holds him tight. And then Lorraine steps towards him and she pulls a large kitchen knife from the waistband of her skirt and she stabs it into his back."

Sam stops for a moment. His breath is short. He pants, swallows, takes a sip of cold coffee, never once breaking contact with Nina's swelling eyes.

"Frame pushes down on Scott's shoulders and he goes to his knees. Then Frame steps away and he falls forward, supporting his weight with one hand. He turns over his shoulder to look at his wife and I can see that his face has turned completely white. It makes his dark stubble look artificial. And his eyes are shining large and white, so large that the pupils and the irises almost disappear. And his mouth is stretched wider than a person's mouth should be able to go. And then the knife comes down. It hits him in the forehead and does not penetrate. The sound is like someone chopping a coconut. The blade glances off and slices a line through his eyebrow, misses his eye and cuts deeply through his cheek. And his face turns down and I do not see it again. And he's got a hand held up to his injury and Lorraine sinks the knife into his back over and over until his arms give way and his chest falls against the floor. Then she steps over him, she grabs his hair and pulls his head up and slits his throat.

"When this is done, she stays there, standing over him. I notice that against the wall there is an oversized stuffed-toy elephant, spattered with dark flecks. And the knife in her hand is dripping. It is covered in so much of the bright red blood that I cannot see any of the metal of the blade. It is like she is holding a strange object made of blood. But we do not stay to watch. I turn and walk back through the hallway towards the kitchen. The others follow after me. Except for Lorraine. We leave the house and go back into the garden and then we climb over the fence. We drop down into the next road and go our separate ways without a word or a glance to anybody else.

"When I get home I get undressed and climb into bed. The next morning I remember feeling tired, like I had not had enough sleep."

Nina drops her head into her hands. She sobs audibly from within the cage of her fingers. She doesn't know exactly who she is sobbing for: Scott, Lorraine, their children, or Sam. When she looks up, her face is wet in patches where her tears have been smeared and red in places where her hands have pressed against it.

"How did you know these people?"

"Their hour with Roberta was right after mine. Sometimes he'd be early and he'd wait for her in the cafe around the corner. We got chatting. Lovely guy..."

"God. When... was this?"

He turns away from her, "It was the night after our first date."

Her words stall. She has no way to express what she's feeling. Sam's face looking back at her is blank and it fills her with horror. And she wants to get up and slap him. To run away. Get as far away from him as she can.

"How can – how can you not have had any… any idea?" she stammers.

And Sam's mask shivers at the edges and then the shivering spreads from his twitching jaw to his lips to his cheeks. And his mouth twists in an unstable curve. A hand sweeps up and latches onto his chest. The fingers curl inwards, the nails tearing at the material, digging in. His shoulders jerk forward and he gasps as his upper body twists and the muscles in his arms twitch uncontrollably. And Nina can only sit and watch him, this display inspiring further horror, but also pity and she longs to reach out to him but her body does not allow her to move from the seat, her fingers clamping onto the underneath of it as if to prevent her from getting up. She sees his hand tighten on his chest, the fingers clawing deeper and he gives a low growl that twists through A-vowel sounds until it becomes a whine. And she sees a hint of red coming through his shirt, staining the depression around his fingertips.

Nina catapults herself up from her chair. Without taking the time to grab her crutches, she leans against the table and stumbles her way around it until she reaches Sam. Her arms encircle him and she collapses onto him and her hand finds his hand and tries to pull it away from his chest. She has to bring her other hand to help it and she mutters "Stop it, stop it, darling stop it," into his ear as she eases the wounding fingers away from him. And his hand drops heavily into his lap and she hugs him tightly. And then his arms find her. And they hold each other like that for some time until sobbing and desperate breaths become slow and normal and they are just there in each other's arms with nothing else intruding. They fall into a silence inside of each other's embrace.

The squawk of a siren from outside splits their sanctuary. Nina watches an ambulance pull away from the scene below the window. Her hand finds her face and wipes away the moisture there as a new curiosity takes her and she lifts her head up to see better.

"Sam look," she says.

In the street below, the police have set up a cordon. They are directing traffic around the crashed vehicle. A temporary traffic light is under construction. There are several police vehicles pulled up onto the pavement. Yellow hi-vis jackets outnumber pedestrians. The police officers walk around the scene. Some are talking into radios. Others are taking statements. Some just sip coffee. The newsagent sits to one side, wrapped in a silver heat-blanket, a bizarre cast-off from a sci-fi B movie, while an officer feeds him fluid. It is like watching ants swarming the body of a dead crow.

"She's closing in on us," says Sam.

A shiver goes through Nina, "You don't think..."

"Car crash. Police cordon. Right outside our door. Look at it."

"No, it's, it..."

Nina feels a twitch in her eyes like an itch. She tries to lift herself out of Sam's lap.

"Help me. Can you help me up?"

He loops his arms under hers and stands. She leans on him and gets back to her chair. Sam reaches for the notes with the names of police officers written on them. He reads through them, looking up and down between the scene on the street and the list. He begins to point at individual officers, naming them.

"But how can you know? You said before you don't know these people."

"I recognise them. From the basement. From the group. I recognise them now."

"And you can put names to them?"

When he looks at her there is a new clarity in his gaze. It is that same, even look; the way he looked when he was telling the stories.

"What, you think I'm making this up?"

She shakes her head. Sam stands watching the scene below unfold. Looking at it, Nina can't help but find his opinion confirmed: the police certainly appear to be digging in.

"Well what is it? Why do you think they're there?"

"They control the area. They can do what they like. Or let someone else in to do it."

"We should get out of here."

Sam's head whips round.

"You want to just walk out? While the place is crawling with them."

"Well they're not going to go until they've finished whatever they're here for are they? You think we should just sit and wait?"

"No, no, I..."

"Look, if you're worried about what might happen when you go, then maybe it should just be me. Maybe I should go alone."

"Nina." Sam's face is wrought with concern. He arrives beside her, crouching to look into her eyes. "Honey. I can't let you go out there with no-one to protect you."

A smile creases her lips. Her fingers brush his cheek,

"I know you want to protect me, but think about it: Scott, Lorraine. If Roberta's going to strike at me through anyone, surely it'll be through you."

"I told you before, I could never hurt you."

"Shhh," her fingers press against his lips. "It's a lovely, it's a romantic, it's a beautiful notion. But that's all it is, Sam. It's just what you want to believe. You don't have any evidence for it. Not really. Do you?"

His eyes close and his lips form a kiss against her fingers.

"Okay. You're right. You should go."

Sam gives her the saddest little smile, kisses her forehead and then walks away. He goes into his bedroom and he closes the door behind him.

And Nina sits there, alone. She finds herself not overcome by any emotion. Tears do not come. Instead she sits erect in her chair and looks around, her head feeling clear. She is alert and aware of everything. It feels like there is a cool breeze about her ears. Her eyes jump from place to place in the room. From the window to the coffee table and the couches to the clock on the wall to the door to the hallway and beyond it the door to the outside world. And then back towards the bedroom. She feels eerily present. Like this moment is one in which a great deal of power rests upon her decisions, the consequences of which, once it has passed, will be very difficult to repeal. Perhaps even impossible. Because a moment like this will not come again. And she thinks about that. Thinks about what she might do, where she might go. And the thought does not require a massive amount of effort or concentration; she moves smoothly from one idea to the next, examining each of them and evaluating them with a peculiar detachment. She alights upon the moment immediately preceding this one. She thinks about how easily Sam gave in to her once she had outlined her case. Once he could see that her leaving made sense, made unavoidable sense. As soon as he knew that if he loved her he had to let her leave, he just left. And that's why the decision was easy: because he loves her.

The door to the hallway. It looms large. Just a few steps away.

All she has to do is pick up her crutches and go.

She picks up her crutches.

Chapter Nine

A CRAWLING SHAPE

“If I leave now she’ll have won, won’t she?”

Sam is curled up on the bed with his face buried in his knees. From the doorway, Nina can just see the curve of his back, the spine a sharp ridge under the tight fabric of his shirt, cuts up through the planes of his shoulder blades.

“Because if I go, if we just part, then we’ll never be able to be together again. Which is what she wants. Because she knows without me you’ll come back to her. You wouldn’t have left her.”

“Yes,” says Sam, his head still hidden behind his gathered shoulders, “that’s exactly right.” His voice has a muddy quality, his throat cloying with tears. “B ut you have to.”

He feels her arms close around him, her body fit around the shape of his. Her fingers find his fingers.

“I don’t think we’re there yet.” Her hair falls across his face in a cool, silky curtain. Her lips, soft and warm, find his cheek. They press against it and stay there. “We’ll get her Sam. I promise.”

“Thank you,” he breathes.

"Jesus, Sam."

Nina extracts a packet of something unnameable from the fridge and, dangling it from the end of her fingers, wheels it around to the bin.

"Don't you have anything edible?"

"Um..."

Digging in a cupboard, he drops a bag of pasta onto the counter top. She looks at it with a resigned sigh.

"I suppose it'll have to do." There are some intact if wrinkled vegetables. "Let's use these," she says pointing at peppers and onions that she sets about chopping. Things with more longevity than others. Each vegetable presents its own unique problems and flaws: dips and hills that frustrate Sam's hand. He can't get into the swing of it. Perhaps there are other things nagging at the back of his mind. And of course there are. Very heavy things, not so much nagging as screaming. Yet there is something about putting his hands to use, about standing with Nina in this part of his flat that he so seldom inhabits. It lifts him. And for both of them, it is like they have stepped out of the mire of their situation and now are just being normal, being real. Making a meal together in the yellowy glow of the kitchen's single strip light. It's nice. Sam looks across at Nina as she chops the onions. He sees moisture glisten at the corner of her eye and she lifts the knife-hand to wipe the tear away with the back of it. She catches him looking at her and they share an easy smile. She looks so beautiful there, crying. He has seen her shed tears so much recently but this time she does it with a smile on her face.

"I think I've got a bottle of wine somewhere," he says. "Do you fancy a glass? I fancy a glass."

By the time the buzzer goes they are halfway through the cheap red.

"Seven on the dot," Nina says, looking at her watch. "She never changes. Always bang on time."

"I make it seven-oh-one," Sam snorts.

He gets up to answer the door. Nina pushes herself up in her chair to look out of the window. On the street below, she sees the police officers pacing around their cordon. The old red Volkswagen still has its nose planted in the window of the newsagent's. The newsagent himself is long gone now and pedestrians show frustration rather than interest as they are forced to cross to the other side of the road. Cars slow as they pass, and then continue on their way. Waiting on the top step, directly below the window, Sandra watches the cordon from across the street. Inviting her over for a meal was a good idea, Nina thinks.

She hears Sandra introduce herself to Sam at the front door. She is the kind of person who always sounds bright and cheerful. When she walks in, her very presence transforms the room. A small woman in a navy coat, her dark hair flicks up just below her chin. There's a big smile and a squeal of excitement as she sees Nina for the first time in a year or so. It makes Nina realise how insular this flat has become over the last twenty-four hours; its own hermetically sealed world, where nothing comes in and nothing goes out and the same air cycles around being breathed and rebreathed. Only when an ecosystem has been undisturbed for a long time can the arrival of one organism have such a dramatic effect.

Nina starts to rise to greet Sandra, levering herself up and reaching for her crutches. The smile drops off Sandra's face and her mouth hangs open. But it is only for the briefest second. The smile returns and she's coming towards Nina saying, "No, no, no.

Don't get up."

And Nina is relieved to be able to let herself back down in the chair. Sandra throws her arms around her. A light floral perfume.

"How are you?" she asks as she pulls away, and continues as if it wasn't really a question anyway. "Sorry. I kind of forgot. Gosh, that's terrible."

Nina smiles and cocks her head into a shrug, "Yeah, well it happened. Want a glass of wine?"

They are halfway into their pasta and the bottle of wine is gone by the time Sandra brings up the business of the evening. The pleasantries have been really pleasant. The injection of some other company into this intense space is something Nina feels was very much needed. And it is with a collective sigh that they sink in and listen as Sandra gets serious, her bubbliness maintained but transmuted into a more professional mode of speaking. Her hands clasp in front of her on the table, engagement ring a bright sparkling notch between her fingers.

"So Sam, I take it that you've decided you're willing to testify."

"Er," he looks sideways at Nina, "we haven't really talked about it."

"We just thought it would be good to talk to you," Nina summarises.

"Oh. Okay. Well, really what we need is for Sam to come forward. I mean we can't get a restraining order for Sam unless he asks for it himself, and that means having to get up in court and talk about it. Nina, we could try and get one for you, but it sounds like that's not really the locus of the problem."

"So what exactly do we need to do?"

Sandra chews a forkful of pasta before answering Sam.

"We need to present evidence to the court that a temporary restraining order is necessary. Now, if there were any physical or recorded evidence, or perhaps calls logged with the police that could provide documentation of ongoing harassment by Roberta, maybe the emphasis on what you have to say wouldn't be so great. But we don't have any of that. All we've got is your testimony, Sam, as the complainant and Nina, yours will back up what he has to say."

Sam exchanges a frown with Nina. It's all very uncertain. He doesn't know what she's told Sandra, how clued-in she is.

"Why don't you tell us how the case looks," says Nina, reading his mind, "from your point of view."

"Okay, sure." Sandra pulls out a cardboard folder out of her bag. She opens it and glances over three sheets of A4 covered in illegible scrawl.

"So Nina tells me that you made the decision to leave therapy several weeks ago and that Roberta Klein, your therapist, was not keen on allowing you to do so. But you insisted, and were able to terminate your therapy. I note that a variety of techniques, bullying and intimidation were used by Roberta to try and keep you there."

"Like when she told me that if I left I'd never happy."

"Mmm." Sandra stops to think for a moment and places her pen on the paper next to the note. "That's good. It could help us. Anyway, so you quit, and on a number of occasions she appeared to threaten you or approached you to try to persuade you to come back into therapy, is that right?"

He nods.

"And there was one time she used her pull with the police to have them release you into her custody?"

Sam nods.

"You were arrested for having stolen her notes, am I right?"

He nods again.

"This is tricky. We need to show that there was sufficient motivation for you to have broken into her house in the first place. That you were driven to it in desperation – otherwise it's something that helps her more than it helps you. It would be really useful if you could tell me exactly why you felt you needed to take them."

Sam and Nina look at each other. As Nina expected, Sandra is honing in on the gaps in her account, of which there are many. Nina expected it; Sam didn't. And she's not sure how it is sitting with him.

"When she took you from the police station," Sandra continues, "what did she do or say at that point?"

"We went to an all-night café place. She tried to smooth things over between us and persuade me to come back to therapy. I told her I wasn't going to."

"What's important is how she tried to persuade you. Did she use emotional blackmail or..."

"No. She just pretended everything was normal."

"What do you mean by normal?"

"After what had happened."

"That's what I'm getting at Sam. What did happen?"

Sam has clammed up. His breath fits tightly through his nostrils, his mouth is sealed shut, his arms folded. Sandra leans forward in her seat, her pen tapping her notepad. Her eyebrows are pushed together and her piercing dark little eyes search his blank façade for an answer. She is good at this. Digging out things that vulnerable people and victims don't want to talk about. It's what she does every day.

"What do I tell her?"

The small enquiring eyes switch across: "Nina?"

"Sandy, there's a lot that you don't know. That we haven't told you. That," she pauses, words on the tip of her tongue, weighing them carefully before dropping them, "I decided to keep from you."

"Right." A tight smile. Two decisive taps of the pen on the pad. Now we're getting somewhere. "I think you'd better tell me, don't you?"

"I think they'd have trouble believing a lot of it in court. So much is circumstantial and some of it, well, some of it sounds really crazy."

Sandra holds up her hands, pen rotating between the first and second fingers of her right.

"Hey, I'm not judging. I'm here for you guys, you know that. You just tell me everything and then I'll figure out how we put it forward. I think between the two of us we've got that covered?"

Nina nods her agreement.

"Sam?"

"What do I tell her?"

It's the same question. This negotiation has happened between the two of them. For him the question hasn't changed. He's placed himself in Nina's hands.

"Tell her everything," Nina says, "Start from the beginning."

Sandra sits there writing everything down. She doesn't blink. Doesn't show any reaction to anything Sam says other than to look up at him, nod, and look back down to write a note. He tells her everything; everything but the keys.

When he is finished, Sandra says,

"Thank you, Sam. I think we've got plenty to go on there."

Her movements business-like and efficient, she closes up her folder and puts it back in her bag.

"Well," she says, standing and holding out a hand, "It was lovely to meet you Sam and I'm sure we'll be able to get something moving soon."

"You know, I'm still not sure about this standing up in court," he says as he shakes her hand.

"Let's cross that bridge when we come to it."

"It's just I'm not sure if I'll be able to trust myself."

Sandra doesn't answer this. She gives a curt nod and a smile. Nina notices that her usual ebullience has completely dropped away. Her smile is not the kind of smile a person has when they are genuinely cheery, it is the smile that they use when they are tolerating someone.

"Nina, do you want to see me out?" and Sandra's staring down at her now.

"Are you okay with the crutches and everything?" says Sam.

"Yeah, I'm fine." Nina starts to get up and Sandra goes to support her arm, "Sandy, I'm fine. Sam do you want to start clearing up?"

In the hallway, Nina closes the door to the lounge behind her. She takes Sandra by the arm, stopping her just before she reaches the front door. She leans towards her talking in a harsh whisper.

"Don't you want to talk about it? Discuss how we're going to put things together? You could have tried a bit harder to persuade him to testify – don't you do that all the time? Reluctant witnesses and stuff, it must be a daily thing for you."

"I need to sleep on it." Sandra turns away from her and opens the front door. "Walk me to the lift will you?"

Nina indicates her crutches with a puzzled frown.

"Just..." Sandra nods pointedly towards the corridor beyond.

Nina follows her outside. Sandra pushes the door to and then walks halfway down the corridor. She stops and turns to Nina, waiting for her to follow. Nina huffs and puffs as she hobbles over to her, wondering why her friend is putting her to this trouble.

"What?"

"Nina, I'm going to ask you a very important question. And I want you to take a moment to think about it before you answer."

"Okay."

"Do you believe all of this?"

The question is not a surprise to Nina. But it is something of a shock. Perhaps it had been unfair of her to expect her good friend to accept this outlandish story unquestioningly, nevertheless realising that Sandra does not believe it at all carries a bit of an emotional sting. A slap in the face from someone you care about always does. And deep down she also knows that part of her reaction comes from her own scepticism which, most recently, she has been making a conscious effort to suppress. Maybe that was what she was really looking for when she brought Sandra into this: an objective opinion. Indeed, the very act of taking the matter to law – although perhaps a secondary objective – is a way of proving the veracity of Sam's ordeal. Public acceptance. Nina looks into Sandra's dark eyes. Their sparkling intelligence. They are a razor of truth. To have these powers of perception employed on her behalf is in fact a great comfort.

"I think so," she says.

And Sandra bites back without hesitation: "That's not good enough."

"What on earth do you mean?" Nina scoffs.

"You need to believe him absolutely."

"Do I, Sandra?" Despite her better judgement, Nina is annoyed now. Her hands twist on the crutches' grips, elbows jutting. "I mean, so what if I mostly believe him? If it turns out I'm wrong about things it'll come out in the wash. The truth is the truth and however I would like things to be, if I'm wrong, well, I'll just have to live with that."

"You know better than that. You know damn well." Now Sandra has her hands on her hips and her head is jutting forward. Nina has never seen her friend in her professional capacity, but she guesses that she is a formidable opponent. "There are two reasons why you need to believe him. And they're both really important. You need to be rock solid or everything you're doing here is just going to make matters worse. For everyone, including Sam, and especially for you. Which, by the way, is all I really care about here.

"Reason one – and I find myself surprised that I'm having to tell you this – is that if we were to get any of this past a judge we'd have to rely on your testimony to back up his. And it's not enough for you to just say the right things, you've got to believe them. It's not like acting for a client. I mean sure, yeah, there's a chance that if we make the right selection of material we might get an order through without our claims being subjected to too much scrutiny. But it could easily go the other way."

"Yeah, okay, fine."

"Let me ask you something, Nina. Apart from the moment where Sam was perched on the window sill, apparently under hypnosis, is there anything, anything at all that you have seen with your own eyes – anything that would corroborate any of this?"

"Well, like I said, some of the information..."

"Not information. Things you've seen. Real things."

Nina looks down at the floor. She shakes her head.

"But you were definitely stalked. And you were most certainly hit by a car. These things are hard, cold facts. And pretty much the only ones we've got, I might add."

Nina looks up. A fluttering of hope. Sandra could be onto something here. Maybe there's a way of tying these things together, something that she might have missed. Any link – that's all they need.

"Yes, right." She almost dares to smile.

"See," Sandra's cheek jerks up in a little wince, "this is where reason two comes in. And its difficult," she scratches the back of her neck as she considers her words, "but it's fundamentally the most important thing. It's the only thing that matters. To me, at any rate. And you should be thinking about this above and beyond anything else." Sandra stops. She narrows her eyes and breathes out sharply through her nose. She's building herself up to something.

"Spit it out Sandra."

"Have you any reason to suspect that Sam might have been responsible for those things? The things that happened to you – ?"

Nina almost laughs.

"Because I don't think he's stable."

"Well, he's been through some traumatic..."

"Yeah, yeah, yeah, I know. And at times his behaviour, the way he talks, his vulnerability his insecurity, lack of confidence – at times that seems consistent with some of the things he's talked about. Being abused physically, mentally; pursued. I see people everyday who have been through stuff like this and I know what it looks like." A breath. "But at other times, Nina, he's, well he's almost maniacal, he seems delusional, he'll rattle on about things to exhaustion – which, by the way, is much more in line with the way abusers tend to talk, people who are trying to justify things that they know are wrong – people who are trying to convince themselves. And sometimes he seems dispassionate, as if none of this has ever touched him. As if..."

"As if it hadn't really happened."

"Right." Sandra nods, her eyes wide. "It's like he's mythologising, building a whole story in his head that gets increasingly elaborate."

"No, wait. I wasn't agreeing. I was just..."

"Finishing my sentence."

She gives a wry half-smile. Something passes between them. An understanding. Nina knows how she sounds, how it's coming across. And the fact that she hates that is an indicator of just how conflicted she is.

"Okay, whatever. So you don't believe him. Fine. I'll find someone else who can help."

"Nina, don't get me wrong," Sandra takes hold of Nina's shoulders. She smiles in the way that only people who really care can smile, "I'll help you. I'll do everything I can. But I just want to know that you're fully aware of the situation you're putting yourself in. Fine, believe in Sam, support him. If that's what you want to do, I won't question it. But keep your eyes open. You're in his flat, you're injured, you're kind of at his mercy. Nina, do you really know if you are safe?"

Nina's tight smile masks the grinding teeth beneath it, "Thanks, I'll... Yeah."

Now that she has said what she needed to say, the awkwardness of the moment settles on Sandra fully. She hides it behind a hug, "I'll be in touch."

And then she lets go and walks straight for the lift without waiting for any kind of response. Nina watches her hit the button and wait, her foot tapping impatiently, itching to get out of here.

"Sandy."

She turns. Her bubbly smile has returned but it is tinged with something uncertain.

"You're a good friend."

And it brightens.

The lift doors open. With a wave she is gone.

The table has been cleared. Sam is sitting in an armchair, his arms and legs spread out, slumped there like a big lazy spider. His face is downturned, his brow shading his eyes. His mouth curves grimly towards his chin at the edges. Nina watches him for a moment. She notices the frayed bottoms of his trousers, the dirty trainers, the rolled up shirt sleeves, a dinner stain, the dark crescents under the end of his nails, the stubble beginning to bed in, growing just past fashionable and edging into slothful. She finds herself lost in contemplation of him; trying to glean hidden messages from his physicality as if, like Sandra, she could read the truth of a person without really knowing them at all. She doesn't know if being this close to Sam, knowing him better than anyone, puts her in a stronger or a weaker position. Better than anyone? There is one person she can think of who knows him better even than she does. Something slithers down her spine. She looks down and notices that the hairs on her arm are standing up.

Slither. Shiver.

"She doesn't think she can help, does she?" Sam says in a flat tone, his attention lodged in some invisible hollow beyond the wall.

"She'll, um, she'll do what she can. She said it would be difficult, but..."

"She's not going to help."

"No, Sam it's not..."

"She doesn't believe me. I can tell."

"Goddammit, Sam, if she doesn't help I'll do it myself. I mean what am I? Scotch mist?"

Irritated, she engages a clumping trajectory towards the bathroom.

"If she doesn't believe me, then how can we expect anyone else to?"

Slam! The sound of the bathroom door makes Sam jump. Shakes him out of his dolour. He sits up and mumbles

"Sorry," then louder: "Sorry."

Nina's crutches clatter to the bathroom floor, echoing off the tiled walls. She leans back against the door and her body shakes as she exhales. And then she notices herself beginning to slide. Her hand grabs for the dressing gowns hanging on the back of the door, but they flip off their hooks and drop to the floor. Before the slide reaches critical mass she pushes herself away and hops over to the toilet. She knocks the lid closed and sits down, burying her face in her hands. *Goddammit*, she thinks. And she looks up to see her face reflected back at her. *Goddammit, I'm up and down like a yo-yo.* It's like having the symptoms of being bipolar without actually being it. And Nina begins to wonder if by putting herself through these violent extremes of emotion she will eventually manifest the cause.

The atmosphere in the flat has changed since Sandra left. It's partially that feeling of emptiness when guests leave. But it's also a pall of disappointment and futility that hangs over the place. Sam and Nina do not have much to say to each other. They move past each other in a cold silence. The only words that pass between them are utilitarian. When their eyes meet or they feel each other's gaze on their backs, it feels barbed. Accusatory. After a while Nina can't take the bad vibe any more. Even the television doesn't shift it. She announces that she is going to bed. Sam switches off the TV and informs her that he is going to do the washing up before he goes to bed, although he does not get up from his armchair and shows no sign of doing so. He's just sitting there staring into space, exactly the way he has been from the moment Sandra left.

When Nina leaves the room, Sam feels like a scratchy woollen blanket has been removed from his chest. He can breathe easily. And he stretches out his languorous arms and legs and his eyes snap out of space and back into the room. He looks around him, trying to remember how the flat used to be, back before Nina's first decluttering sorties. It's better now, he's sure of that, but in some ways he misses the close, nest-like feel of the place when it was more full of stuff. It never mattered what the stuff was, just that it was his and it surrounded him, it made him feel at home. He finds himself on his feet. Then in the kitchen. He puts the kettle on. He stands watching as it heats up, begins to simmer, comes to the boil and clicks. He makes a cup of coffee, moving so slowly that by the time he pours the water is no longer steaming. He opens the fridge. The milk stands out against the emptiness. There are a couple of eggs on a saucer, the hairy end of a piece of Brie, a tube of Swedish cod roe paste and a nearly empty tub of spreadable butter. He takes the milk out and pours a drop into his coffee. There is only the tiniest amount left sloshing around in the bottom of the carton, so he upends it into his mouth. The coffee is strong. He's drinking it more for the flavour than for the caffeine but it's going to keep him up for some time. Not that he has anything to do. But he doesn't really care.

Sam crosses the lounge to look out onto the street. The police are still out there. The car has been removed and the front of the shop stands open, exposed to the elements. It's like a hole in the side of an aeroplane, all the contents of the interior blown outwards. He wonders if anyone was hurt in the crash. Who was the driver? Was there anybody in the shop at the time apart from the newsagent? He suspects that there wasn't. He suspects the newsagent was in on it. He has always been suspicious of the newsagent. Always standing there outside shop watching him. Never a friendly glance or a smile. Up at all hours. Never away from his work. Until now. Now the newsagent's private space is open to the world. You could walk directly into it without using a door. It is a continuation of the street. And the man himself is removed from it, taken to a place that is not his, like a fish out of water. His habitat is destroyed, he can never return.

The flat still smells of the oniony dinner they ate earlier. He opens the window and cool air blasts upwards. Eyes closed, he lets it blow around him, opening his arms and body to the elements. The night air accompanied by the roaring of the city is like a waterfall. He washes himself in it and its freshness combines with the caffeine to bring him right to the surface of himself. The shreds of the desultory evening blow away from him like a tattered cloak. He takes deep, indulgent breaths and lets them out long and slow, hearing them sigh above the traffic noise, the sound of distant sirens, footsteps on the pavement below, the chatter of police and their radios. No. Not above it. With it. His breath blends with it and becomes a part of the soundscape. There is no moment at which his breath ends and the other sounds begin. They are one. He breathes in the city.

Sam opens his eyes and looks out over the tops of the buildings. Sees the low-rising commercial structures, the higher domestic ones, spotted irregularly with lighted windows. The way they are interspersed with darkened ones makes them appear like some kind of code. Beyond them, taller buildings still – the city – rise up and threaten the skies. They are confident, brash and shiny in all their height and glass. Each one a Tower of Babel. His gaze follows them down and then draws in from the horizon-hugging cityscape to the closer buildings that define this part of London. From street-level they appear to be the walls of the world, beyond which there is nothing else, but from up here he gets a real sense of just how small he is, how his area is but a few streets within a city so sprawling that it seems not to have an edge. And then, below, back, back, back to the newsagent's, to the chaotic pavement in front of it.

And there they stand. Eight police officers. Some men, some women. Some in yellow hi-vis jackets, others in their white shirt sleeves with their black stab vests. And they are standing in a line. A line exactly straight, corresponding with the edge of the pavement. They stand with hands gripping lapels, thumbs hooked over vests. And they are all looking in the same direction. Up. Right towards. Straight at. Sixteen eyes. All of them locked upon Sam. Their expressions are vacant, soulless, as if they were not human beings at all, just very precise imitations of them. And in their combined gaze there is a sense of threat so palpable that it sends a wave of fear rolling towards Sam that rocks him back on his heels. And he stands there, looking back at them, feeling like he could be blown away at any moment by the tiniest wrong-facing breeze. That a swirl of air in the flat behind him could push him out of the window and send him tumbling to the pavement below. Their gaze carries more than just the power of a combined look. It is a two-way communication. A channel through which something is simultaneously projected at Sam and sucked out of him. Until he is completely powerless. Until he is nothing but a husk.

Chapter Ten

IT WRITHES

Sam is asleep beside her. The curtains are closed and no light penetrates. She can just make out the grey shapes of the cloth shifting in a listless shade. She thinks she must have woken in the middle of the night and considers going back to sleep. Until she catches the orange digits staring out at her from the clock. It is 7:59. Morning proper. Time to get up. With a sleepy grumble, she gets out of bed, wiping the sleep from her eyes. The crutches are heavy in her hands and walking with them seems to slow her even more than it normally does. Everything about them is uncomfortable. The tops jutting into her underarms, the grips hard and harsh in her hands. And she walks with an uneven lollop that jars her with every step, jangling her head so that whatever thoughts are starting to form in between movements of the crutches are eliminated by the violence of the lurching step. She feels like a goldfish with a three second memory.

Beyond the bedroom door the darkness persists. The lounge is like a cave. In the kitchen at least, there is daylight. But it is a thin anaemic light and outside a drizzle falls and she looks out at the brick wall of another block of flats. While she waits for the kettle to boil she finds herself coming more fully into wakefulness. And when she gets there she notices an emptiness inside her that she has not felt for years. Not since the time when she was stalked. When she was pursued everywhere she went and it felt like there was nothing she could do about it and no-one who could help her. All of her qualifications, her knowledge of the law, her general capability in life – it all meant nothing in the face of one man who did not care about any of those things and who would keep following her no matter what obstacles were put in his path. Until he was locked away. She knows he'll get out one day, but she filed it away long ago, telling herself that when that day comes he will have forgotten about her, or been rehabilitated, or moved on, found a healthier way to live his life. But it's that feeling. Like she could do nothing. That's what she feels now. She can't even get a restraining order. She's a barrister, she works with the law every day. It is the stuff of her craft. She knows its shape, feels it mould to her fingers as she manipulates it. But now it is intangible. And there's nothing she can do. And this knowledge, this thing that she isn't quite willing to accept, that swells within her despite herself, it festers into a bitterness. An anger. And the first thing she thinks about is Sandra. Her bile flows towards her. She can't reconcile the fact that her friend, a woman who is supposed to do anything in her power to help her, will do nothing. It wells up in her, bubbling and frothing, she wants to grab Sandra by the hair and drag her kicking and screaming to...

The kettle boils. The click, the subsidence of the bubbling sound, it soothes her, ebbs away. And as the hot water dissolves the pixel-like granules of coffee into a rich brown liquid, she corrects herself. It's not Sandra's fault. She knows that. If Sandra could do anything, she would – and she will, if she thinks she can make it work. But even if she did, keeping Roberta away from Sam physically seems hardly worth the effort. What are they going to do? Take out a restraining order against every one of her clients? Nina imagines saying that in court, imagines the judge's face, imagines him stifling laughter as he responds to her.

She opens the fridge: no milk. And her temper's back. Slam. Fridge door echoes around the kitchen. Sam. Sam. Fucking Sam. Isn't he the problem here? If anything's missing it's coming from him. He's giving her nothing to work with. Every time she tries to suggest a course of action he steps on it. And she knows, she knows it's not his fault but the whole damn thing is so deeply frustrating.

The emptiness, that emptiness is still with her. And she realises now that it's not just an emotional sensation but a physical one. A gnawing hunger in the pit of her stomach. She opens the cupboard and finds a box of cereal, but then remembers that there is no milk. The contents of the fridge flash through her mind. Like Old Mother Hubbard's cupboard. She imagines standing at the supermarket checkout with them: two loose eggs, the end of a piece of mouldy brie, a tube of cod roe paste and a near empty tub of spreadable butter. The beeps as the checkout worker scans each item, too bored to even raise an eyebrow. She considers frying up the eggs but figures she should probably wait for Sam to get up so they can share them before she sends him out to the shops. She leans back against the counter top and takes a sip of her black coffee, balking at its bitterness, and then decants it into her water bottle.

Sets the bottle on the table in the lounge. Looks around for a paper or something to read. But there isn't anything. So she sits down with the bottle of coffee and takes another sip. It's hot, burning on her lips and the back of her throat as she swallows it. It's too dark in here. Too dingy. Too frigid. And in spite of the discomfort and the effort, she gets up. Hobbles to the curtains and throws them wide.

If anything it gets darker. The whole window has been sealed off in black plastic. A bin liner taped over the glass. Nina reels and staggers back a step. What the fuck has he done? Why has he done it? She pushes at the edge of another curtain with a crutch. The same thing on the other window. He must have done all of the windows, even the bedroom windows, while she slept.

"Saaaaam!" She screams at the top of her lungs. And she screams it several more times. The sound of her voice fills the space, so that it doesn't seem so empty or cold anymore but full and hot. And when she stops, that feeling is sucked away and the emptiness of the place billows with its silence, with the absence of her echoes, so that she feels compelled to fill it again.

Until Sam appears at the doorway to the bedroom. He stands there blinking at her in a t-shirt and boxer shorts, rubbing his thick dishevelled hair. And he mumbles something like,

"What is it?"

As if he had got up on an ordinary day and was going to go to the toilet and take a long morning piss and that's probably of more importance to him now than her obvious distress. So much more important that he hasn't spared the thought to connect that distress with the fucking weird thing that he must have spent all night doing. She glares at him, gesturing towards the window.

"Oh, um," continuing to rub his head, gummy eyes searching the floor, "I, er, they were looking in, you know, watching us, so I thought I'd stop them seeing in, you know."

"You could have just closed the curtains."

"I wanted to be sure," he says, shuffling past her to the bathroom.

Nina stares after him in disbelief and then slumps down on a chair. That long morning piss echoes through the door.

He comes out and he seems to be more awake and as he crosses back towards the window, not looking at her, he says "It was the way they were looking at me. You should have seen it. Actually, I'm glad you didn't. It was really freaky. They were all just standing there in a row, staring at me. I was so scared they might do something, or they might see something. I don't know what it is. It's like they're stealing something by looking at us."

"What?"

But Sam ignores her. He pulls back a curtain and makes a tiny tear in the bin liner and peeps through it. "Yep," he says. "They're still there."

And Nina feels a shiver go through her. The Sam that's so concerned for her, that looks after her, where is he? His care seems to have disappeared now, as if he can only exist in one sphere of attention at a time. And right now it's one of obsession. She doesn't feel like going over there and standing next to him with their arms and their heads brushing against each other as they take turns to look, so she makes her own hole in a different window, keeping the table between them. And sure enough, there are the police officers. There aren't as many of them and the shop window has been boarded up, but the cordon is still up. Two officers are standing outside and another one walks out of the shop, says something to the others and goes back inside. It is odd. That it would take them this long to deal with something like this. Are they investigating the scene or are they just clearing up? If Sam is right, then they're using the disturbance to maintain a visible presence outside the flat for as long as possible. And what could they be doing that for? What does Roberta hope to achieve?

"Is that it, Sam?" she says with her eye still glued to the window. "You were scared so you blacked out the windows. Is that really it?"

When he doesn't answer, Nina pulls away from the peephole. Sam is standing with his arms folded.

"It wasn't was it?"

"There was something else," he says. "I was worried that they might try and put some kind of message through to me, you know, like a code word, like using a sign. When they had their whole attention on me it was like they were trying to communicate with me in some way. It was like the silent communication in those darkened rooms. When we would all just sit or stand there."

And for a second time this morning, Nina feels afraid. Caught between fear of what terror Roberta might wreak and the fear that this is all the product of a confused mind. She can't think of anything to say back to him. She can't even look at him, for fear that her face might betray the conflicting notions within her. She looks back out the peephole, studying the scene.

"You know something," she says after a while, "those are different policemen."

"I know," says Sam. "They've changed shift. But they're still hers."

"You recognise them?"

"Mm-hmm. See the two at the front? That's Gregory Jones and the other's Mike King. The one that went inside a moment ago, he's Jordan Phelps. They're all on the list."

They don't look like anything other than ordinary police officers. They have that self-assured air about them, and at the same time seem moderately bored. But then that's the thing isn't it? They aren't anything but normal police.

Nina withdraws to a chair and checks the list. And sure as his word, the three names are on there. It occurs to her that Sam seems to have a greater degree of certainty about who these people are now. He is putting names to faces unquestioningly, whereas before he had to summon vague scraps of memory from his subconscious with great difficulty and mental effort. She wonders whether this is the cumulative effect of more and more pieces coming together and is about to mention something when the thought is washed away by the redoubling of the gnawing hunger in her gut. Footsteps cross behind her.

"We should make some breakfast," she says. "There's a couple of eggs – not much, but I'm pretty hungry. We're going to need to go shopping."

Sam doesn't reply.

"Sam?"

She twists to look over her shoulder but she can't see him. Then twists over the other and still she can't see him. He's standing in the blind spot directly behind her chair. She hears his footsteps and then feels his hands on her bare shoulders. His chin rests on top of her head. His breath teases her hair.

"Hmm," he says, and she feels the vibration of his words through the top of her head, "That's a problem. I hadn't thought of that."

Beneath his hands her shoulders start to itch, his breath in her hair feels like insects crawling through it. She doesn't know why she feels this irritation but there's something, something in his tone that she doesn't like at all. She twists away from him and turns in her seat to look up at him.

"What's a problem?"

"Well we can't go out, can we? Not with them there."

Sam can't quite meet her eyes. His cheek is jumping like he's trying to dislodge a mosquito. His mouth twists into new configurations every second. Nina can't have this. She needs him focused, sensible, but the longer this siege goes on the more she feels like she is losing him to irrational emotions and paranoia.

"Sam," she grabs his head and turns it towards her. "Sam, listen to me."

And he kind of looks like he is but his pupils occasionally jump to the side, over her shoulder, towards the window.

"How long do you think we are going to wait for them to go away? They're the police. They can stay there as long as they like."

"Maybe. But maybe they can't. I mean whatever they're doing there they have to justify it to their superiors don't they? There's only so long they can string it out. It was just a car crash. Maybe more. Maybe they'll tell them it's a robbery or something but still..."

"Okay, and then what? Let's say they leave tomorrow. What's to say that she won't have other people out there, people that aren't even so conspicuous." It sounds so ridiculous coming out of her own mouth. She can't quite believe she said it. And as soon as he replies she wishes she hadn't.

"Yeah. Yeah, I know." He bites his lip and looks down at his fingers, which are fidgeting against each other, clicking the nails and picking at their quicks. Nina finds her attention drawn there and the fidgeting is like a buzzing light or like watching ants crawling over each other. His pale sweaty fingers, their dirty nails becoming granulated and she notices crumbs on the side of his palm.

"Stop that!"

She grabs hold of his wrists. And he does as he is told, looks at her like a scolded little boy.

"Look, if you're not going to go out there, then I am. Is that what you want? I've got a broken fucking leg and you're going to make me get up and go to the shops while you sit here curled up in a corner biting your nails? Is that it? Is that what you want?"

"No, no, no, but I..." he breaks away from her and walks over to the corner of the room, tugging at his hair, trying to figure out what to say to her.

"Fuck it, I'm going."

And she drags herself up from the chair and takes hold of the ungainly crutches and begins the haul across the room towards the hallway. The door is closed and she has to set one crutch aside and lean heavily on the uncomfortable rest of the other as she twists the knob, then hop-shuffle backwards as she drags the door towards her, finally flinging it open.

She doesn't see it so much as feel it. An image that empties her stomach and sends acid scouring up through her heart. The hallway chest. Lodged in front of the front door. She feels the flat closing around her, becoming hot and stifling and small. Her first thought, illogically, is how did she not hear him dragging the thing across the floor in the middle of the night. How did it not wake her up? Then a crushing sense of disappointment in him. He's not thinking clearly at all.

She hears his feet crossing the floor towards her.

"They were in the corridor," he says. "Last night after I put up the bags to block their view I was just about to go to bed and then I heard their footsteps out in the hall and I could hear them talking."

Nina shrinks as she listens, her back to him, her shoulders rise and she curls her head into her chest, hoping, hoping one thing: don't touch me Sam, don't come near me.

"I don't know what it was they were saying but their voices were coming through the door and I knew they were getting closer and all I could think was, this is it, they're closing in for the kill. And I thought they've got a key. They've probably got a key, just like I have keys. So I had to stop them."

"Move it." Her eyes are closed, her teeth gritted. "Just move it."

And for the second time this morning her words are met with empty silence. Like there's no-one there with her. Like it's just her and these walls shrinking towards her. And Sandra's words come back to her:

You're in his flat, you're injured, you're kind of at his mercy. Nina, do you really know if you are safe?

And she asks herself that question again and again in her head: Do you really know if you are safe?

And the chest of drawers in front of the door then, right then, is a visual and practical representation of this idea in one cogent image. If he won't move it, if she can't get him to, if he won't agree to it, there's no way she can move the heavy piece of furniture herself. Not in this condition.

"Please move it."

But still, he says nothing.

And when she has to put herself to the effort of turning to look at him, she thinks surely he knows how hard it is for me? Every movement, every unnecessary step I have to take. Surely he should be showing more concern?

She finds Sam's eyes shut. His hands are clasped in front of him and she can hear him inhaling deeply through his nose. She can almost see him counting down from ten, the numbers flashing up behind his forehead. He opens his eyes and even though there is a tremor in his body, still the twitching in his face, his eyes are clear and level and staring at her.

And when he speaks, it is in a steady monotone, "I don't think that's a good idea."

He's terrified. He's clearly terrified of something. She has no idea though whether it's what is outside, or what is in here. What is happening right now in front of him. Because he must know it as much as she does, that he's stretching her thin, that the longer he pursues this line the greater risk he stands of alienating her? Nina makes up her mind there and then, staring at the trembling man standing in his boxer shorts in front of her, that if that happens, she is not going to let herself be persuaded back from the brink.

"You realise that you're making this impossible," she says.

"What?" He looks genuinely confused – maybe none of this has occurred to him, maybe it was just her projection. Has he even spared a thought for her?

"I'm here for you. I'm giving everything to you. But we have to do something. We can't just hole ourselves up in here and hope it'll all go away. If that's the line you want to take, Sam, then you're going to have to do it on your own."

"I know, I know. I'm sorry. I don't know what else to..."

"I need to eat, Sam. We need to eat."

"Can't we wait just a little bit longer? We," he licks his lips, there is a smear of sweat on his brow, "we, we need to pick our moment."

A pain slowly swells in Nina's leg and she feels it radiating up through her thigh. The emptiness in her stomach grows and the heat of the flat becomes unbearable. And now her head feels light. So light it might float away from her shoulders and pop on the ceiling. She hears a crutch hit the floor. And then she collapses.

She blinks and her eyelids stick sweatily together. His face hangs above her like a great moon in this day-darkened bedroom. It radiates a self-satisfied glow, absorbed in the process of mopping her brow. Perhaps it is unfair to judge him in this way, but where was his care and affection a moment ago? It seems completely unrelated to her. A part of the tapestry that he is weaving inside himself, in which she is just a figure, just another piece of cloth that looks and acts like her but is not her.

He sees that she is awake and says, "Hello you," with a sweetness that makes his words ooze between his teeth.

And she starts to say his name. It is hard at first and her throat sticks together allowing only enough space for the consonants to escape, "Sm... sm... sm..."

He takes a glass of water from the bedside table and holds it to her lips. She sips and some spills over her chin. He wipes it away with the same damp cloth he was using for her brow.

"How long have I..."

"Not long. Are you okay?"

"I think so."

"Do you want something to eat? I could make you some eggs."

"Have you been to the shops?"

He pauses, looks up and to his left. Is he considering lying to her? Obviously he hasn't been, otherwise he'd have offered her something other than eggs.

"Not yet," he says. "But I will go. Soon."

She watches him walk out of the room. She wants to believe him. She wishes she could. He might mean it in this moment, but in another he'll be off somewhere else, a different person.

She hears something dripping. The bedroom is dank. She longs for daylight. It is like being buried somewhere roomy, where it seems like life is possible. But no tomb is roomy enough. She thinks of the last moments of Egyptian slaves, closed up alive in the pyramids of their dead Pharaohs. Nina pulls herself up to half-sit, leaning against the wall, the pillow at her back. The moist cloth on her forehead is chilly and clammy. She sniffles and feels a drop of liquid curl back inside her nostril. And all she can think is, what the hell am I doing?

Gregory Jones, Mike King.

The way he said it. The way those policemen's names just tripped off his tongue. It's like he had known them forever. He didn't need to refer to the list or pause for thought. It occurs to Nina that since making the decision to support him, she has only undertaken investigations on his behalf. Perhaps now is the time to start making some inquiries of her own, for her own sake. For her sanity, if nothing else.

She picks up her phone from the bedside table.

"William, hi."

"Miss Trevanion, how can I help you?"

"I need you to do something for me. It's a bit of an odd request."

"Whatever you need."

"Do you think you'd be able to send someone down to where I am. There's a police crime scene outside, well, it was an accident but, anyway, I need to check out the police officers there. I need their names."

"Course. I'll send Tim down right away. What's the address?"

Nina furnishes William with the address and thanks him profusely for his help. She puts the phone back on her bedside table. Her arms wrap around her and she shivers. She needs to get up, move about. She is not entirely sure why she fainted, but it was probably a combination of hunger, exhaustion, emotional stress, physical trauma. Whatever, she feels okay now and she can't stand staying put any longer. Flinging back the duvet, she looks around for the crutches. Sam must have forgotten to bring them from the other room. She sighs. Contemplates calling for Sam to aid her, but for some reason she'd rather do it by herself. She swings her legs over the bed, leans on the bedside table to pull herself to her feet and then begins to hop.

The crossing to the bedroom door is nerve-wracking. There's a stop halfway across at Sam's desk, but in spite of that, there are at least two points where she nearly loses her balance. It's something she's never really considered before, but for a tall person the idea of falling to the floor is probably much scarier than it would be for a smaller woman. She could do with softer more ample curves to cushion her fall. With every hop, she imagines the clatter and shattering of all her long and vulnerable bones. But she reaches the bedroom door and there are the crutches, only a few short hops away into the lounge.

She is on one leg, bending down to pick one up when she falls. Her hand flies out to protect her head, which leads the descent, the wooden floor coming up at her in slow motion. She feels a jar in her elbow. And then her shoulder follows and there's a smack as her hip hits the floor. None of it is quite as bad or as painful as she had imagined. But still, it feels like a massive setback. She'll have to get back to her feet from the floor, which won't be easy. And then there's the humiliation. She is incapable of basic functions. Sitting on the floor there, she feels like a baby marooned on its play mat. And before Sam rushes in to check she's okay her cheeks are already burning red. She shrugs off his concerned enquiries and grumbles as he helps her to her feet. He's great at playing the good boyfriend, but he seems a little too glad for the opportunity to show it.

"I need to get dressed..." she mumbles.

"Your eggs are ready," he tells her when she's seated back at the table.

Back at this table in the same fucking chair. Ants are crawling under her skin and all she wants to do is get up and run around and shake them off, feel fresh air against her face. But she can't: even if she could get outside, the best she could hope for is an accelerated hobble. And so instead, she sits here, suppressing the feeling while Sam brings her a plate of scrambled eggs with a smile on his face like he's fucking perfect.

"Aren't you going to eat something?" she asks him. "You must be starving."

"I could have dry cereal and cod roe paste," he chuckles. He chuckles! As if there's any humour to be found in this situation. "But I'm not so hungry now. I think I can wait."

Nina narrows her eyes,

"Are you rationing? You want me to think that was some kind of harmless joke but you're rationing aren't you?"

"What? No! I just meant I'd wait until I've been to the shops, that's all."

"Hmph."

Nina shovels a forkful of eggs into her mouth.

"Well," she chews, analysing the eggs to pick out the next good-looking yellow cluster, "I'm just eating here, so you might as well go now. I'll be fine on my own."

Sam nods. He gets up and crosses to the hallway door. But before he reaches it he turns in a wide circle and returns to the window to peer through a peephole.

"Mmmm," he growls, "they're still there."

"And?"

"Well, we should probably pick our moment."

"They're not going anywhere Sam." She can't quite believe they're still playing this game.

But he doesn't respond to her irritation at all, he just keeps staring out of the window.

"Will you just go to the fucking shops!" She spits scrambled egg all over the table.

Sam turns to look at her. His expression is dispassionate, his eyes hooded.

He turns back to the peephole.

"Fuck's sake," Nina grumbles to herself. And she shovels what's left of her eggs into her mouth. Her fork bounces off the table when she throws it down, the clatter ringing across the room. This gets Sam's attention. He gawps at her. Maybe he really wasn't aware of the tension hanging on her words. But Nina doesn't care. Her movements are brusque. The chair scrapes. She yanks herself up. Her crutches thud across the floor with a series of rapid clunks as she swings herself towards the hallway. Sam watches her go. He turns back for a quick check of the peephole and then he follows her.

Nina's crutches lie abandoned on the hallway floor. She has manoeuvred into a back corner of the chest, bracing herself against the wall. She has some stability there and can get good purchase. Working the corner of the antique chest out a little bit, she slips into the gap and leans her weight against it. It grunts and strains, wood creaking. And then there's a heavy scrape as the corner pivots forward. Nina falls against the chest, breathing hard from the exertion, sweat breaking out on her forehead. She lies across the flat varnished top, arms outstretched, head to one side, catching her breath. But instead of relief she begins to feel fatigue in her arms and legs. Before she can succumb to it, she pulls herself up, her skin peeling from the wood with a sound like sticky tape.

Standing on one leg and holding herself there with her arms, she locks eyes with Sam. He is standing in the doorway to the lounge, his expression inscrutable. She stares back at him, daring him to stop her. But he doesn't. She turns around and scoots out a little, still holding herself up with one arm against the chest. Grabs the door handle with her free hand and twists. She pulls it towards her. The clunk comes sooner than she expected. It won't move any further. All of her exertion has only earned her a few inches of leeway. She puffs her cheeks out and frowns. Then hops around in an ungainly circle and repositions herself for a second shove.

"Nina..."

But she ignores him. This time she doesn't have quite the purchase that she had on the first push. She has to rely on her good heel shoved up against the skirting board. Leaning into it she strains to get some movement. And then it comes. A lurch. Dragging forth, making a dark groove on the wooden floor. The space opens up in front of her and with her support removed Nina drops forward.

The wood smacks up against her with a stinging slap that runs from her face all along her body to her feet. Her leg hurts like hell and there's an ache in her head where it lies against the foot of the chest. Still running on adrenaline, she contemplates getting up. She turns over and sees the chest towering above her. From here it looks as big as the whole apartment block does from the street outside.

And lying there on her back, wedged between the partially open door and the chest, tears start to come. She doesn't want to cry. She wants anything but. But she can't help it. She hears Sam coming nearer with words of conciliation and concern and she covers her face. And Sam's saying everything's okay and not to worry about it and as his arms come down to hold her she pushes them away, her wet shiny face exposed in flashes between the flailing of her arms and the return of her hands to cover her shame. Sam steps back, his hands fidgeting at his sides, unsure where to put himself.

Nina's breath stills and the tears dry up. Wiping her face, she drags herself into a sitting position. Her back against the leg of the chest to keep herself as turned away from Sam as possible. She wipes her face until it is not wet anymore, just clammy. And blinks through the remaining blurriness left by the tears until her vision clarifies. And there, in front of her, is the door. Open enough for her to get through, maybe even with a few inches to spare.

Sam crouches down beside her and the apologies begin. But she isn't hearing him. She's just looking out into the corridor beyond. The faded wallpaper, the grey lino floor, cheap fluorescent light. The corridors in this building are narrow but right now they feel as expansive as the plains in some country much larger than this cold, wet island.

His arms close around her and although she doesn't want to be held, they are tender and his grip is a gentle caress that guides her around to face him. And then she's looking into his eyes and they are large and dark and deep, their colour shifted from their ordinary tincture to a richer brown full of sincerity and warmth. His face around them disappears and it's just those rings of white and brown and black searching deep into her soul. Their communication is transcending the verbal, ideas and feelings flowing between their minds. And she hears him think, "I'm sorry, I really really, really am. I didn't realise how I was being. I didn't know how important it was to you. Well, yes I did, but I've become so selfish, so self-absorbed and I can't believe that I just put you through this and" and it is only when his words trail off that she realises that his lips are actually moving. And there's a great surge of happiness within her as for the first time since some point yesterday she feels like they have come into each other's company again. They are with each other now the way it is supposed to be and there is give and take and sympathy and care and

A phone rings. Nina feels the vibration in her skirt pocket. She wipes the back of her hand across her face and sniffles.

"It might be important."

"Sure," he says, and stays, his arms around her, their arms tangling through each other's as she raises the phone to her ear without breaking eye contact. And his smile is broad and deep and sincere and it fills her with a nourishing strength while she listens.

"Hello, Ms Trevanion? It's Tim here, Tim Bennett from Chambers."

And even as she listens Sam is staring into her eyes and smiling that beautiful smile and she is still held inside those deep sincere orbs and she doesn't want to let go doesn't want to break out of them even though her heart is sinking and there's a feeling inside of her that's like poison.

"Thank you, Tim." Her words come out on their own, as if spoken by someone else. "That's very helpful."

"Do you need me to come up for anything?" says Tim.

"No. No, thank you."

"Okay. Bye then."

And it's only when the line goes dead that she thinks to say, "Bye."

And now she can't look at Sam. Her lip trembles and she shades her face with her hand because she doesn't want him to see what is about to happen to it. And she tries to hold it back. Tries to hide her emotional collapse with all of her might but in such proximity it's so hard.

"Nina, what is it?"

And all she can think is shut up, shut up, shut up. Don't ask me to tell you. Let's stay right where we are in this moment and never leave it. But the moment is already gone, disappearing rapidly into the darkness like a train moving away into a tunnel.

"What's wrong? Who was that?"

And then out of nowhere she looks up at him, composed, and says, "The police officers downstairs. They're not who you say they are."

Sam's face twitches as if someone had just flicked water in his eye. A silence descends between them. She knows this is going to shatter his whole world; he's not quite there yet.

His arms tighten around her.

A spike of alarm. What's he doing?

And then she realises that he is trying to lift her to her feet. In the absence of a reaction to what she has just told him all he can do is to reach out to help her. And that only makes it more painful. That underneath all of his chaos and confusion and craziness, there's just a good person. A warm, caring person that doesn't deserve any of this.

Nina holds onto the chest while Sam fetches her crutches. He leaves them leaning next to her without meeting her eyes and walks away into the lounge. As he goes she can hear him muttering,

"Maybe I just got mixed up about which ones..."

But she knows he didn't. She takes up her crutches and finds herself standing in that small hallway, alone with a displaced chest and a row of coats on hooks and an open door. Looking out into the corridor she can see almost all the way down to the lift. It's an open highway leading away, far away from this ever-shrinking flat with its stale air and blacked-out windows. She picks up the smell of cooking: someone's making curry. In another flat further towards the lift a child is laughing. And even that stagnant space that is nothing more than a passage, an unloved place that nobody lays claim to, is more welcoming than the dank darkness behind her. All she would have to do now is walk away without saying a word to be free of all of this forever. The bright light of the morning is just a couple of minutes away. A lift journey. She can picture the doors opening and the light flooding in through the glass entrance door. Burning bright. Full of life. But she can't walk away. She can't leave him hanging like this, answerless. The way is clear now. She can leave any time she wants. She closes the door and returns to the lounge, to the chill, to Sam.

He is standing over the table, leaning on his hands, his head disappearing behind the raised planes of his shoulder blades. White t-shirt, boxer shorts, hairy legs. He almost looks strong in some way, like a general standing over a strategic map. Hearing her come in, his head jumps up and he turns to face her. There is a tension in his jaw, the muscle ticking under the skin.

"Who was it?" he asks. "On the phone?"

"Tim. He's a clerk at chambers. I had him go and check out who they were." It feels confessional. Confessing to a betrayal. Yes, I was a member of the Communist Party.

"And who are they?"

"Michael Kent, Peter Rushkin, George Greenwood."

Sam returns to contemplation of the list.

"They're not on there Sam."

"But it can't," he says from between his shoulder blades, "that can't be right."

He walks towards her.

"I can see it in my head. They're here. Right here." He holds a finger to his temple as if the sentiment requires illustration. "Faces. Names."

"Since when? You weren't even that sure about it yesterday."

His eyes squeeze shut and he runs a hand through his hair and he takes a long slow breath through his nose. His whole body is drawn tight, like there are steel cables running through his limbs. He whirls to a window and rips down the bin liner. Light floods in and outside, the boarded-up newsagent's stares blankly up at them. Two police officers – probably Michael Kent and Peter Rushkin – are taking down the police tape.

"You see?" Sam's eyes bulge, his outstretched arm shaking spread fingers at the window. "You see!" His fists ball in front of him, drawn in towards his chest and his head juts towards her, the veins popping out on his neck. "It looks," he seethes, spit flecking his lips, "It looks like they're winding it all down. Like nothing's happening. But even as we sit here they're closing in. It looks like it's all calm. But they're stepping it up. That's the fucking genius of it."

"Okay. Okay. So what do you want to do about it?"

He freezes, his mouth open. Processing everything. But whichever way his mind turns he can't see a solution. Nina knows this. Of course there isn't a solution because none of it is real. That's why he has always refused to act. And that's the only way to diffuse him, to calm him down. Push him to one end of the delusion and he'll be forced to retreat in order to preserve it. But if none of it's real, Nina thinks, then that probably means he...

She puts the thought out of her mind.

"Sam, come on. Just sit, okay. Let's talk about it."

"I don't know what we're supposed to do. I, fuck, you don't even bloody believe me. What's the point? I might as well just sit here and wait for them to come. Or maybe I should go back to Roberta and ask if I could start therapy. Is that what you want?"

"No. Of course not. Don't be stupid."

But he's still pacing up and down the room puffing and panting.

"What if," she ventures, "what if it was all part of her plan? What if she suggested certain things to you and then, and then you just, well, took over. After all, isn't that what she wants? For you to doubt yourself. So that you'll come back to her."

He stops pacing.

"We have to work with what we know," she says, "with what's real. What we can touch."

"You're saying that everything I've seen," he says, arms folded, head shaking, "everything that's happened to me, that it's not real?"

"No. Not at all. I just think we should work from the ground up. Especially when it comes to these recent things, these remembered memories. I don't know how reliable they are. They're curled up in there with all that other junk that she's put in your head. Start from the beginning. Assemble the facts. Like it was for court, like we did with Sandra."

"Oh yeah, and where did that lead?" His eyes widen. "Wait. That Sandra. She's working for Roberta. Obviously. I mean maybe your man is too. The one from chambers. How do you know he's not?"

Nina lets out a long slow sigh. This is pointless.

"You know what, Sam?" she says. "I'm just going to go home. You take a couple of days to calm down, think about it, and then we can have a proper chat."

It's like a comedown. The whole bubble of everything that they've been in for the last few days. It's all just gone with the flooding-in of the daylight. The sun comes up and the night of crazy fun is over. The magic dispelled. And all that's left is a cold empty world with nothing to look forward to. Nina hobbles across the lounge and through the door into the hallway and as she moves she feels cool air breezing past her ears and there's an uncomfortable, greasy feeling in her gut. But it's nothing she can't ignore for now. And behind her, the image of Sam in his boxers leaning against the back of the couch dissolves and disintegrates until there's nothing behind her but an empty flat. She moves around the chest and takes hold of the door handle.

Sam's arms close around her. She protests, telling him to get off her. She can smell the sweat of his unwashed body. Feel his stubble scratching against her cheek. His morning breath washing over her ear. For a moment she's thinking, oh no, I've gone and done it now, I've flicked the wrong switch and he's going to flip out on me. But that's the problem with Sam. He's too nice. Even when he's off his rocker all he can do is beg and plead with her and he's whispering into her ear saying "Please, wait, we can talk about it, let's just sit down and talk about it, okay? It'll be fine. We'll do it your way, look at the facts..."

"No, Sam. I want to go. Can you just respect that?"

He rests his head on her shoulder.

"Please," he breathes, and the word enters through her skin. And despite herself, she acquiesces.

"Now let go of me."

And he does. She turns and hobbles back towards the lounge.

Heavy scraping sound. She looks round just in time to see the chest slam flush against the door. And it all comes flooding back. The adrenaline, the pumping of her heart. Her body telling her that now is the time to run. Get out of here. Take the blood from the stomach and flush it into the legs. Her legs. Here's what you need. But her legs aren't working. Not both of them, anyway. Sam must see the fear in her eyes because he adopts a casual posture, leaning against the chest and patting it with the palm of his hand and shows her his most reassuring smile.

"Just in case," he says. "In case I'm not wrong."

It doesn't reassure her. She thinks of those old horror films where the werewolf begs to be locked up alone in a room on a full moon. Only right now she's locked in with him. And the moon is full.

You're in his flat, you're injured, you're kind of at his mercy. Nina, do you really know if you are safe?

Chapter Eleven

THE ANGELS, ALL PALLID AND WAN

Nina once again finds herself thinking about the last moments of Egyptian slaves; imagining being in a tomb. The fact that she is on the sixth floor of a block of flats in a busy city in the brightness of mid-morning is irrelevant. It could be anywhere. Or nowhere. The rest of the world is as faint as a dissipating dream. The walls in this darkness fade to shadows, but if Nina could see them more clearly, she is sure they would be dripping with the kind of condensation that clings to the edges of tunnels and sewers. The only light in the place comes from the one window that has had its black-out bin-liner pulled away. The curtains are now closed, softening the aperture, so that it becomes a faint rectangle of light filtered through cloth. It hangs there at the back of the room, some distance behind where Sam sits on the couch. The curtains shift slightly, giving the impression that the rectangle of light is fluid, floating alone in the darkness, above and behind Sam's head like a projector screen on which his thoughts might play out. But there is nothing on the screen; it is empty. Sam's face is tilted down into his lap as if he is meditating. The light behind his head and the inclined angle combine to cast his features almost entirely in shadow. The uneven tufts of his hair are picked out like a ridge of mountains, shifting when he moves. The bridge of his nose, his eyebrows, catch what little light reaches them, forming a cross like the front of an ancient helmet that defines his whole face even though most of it is absent. She sits in an armchair facing him, her good leg folded on the cushion beneath her. In her lap, her hands hold each other and gently shift around, fingers probing around fingers.

Sam's voice slithers out of the darkness as if belonging to something other than himself, disembodied from his invisible lips. They must be moving, Nina thinks, although she cannot be absolutely sure.

"Are you the therapist now? Am I the patient again?" he asks. There is nothing facetious in his tone. It is a wholly innocent question. The kind that a child might ask its mother.

"No," Nina answers. "It's about finding out what's real. That's all."

"Yes."

No more words come. She waits for him to speak, staring at that blackness, wondering when the next sounds will emerge. And sounds do emerge. But they are not words. Not at first. There is a series of small verbal clicks, mini-groans, the kind that emanate from the back of the throat and tend to indicate a nagging discomfort.

"How long have you not believed me for?" he asks her.

Nina opens her mouth to answer but then stops, thinking carefully. This isn't just a question, not a normal question, a question like where is the nearest bus stop or what time are we meeting or have you eaten or what would you like to drink. Her mouth shuts. Her face contorts.

"It's not that I don't believe you."

"How long?"

This is not the time for equivocation. He sees straight through it. Like a searchlight in the dark. He is obscured, she is lit up like a beacon.

"I don't know. I suppose I've always been worried. Maybe since I met Roberta."

"Worried that she might be right."

"But that doesn't mean I think she is. Not in the least. I don't trust her at all. But I have to allow for the possibility."

"That all of this might be in my head."

"Yes."

His head does not move. The ridge of his shoulders is a bright line making his body a shape cut out of blackness. The rectangle of light wavers over his shoulder.

"And if it is all in my head," he says, "does that mean that you think that I followed you? That I ran you down with my car? That I did all these things?" And even though this eventuality must be entirely distressing to him, his measured tone betrays no emotion.

"Not necessarily," she says.

"But you have to allow for the possibility."

"I know that you were probably in a car crash. I do not know if your Rosanna exists. I do not know if Neil Allen really exists. I do not know if those keys you have open the doors you say they do."

"If I was you I wouldn't believe me."

"But you're not me."

"You want to believe me. Why?"

"Because I love you."

Nina thinks she sees the cross of light that frames Sam's face twitch. She has never said these words to him. And now that she has she finds herself feeling nervous and exposed. She hoped they would have made things better but they have made things worse. She is desperate to hear something from him. For him to reciprocate, or at least acknowledge her gesture. But he doesn't. And after a while the silence becomes unbearable and she feels the need to talk, to move on.

"I think that Roberta's got you so confused that you don't know where anything stops or begins. Sam, she's got me just as confused. I don't know. But I think if you're going to be able to see anything clearly you're going to need to be really honest with yourself."

His breath is loud. Deep in and deep out through his nose. The sound of emotions being contained, controlled. The hiss in. The hiss out.

"That's what I am trying to do."

"Are you?"

The breath catches. It is held for what seems like an age in darkness.

"Caroline," Nina says. And his breath comes out in one long stream. Like vomit. "How come you can see, you can 'recover' so much buried stuff and yet the one thing, perhaps the most crucial event in your entire life is completely blocked out to you? No. It's not even blocked out. It's invisible." And she finds herself firing up, the adrenaline that began as nervous energy when she was approaching this subject is now a surge of strength, propelling her onwards. "I think a lot of this stuff is just a sideshow. A distraction. Maybe you invented some things, maybe you didn't, but at some point you started making stuff up for yourself and why? Because the more you lose yourself in that fantasy the less you have to face up to the fact that there's something, something really sad and horrible in your past. So horrible that you can't even acknowledge it. And this despite the fact that there's hard evidence right here on paper and –"

Sam's face tips up into the light. His eyes are two hard glossy beads. His mouth is fixed in a bitter aspect as if swallowing something sour and his nose wrinkles like an alligator's spine. It stops her dead.

"Well thanks for your armchair opinion."

"And fuck you too." The words are angry, but there is no loss of control. It is a reprimand that is necessary. "You asked me what I think and there you have it."

They stare at each other. Neither moves.

"Caroline," Nina reiterates. "It's all about Caroline."

"Yes it is."

Nina is a statue. Is this what they call a breakthrough? Or is it something else?

"So that's it. It's all about Caroline and I made the whole damn thing up and, yes, I stalked you and I ran you down in my car without even realising what I was doing. Do you still love me now? Even if I came right out and said that? Then where does all your affection go? Can you love something that's killing you?"

"Sam, I don't even know what you're saying. I don't know if this is a confession or a tantrum or something else or what."

"Well if you don't know I don't know how I can help you."

"I've already told you. Think. Think really hard. Go back. Right back. Think back through all of your time with Roberta. Everything she ever said to you. The hallucinations, the episodes, the time when you were attacked in the night, Neil, Rosanna, what did she say to you about Caroline? What did she say to you under hypnosis? You say you're awake now, so use that. What do you think was really suggestion and is there a jumping-off point? There must have been a time when... when it became more comfortable for you to believe in the idea of what she was doing to you than to face up to the truth."

His head snaps up to the side, the outline of his profile suddenly visible. One eye glittering out of the shadow. It shines, that eye. Shines a liquid white. A wet gleaming. He takes in a sudden breath and holds it.

"There was no jumping-off point," he says.

"Oh, come on Sam."

But her petty admonition goes ignored. Because he's in the middle of something deeper. A switch has flicked in his mind. And it is only as he sits there with his head held up at that weird angle, perfectly still, made more of shadow than light, like the body of a bog person lit by museum lamps, that Nina understands that now the process is going through. He's deep in contemplation of something up above, beyond them, something floating where that rectangle of light hangs above his head, inscrutable and blank to her, but he is inside it, reading it, probing. He's pushed himself there. And he's done it for her.

"There was no jumping-off point because I was never ready to think about Caroline. I thought that if I left it tucked in the back there I could just get on with my life, be with you, become a new person. But it kept coming back to me. It kept on coming back. Which is why I was so ready to believe Roberta. Anything she told me. That's what made me hold the gate open. And to be honest I have no idea if she really ever wanted me to confront Caroline because that was what made me so ripe for her, so vulnerable to her. And so instead of encouraging me to go deeper into it, she introduced another idea – another dream, and she'd guide me from one to the other, as if they had the same origin, as if they occupied the same space in my head. Twin dreams. Only one was real and one was not. Yes, they reflected each other. Both involved a woman, both involved death. But one was in the past and one was yet to come. It was an implant, preparation for reality, not analysis of it." And he turns back to Nina, his face disappearing into shadow again. "But I never had to jump off. She just had to keep me swimming in the direction I was going in."

"Yes." A nervousness swells inside Nina. They are about to move into new territory, darker and more dangerous than anywhere they have been before. And at the same time, a great sense of pride in him grows in Nina. Maybe he can do it. Maybe he really can do it.

"None of it was real," says Sam. And Nina feels maybe he is going too far, maybe they should stop and explore that further, but she doesn't want to interrupt his flow. "And all I ever had to do was stop, go back. Go into the other dream. Into that other space where Caroline still lives and breathes her last breaths and let the movie play out in my memory that little bit further." He leans forward and his eyes emerge like black diamonds twinkling in the dark, looking right at her, right into her.

"What was the dream, Sam? What was the other dream? Tell me about it. Go to that place."

The shutters come down. The black diamonds are sheathed and his head tilts down as he sits back and is all but enveloped in shadow, as if he really is leaving this place. Folding out of it and into another.

Sam closes his eyes.

The first thing to go is Nina. Then the furniture, then the walls, the windows. He is aware of the hushed sounds of traffic beyond the window, and then like any persistent noise they disappear until everything is completely silent.

And with that absence of sound there comes a closeness. The air draws more tightly around him, becoming thick in his throat. His chest tightens and for a moment he worries that his breathing will stop entirely. But it doesn't.

Then before him there are several lines. A midnight blue. Outside the sun is going down and twilight is split into a series of parallel strands by the half-open blinds. The blue lines. And the orange lines between them. The blinds turned orange by the interior lamp. Daylight and artificial light jarring next to each other, the colours clashing, making them both unnatural. And as if it belongs to someone else, he watches his hand rise to twist the cord. And the blue dwindles into thinner lines and then disappears completely. The orange fills the window. With the shutting-out of the outside light the room sinks into a soft darkness with that yellowy orange tinge to it, as if it is dirty. His eyes begin to adjust and the floor lamp blooms until it becomes a glow radiating against the wall, over the blinds, on the backs of the hands that do not look like his. He sees the veins standing out, the angle of the light casting larger shadows, making the veins look bigger, the hands look older. The pores seem more prevalent and open, giving them a sweaty cheese-like appearance as if there is something wrong with the flesh itself, something rancid.

The air tightens further in his throat and now he really is struggling to breathe and he feels a sense of outrage at this closeness, this stuffiness, that this place is the last place his wife will ever see. This place with no air, no view, no life. Perhaps she is already dead. Perhaps they both are. Perhaps this is a waiting room at the entrance of death, where he's sitting with her but will not be able to accompany her any further once she decides to move on.

He leans into the blinds, willing himself to pass through them and through the window. Wanting to run but with nowhere to go. And he begins to hear her. That wet, susurrating breath. The hiss out with a wheeze and then the intake that upon every hearing could be an ordinary, deep breath, until somewhere near the end of it, it catches, with a chest-infected catarrhal sound like a net full of wet gravel being dragged through thick mud. And every time he hears that it sinks straight into him, as if the sound was emanating from his own lungs and he feels the pain of the imminent thing again and again. The pain that only pales when it is laid alongside the pain of her existence. For now he turns and he sees her there. That bed, floating in the pool of stale light. The bed that hovers above the darkness of the rest of that room, which sinks away for an eternity at all edges. Caroline is so thin that the shape of her body under the sheet is nothing more than a crease that could be straightened out by pulling the bed linen taut. And he draws towards her and sees her head. That nest of luxurious blonde hair that still looks as beautiful as it ever did, only the skull to which it is attached is now a parched, yellow bulb, the edges of which can be glimpsed through the hair when the light catches it at the right angle. Her skin is vacuum-sealed over the cheeks and nose. The eye sockets sink back. Shadow pools inside them and Sam can only just make out that her eyelids are closed, wrinkled like dry leaves as if the eyeballs themselves – her beautiful eyes – have become desiccated and are no longer even present. It looks like she is already dead. Beyond dead. Mummified. A thousand-year-old corpse. A bog person. And yet those sickening breaths are still forced in and out of her by some unknown and sadistic power that won't allow them to stop. And the slight incline that marks out her breast rises and falls so minutely it could be the heartbeat of the mattress. A skull. No body. A skull perched on a pillow above a rumpled sheet. And a sucking sound, intermittent, timed in 5/3 like a telephone ringing, an interval chosen to be the most irritating and irregular-seeming of regular intervals.

He stands at the foot of the bed looking down upon his wife. And he has to force himself to associate this figure with the person that he loves more than life. Because right now this does not look like her, but like a special effect from a horror movie. But he can still see it, if he tries. If he joins the dots, if he mentally fills in her cheeks, brings back the colour and eliminates the cloying odour, the pungent staleness of breath and wasting. Can he do it? Can he bring her eyes to open, let those great glassy orbs rise up with all their depth and wonder and splendour? Can he see her as she was even a month ago when she still at least resembled herself? Or back before then, when they were on holiday in Florida, both ignorant of the imminent terminal diagnosis, she in her bikini, glowing bronzed skin in the bright, bright American sunshine of the Sunshine State. And her youthful face with its round freckled cheeks is inflamed with rage and blue eyes electric and flaring as they argue about something so insignificant that he cannot even remember what it was. And as stupid as that argument might have been, he wishes he could now remember it – almost as much as he wishes they had never had the argument that marred their last perfect time together. Although, in a way, as a memory its flaws only make it all the more valuable – like an off-cast stamp to a collector.

And back, back, back before that to see her laughing brilliantly and draped in a floor-length black evening dress, her shoulders not yet tanned are pale and bare and stand out like marble reliefs from the velvet beneath them, the light dusting of freckles again an imperfection that only makes them more perfect, giving them a kind of impossible softness and firmness at the same time. And diamonds sparkle, dangling at her ears in the bright ballroom full of chatter and glamour. Black diamonds. Her lips are parted, a deep glossy red, teeth pearly white as she laughs and laughs and laughs.

And now her head lies back on a pillow and she's not laughing, but her mouth is open in exhilaration. She's transported, the shackles of civility and demeanour are cast off and she is purely herself. Reacting without censure to the pleasure that pervades her whole body. She is in her wedding dress and the white shimmers, bunched up around her thighs where the creamy skin appears more richly coloured against the virginal fabric. A diamond sparkles on her finger as her hand frames his face and then moves up onto the top of his head and pushes through his hair and moves him down. Down to the heat and warmth and the soft hair and the pink and wet opening. An opening from which children will come. One day. Maybe. The white fabric falls around him, enveloping him; the starchy crinkling of petticoats and all those heady and beautiful scents, a rich, rose-based perfume, the sweat, an intensity that he inhales as he becomes lost beneath her skirts with only her cries to connect him to the real world. And everything fills in white. White is all he can see.

White curved around, hugging her shape. This anonymous woman in the university line. Her bob-cut hair, the way she used to wear it before she grew it out, just curling past the edge of her tight, white polo-necked top. He watches her. He waits. His turn comes in line and he lets the person behind him go instead of him and she turns and he sees her face. Her face: it was a gentle oval, glowing from within, it tapered to the bottom of her chin and moving up from there, her lips puckered in a dark red cupid's bow, a button nose dusted with freckles, her cheeks were wide and high and full, youthful, almost child-like, providing space for those large eyes, the delicate swish of thin blonde eyebrows above them, arcing with a flourish over the wide ovals that shone with unsullied brilliant whites and inside them a pearlescent blue that was as loud as it was deep and the black pupils always large as if she was on some kind of drug, the eyes in which he could drown and happily float there not caring whether he was dead or alive as long as he was there. And at the heart of those black, black pupils there was a prick of light, something that at first glance could be taken to be reflected light, but was in actual fact coming from within her. Two pricks of light. Like distant stars. That grew the more he stared into them. Grew and expanded until they became brilliant white and the light pervaded her features, burning out from beneath the skin so that the face became not so much a face but the impression of a face, like the afterglow of fireworks and if he closed his eyes he could still see it, the shape of her face burned in brilliant white into the backs of his eyelids. There forever as it is to this day.

But that was her face then. And now it is gone, wasted. No full cheeks, no plump lips. Everything thin and wasted. And as he stands over her and tries to see the face that he holds in his memory, that grins next to his in a hundred pictures and wedding photos, he cannot. It is not there. It has gone forever. And he does not know if it is because of his pain at this loss or her pain at having lost it – at having to exist in constant agony with only the certain knowledge that death will come, an existence so uncompromisingly bleak that death is its most redeeming feature – that without thinking or rationalising or even speaking to her, he draws the pillow out from under her head as gently as one would take a newborn from its crib.

And he is not thinking. There are no tears. There can be none. His eyes feel wide and dry as if the lids have been scorched away and they are not liquid but just two peach stones sealed into his head. So he cannot cry. And he lifts the pillow in front of her and brings it down over her face. Then stops. Not out of indecision or regret or second thoughts, but just on the off-chance that in lifting it away he might be allowed one more, one last glimpse of her face, her real face, her true face. But when he removes the pillow he does not see it. Only the paper skull. And he feels the sorrow redouble in him. And his own eyes close and he feels the feeling that usually precedes tears, the tingling and pressure at the corners of his eyes. But still none come. He just shudders in silence with the pillow in his hands. And when he opens his eyes – her eyes are open too.

Her eyes.

Large and blue and pearlescent and white and the black pits of her pupils with the twin pinpricks of light shining inside them, just about there, just about still there, twinkling like distant stars. And it steals his breath. Because he sees in that moment her entire essence and that under that paper mask Caroline is there, still very much there. And even though he knows she would want this too, it is impossible to stare into those eyes and not want to keep staring into them forever, even if the rest of her were to melt away, or crumble to dust and blow away in the wind.

"Caroline," he whispers, "Caroline, Caroline, Caroline," until the name has no meaning and is nothing more than three meaningless syllables. And he sees her eyes just staring at him there, not even moving but fixed on him and within them he can see the certain knowledge of what he is about to do and that she has recognised the action that he is taking and in its acknowledgement there is nothing but love, love, love and understanding. She is cheering him on, encouraging him. Screaming for him to cover her and take her out of this once beautiful world that has now become a parched desert in which she lies like a dead bird to bake in the sun.

And so he lowers the pillow over her face, covering the eyes, this time for good.

And for a moment he thinks he hears the ghost of her voice whisper "No." but it does not stop him. He is so steeled, so prepared to go through with this horrible task, to take on the weight of its guilt so that he can give her the gift of a few months' reprieve from the worst pain she will ever experience, that nothing can stop him. He cannot register a second thought or any thought, he can be only purity of action and intent. The decision was made. The trigger was pulled the moment he closed the blinds and stepped away from the window. The moment he twisted that cord and the reflection of himself in the space was closed off line by line until it was nothing. And he leans full forward, letting his weight drop down onto the pillow.

She has not even the strength to put up an instinctive struggle for breath. He stands there, leaning down on the pillow for hours, days, weeks. And there is nothing to tell him when it is finished. No going limp. She is already as limp as it is possible to be. No death rattle, no cough or shudder. Just the very same stillness that was there before. The stillness where the only action she was capable of other than breathing was to open her eyes to look at him one last time. And to allow him one last look at her.

And he only knows it is over because the room feels emptier. The stuffiness has gone and his breath begins to come easy and clear. And when he stands and removes the pillow, the thing that is there really is just a paper skeleton. There is nothing of her left in it. And only then, beginning immediately to reminisce, does he come into contact with her last action – the last thing she ever did on this earth.

What was that she said?

No?

His body begins to waver. To weaken.

And the curtain comes down.

Sam is enveloped in a blackness. A soothing blackness from which part of him hopes never to return. It is a thoughtless, imageless state. There is nothing but the endless depths and the swishing sounds inside his skull. The faint noise made by the movement of blood around the body, sometimes picked up as it circulates around the ears if you listen really closely. It is a hush. A whisper. An aortal rhythm, a liquid sluice. He floats in a timelessness. A nothing.

And then, slowly, the sounds begin to invade. The swirling of his body becomes the dull burr of traffic on the outside. Far away and muffled. And there is a vague sense of disappointment as he feels the world coming back – not a tangible thing, nothing as strong as anger or regret, just a deflation. He is unaware of his eyes opening, but following after the outside sound, comes light. There is not much of it. It is a thin anaemic light, like the first layer of wash on a watercolour. It picks up just the bumps and edges of things beneath it, making shapes not out of the things themselves but out of the hollows and depressions around them. A landscape made out of shadow. The walls first, filling in as boundaries to the space. Furniture begins to appear in the wash. Wooden floorboards telescoping towards him from the back wall. The television sits black-screened across from him. The screen is a window, reflecting some things back at him. Things that are not quite clear yet. He should see himself in the space but instead all he sees is an oblong of light floating behind a mass of darkness. And then the armchair grows out of the dark, off to one side of him. On it he sees the curled-up figure staring at him. Like a cat. She is there in all her elegance and sleekness. Her black hair lies across her shoulders in a lustrous curtain. And from within he can see the shape of her face peering out at him. Her lean, strong face. The resolution and solidity, the power it contains. To hold him up. Comfort him. Reassure him. Hold him steady like iron bands strapped around him to keep him from falling apart.

Nina says something to him but he does not understand it. He thinks she's asking if he's okay but the words don't have any meaning. They are just sounds. He does not know what causes her to rise from her chair. Her cat-like grace is shattered and stumbling. The crutches, like the borrowed limbs of a less elegant creature, carry her over to him. He can feel the warmth of her body beside him in this cold place. It wants to envelop him, or he wants it to envelop him. But for now he can only sit. And she is beside him but his gaze is still locked ahead, away. At the blank screen of the television, wherein he sees them both reflected. The images of themselves, aping real life, off in another space inside the TV screen that is the same as the space that surrounds them but is smaller and far away and locked within that square and no more real than any of the ideas that might inhabit a person's head at any one time. He can see her, curled up on the couch beside him, her plaster-cast leg dangling down, the other tucked up under her. Her hand moves to his arm and rubs it gently, as if trying to wake him from a sleep and as if reality in some way magically corresponds to this false image he feels the warmth of her hand, the gentleness of her touch. And now he hears her voice, her breath brushing against his ear. She is not just asking if he is okay but she is saying something more important to him, something that he needs to hear.

"What was the dream?"

"It was not a dream."

Sam hears his own voice. Hears the words. But on the television screen he cannot see his lips moving. His own face is obscured. A black disc framed by a ring of light.

"It was not a dream," he hears himself say again, "it was a memory."

He can hear Nina's breath. Hear it and feel it against his ear. It is reliably constant. There is a certain quality to it, a note of restraint. Something anticipatory. She is waiting for him to elaborate. And then he hears his own voice again,

"She said no."

And those three words repeat and repeat until he is not sure whether each repetition is a fresh utterance or just an echo of the one before reverberating off the walls of his mind. Or the walls of the flat. Or reflecting back from the television screen.

"She said no.

"She said no.

"She said no.

"She said –"

"Who?" Nina's voice breaks the repeating circuit, "Who said no?"

Brought back from the reflected reality opposite him by the sound of her voice, by her fingers spread on his shoulder, he turns to her. She is not looking directly at him. Perhaps while she was waiting for him to reply her attention wandered and she turned away. Her hair hangs around her face, masking her. Sensing that he is looking at her now, she turns to him. Tapered fingers rise to tuck the hair behind her ears.

And like the sea pulling back to reveal something hidden beneath the waves, her face emerges. The olive skin, the strong cheekbones, the straight nose, the wide lips pink and parted. She exhales and he feels her breath against his face. But he does not notice any of it. Because within the shadowy hollows created by those high cheeks and the elegant arch of those shrewd brows, her eyes draw him in. And the face around them drops away and they become so all-consuming that within her grey, studious irises, he is not really aware that he is looking at eyes at all. Just that he is sinking into something. A something so broad and deep that it has no boundaries, no end, like the city that seems to go on forever.

And in the centre of those pitch-black pupils, he finds something. Two little beads of light that glitter like far away stars. Only they are not stars, they are her soul duplicated through two windows. At least he thinks they are her soul, but he cannot remember ever seeing this thing before. Not in *her* eyes. They stay back there, twinkling away, tantalising, asking him to draw closer. They are so familiar, so close, like something that he carries around inside of him. Something that has been with him much longer. Long before he met Nina. It is a soul. But it is not her soul.

Sam feels himself pulling away in fear, in awe of a beauty that he had never expected to see again, and whose re-emergence makes him question whether he is even alive. How could it be here with him, now, in the real world. Right here on this couch. And he feels his focus reeling back. The edges of Nina's eyes come into view. Boundaries, shapes, circles within circles. The pupils are wide, dilated as if on some kind of drug. And then, around them, the irises, not grey but blue. Bright blue. Electric blue. A blue that shocks him with its purity. The whites are unblemished and shining, as clean and as perfect as if they had never been used.

No-one has eyes like that. No-one but *her*. And even though, as he sits back, he sees that it is still Nina's face that frames them, her long black hair cutting around and rendering it sharp and clear, he knows that it is nothing more than a mask. It is not Nina that inhabits it. He doesn't know what has happened to her, where she has gone. But she is not here. Not any more. And he doesn't care. It is a knowledge, a recognition that sends such a trembling through him that he can barely bring himself to speak the word. He has never felt more elated. Or more afraid.

"Caroline?"

Her focus has begun to wane. She has been staring at that silhouetted figure – ridge of shoulders, rocky peak of hair, head hung in blackness – as if she might be able see the cogs and machinery whirring away within it if she only stared hard enough. But she has seen nothing. Only stillness. And so despite willing herself to keep searching, her eyelids have become heavy.

And then, just as she is about to drop off, something changes. She can't tell exactly what it is. There is no exterior physical sign of it. His face is still obscured, his body has not moved. But there has been a shift. Perhaps something in the motion of the oblong of light behind his head. Perhaps nothing. Perhaps something in her mind.

"Sam," she says, softly at first, "are you okay?"

And there is something very subtle, a motion, a lolling of the head. A wet sound in the back of his throat like a man drowning in three inches of water.

"Are you okay, Sam? What's going on? Is everything alright?"

Still, he doesn't speak, but the rotation of his head becomes, if not larger, then looser. She catches a glimpse of his eyes and they are staring away as if he is not looking at anything. Like a blind man.

She sits down on the couch beside him, tucking her good leg under herself, the plaster-cast dangling onto the floor. She can see his face now and although his eyes are open, he is in a state of deep repose. The muscles of his cheeks are relaxed, the stubble-coated jaw loose, his mouth open a crack. She can hear his breathing coming long and slow in and out. He still seems far away and she reaches out to shake him gently. The flesh of his arm feels loose, like a filled stocking. His shoulders are devoid of tension and there is a warmth to him reminiscent of someone who has been curled up under a duvet for an entire night's sleep. She presses her lips close to his ear,

"Sam? Sam can you hear me? What's going on? Are you okay? Speak to me?"

But he does not react. Looking at his eyes from the side she can make out their curve and the dim light comes through them and makes them glassy, like marbles. She wonders what he could be looking at, where he is, what he is seeing. In his pupils she catches what could be the reflected square of the television screen with a small couch inside it on which there sit two miniature people that look a lot like them. Reflected and reflected again. But it is a fleeting thing. A fancy. "Where were you Sam? Was it the dream? Which dream? What did you see? What was the dream?"

Sam's face does not change, but its lips move by themselves.

"It was not a dream."

It is not a conversation. If he is hearing her, it is an automatic thing, not a question-response. Just an input of data that combines with other factors and then, maybe, when he is ready, produces a commentary on the situation. He is not talking to her. He is not talking to anyone. Not even himself. She watches the still face, waiting for its next output.

"It was not a dream," he says again, "it was a memory."

Something is happening. She leans in closer, her hand spreading as it moves up to his shoulder.

"She said no."

The words have little meaning to her. Without context, they are just abstractions. But he does not elaborate and after some time waiting for him to continue, feeling the curiosity building inside her like an itch she wants, no, needs to know. Needs more.

"Who?" she says. "Who said no?"

His response is a long time in coming. The itch is not scratched. It is too great an irritation. She needs to move, can't keep her eyes trained on him any longer. And so she looks down at the floor. Blinks. Rubs her eyes.

She turns back to him, tucking her hair behind her ear. He is looking right at her with eyes open wide as if transfixed by a bright light. His face looks gaunt now. And as he stares into her eyes, his own appear to widen impossibly. His cheeks become hollow and his mouth hangs further open by degrees. His breath washes over her, still reeking of the morning, of unbrushed teeth. She wrinkles her nose, fighting an impulse to pull away. She can't break eye contact with him now. He is going through something. It really does feel like something is about to come, something terribly important and valuable and useful.

Is this it? Nina thinks. The breakthrough, is this what it feels like? It feels somehow marvellous, like an immense relief of pressure. Freedom from slavish thoughts. A new horizon. Perhaps she has done it, perhaps now she has really done it. She has saved him. The truth is about to come out, and when it does they can move on. She doesn't know where to, but anywhere is better than here.

Something changes in his face. The hollows become more hollow. Shadows filling in from an indistinct grey to a deeper black. His skin looks like anaemic rubber aged to the point just before it begins to crack. His eyes are dancing, patterns visible within them as his pupils expand and contract. Something has taken hold of him. It is a definitive change. Not the kind of change he has talked about when Roberta takes control, not the same vacancy that Nina saw when he was sitting on the window ledge. This is different. So very different. He's definitely there. Perhaps more there than he ever has been. But something inside has snapped. She can almost hear its broken pieces pinging apart. And as his lips try to move, drawing together in a vain attempt to form words, something dark and curdling drops through Nina's stomach. And she can sense the imminent arrival of that thing, the thing that is waiting to emerge from within its chrysalis. She doesn't know what it is but now that it is coming she knows that she doesn't want it. She doesn't want it at all.

"Caroline?"

The last word she wanted to hear. And upon hearing it her whole world crumbles.

"No."

Is all she can manage. She wants to reach out, grab him, shake him, slap him across the face. But all that comes out is that word. It means no, I am not Caroline. And it means no, I don't want this to be happening.

"Why are you here?" says Sam. "Why did you come back?" And there is something rumbling underneath his voice, deep within his body. She can see the tremor under the skin of his face and in his hands, she can feel it in his shoulder where her hand rests and from which she now withdraws it. His breath shudders and rattles within him. She worries that whatever it is under there, that thing is going to shake him until it tears him apart.

"Sam, it's me, Nina. I'm not her. I'm not Caroline. You need to snap out of this. Now."

"I have missed you. So, so much."

There is absolute certainty in his stare. And Nina knows that her words are not achieving anything. Sam is not hearing them. He reaches out with trembling fingers and it makes her shiver and want to shrink away, but she doesn't. There is no way to avoid him without getting up off of the couch, without breaking contact. And maybe that's not what is needed right now. Maybe he needs this, he needs to go through it. His arms close around her, holding her loosely. He is gentle and soft and trembling and his body feels cold all of a sudden. Colder than it can surely be healthy for a human to be. And yet the sweat is beading and starting to drip from his forehead and run along his nose.

"I'm sorry," he says, burying his head in her shoulder, "I'm so sorry." And she can hear him sobbing.

Sam looks into her eyes again and now Nina is unable to do anything but look back at him with a catatonic terror.

"Speak to me," he says, "Please speak to me. Don't just look at me like that. I can't bear it. I know," he gasps, recovers himself, "I know I did you wrong. I'm sorry. I really, I am, but I thought it was what you wanted."

Nina forces her shaking hands to reach out and take hold of him,

"Sam. Sam, Sam, listen to me. It's alright, okay? Everything is okay. You just need to, to take some deep breaths and..."

"... but you can't just sit there and stare at me in silence. Why did you come here? You came all this way not to even speak to me?"

"Sam are you listening. Listen to me!"

"To torment me? Is that it? Is it revenge?"

And Nina has lost the ability to speak, all she can do is shiver within his embrace, wishing she was anywhere but.

His eyes soften. His mouth closes and his face seems warmer, gentler. "I'm sorry. I know you'd never do that."

And in his stare there is something richer and deeper than she has ever seen before. He has never looked at her like this. No-one has.

"I love you," Sam continues, "I love you so much and I've still loved you all these years you've been gone. And I know you wouldn't come here to do me harm. You couldn't do that to me anymore than I could you."

Nina's skin crawls. The resonance of the words. *I could never hurt you*, he had said to her. And now he echoes the sentiment, but he's speaking it to Caroline, to the woman he did hurt. A woman he loved. That he killed. And even though he was trying to spare her pain, he still can't face up to that fact. And now Sam is drawing his arms tighter around her. A nausea rises in Nina, she can taste the acrid sting of stomach acids at the back of her throat and where his body is in contact with hers there is a churning as if her very flesh is rebelling against his touch. But she tries to hold on, to keep her senses, to manage the situation. She raises her hands to cradle his face and says,

"Sam. Sam listen to me," and a stream of conciliatory words comes out of her mouth but she already knows they are lost on him. And he's looking at her with such affection that she can't help but to want to help him, despite the intense wrongness of the situation and the warning signs flashing red in front of her eyes telling her no, no, danger, get away.

Sam's head inches towards her. His hand moves up along her back creating an undulation of discomfort all along her. His grip is so tight. And the hand reaches the back of her neck, moves through her hair and tightens its grip. She's thinking no, no, I don't like where this is going. And his head is pressing closer to hers and his grip is too strong for her to pull away and he whispers words of undying devotion and he presses his lips into hers and the stale taste of his mouth invades her own. She twists her head away from him, around and away and he folds forward on top of her, his weight bearing down until she sinks onto her back. The crutches, leaning against the couch, clatter to the floor beside them. She squeezes her eyes shut. He moves above her, his body pressing down on her. His knee pushes in between her legs, forcing them apart. And she can feel him stirring against the inside of her thigh. His mouth is moving along the side of her face, placing wet kisses, his tongue darting in and out. And all she can do is lie there whispering for him to stop and knowing that he won't hear it and the whole time she has her eyes shut tight.

But then he does stop. The motion, the stirring, the mounting arousal and the coupling movements of his body. They all stop. His hand seizes her face, "Where have you gone?"

She doesn't know what he could possibly mean but she can't bring herself to turn and look at him, to return to that hot embrace, to the closeness of his face.

"Don't do this to me," he says, "I know you're there, just, don't hide from me. You can't show yourself to me like that and then go away again."

She tries to resist as he turns her to face him but her neck is not strong enough. She feels as if something will pop or break inside it. And then her head is being pushed back into the cushion. She keeps her eyes screwed shut. His hands paw at her face, beseeching her – no, not her, Caroline – to come out. His fingers and thumbs spread over her eyelids and pry them apart. Nina stares back at him with her lids pinned, her eyes wide and large, like eyeballs in a skeleton and her mouth peels back from her gritted teeth as she twists and writhes and grunts under the weight of him.

He flushes with ecstasy, "There you are." An epiphany.

This is more than just a confusion of senses. He really believes that his late wife is inhabiting the woman in front of him. And he's willing to use Nina's body as a vehicle to commune with Caroline, with no more compunction than he would use a machine. His hand roams down her collarbone and over her breast, slipping up under the shirt. And something starts within Nina that is at first a hiss through her teeth and then a thin whine, rising in pitch until it becomes raw noise, surging out of her in an unending scream. And even this Sam doesn't hear as he folds her skirt up and his fingers grip the elastic of her knickers. Her hand flails around on the floor beside the couch until it finds a crutch, closes around it and brings it up hard into Sam's ribs. He makes a hollow exhalation and twists away from the blow – Nina slides out from under him and tumbles onto the floor. On her hands and knees, she scuttles over to the armchair and hides behind it, the crutch clamped in her white-knuckled hands.

She peeks over the edge of the chair. Sam is curled up on the couch, holding his stomach, trying to get his breath back. Nina watches, shaking. The wood of the crutch is slick in her hands.

"Sam, you have got to back the fuck away." The voice comes out of her strong. Somewhere under the fear, the fighter in her has surfaced. She needs to keep this distance between them, keep him over there until he calms down.

He makes a noise. A winded mumble. A wheeze-word. And then a long groan comes out of him as he twists onto his knees, his hands groping along the cushions of the couch, trying to find some stability.

"Is," breath, breath, breath, "is this," breath, "what you want?" He looks at her. Bitterness. Words hard and dry. "Did you come here to punish me?" He swings his legs out and sits doubled-over, holding his stomach. Takes a few deep breaths. His eyes burn her. "Haven't I already been punished enough? How many years do I have to go on living and reliving this? You want me to just carry on forever with you in my heart like a – a cancer! If you're not here to be with me then you can at least let me go."

"I'm not punishing you. *I'm* not doing anything."

"Why don't you just come over here? Come over here, yeah? We can, we can be together and..."

"Sam, snap the fuck out of it!"

He pushes himself to his feet. Standing for a moment, glaring at her with a frightening anger, he wavers and then drops down into his seat again. How hard must she have hit him? And it was only the one blow. But she can see that he's already preparing to get to his feet again. Her fingers fumble through her pocket and find her phone. She takes it out. Looks at the screen. The thought of making the call sickens her. It's the last thing she wants to do but she can't see any other choice. She doesn't know who else she can call. There isn't anyone to call. Not that can help her now. And as Sam finds his feet again, her thumb hits 9 for the third time. She speaks hurriedly into the phone as he takes increasingly steady steps across the floor.

"Has he hurt you?" asks the operator.

"I don't know, I don't know what he's going to do," she says over again as he advances, his long body blocking the oblong of light behind him until he is a towering silhouette. Nina's voice trembles and she can barely pronounce the words she is trying to say, and then she doesn't even know what she is saying. The phone slips from her hand and she shuffles backwards across the floor, dragging the crutch with her. Sam looms over her, faceless, featureless, a body made of shadow, its only expression in the aggressive curve of its back, the jut of its head, the curling of the fingers that rise at his side. Her back hits the wall. Beside her, the TV table represents an opportunity to pull herself to her feet but she doesn't know if she is better off curled-up down in the corner or standing. She holds the crutch out in front of her like a spear. And when Sam lurches forwards she swipes it at him. But her position is so weak that it is little more than a feeble swish. He comes again, admonishing her, telling her to stop it. She stabs with the crutch and he steps back. His arm sweeps for it. She whips it up and away from him and then brings it down into his face. Sam howls and totters backwards. He staggers around the room doubled-over, his hands holding his face. A strange dance.

Nina takes the opportunity to get to her feet. And she hobble-hops as quickly as she can towards the hallway. Throwing the door open, she sees the chest. She had forgotten all about it. Defeat floods through her. She looks over her shoulder to see Sam walking towards her. His nose is inflamed, bloodied, his eyes shot through with tears. He wipes his sleeve underneath it, smudging the trickle into a smear along his upper lip. She turns away and lurches over to the chest, shifting herself around it, trying to find a way in, to get behind it and push.

"Nina."

Her name. It sends a shiver through her. A wave of elation. She can't help it. Euphoria claims her and she turns back to Sam.

"Sam, is that really... are you okay?"

"Nina, it's alright. You don't need to. Just wait a moment okay." And he sniffles back blood and wipes his nose again. Looks at his hand. At the livid red stripe across the back of it. And when he looks back up at her, his eyes are wells, brimming, full of confusion. "I don't know what's happening," he says.

"You need help. We need to get you some help."

He freezes. Shrinking away.

"Not her."

"No. No, not her. We'll get you someone else."

He snorts back liquid sludge and his mouth curves down, the corners finding deep places at the bottom of his jaw. His lips part, trailing strings of blood and mucus and he makes a sound. It is a sound that comes from somewhere right at the bottom of him. A sound of whatever it is inside being torn apart, tearing itself apart. The splitting of a tectonic plate. Confusion and anguish grinding against each other in a low gurgle that twists and wails into a throbbing ululation without tone or pitch. The sound of his soul being wrenched out of his mouth and dragged through the dirt. His knees buckle and he sinks into a sort of crouch as the terrible sound echoes around the room. Fills it. The edges of the noise so ragged and raw that Nina fears that his throat is tearing. It is not a human noise. It is the noise that is left behind when the humanity has been ripped out.

Sam sinks to the floor. On his knees, huddled over, his face against the floorboards, the sound dwindles until it is a barely audible hiss. He crawls along the floor towards Nina. She watches as he inches towards her. Her heart is broken. Even watching this pitiful display, there is no pity in her, only the deepest sorrow. She looks at what Sam has become and it makes her, too, want to curl up and die in a corner somewhere. He draws near and she can see that behind him there is a shimmering trail of mucus left by his face along the wood. His arms close around her ankles and he hugs to her legs. Somewhere around her knees, she can feel the dampness of his face through her skirt. And although his body is wrapped around her, she does not feel any shaking or trembling. She does not even feel the beating of his heart. It is as if nothing beats within him. She looks down at the top of his head, the thick messy hair shoved into uneven spikes. Pointing up like the top of a coconut. She reaches down and places her hand on it, letting her fingers push through it. And all she can do is stand there like that and stare down at the top of his head. And tears begin to run down her face. There is no twitching, no creasing of her expression and she does not attempt to wipe them away. They run out of her eyes as if someone has left a tap on. And she watches the drops splash down onto the back of her hand, soaking into his hair.

A wooden sound.

Knock, knock, knock.

Oh, thinks Nina. Voices come through the front door. They are asking if she's okay. They are telling Sam to open the door.

"There's a chest of drawers against the door," she says. "You'll need to break it in." And she expels a useless sigh, lifts her head and stares away at the empty flat, thinking about all the time they have spent together there, trying to see past the fog of the last forty-eight hours.

"Are they here?" A small voice says.

"Yes. They're here." Her vision defocuses, the flat becoming misty through a wash of tears.

His hand finds her thigh. Grips it. The fingers digging in. She smiles sadly and reaches down to hold it. But he shakes her off. His other hand clamps onto her waist. The other above her hip. She feels a weight drawing on her and realises that Sam is climbing up her, pulling himself to his feet. She looks down, to reach out to him, to help him.

Bared teeth meet her gaze. Gritted, grinding teeth in a face flushed with red and raw. The cheeks shine wet and the eyes, the eyes are blistered and cracked. The vessels in them are like fissures in the surface of the world. Magma showing through. A claw grabs her breast and squeezes so tight that she lets out an involuntary cry of shock and pain. And then that face is right in her face. A mask of loathing. She feels the heat radiating out of it.

"You."

The word is squashed through the grill of his mouth. And before she can react. Before she can even understand, his hands clamp around her throat.

"You."

And they constrict. She lets go of the crutch and claws at his tightening fingers but they are unbreakable. They are crushing the air out of her and he presses his face into hers, not in a gesture of intimacy but as if he is trying to erode her, consume her, his forehead butting against hers so that it makes her head rock back. Her mouth strains wide, and a dry sound like a reverse cough comes out as she tries to suck in air that will not come. The pain in her throat is dark and bitter and he butts up against her again, the rocking of her head doubling the pain.

"You," he says again, "You you YOU!"

And whether it is because the light is already beginning to fade, because she cannot bear to watch the world die or because she cannot bear to see the murderous rage flashing in front of her, she closes her eyes. Her legs buckle but she does not drop, she is held up by the hands that are closing together as if they could push through her neck. And all sound and all light and all of it – everything is shut off. It disappears. Until there is nothing but the pain and the blackness. And then, not even the pain.

A flashing of light and bodies. A wheeling disorientation. Impact and wall and floor. The ceiling lamp spins like a Wurlitzer. Harsh voices echo through, shooting in and out like cars in a road tunnel. A pair of heavy boots steps across and the field finds itself.

Sam is coming round, the blaze of hatred has faded, the red mist dispersed as if by a heavy rainstorm. And now there is only confusion and fear. This, Nina can see in his eyes as two police officers hold him down and he does not resist, he just gives himself over to the hopelessness of it all. They lift him like a ragdoll and one of them looks down at her where she lies in the doorway between the hall and the lounge and tells her that they will send someone for her and to stay put and try not to move. She watches as Sam is hauled out through the front door and as she does, she feels nothing, no emotion positive or negative. All she can do is see. All feeling has been wrung out of her. The officers pause in the doorway to re-orientate themselves and get a better grip on Sam before moving him out into the corridor. There are only two of them. They need to make sure they have him. And Nina notices that Sam's eyes are trained on one of them. A man. A tall man. Sam is glaring at him, and his face is slack and yellowing in the grip of a fear that has robbed him of the ability to do anything. Except an utterance that she hears come out of him in a mumble that is only just distinguishable to her, perhaps because she knows him well enough to decipher it –

"You," he says to the policeman. "You're Frame. Jonathan Frame."

But the man does not understand it and pays no further attention. And even had he heard it, he is not Frame.

And then they are gone. And Nina sits alone as the echoes of struggle recede and the flat becomes silent. Like a box buried deep underground. And she lies in the cool stillness of it, feeling nothing, not even the pain that she should be feeling. And for a moment she wishes that no-one would come to rescue her or make sure she's okay. And that they would leave her here forever to slowly sink into the floorboards and become dust.

And all she can think about is the word.

YOU.

It runs around and around the inside of her skull, ringing with a persistent nagging repetition, impenetrable, incomprehensible. The word refuses to be pinned down. Every time she finds a meaning, tries to hold onto it, it slips away from her.

YOU.

Is it an accusation of betrayal, that he believes she has colluded with Roberta and her people?

Or was it something else? Was he even speaking to her? Was he speaking to Caroline? And if so, was it a message of hatred, or a message of love? Or the pure frustration that he is not allowed to *be*. Not allowed to live. Because ultimately he still loves her.

And that's what stops her feeling. The very notion that she was nothing more than a blank screen, an oblong of light onto which an image of something else was projected. Because the overwhelming thought, the thing that she can't get away from, is that Sam, the Sam she knows, really never could have hurt her.

Because he didn't love her enough.

Chapter Twelve

THE MIMES BECOME ITS FOOD

"I know it's a horrible thing to contemplate but the sooner you get off your arse and do it, the sooner you'll thank yourself for doing so."

Nina squints away across the restaurant, avoiding Sandra's well-meaning stare. She wipes a stain of red wine from her lips. Framed by the golden glow of plate glass window lights, diners chat and laugh with each other. All of them couples. Or at least she assumes they are. She wonders what she is doing in this smart restaurant, surrounded by romances at various stages in their evolutions; some just beginning, others no doubt nearing their ends, whether the participants can see it coming or not. She wonders if Sandra brought her here intentionally to frame the topic of this discussion, to put her in a place where she'll be receptive, where she'll feel her loneliness strongly enough to make her jump up and ask if there are any single men in the room. Because if that was the plan, it's not working. She isn't there yet. All it makes her do is reminisce.

Although at the back of her mind she's aware that she is telling herself this – that this is what she wants to hear, that she's trying to keep herself inside that bubble of despair for one reason or another. Perhaps because it's all she's got.

"I don't know," she says.

"You never know until you try."

The truism makes her smile.

"Hey, you might even have fun."

"I think we need something stronger," Nina says, and tries to catch the eye of the wine waiter.

There's something reassuring about being in a place where everyone is so eaten up by their own shit that interaction with anybody else is optional. He's sitting on a bench with two other people whose names he has not bothered to learn. They are all wearing tracksuits and trainers. Leisurewear, they call it. It could be a lot worse. It is beautiful here. The bench is on a patio overlooking a steep grassy slope of a garden. And beyond it the whole countryside rolls away until it becomes the city. It glitters there in the far distance, only just visible, like a faded memory. The young man to his left smokes a roll-up and stares at the ground. The elderly man to his right coughs dryly into his fist. His face is liver-spotted, the skin around his eyes sagging so much that it almost covers them, as if it has worn more care than it was ever designed to support. Nobody says anything. They have nothing to say to each other that isn't about themselves and nobody else is interested enough to listen. It's a perfect compact really. Every day people try to make them talk, as if by doing so they might actually be able to change something. Sam leans back on the bench. He looks at the young man. And he looks at the old man.

Sausages, mashed potatoes, steamed veg and peas. He closes his eyes and listens. The only sound is clinking cutlery, the scraping of knives and forks on plates. The dining hall could be empty of people, populated by poltergeists. He opens his eyes, half-expecting to see the cutlery moving by itself. It shocks him to find the room full of people in tracksuits, eating their food like it's a chore.

"It feels like ages since I've spoken to anyone," says a teenage girl. He hasn't bothered to learn her name either. The fact that she takes no care of herself does not stop the glow of youth from coming through. A loose strand of hair clings greasily to her cheek. As she speaks, she pushes the strand into her mouth and sucks it, her finger and thumb pushing it up and down through her lips. "I mean, I speak to people, but they don't hear me. And when they say something back I don't hear them. I almost find it a relief that in here no-one really tries. Do you know what I mean?" She looks around at the group. Many of them have their faces turned down into their laps, fiddling with their fingers or the hems of their garments. Sam stares back at her with clear, unwavering eyes. The girl completes the circuit and her large eyes return to the therapist, looking up at him.

He looks at himself and it is like looking at another person. A person whose expression is flat and devoid of emotion. Whose eyes are dead. He cocks his head. The other guy cocks his head. And then without giving this reflected person any further thought, he turns out the bathroom light.

A security light comes on outside. Filtered through the curtains, it spreads a bright wedge across the ceiling. He wonders if the light actually changes the ceiling to that yellow-orange colour, or if its usual whiteness is an inherent part of its makeup. When it goes off the wedge shape remains, only it is a dark blue. Lying in bed at night he can stare at it for hours, meditating upon the change in colours. He finds a kind of bliss in this simple contemplation. There was a time when he might have seen a blank surface like this as a kind of canvas on which to project thoughts. A place where he could imagine and re-imagine. But for now there is nothing. Only the calm stillness of the night. He does not think of anyone. Anyone living or anyone dead.

"Nice to see you again Miss Trevanion," says the wine waiter. She flashes him a jumpy smile. He walks away and her eyes linger on the straight lines running up the backs of his trousers.

"You come here a lot?"

She turns back to her date, flushed, "You don't need to pick me up." It comes out too sharply. "That is, I mean, we're already here."

"Yes," he chuckles, dimples creasing his cheeks, "you're right, that did sound like a pick-up line, didn't it." He hunches his shoulders and waggles his head, putting on a husky voice, "Come here often, luv?"

She can't decide if he's funny or if he's trying too hard. But his smile is nice. Nina breaks eye contact and takes another sip of her wine.

"So, erm, Sandra didn't tell me what it is you do," he says.

She smoothes out a ridge in the tablecloth, "I haven't been on a date in a long time."

"Oh."

"That's why it bothered me. What the waiter said. Makes it seem like I'm always coming here on dates."

"Well, hey, maybe it's not that important."

"It is important. To me."

Now it's his turn to smooth out a ridge in the tablecloth.

"I always choose the wrong men," she says. And immediately wonders why she said it.

"Well," he looks up at her, that smile again, "You didn't choose me."

His face retains all its roundness and that big smile spreads further, opening as it reaches the apex of its ecstasy. His forehead gleams in the darkness as he moves above her. Every last ounce of breath is squeezed out of him by the shuddering of his body. And then he rolls off her onto his back. He lies there catching his breath, his chest hair curling into sporadic wet coils. Nina props herself up on her elbow. He turns to her and his smile is kind and gentle. He reaches up to brush a hair out of her face, his eyes twinkling.

"Hi," he says.

She doesn't reply. Just gives him a little smile. A warm one. And then takes hold of his wrist and moves his hand away. She holds it on the pillow, her fingers playing in his.

"I really didn't expect that to happen."

"Me either," she replies.

And he stares at her, his fingers tracing hers back. His smile is spreading. It is so open. His emotions and thoughts writ large. Now it's talking to her in images. Things flashing through his mind. Already he's beginning to think about futures. Time spent together. Their next meeting. Their next sex. Certain things are being taken for granted. And the smile in his face is becoming so large it's offensive. It's a great, smug curve, the smile of a cat with its cream. She imagines his mouth opening to a size larger than her head and swallowing it whole.

"Thank you," she says, "but I need to sleep now." The penny hasn't dropped yet. So she adds, "Sorry."

And his smile pops like a balloon, "Oh. No, it's fine. It's just I thought..."

He's unable to look at her anymore. He pulls the quilt back and gets out of bed. She closes her eyes while he's still getting dressed.

She feels his lips kiss the side of her head. Hears the bedroom door close. And is asleep before the sound of the front door follows it.

There's a knock at the door. He must have overslept. It's so easy to lose track of time in this place and there is rarely anything more worth doing than sleeping. Sam blinks gummily at the door. A square-jawed man in a white smock jacket is peering in at him – another person whose name he has not bothered to learn, but whose face he has seen day-in day-out.

"Morning Sam," says the nurse. "It's time for your session."

Sam swings his legs over the edge of the bed. He stretches and lets out something halfway between a yawn and a roar. The nurse chuckles and leaves him to dress.

Sam navigates the corridors on autopilot. He has been in here for long enough now that he accepts it as a given: this is the world, this is the way it is supposed to be. He has let everything else recede. And he's fine with that – at least here he can't fuck anything up. The corridor is reassuringly bland. Its grey carpet and clean magnolia walls offer a reliability that he enjoys. He moves slowly past the doors of the other patients' rooms. Each one is the same, nothing changing but the number on the door.

In the main part of the building the corridors are wider. Paintings by residents hang on the walls. Some are not bad, others are like children's daubs. The good and the shitty hang together with nothing to distinguish them. They have not been selected for their quality. They are there to make the people who painted them feel proud of what they've done. There could be one other criterion, he supposes, which is that they are anodyne to a piece. He's seen the kind of things that can come out in the art room and though a good proportion of it is calming, therapeutic in nature, there is a certain section of work that is not represented here. There are landscapes, there are portraits, there are still lives but they are all paintings of nothing.

The receptionist, another person whose name he has not bothered to learn, tells him to proceed to room five. He nods and follows the corridor along. Reaching the room, he opens the door and moves through without pause.

"Hello Sam."

He sits down in his chair.

"You're late, you know."

Sam doesn't say anything. He sits there, still as a stone, waiting for the tide to wash over him and recede. As long as he can hold still like this, there's nothing she can do. She cannot touch him. For as much as those searchlight eyes scan his expression, his skin, his posture for some clue as to what is on the inside, they have no actual power to penetrate. If he gives her nothing, she can do nothing with it. He stares back at the flabby round face framed by its red-dyed curls. The deep black eyes like coals in a snowman. The maternal body, the ample bosom. Her hand plays with a silver brooch on her voluminous black cardigan: a spider. And as she scrutinises every pore, looking for a crack where she can get in, a tiny smile twists her puffy lips. He sees the light down on the top of her lip. It is not a friendly smile. It is not angry either. It is the kind of smile a gladiator might have when he's squaring off against an opponent. Or a lion before it eats its first Christian.

"You know what," says Roberta. "I'm not going to try anymore. You can sit there for as long as you like in silence. Just know that I'll be here, twice a week, for as long as you're in here."

Sam keeps his face as still as he can manage. Trying not to let slip anything that could be interpreted as a reaction. Nothing to be picked over. Nothing that can be analysed.

"And how long that is, well, it's entirely up to you. You do the work and then we can get you out of here, get a fresh start. But as long as you're just going to sit there saying nothing then, well, I'll just assume that you're happy right where you are."

Her face freezes in the kind of passive-aggressive smile that can only be born when someone's facial muscles are pulled tight by anger and frustration. But then it's gone. And she's easy again, understanding and open-looking. She cocks her head at Sam and shrugs. And then she reaches into her bag and takes out a book. Placing it in her lap she opens it, removes the bookmark and tucks it into the back of the jacket.

"Just let me know if you want to say anything." Her eyebrows rise and she nods with such sincerity and goodwill that it makes Sam want to leap up out of his chair and tear her head off. But he doesn't. And Roberta looks down at her book, the red curls swinging over her face, hiding the searchlight eyes from him, and she begins to read.

And Sam sits, straight-backed, watching her read, waiting for the session to end. She turns the pages, one every couple of minutes. And every movement, every sound, every brushing of paper, provokes a deep irritation in him. But still he does not move. He's not going to give her anything, not if he can help it. But even now, after months of silence, he suspects that this is not enough. That she can see through him. He's not making it easy for her, but with every day that she sits here she gets closer and closer, further and further in. All of this, this act, this ploy, it's just to distract him, make him look the other way while she reaches in and opens up the back of his head and tinkers around. This book thing, it's only the latest trick to convince him that she's not looking. But he knows that she is. And he knows that she knows that he knows. Because if she didn't, how else could she have figured it out? She said it. She's got it now. *I'll just assume that you're happy right where you are.* In four months she hasn't made this conclusion before. This was not an admission of defeat. Quite the opposite. She wasn't just telling him that she's not giving up. She was telling him that she sees him. Because she's right. For now there is nowhere else that he'd rather be. Free he might not be, but this is the furthest away from her he can put himself. He's in the palm of her hand, but beyond her grasp. It's not ideal, but it works. If he can't get away from her, then he's happy to remain here. Right here where she cannot touch him. A thorn in her side. The itch that she cannot scratch.

Lights Out is the kind of club that a single woman doesn't normally go into sober. It's a place where you end up after a long night drinking with your friends when everything else is closed. And with each step down into the red light that bathes the entrance corridor, Nina feels the club's atmosphere seeping up and covering her, as warm as it is disgusting. Like wading into sewage.

Weak blues and reds pulse over the middle of the main room. which by virtue of an absence of furniture is nominally the dance floor. The heat is fierce. It is thick with bodies and hectic with wild movement there; all faces in shadow, flicks of hair catching the light, hands raised and pointing to the ceiling. The music is the worst kind of cheesy pop and it is half-drowned by a clamour of voices. Breathing in here is like taking in hot breath directly from someone else's mouth. There is a scrum at the bar. Nina grimaces. It might take her a while to get a drink. But she's tall and she's a woman – built for getting served.

"You wanna buy some coke?"

She turns. A dirty, pitted face that looks like it has been slammed in a door towers over her. She moves hastily away towards the scrum, scanning the shadowy bodies for an entrance point. The brightly lit bar casts them into a homogenised silhouette like they are one huge creature with many, many body parts. Only the four barmen are clearly illuminated. They are not the bright-eyed youngsters that she's used to being served by in London bars; they are grizzled men who look like they have all done prison time. Nina is about to plunge into the mass, but stops. Turns round. The dirty man is a little further away than he was, blue light flashing on his face like lightning on a buoy at sea. She pushes towards him, bodies heading barwards brushing against her. Warmth, firm flesh, breathy smells of alcohol and cigarettes. He's looking the other way when she gets to him and she has to tap him on the arm to get his attention. She nods and his grubby hand grasps her arm and his rank breath washes over her ear, "Follow me."

He moves away immediately. She tries to keep in the wake that he carves through the crowd, watching the outline of his shaggy hair standing higher than all the other heads.

They rendezvous around a corner. It is even darker here than it is in the rest of the club. People stand around in small groups. No dancing, just drinking, talking and smoking as if the smoking ban never happened. She hands over fifty quid and he presses a small fold of stiff paper into her hand. She pockets it and turns away from him without further acknowledgement and looks around for the women's toilets. But all she can see is darkness and bodies. A large hand falls on her shoulder and she feels that shitty breath on her cheek again.

"That way," he says and the nicotine brown fingers point towards another room further back. He grins at her, his split lips pulling back to reveal a row of yellowing piano keys.

An archway leads through to a smoky haze where a collection of characters not dissimilar to the dealer loiter around a pool table. The tiled floor is brown with dirt. The red walls are stained with drips as if the paint is melting. The ashtrays are all full. Nina heads straight for the toilets, feeling the eyes of rough and scarred creatures all over her like groping hands. She contemplates what it might be like to sleep with one of these men, to press herself up against their filth.

Next to the women's toilets, a short fat man with cauliflower ears and black-ringed fingernails has his arm around a weasel-faced woman who belches a cigarette smoke guffaw. Then Nina notices her fag-hand stroking a pregnant bulge that peeks out through her tight top. She mumbles an excuse-me and squeezes around them to get into the bathroom.

Toilet paper trails across the wet floor, mulching to a fibrous white paste. Nina goes into the first cubicle she comes to. Locks the door behind her. The stench of urine burns her nostrils. The toilet seat is wet. The water in the bowl is brown. Folding her fingers up inside her sleeve, she uses the cuff of her coat to flush the toilet. It narrowly improves matters. She uses the only remaining piece of clean toilet roll to wipe the top of the cistern, then opens the fifty-pound paper fold and tips out a quantity of granuley white powder onto it. Using an old gym membership card she chops the coke into a finer powder and rails it into two thick lines, rolls up a note and sucks one back.

The coke shoots up her nostril and stings her sinuses. There is a bitter tang at the back of her throat and then a soapy taste that hangs around the roof of her mouth. She is awake. The stiffness in her neck and shoulders disappears and she moves her head fluidly left and right. She immediately takes the second line up the other nostril. It's dripping now. That bitter taste falls through the back of her throat, which is becoming numb by degrees and feels like it might stick together. She badly needs a drink and reaches into her pocket for a half bottle of vodka. Takes a couple of quick swigs and feels it mix with the coke and a bright vibrancy throbs within her. She feels taller. Powerful.

Coming out of the cubicle, she catches herself in the mirror opposite. Stops. The picture there is clearer, as if layers of softening filters have been peeled away. She doesn't notice the dirt and the cracks in the glass so much anymore. It's just her, standing in that silvered mirror in the middle of this bright white space of tiles and cubicles. Bass thuds through the door from the club beyond and she feels it deep in her body, pulsing through her limbs, right into her core. Her hair shimmers black and glossy. The strong cheekbones give her face a predatory aspect and her skin looks lustrous. Her eyes are grey and sharp and clear, the pupils looking back at her enlarged and keen. A hunter's eyes. She reaches up and watches dark red nails brush across her cheek, feeling the warmth from within her firm skin. She takes off her coat and folds it over her arm. The straps of her black dress cut clean across her shoulders, as erotic as the straps on a garter belt. The neckline plunges deep, her breasts swell inside it. She watches her gleaming nails move along its edge, sniffing back and tasting the coke again as her red lips gleam into a pout. She doesn't hear the door open, but the pregnant woman appears in the mirror and then crosses in front of her, cutting off her image momentarily. She catches a glimpse of the weaselly face as it passes her.

"Y'alright?" the woman says and then disappears into a cubicle.

"Yeah," Nina replies after a moment's thought. She'd normally be embarrassed to have such a private, sensual moment stepped in on in this way, but realises with some relish that she is not embarrassed at all. "Yeah," she says again, feeling the word well up from her lungs, brush through her voice box and emerge rounded and warm and full from between her lips.

She clips with a quickened, stronger stride through the pool room, turns through the arch and plunges into the darkness beyond. Back to where the normal people are. Or if not normal, at least less totally fucked and horrible. She feels the pulse and heat and sweat of the collective body of people around her. Now, with her coat off, she can feel it against her skin. Her barriers have been stripped away and she can enjoy the raw, unashamed sex of the place. She feels the bodies pressing against her, against her bare arms and shoulders. A loose hand cups her breast and she shivers, her skin goose-pimpling as she moves on.

She could get into the crowd and dance. She feels drawn to it, but there are other things on her mind. She wants what she came here for. And so she finds herself in the quieter, darker space where the deal was done. Here, there is more room between people, the groupings are smaller and there's a chance to actually make some contact. It seems more likely that the type of man she's looking for might be located here. Someone alone, someone perhaps a little bit shy but still looking to pick up. The darkness is near total, shapes illuminate in brief flashes as the echo of the disco lights washes in from around the corner. There are couches here made almost entirely of black gaffer tape. The only people making use of them are a couple tangling in the corner, his hand disappearing beneath her dress. The other denizens are not dancing or swaying. It's as if they are not even talking, like they are asleep on their feet, communing by some kind of telepathy. Or perhaps in silent contemplation, not communicating directly, but with the same thoughts going through each of their minds at the same time.

Nina's eyes search among them until she lights upon a man standing alone near the back of the room. Without a thought, without stopping to gather her nerves, she moves towards him. She feels her eyes widening, lashes fluttering like the fronds of a Venus flytrap as she closes in. Drapes her hand on his arm. He turns towards her, his lips playing in a nervous smile in the faint flickering of a red light.

"Hi," she says but he doesn't hear her and leans in closer and shouts, "What?"

She moves her arm around his back and leans into his ear. But before she can speak she feels him move away. She looks up to see another woman beside them. Short with an aggressive bust and a proprietary pout. The guy gives Nina an awkward smile of apology as he is dragged away from her. She spits curses after them at an ordinary speaking volume, knowing full well that no-one will be able to hear them.

And she finds herself alone in the back of the dark room. She turns around to see the sharp silhouettes of the loiterers all around her. Beyond them disco lights flash over the heaving undulation of flesh on the dance floor. She looks around for a new target. And slowly works her way forward through the still bodies. When the light plays over their features, she notices that none of their lips are moving. They do not even appear to be looking at each other. Occasionally a hand or an arm will stir through the light in slow motion. Perhaps this is the wrong place, she thinks, and weaves towards the dance floor.

She can see it looming larger. Still framed by blackened statues, as if they are standing guard, creating a boundary between the throbbing life beyond and the stagnant limbo that she now inhabits. She is about to stride through two groups of these silent sentinels, when a man steps in front of her, blocking the way. She stops and turns side-on to let him through. It takes a further flash of light for her to realise he is not moving. He is looking right at her. Is this it? The pick-up? From what she can tell in this light, he is well-dressed with a neat haircut. Handsome, she thinks, although she cannot see him so clearly, wearing a suit, tie loosened, collar opened. The texture of a day's stubble prickles along the line of his jaw. She stills her motion, re-orientating her intention and places a hand on her hip. Cocks her head, her lips curling into a coy smile. Her hair brushes along her bare shoulder. She thinks should she, and then why not, and bites her lip. He leans into her and she feels the stubble brush against her cheek.

"Hello," he says. And she turns directly into the incline of his head, so that their faces are only inches away from each other, their lips almost touching. His eyes flicker between black hollows and clear whites with rich brown pupils. She doesn't return the greeting. Just lets herself hover close to the man, feeling a tension starting to grow within her as their bodies almost touch, the heat emanating from him. She slides her hand inside his suit jacket, up around the ribs and feels the smoothness of his shirt, the firm muscle beneath. She can smell the spice of his aftershave. She gives him a moment to move in. But he doesn't. He just stands there, an inch from her, a wry smile on his lips. He's going to make her do it. She closes the gap between them and his mouth is hot and she tastes the sweetness of mint and the dirt of cigarettes as his tongue invades and fills her mouth.

She pulls back, her body now pressed into his. His hand on the back of her neck, fingers wrapped through her hair. Her arms around his back. She doesn't want to waste time. She is about to suggest they get out of there and opens her mouth to speak but before she can he says, "It's Nina isn't it?"

She feels something swirl down in her gut. Not an unpleasant sensation, but an odd one. An exciting confusion as she tries to place him.

"Do I know you?"

"Not really," he says, mouth spreading into a grin that shows his teeth. A crocodile grin. Still holding to him, she leans back to get a better look at him. The lights flash and bit by bit she pieces together his face. Each flash giving away another detail that she holds onto and keeps, combining it with what she already has. Flash. Dark brown eyes. Flash. The robust line of a roman nose. Flash. Flared nostrils. Flash. Mouth curled in a cruel smile. Flash. Stubble on the line of a hard jaw. Flash. Acne-scarred cheeks. Flash. The haughty upturn of his lip. Flash. The thin lip, cruel and flattened. And with every detail it begins to sink in. Perhaps not cognitively at first. She knows it more with her body than she does with her mind, which has for some months been turned away from these kind of thoughts. And the feeling of recognition is growing inside her, and rising from that the churning in her stomach becomes nausea. An unbearable irritation tingles in her arms and across her chest. She tastes the bitterness of cocaine in the back of her throat. And then rising bile. She goes to step back but his arm curls around her and pulls her sharply towards him. His hand clutches her buttock. Her eyes are wide, her face frozen. Ice in her veins.

"Neil," she says. "Neil Allen."

And his crocodile grin widens, lips pulling back and teeth parting. He lets out a braying laugh. An arrogant, hoarse sound that she can feel blasting against her face. And never once does he break eye contact. He holds her to him and laughs right in her face.

She pulls her arms from around him. Her coat drops to the floor. Her flat palms beat against his unyielding chest, then turning to fists thumping and still he doesn't let go. He keeps laughing until the bass and the hum of conversation are obscured and all she can hear is the roar of his laughter. She twists and turns and bucks against him. And only after watching her struggle for some moments does he release her. She stumbles backwards. Almost falls. Drops into a crouch. Hand on the floor keeps her on her feet. Looks up at him. His silhouette towers over her, arms folded, face caught in flashes gloating down at her. And around him on either side are the black statues of people like sleepwalkers in the midst of the throbbing life of the dance floor beyond. None of them look. No-one takes notice of the fact that a woman right next to them has almost fallen on her arse.

Nina thrusts herself to her feet. She pushes past Neil, swooping her coat up on the way, and begins to shove through the asphyxiating sea of the dance floor. As she goes, she looks intermittently, frantically over her shoulder and sees him standing there, looking on after her. Then she doesn't see him. He is lost. Then he is there again. Closer. Moving steadily after her. She barges her way out through the door into the coat-check corridor and stumbles, almost falls up the stairs.

Bursting out onto the night-time street, she takes off her heels and runs. Runs through the wetness and the reflection and counter-reflection of slick orange lights. Cold air shocks her lungs as it pumps in and out of her in irregular, stuttering breaths, propelled by a blind panic that blurs everything into one smear of light and dark and rain and terror. She doesn't know where she is going. She just runs, never looking over her shoulder. Not once. Never looking back.

Review This Book

If you enjoyed *You Are Not You*, I'd be really grateful if you would consider leaving a customer review on Amazon.com. Reviews are crucial for any author, and even just a line or two can make a huge difference.

This is my first novel, but there are more on the way. For updates on upcoming work, you can sign up to my mailing list, which you'll find on my website: simonrosenberg.co.uk.

You can contact me directly at simon@simonrosenberg.co.uk.

About the Author

Simon Rosenberg is an author, screenwriter and director. He was born and raised in Birmingham. He has been living in London for more than a decade. One day he'll get out.

Acknowledgements

I would like to thank the following people for their help with *You Are Not You*:

Jacqui Jackson, copy editing. Joanna Chisholm, typesetting and interior design. Becky Pickard, ebook creation. Vince Haig for the cover. Chuck Regan for his fantastic artwork on the first version.

Dan Jacobs for the internet.

Rick Halsall and Tom Odell for their work on the trailer. Genia Davy, Fiona Dennison, Juliette Odell, Madeleine Odell and Hannah Sassoon for appearing in it. Charlotte Jo Hanbury for her vocal talents.

Jon Spira for his advice and for getting me to change the title.

Dave Taylor for keeping me going.

Michael Leventhal for publishing advice and people.

Tom Barbor-Might and Adam Randall.

All of the early readers. There are too many of you to name here, but your feedback was invaluable.

Past and present staff at The Adam and Eve, Mill Hill, where this book was mostly written.

Edgar Allen Poe.

Hannah, Mum, Ben & Jerry, Grandma Ann and Stewart.

And always remembering Dad and Grandma Anita who are largely to blame for all of this.

32233464R00273

Printed in Poland
by Amazon Fulfillment
Poland Sp. z o.o., Wrocław